D1153314

David Hargreaves studied history at Worcester College, Oxford, before becoming a history teacher, first at Stamford School in Lincolnshire, then from April 1986 at Westminster School in London, where he became head of the sixth form and a boarding housemaster. He taught at Westminster for a total of twenty-eight years until 2014. He now divides his time between running his education consultancy and writing, and is a governor of a London preparatory school. He publishes regular articles on history, including a weekly essay about the First World War published in centuryjournal.com. He lives in north London.

With special thanks to
Chris Liddell and Renee Harbers Liddell

With special thanks to
Dennis and Charlotte Stevenson and their family

With special thanks to:

Christopher Alcock
Veronica Berman
Nabeel Bhanji
John Crewe
Marianne and Mike de
    Giorgio
Angela Dean
Helma Diffey
Robson Family
Arthur Fincham
Mary Gibson
Christine Hanway
William Hanway
Gavin Henderson
Claire & Robin Hilton
In loving memory of Fabian
    Garcia Miller
Dylan, Carey, Harry and
    Alex Jones
Jack Kember
Jennifer and Ewan Labrom
Alan Leibowitz

Alex Letts
Ning Lim
Robert Lister
Cecilia Loo
Mandy Merttens
Andrew Miller QC
Isabelle & Andrea Morresi
Serena Nuttall
David Owen
Alex Panayides
Stuart Proffitt
Will, Gen, Josh and Amelia
    Rosen
Ben Shillito
Simon Stanley
Barbara Weiss
Tom Weisselberg
Nancy Wood
Richard Wynne-Griffith
Alina Young
Sam & Annie Younger

UNDER THE TABLE

David Hargreaves

Unbound

This edition first published in 2018

Unbound
6th Floor Mutual House, 70 Conduit Street, London W1S 2GF

www.unbound.com

Text Design by Ellipsis, Glasgow

A CIP record for this book is available from the British Library
ISBN 978-1-78352-441-9 (trade hbk)
ISBN 978-1-7835-2442-6 (ebook)
ISBN 978-1-78352-440-2 (limited edition)

Printed in Great Britain by Clays Ltd, St Ives Plc

1 3 5 7 9 8 6 4 2

For my family – past and present

Dear Reader,

The book you are holding came about in a rather different way to most others. It was funded directly by readers through a new website: Unbound. Unbound is the creation of three writers. We started the company because we believed there had to be a better deal for both writers and readers. On the Unbound website, authors share the ideas for the books they want to write directly with readers. If enough of you support the book by pledging for it in advance, we produce a beautifully bound special subscribers' edition and distribute a regular edition and e-book wherever books are sold, in shops and online.

This new way of publishing is actually a very old idea (Samuel Johnson funded his dictionary this way). We're just using the internet to build each writer a network of patrons. At the back of this book, you'll find the names of all the people who made it happen.

Publishing in this way means readers are no longer just passive consumers of the books they buy, and authors are free to write the books they really want. They get a much fairer return too – half the profits their books generate, rather than a tiny percentage of the cover price.

If you're not yet a subscriber, we hope that you'll want to join our publishing revolution and have your name listed in one of our books in the future. To get you started, here is a £5 discount on your first pledge. Just visit unbound.com, make your pledge and type **table5** in the promo code box when you check out.

Thank you for your support,

Dan, Justin and John
Founders, Unbound

Chapter One

Dominic: Avila House, January–February 2014

'I may not be an alpha male,' said Dominic, with a forced casualness, 'but – really – breast cancer?'

'I'm afraid so.'

He looked down sceptically at his chest which had been stripped bare for the purposes of examination. His left side felt very tender but, as midriffs went, it looked unremarkable for a man in his sixth decade: no moobs, at least, but only a historical trace of the muscle definition it had once boasted.

'Well,' he said slowly, 'goodness me. I didn't even know men could get breast cancer.'

Mr Seymour, the oncologist, sat opposite, looking appropriately serious. He was a short and powerfully built man of about fifty with a generous crop of silver-grey hair. Through the garish 1950s redbrick casement, the afternoon blazed with a defiant optimism.

'It's rare, I grant you, but not unknown.'

'Also vaguely insulting,' said Dominic, essaying a lightness he did not necessarily feel.

Mr Seymour gave a small, uneasy smile.

As a veteran of breaking bad news himself, Dominic could only admire the consultant's deftness – he had spoken in a measured tone, as one thoughtful man to another. Had he been gauche or flustered, or had he perhaps dropped his papers at the critical moment, Dominic might have had to deflect his own feelings and concentrate instead on feeling protective or sorry for him. Now all he could do was reflect on what he had been told.

A silent fifteen or twenty seconds passed which were broken by Mr Seymour, who suggested in tones of quiet encouragement, 'You must have some questions.'

'Must I?' He thought for a moment. 'I suppose I must. How rare?'

'Sorry?'

'Male breast cancer. How rare?'

'Ummm, about one per cent of breast cancers occur in men.'

'And how many are fatal?'

'There are about three hundred deaths a year. '

Dominic kept his face impassive. Momentarily, he allowed his eyes to search the room, as though it might provide answers. The sign fixed to the door had described it as a 'consulting room', and NHS bulk-buy furniture had been deposited within it without much sign of interest or care. There were two hard chairs opposite the desk, one of which he occupied. Mr Seymour's was more elaborate – a clumsy recognition of his status as a consultant – upholstered in royal blue fabric, and with a swivel mechanism.

'So,' Dominic asked, 'what happens now?'

For the first time, Mr Seymour tensed slightly. Dominic was aware that the nurse, who had been affecting to concentrate on the contents of a buff envelope, was listening intently.

'Well. As you know, we did the scans because of what we

found when we examined your lymph nodes – that is, under your left arm, when we first saw you – what is it? Twelve days ago?'

Dominic nodded.

'It isn't good news, I'm afraid. The cancerous cells have metastasised quite aggressively.'

'I see.'

'We should start discussing treatment straight away.'

Dominic gazed at him, quite still.

'It's a question of working out how you are going to cope practically. Is there anyone who will be able to help at home?'

The nurse had given up pretence of doing anything at all other than staring at Dominic. She looked the very soul of compassion and, he realised, with a stab of humility, this was for him.

'I am sorry,' said Mr Seymour after a pause. 'This is a great deal to take in.'

Dominic was aware that he was trying to assemble an idea, rather than struggling for composure. 'Do I have to accept treatment?' he asked quietly. 'I'm pretty sure that I'd rather not.'

Mr Seymour shook his head. 'No, of course not. Not necessarily. But that's not a matter for making any decisions on today. That's . . . that's for when you've had time to digest the news.'

There was another longish silence. Unbidden, the nurse appeared at his side with a plastic cup of water which, to his surprise, Dominic found himself sipping gratefully.

'I know I want to protect what's left of my life,' he said finally. 'I'll take anything that's going to control the pain and to keep me calm. But I've no desire to spin things out if I'm just going to be miserable.'

Mr Seymour said nothing but nodded sympathetically.

Sly bugger, thought Dominic. He thinks I'm going to come begging for treatment once I'm past the first shock. But I won't.

'I'd like an idea of how long I can expect to live,' he said finally, his voice sounding unnaturally slow and calm, even to his own ears. 'I don't have a family, but – well – there are one or two people who are going to need to know.'

'Of course. I imagine you'll want to talk to Fr Maybury, for one.' Mr Seymour was a long-standing St Asaph's parishioner.

Dominic nodded. 'But not quite yet,' he said, 'I need a day or two first.' He gestured ruefully. 'Anything I say at this moment is bound to be a bit of a cliché – I need a bit of time to get my head round it.'

'Of course.'

'I'd also like an answer to my question. How long?'

Mr Seymour folded his hands. 'I understand that. You also know I'm bound to hedge. Everybody reacts differently to the disease.'

'And you know I'm bound to push you. How long?'

The consultant grimaced, perhaps realising he had come against someone of strong will. 'In my experience of patients who've decided against treatment for this kind of cancer, most have lived a good life for a year or more.'

They always over-estimated. Somebody had told Dominic that. Had it been Cara? Janey, even? Somebody well-informed, anyway. Six or eight months, he thought. Where were they now – January? Dead by Christmas, for sure. Finally absolved of the need to send cards.

'Thanks,' said Dominic, even more quietly. 'It helps to know.' He stood up and asked in a voice more like his usual what he needed to do next.

Mr Seymour looked at the nurse, rather as if he needed a prompt. She said something about Dominic's medication, and about him needing to come to the dispensary on Monday.

'And you and I can meet again next Friday, can't we?' he said, a little too heartily, speaking over her.

'That's fine,' said Dominic.

'Good, good.' He turned to the nurse. 'Ella – could you arrange for a taxi for Mr da Silva?'

Dominic protested, smilingly, he wanted to take the bus. It was nothing to do with money, he assured the consultant, just habit. Eventually, he shook hands with them both, having agreed to come back in a week's time to discuss his decision. He could always change his mind, he was told.

'I'm a bit worried about you having to take all this in by yourself.'

Dominic smiled. 'Don't be. I have good friends. They'll step up.'

Practicalities, he said to himself, as he stepped on to the double-decker that would take him back to the centre of town. Concentrate on practicalities.

His will had first been written twenty-five years earlier, but he had made a point of revising it every couple of years, and so it was reasonably up to date. A bigger problem was what would happen to Avila House, the hostel for the homeless – or those otherwise on the fringes of life – where for over twenty years he had been warden.

His mind went back to – when was it? 1992? 1993? Avila House had consisted of no more than the old Victorian mansion and a couple of Portakabins in the asphalt yard at the back. It had been out of these that he and Breda Devlin had attempted to administer a home for twelve men, some recently out of prison, and whence many were destined to return.

The house had been a seminary until the late 1970s, by which time the flow of eager young prelates, mainly from Ireland, had dried up almost altogether. The diocese had tried to sell the house on several occasions, and it had been lying unused for months when squatters moved in during a particularly bad time for the town in the 1980s. The bishop, anxious to raise some funds for the struggling parish, prepared his lawyers to order an eviction. But Father Maybury, then the newly appointed parish priest at St Asaph's, had counselled caution. Times were hard, he said, and the government appeared uncaring to those left in the wake of the hubris that seemed to have overtaken Britain. A few thousand pounds were raised and the hostel opened its doors for the first time in March 1993.

At once problems had erupted. Hostel wardens came and went with even greater rapidity than the residents, occasioning, as the bishop noted irritably, greater trouble. Within six months there had been one stabbing on the premises and one attempted suicide. The only clear legacies were a burgeoning trade in proscribed substances and ruptured relationships with the local community. On the Feast of the Assumption that year the bishop summoned Fr Maybury and told him he wanted the hostel closed by the end of the month.

Predictably, the priest pleaded for time. 'I have an idea,'

he said. 'There's someone I know who just might turn the whole thing around.'

There were roadworks just outside the big Iceland warehouse, and the diesel engine of the bus was left ticking over for almost ten minutes. Dominic found himself speculating about the intentions of two women emerging with trolleys stacked high with hamburgers and firelighters. It seemed the wrong time of year for a barbecue.

Hardly my business, he thought. His reflexive interest in other people seemed more than ever superfluous, but it was still there – for now. I have terminal cancer, he told himself slowly. I will be dead by Christmas. It would be an effort to say the words out loud.

He thought about the evening that lay ahead. Even though friendship was immensely important to him, the habits of a solitary life were ingrained. Roy, the assistant warden, was on duty in the hostel, so he would have no duties before the morning. As the bus turned in to Friary Lane, his gaze wandered from the top deck to Marks and Spencer.

An extravagant supper, he suddenly thought; that would be an appropriately defiant gesture. In the light of the day's momentous news at least there was no incentive to economise. Impulsively, he stood up and rang the bell. Inside the shop, he chose a baguette, cherry tomatoes, green salad, dressed crab pâté, and a small rump steak. Then, feeling cheerfully naughty, he picked out an egg custard tart sprinkled with cinnamon, and a half bottle of Rioja.

As he queued at the checkout, he felt himself salivate, but then the brief euphoria subsided as suddenly as it had arrived, and he felt almost too tired to remain standing.

He rang for a minicab, which deposited him at Avila House.

As it swung into the forecourt, Roy was standing at the front door, holding an old VHS player, which Dominic vaguely recalled having seen on the upper landing. Lacking hands to open the taxi door, he made a pantomime show of regret. Grateful for having a reason not to make conversation, Dominic nodded his understanding and prepared to carry his shopping up to his flat.

Avila House had transformed itself since the early days. Instead of the original complement of twelve residents, there were now thirty-six, each with their own room in the large purpose-built block constructed on what had once been the back garden. The old house was now given over to a range of offices and workshops.

'Here, Dom. I'll carry that.' With classically inconvenient timing, Lewis – the most obdurately unemployable and long-standing resident – suddenly materialised at his side. He was a floppy, overweight man, rather older than Dominic himself, but with an adolescent's anxiety to be included.

'Oh, that's nice of you. I'm sure I'll be fine.'

'No, no. Let me.' He made a beeline for the bags.

Sighing inwardly, Dominic prepared to write off the next twenty minutes. Lewis considered himself an intellectual in a Sargasso sea of philistines, and Dominic was one of the few people who was prepared to listen to him expiate on a disconcerting range of subjects. 'Have you heard about that President of Nigeria?' he now asked him.

Dominic shook his head, thinking inwardly that he very soon would. Fortunately, at that moment Roy emerged, claiming he needed help in identifying the owner of a mystery anorak, and took Lewis away.

His supper was easily made, and every bit as good as he had hoped. The two glasses of Rioja, enjoyed while stretched out on the sofa, made Mr Seymour's news seem remote. Thank God for iPlayer, Dominic thought, as he settled down to catch up with recent episodes of *The Apprentice*.

In the small hours, of course, he lay awake.

Bad news could be quite exciting. At the time of his disgrace a quarter of a century earlier, any blame or reproach lay at his door, even though most people had tiptoed carefully around the scandal which had enveloped him. A sudden and aggressive cancer wasn't like that. Once again, it gave him an excuse to do what always gave him comfort – organise his life and, where possible, control it. He thought now with some satisfaction of the tasks that lay ahead: tell friends, inform the bank, fix hospital appointments. And while he dreaded to be the occasion of sorrow to those whom he loved, he was stimulated by the thought of the attention he would now receive. Come off it, da Silva, he told himself – this isn't mainly bad news: I'm being spared a lonely and directionless old age.

The thing was that he didn't feel ill exactly. Tired most certainly. But still curious about the future. It was bewildering and incredible that there were narratives in which he was deeply interested, to which there were resolutions he would not live to see.

Somehow, his mind refused to dwell on the people he knew best and loved most, but raced across the more impersonal world of politics. What, he wondered, would he now not know?

Well, all the political shenanigans for one thing. Twenty

years earlier, he'd bought into the whole Blair package, but that was an infatuation which had turned sour. Almost anyone was better than Cameron, though. Assuming there would be no General Election before 2015 – *shit* – he was going to die under the fucking Tories.

Thank God, he thought, for Pope Francis. He'd hoped since the age of about twenty that much against which he'd railed in the Catholic Church would have been expunged in his lifetime: a relaxation of the ban on women priests, for instance, or on clerical celibacy – let alone the old chestnuts like abortion, homosexuality, and contraception. These weren't going to happen, evidently, but every day of his life he thanked God for the new Pope.

His mind moved on seamlessly to sex. The young man on the checkout desk in Marks and Spencer had been absurdly attractive. He chided himself for the thought: insofar as he had been given the death sentence in Mr Seymour's office about half an hour earlier, it might have been more seemly for him to have held his carnal appetites in check. You are incorrigible, he told himself.

He wouldn't have minded a pee, but it would have meant getting up, and he wasn't sufficiently uncomfortable for the effort it required. He put on his glasses and turned vaguely to the bedside clock. 3.20 a.m. *Christ*, he thought, I've got hours of this.

He might as well start to plan his funeral. He vaguely hoped that some of those who had passed through the doors of Avila House over the years might show up – those who weren't dead or in prison, anyway. He smiled as he thought of the hymns best suited to the kind of democratic send-off he would prefer: 'Lord of the Dance', 'Shine Jesus

Shine', 'I the Lord of Sea and Sky'. Hymns calculated to piss off the kind of person he enjoyed pissing off.

Talking of whom, what about his former mother-in-law? He tried hard not to nurse grudges, but the memory of the abrasive mistrust between them had not been quite expunged, even after all this time. It was doubtful that she would attend the occasion, but he enjoyed the fantasy of her discomfort should she choose to do so. What about Janey? They'd never kept in touch, but – well – she had been his wife a quarter of a century ago. Blimey, he thought, why didn't I think of her earlier?

Next morning, all seemed normal. Dominic was in his office from just before 8 a.m., veering between emails, phone calls and talking with the residents who milled in and out. When Fr Maybury arrived, Dominic gestured for him to close the door.

'Something's happened,' he began, and saw the priest's eyebrows arch in alarm.

It didn't take long to lay out the bare essentials, and when he had finished the two men eyed each other in silence across the desk. An oasis of rosewood in a sea of plywood and Formica, it had been donated by the retiring senior partner of a local law firm. Facing Dominic, on the opposite wall, were three watercolours of his old college – one of the main quadrangle, one of the cottages, and the other of the old copper beech by the lake. They had been left to him years earlier by his Oxford tutor. On the desk were photographs of his parents, and another of a youngish man in a QC's wig and gown.

'Have you told Jack and Orla?' asked the priest eventually. He was a tall man in his early sixties, big framed but still powerfully built, with a great head of thick white hair.

'Yes,' said Dominic, his eyes unhappy. 'I rang them about half an hour ago.'

'They'll have been very upset.'

Now he wished he had not tried to use the phone for such a purpose. They were his oldest friends, and their intimacy had been greater in recent years than at any other point. He should have gone to see them, he thought.

'They were.'

'What about your family?'

'I don't really have a family, do I? My parents died years ago and I haven't set eyes on Janey since . . . 1990, I think.'

'Janey?'

'My ex-wife.'

'Ah.' Fr Maybury looked embarrassed. 'No brothers or sisters?'

'None.'

'Wait a bit. What about the nun?'

'Oh yes – Kate. Not exactly a nun, but she runs a Catholic orphanage. My cousin.'

'You haven't told her?'

'The orphanage is in Paraguay. We usually email at Christmas.'

Fr Maybury stretched his lips unhappily. 'You might bring that forward a bit this year.'

'Point taken.'

Fr Maybury looked as if he were struggling to remember something. 'What about the posh pair?' he said finally.

Dominic laughed. 'Posh is a relative term, especially round here.'

'You know who I mean. Great bear of a chap. Beautiful wife.'

'Ah – Digby and Cara. I planned on ringing them tonight.'

After Fr Maybury had left, Dominic washed up the coffee mugs and tried to think what needed to be done. It was Wednesday, he knew, and on Wednesday he and Breda organised fresh bedding.

The reservoirs of self-discipline, by which he had often propelled himself in darker moments, were enough to help him absorb the shock, but they could not inure him against lassitude and exhaustion. The Bishop persuaded him to take indefinite leave, while insisting he could carry on living in the flat that came with the job.

He had, however, been right in what he had told Mr Seymour – his friends did rally to him. That first weekend, Jack arrived in his geriatric Fiesta to take him home for the weekend. He and Orla lived about thirty miles away, but they'd given Dominic the run of the place for the past twenty-five years.

'Decent of you,' said Dominic, as Jack insisted on carrying his small overnight bag out to the car. 'I could have got a bus, you know.'

'Will you shut up?' It was said smilingly, but Dominic knew him to be both intensely shy and emotional.

'What? Me? When I've got such a good reason to grab everyone's attention?'

Jack gave a bleak smile. To anyone else, he looked his full age – Celtic, heavy-set, with a deeply lined face. When Dominic looked at him, however, he still saw the absurdly handsome and clever schoolboy who had befriended him.

'Let's do the cancer bit once Orla's around, shall we?' Dominic said pleasantly. 'Jolly interesting for me, of course, but I don't see why you should have to go through it twice.'

'Good man yourself.'

Dominic smiled. It was Jack's stock phrase of approval –
an Irishism which he had picked up in childhood. Had he
suddenly started wailing and gnashing his teeth, he knew,
Jack would never have withheld support or comfort. But
they'd known each other so well and for so long, there was
much that didn't need saying.

'All right,' said Dominic, once they were on the road.
'General Knowledge test. For ten points – give me the name
of Lord Curzon's governess.'

'Who?'

'Lord Curzon. Viceroy of India? Are you telling me
you've never heard of him? Very odd for someone who
claims to be educated.'

'How am I supposed to know the name of his – nanny?'
The last word was inflected with particular contempt.

'A famous figure, Jack. Subject of a book by Jonathan
Gathorne-Hardy. I'm sorry your reading is so restricted.'

'Oh, *that* Lord Curzon. Let me see – Miss Paraman?'

Dominic groaned. 'You were not supposed to be able to
answer that.'

'No complaining, please. Right now – my turn.'

Orla did not go in for this kind of nerdy emotional eva-
sion, although she was the best of the three of them in their
ludicrous General Knowledge competitions. When the car
pulled up outside the front of the house (they lived in half
of what had once been a Victorian village school), she was
standing by the front door, but did not emerge. Short and
slight, she radiated a determination to be good, and to sub-
ordinate her own needs and feelings to those of others.
Today, however, Dominic could see she was struggling to
maintain her composure.

Their four children were all grown up and lived independently. Dominic was close to each of them, but he enjoyed the undivided attention of Jack and Orla that weekend and accepted their invitation to come back the following Friday.

'Actually,' said Orla, 'what we'd like is for you to come and live with us.' Her copper hair had been cut short recently, and she looked far more severe than she was.

'The Bishop said I can have my flat for as long as I've got left.'

'Come on,' said Jack. 'We'll look after you. Your cooking's shite, anyway.'

'It's not that bad.' He smiled at them. The reflex that had led him to cling to independence was, for now, as strong as ever.

Two weeks later, having accepted Digby and Cara's invitation, he went to see them in their manor house in Sussex – the same house which, when Dominic had first known them both, had belonged to Digby's parents.

It was cold out of doors, but the sun was bright and he lay in a large armchair in the orangery, reading Raymond Chandler.

'If this is cancer,' he said contentedly on the Sunday afternoon, 'I'm all for it. Between the pair of you and Jack and Orla, I'm a pig in shit.'

'Come and stay with us at St Maurice,' said Cara. They had a farmhouse near Avignon. 'We're going to be there over Easter week. We'll look after you.'

'We'll get a nurse,' Digby promised, in his rumbling patrician burble. 'Or, well, perhaps a priest?'

'A bit previous,' Dominic said, smiling. 'But I have a favour to ask.'

'Fire away.'

'I want opium,' said Dominic, 'and a lot of it.'

Digby looked uneasy. 'You're not planning on . . . ?'

'No, of course not. I just don't want to hang around any longer than I have to once everything starts to kick off.' He pointed vaguely in the direction of his breastbone.

'Won't the hospital see to all that?'

'I hope so. I want you to prepare to make good any deficiencies.'

'Ah, point taken. Not a problem, old boy.'

'I need to know you mean it.'

'I absolutely do. Now put it out of your head.'

Back at Avila House, he began to find the weekdays more of an effort. Afternoons could be particularly hard: for so long now, his days had been filled by visits to detention centres, housing departments and cut-price supermarkets – none of them guaranteed entertainment hotspots, but they had soaked up a great deal of time.

Rather like an over-ambitious gap-year student, he now listed books which he had never read or those which he had merely glossed over and made self-conscious efforts to repair the omission. They didn't come to much, however. The Book of Psalms had a couple of airings. So did the poems of Robert Browning, and even the sonnets of Shakespeare. *Swann's Way* was tossed aside after twenty perplexed minutes, as was *A Suitable Boy*. Far more time was expended on watching re-runs of *Frasier* and looking rather listlessly at YouTube.

After a month of this strange half-life he knew he could not put off telling the person who mattered to him perhaps most and prepared, finally, to call Daniel.

Chapter Two
Daniel: Avila House, February 2014

It was a Saturday morning. They sat now in Dominic's flat drinking coffee. Dominic claimed that it had come from the local discount store but to Daniel, a great aficionado of expensive blends, that seemed unlikely. Momentarily casting aside more pressing feelings, he reflected that his old friend and mentor had never been able entirely to suppress the evidence of the more affluent world to which he had once belonged.

Even in the sitting room, which was small and looked out over nothing more glamorous than an asphalt yard, there were giveaways: for one, his old Charles Eames chair and footstool. It had been a gift from Janey, Dominic had told him, by way of mitigation for such a gross extravagance. (Daniel had seen the former Mrs da Silva, of course – but, like so many wives in old-fashioned public schools, she had assumed no independent profile in pupils' eyes.) Then there were the books – mainly nineteenth- and twentieth-century history and literature. Dominic, he thought, might play the ascetic all he liked, but he could never be a philistine.

They talked now about their most recent meeting a few months earlier. It had been at home in Hendon when

Esther's family and his own parents had celebrated Shabbat. It had been evident that Dominic had been delighted to have been asked, and that he had enjoyed the excursion from the habitual disciplines of Catholicism. On that occasion, Daniel had noticed, he had seemed energised and quietly joyful, almost as though he had known something which he did not, yet, want to share.

'Did you know then that something was wrong?' he asked him now.

'Not exactly.'

'What do you mean – "not exactly"?'

'I could feel a lump around my left tit.'

'You didn't feel ill?'

'Just tired. I didn't take it very seriously. Being tired is nothing new.'

'That's because you work all the time.'

'What – and you don't?'

'I'm younger.'

That was true, although the twelve-or-so-year gap in their ages felt a great deal less now than it had when Daniel was a bright and intense schoolboy and Dominic his History teacher. The real gaps between them had less to do with age than circumstance. Daniel had taken silk the previous summer and was already being spoken of as a future Law Lord.

'I still wish you'd told me earlier,' Daniel said, forcing himself back to the present.

'I know, Dan, I know.' Dominic shook his head. 'Believe me, it wasn't through any absence of affection.'

'What were you thinking of?'

'Honestly? I've been scared of upsetting you.'

'I don't care about being upset,' said Daniel. 'I care about you.' To his dismay, he could hear his voice thickening and registered at once the distress in Dominic's face at the sight. Bringing himself under control, he said, 'Are you scared?'

'Not very. Not in the way I would be if I had to go through chemo. Oblivion feels altogether easier.'

'I would be.'

'Ah, I'm looking to be bailed out by my posh connections. My old buddy Digby – that's Sir Digby to you – has promised to procure hard drugs before the pain gets to me.'

'How the hell is he going to do that?'

'I have no idea. But I know Digby. He always delivers.'

Daniel said carefully, 'I've got no scruples about suicide.'

'I do,' Dominic said. 'Once I really am dying, however, a gentle shove would be appreciated. No point hanging around.'

'How can you be so cool about this?' Daniel asked. 'I wouldn't be.'

'You have a wife and daughter, *mon vieux*, so you've no choice but to stay well and strong. Anyway, I need you to be well. I've a big favour to ask – much bigger than the one I asked Digby. Also more legal.'

'Of course. What is it?'

'I need to show you something,' said Dominic, suddenly standing up. Behind the sofa lay an old-fashioned tin trunk that Daniel did not remember seeing before. He looked up at Dominic, whose eyebrows were arched.

'Open it.'

Crouching down, Daniel did so. Inside were piles of diaries, mainly the kind manufactured by Collins and Letts, augmented by a few old school exercise books.

*

Rummaging among them soaked up the next half hour very easily, after which Daniel placed the contents of the trunk carefully on the small table behind the sofa and Dominic went off to the kitchen to make fresh coffee.

'How many years?' Daniel asked when he returned.

'Twenty, give or take a few months.'

'You filled in every day?'

'Nothing like, you'll be relieved to hear. I seem to remember being more diligent about them when I was a little boy. Later on, there were phases when I might write it up two or three times for a week and then do nothing for a month or two.'

'Bloody hell. When did you start writing them?'

'On my tenth birthday.'

'And why did you stop?'

'If you read them,' said Dominic, 'you'll understand.'

Daniel sat up, looking genuinely surprised. 'You want me to read them? All of them?'

Dominic nodded. 'That's the favour,' he said. 'I really *need* you to read them. Carefully.'

Daniel stood up and went over to the table, and started flicking through the pile.

'Do you want me to wait until – well – afterwards?'

'Quite the reverse. I'd like you to read them now, while I'm still around and compos. Then maybe we can spend some time talking about them.' His tone was conversational but Daniel was under no illusion as to how much this mattered.

'Of course I will.'

Dominic looked across at him and spoke in a low and serious voice. 'Listen,' he said. 'I know I'm reverting to teacher mode.' He passed over a big Tesco's shopping bag. 'These cover my prep school years. Don't lose them, please.'

Daniel looked at him. 'Never,' he said. 'I'm good about that kind of thing.'

'I know you are, I've also put in a covering note – just to give you the feel, you know.'

Later they went out for a drive and took in some of Dominic's favourite Warwickshire villages.

'It's annoying,' said Dominic. 'The older I get, the more I love rural idylls. Exactly what I used to despise in the older generation.'

'I wouldn't bank on it happening to me. I only get cities.'

Dominic raised his eyebrows. 'Don't flatter yourself. You only get London.'

'I only get north London, come to that. Anyway, didn't you spend your childhood in London?'

'Hardly. Until I was ten we lived in West Byfleet.'

'Where?'

'You illustrate my point exactly. West Byfleet in Surrey – very genteel in those days. The motif was, ummm – faux-rustique. With a few suburban safeguards like lollipop ladies and monkey puzzles.'

Later that afternoon, Daniel pulled into a service station and parked but did not get out. On the passenger seat lay the big box file. He had promised himself he wouldn't start to read the diaries until he could set aside some proper time, but Dominic had said he had put in a letter as well. Maybe, he thought, he could read that.

He leaned across the passenger seat and opened the file. Four of five leatherette diaries lay inside with a cream oblong envelope on top of them, on which was written his name.

Avila House
Bulmer Road
11 February 2014

Dearest Dan

I blame Jennings. Like thousands of other poor saps who'd read that particular oeuvre *too enthusiastically, I had been wildly excited before I arrived at prep school.*

My parents drove me all the way from Surrey to the distant north for my first day – an all-day drive in those days, made in my father's rather ponderous Rover 3-litre. It was September 1967 and there were long stretches of very slow road because the M1 and M6 weren't yet linked. At one point we pulled over and had lunch on the side of the road, drawn out of pale blue Tupperware containers – all the rage in those days. We ate ham and cress sandwiches and homemade flapjacks, and drank from plastic beakers of orange squash.

We had been told that the school was due to assemble for Benediction at six o'clock. The sound of the tyres crunching on the gravel as we turned into the front drive is very vivid in my ears. So too was the slightly apprehensive voice of my mother who turned to my father and asked him 'Aren't you going to wear a jacket, darling?' He duly obliged.

The diary habit kicked off a few months later –

slowly at first, but seems to have become properly ingrained by the time of my tenth birthday. I was lonely and bored, I suppose, and found it therapeutic to be able to spill my thoughts at the end of each day. Maybe if I'd been at home I might have done that with my parents, but I doubt it. People held back a bit more in those days.

I should add, however, that I never felt remotely abandoned by them. I received at least one letter every week, penned in the slightly guarded but affectionate terms which marked out their generation, and they made termly visits. Of course, I also went home in the holidays. My father had had it much tougher: he had arrived at Hunter's Chase Prep, also aged eight, back in 1929. But my grandparents lived in Argentina, and in the ten years which followed, he saw them again exactly once – when they came to London in 1935 for the Silver Jubilee of King George V.

Bless you for doing this. I am happy and relieved to know these will have been read by someone who loves and understands me. I suppose the simple truth is that I need to remember my life before it's quite gone.

Much love
Dominic

Chapter Three
Daniel: London, March 1991

One memory – brutal and transformative – stood out: 30 March 1991.

He was nineteen years of age, and in his second year at Merton. Insofar as there were ways of measuring such things, it seemed to be going well: his tutor was delighted by his work and, among the rather cautious kind of company to which he gravitated most naturally, he was respected and popular.

He had no girlfriend, however (a fact that tormented both him and, for entirely different reasons, his mother). A couple of earnest college acquaintances had suggested he join them for the Easter vacation in walking part of the Camino de Santiago. He declined, on the basis that he wanted to get laid rather than blisters, and felt the odds were better in London.

Daniel's father had never been to any kind of university and found the ways of such places arcane and effete. After watching his son loll disconsolately round the house for a week, he called in a favour from a business acquaintance and arranged for Daniel to get some work experience at a criminal set in Lincoln's Inn.

Schooled to obedience, Daniel left his parents' house the

following Monday morning and took the Tube from Golders Green to Temple. The traces of panic in the eyes of Mr Barrons, the barrister to whom he had been assigned, and the thinly veiled contempt of the clerks, left him in no doubt that his presence was welcomed by none of them. A token effort was made during his first two days to keep him busy but, on the Wednesday morning, Mr Barrons decided to work from home and advised Daniel to spend the morning at City of London Magistrates' Court.

'Might be interesting,' said the clerk, through whom the message was relayed. 'Never know, do you?'

'I see,' said Daniel. He had long learned to appear impassive even when he knew he was being jerked around, and vented his frustration by walking as slowly as possible towards Queen Victoria Street. Once inside the building, he chose a court at random and sat at the back.

His arrival coincided with the reading of the charge of importuning in a public lavatory contrary to the Sexual Offences Act. All that Daniel could see of the occupant was a balding head and a blue suit which had seen better days.

He had never been in a courtroom before and began to drink in the surroundings: grubby panelling on the walls and on the bench; a rather fussy coat of arms – enough to irk his republican sentiments – and, almost directly in front of him, the dock in which the accused was standing.

After some whispered consultation with a grey-haired man who appeared to be the instructing solicitor, the clerk shuffled his papers.

'Do you plead guilty or not guilty?'

'Guilty.'

'And are you willing for this matter to be dealt with here in the Magistrates Court, or to go to Crown Court?'

'I am willing to have it dealt with here, ma'am.'

'Please sit down, Mr da Silva.'

For a few moments, Daniel tried to believe that this wasn't the same man. Da Silva – not a common name exactly, but there were others. About the same height, true, but then average height was what the word suggested, and most people were somewhere around that. No, no – this guy was bald, almost totally. That's not, Daniel told himself furiously, that's not how I remember him.

Jaw clenched, Daniel reached out for the Court List, a copy of which lay on the unoccupied seat to his left.

0699/59 Da Silva Dominic James Francis dob 07/03/59.

'Well, Mr Jeffrey-Herd?' said the Chairman of the Bench.

'This is a sad case, Your Honour,' he began. 'A tale of a talented young man who has made a most regrettable mistake.'

What followed was unedifying. Mr Jeffrey-Herd described his client as a young man of excellent character but a victim of entrapment. He had indeed visited the public conveniences at Euston station, en route to visit his recently widowed father.

'You mean your client has recently lost his mother, Mr Jeffrey-Herd?'

'He has, Your Honour. Only a few months ago.'

'Please go on, Mr Jeffrey-Herd.'

Mr Jeffrey-Herd did so. His client, whose marriage had recently ended and who was unemployed, had been drinking whisky by himself for most of the afternoon and evening. When a young and handsome man had sidled next to him at the urinals and made, by virtue of a series of body movements, a lewd suggestion, Mr da Silva had succumbed to a moment of weakness.

Miss Holmes, Counsel for the Prosecution, reminded the Bench that the law made importuning for sex a criminal offence. The fact that the young and handsome man was a police officer, said Miss Holmes, did not alter by one iota the culpability of Mr da Silva. She conceded that Mr da Silva was not a predatory offender, but suggested that his behaviour fell way below the standard one might expect from someone who had enjoyed so many advantages in life: Mr da Silva had been to Oxford, after all. He had taught at Groom's, one of the most august schools in the country.

The Bench stirred at the mention of this great name. The Chairman, looking distinctly unfriendly, peered over his spectacles. 'Indeed, Miss Holmes. At Groom's?'

'Yes, Your Honour,' Miss Holmes said. 'At Groom's.' She allowed the word to fall slowly into the courtroom, perhaps for the benefit of any journalist who might be lurking.

Mr Jeffrey-Herd stood up. 'It should be understood that no hint of impropriety attaches to his career there.'

'True,' said Miss Holmes. 'But of course, he is no longer at Groom's. He left there at about the time his marriage broke up, and went to Thailand.' Again, she allowed the last word to fall on the court in a light diminuendo.

The Chairman's eyes narrowed. 'Thailand, you say?'

'Yes, Your Honour – Thailand.'

That was that, despite Mr Jeffrey-Herd's silky efforts at mitigation. Dominic was fined £100 plus costs, and bound over for nine months.

After the Bench had retired, Daniel saw his old teacher leave the dock and walk towards a handsome elderly man with white silky hair, who, judging by the palpable pain and tenderness which was passing between the two of them, must surely be his father. It was an unbearably intimate moment to be played out in public, and Daniel wished very much he was not there. When the coast looked clear, he fled from the court and dived into a cafe a safe distance away.

Over a cup of tea, he tried to get a handle on his feelings. The spectacle in front of him – someone shamed in the eyes of the world and for slightly shabby reasons – saddened him. There was also shock: he couldn't help seeing Dominic through the eyes of a slightly overawed teenager. Only two years earlier, Dominic had been a teacher, he kept thinking, he shouldn't have done this.

Daniel had suffered at Groom's. His Housemaster had once described him to the Matron as a 'clever little Jew'. Those were the exact words, and they had been uttered without the least embarrassment, although (he supposed) he had not been intended to overhear them. Over time, he schooled himself to ignore the low-level antisemitism that emanated chiefly from the younger boys and the older masters, but found it harder to forgive their philistinism or the absurd quantities of time he was required to spend playing meaningless team games.

At the start of his O-level year, he had changed History teachers, and thus Dominic had come into his life. Daniel's first impression of Dominic was that he was funny and kind and had no favourites. That marked him out. He also worked hard – essays were always marked by the next class. He had a whole repertoire of daft theatricals: the Ministry of Silly Walks (he liked to walk on desks or collapse under them, feigning despair at the stupidity of his pupils) and the Ministry of Silly Voices (Mussolini, Gladstone, Churchill, even – rather riskily – Gandhi). For A-level pupils, Daniel was to discover, he toned it down. Less knockabout, more stories.

For Daniel, the arrival of this upbeat soul had been a blessing. Mr da Silva had quietly guided the pupils in his classroom into a semblance of care for one another, a near-miracle brought off by the simple expedient of being nice to all of them. Incredulous and grateful, Daniel developed the habit of hanging around at the end of class, usually with an invented question, in the hope he could strike up a conversation and prolong the time of grace. Other boys (girls too, once they joined in the sixth form) did the same. Mr da Silva seemed pleased to see them all – he seemed quite without fear or favour. Nothing that he had ever done in sight of Daniel had ever been less than fair and fond.

In the days which had followed Dominic's ignominious appearance in court, Daniel tracked down an address for him (not easy – his old school, ever-sensitive to adverse publicity, was trying to erase all memory of him but Daniel persevered). He sat in his bedroom and, painfully slowly, wrote a short letter of support. He also suggested that, next time Dominic was in London, the two of them might meet up for a meal.

It would have been a hard letter for anyone to write, and Daniel felt emotionally drained by the time he dropped it into the letter box at the end of the road. He knew, nonetheless, that he was doing the right thing. Having sat, bored and resentful, through many school chapel services, one line from the Book of Samuel had stayed with him: 'He that honours me, I will honour.'

Chapter Four

Dominic: London, March 1991 and
April–December 1989

Sprung from the dock, Dominic would have gladly taken the Tube, but he could see that his father's emotion and exhaustion exceeded his own. There were no cameras or reporters, fortunately, and he and his father piled into a taxi without anyone paying them attention.

'Euston,' Dominic told the driver. He saw his father flinch slightly at the sound of the name. For a moment they looked at each other nervously.

'It's all right,' Dominic promised. 'I'll behave this time.'

His father laughed softly, and so did he. It was the first good moment they had both enjoyed since his arrest. On the train back home, the elder Mr da Silva slept, leaving Dominic to his own thoughts.

His solicitor had harrumphed a good deal after the case ended, using words like entrapment and muttering about a travesty of justice. Perhaps, thought Dominic, he had been rather unlucky, but his guilty plea had been heartfelt and general. Any chance of going back into teaching was torpedoed, of course, but his instinct just now was not to mind. Something menial but useful was what he wanted. It was time to atone.

The train juddered to a halt just outside Bletchley – there

had been an engine failure further up the line, apparently – but his father slept on placidly. In the last few months, the older man had lost his wife, and had had also to endure the grief of watching his only son throw up his job, give up on his marriage and most recently surrender his good name. When Dominic woke up in the small hours, as he always did, his grief was mostly for the suffering he had visited on his father, rather than upon his wife – who had opted, after all, to move on.

Now, confined to a stationary railway carriage, Dominic allowed his thoughts to roam more widely. Two years earlier he had been running his own department at a school that considered itself one of the best, if not the very best, in the country. He had had a wife too, for whom he cared deeply, and had felt himself to be useful. But then the shadows had closed in upon him, and he had felt himself distrusted, even vilified, by colleagues, and school became unbearable. Janey had been disconcerted but definitely not sorry to return to London. He had left Groom's as soon as he'd served out his obligatory term's notice.

In fact, their first few months in London had been happy beyond both their expectations. In later years, his memory of this time tended always to return to a warm Sunday morning in May, about six weeks after they had moved in, when Janey had emerged from her bath to find Dominic curled up on the sofa engrossed in *The Mill on the Floss*.

It was a cameo, of course, but at the time it had felt good. One reason for that was that a couple of days earlier, they had completed on the sale of their house and a substantial sum of cash had winged its way into their building society account.

'Let's wait a bit,' Janey had said.

'Meaning?'

'Let's not buy anything else yet. I think property's peaked. For now, anyway.'

'Good idea. Anyway, I like it here.'

They were renting a one-bedroomed flat in an unexpectedly pretty Georgian terrace just off the Old Kent Road. He had spent a couple of days hanging up some of their paintings, made a modest outlay on window boxes and shrubs and even planted some polyanthus and violas in their tiny little garden.

'You old homemaker, you,' Janey said smilingly when he pointed out his handiwork.

'That's me.'

The contrast between the unrelieved pressure of Janey's days and of the freedom of his own was still a bit of a joke. Nor had he abandoned the habits of diligence – not yet anyway. A tutorial agency sent him occasional A-level students, usually refugees from posh public schools who had been expelled for unspecified drug offences. And there was a course in Aristotelian ethics advertised at the Senate House to which he had sent in an application.

'What on earth do you know about philosophy?' she enquired.

'Nothing. It annoys me. And I like saying it anyway.'

'What?'

'Aristotelian ethics. Tell your lawyer chums. You wait – they'll even want me at their dinner parties.'

'Maybe. But they want me in the office first.'

'No day of rest for you, my darling.' He prepared a rabbit stew for their supper, but in the event she didn't get back till ten o'clock that night, so he had eaten his portion alone.

In theory, he liked dawdling over breakfast, reading the paper at length while listening to the *Today* programme. In practice, he was way too anxious to cope with leisure unless he felt he'd done something to earn it. Janey seemed prepared to tolerate his unemployment (for a period at least), but he knew he needed a plan.

That was how he came to write the book – nothing to do with scholarship or vaulting ambition. He needed something to fill his days. Anyway, he'd always been a bit of a Nazi obsessive and, judging by the bookshelves of Foyles and Dillons, there was a market for such things. He decided that the one subject area in which he possessed some knowledge and insight, and in which there was no popular best-seller, concerned those Germans who had stood up to the Hitler regime.

Janey had been enthusiastic, perhaps, he guessed, because anything that absorbed his energies released her from the obligation to feel anxious about him. More practically, she had put him in touch with a friend of her mother's, a publisher in Bloomsbury with a reputation for niche historical books. A few days later, he had cycled over to a shabby office on the third floor of a house in Charlotte Street. There he had been greeted by a portly septuagenarian who had introduced himself as Lionel Kleinsman.

Diffidently, he outlined his ideas.

'Tell me,' Mr Kleinsman said when he had finished. 'What makes you interested in this subject rather than any other?'

Dominic had thought for a moment. 'It's the fear they

must have endured,' he said. 'The loneliness. I keep thinking about that.'

The older man had nodded, almost respectfully. 'Good,' he had said. 'Write me ten thousand words and a synopsis, and I'll tell you if I think it's worth a book.'

There was a good deal of research material accessible to him in the British Museum and he started to put in very long hours, leavened only by workouts at a gym off the Old Kent Road. When he arrived home, he was always deliciously tired, and that helped to offset any loneliness he felt if Janey was still at work, which she almost always was.

Six weeks to the day after his first meeting with his publisher, he had returned to Charlotte Street. Mr Kleinsman was sitting on a stained brown chesterfield in his office with Dominic's manuscript at his feet.

'Sit down,' he said, smiling. 'This is good.' He gave Dominic a cheque for five hundred pounds by way of an advance, and told him he wanted a completed manuscript within eighteen months.

His own book deal. He had been proud of that little bit of success. When anyone asked him what he did, he could claim he was a writer. Janey took him out for a curry to celebrate – it had been ages since they'd had an evening out together. She was so snowed under at work that she could only take a week off that summer.

They spent it in Tuscany with two other couples in a large farmhouse in the Val di Pesa and Dominic put himself out to ensure she relaxed and enjoyed her precious leisure. In reality, it had been a bit of a strain: he was the only one not a lawyer, and so conversation was almost invariably shop. His curiosity was too slight for him to work hard at finding a point of entry.

'Do you mind?' Janey had asked him, slightly insincerely, after a particularly intense discussion on antitrust law over the spaghetti alle vongole.

'Not remotely.' Lawyer-talk provided a perfect cover for him to spend his days working on the book.

By late autumn, however, the bracing daily routine of library and gym had come under strain. One lunchtime in mid-November he had taken an unusually long stroll from the British Museum up to Soho, trawling past the sex shops of Old Compton Street. He had told himself, tentatively pushing open the doors of one of them, that he was merely curious, and peered with an apparent detachment at the counters devoted to the interests of gay men. He returned there a few days later, this time purchasing a generous selection of magazines and videos that he secreted in the little garden shed.

Poring over their contents had helped fill in some solitary evenings, but it had also unsettled him: ten days later, with Janey away in Edinburgh for a couple of nights, he took a Tube to Clerkenwell where there was a sauna catering to his needs. A few days later, in the hot tub, he met a young builder from Stratford who seemed enthusiastic to pursue the acquaintance.

It was only after he had left that Dominic focused on the potential risk he had taken – not only with regard to his own health, but to Janey's. He turned up at the local sexual health clinic the following day, where he found the doctor unmoved by his remorse but anxious to establish facts. It was far too early to detect any infections, but, by way of a pre-emptive cure, a sharp needle was inserted into both of his buttocks, and a course of antibiotics was prescribed.

'No sex for a fortnight,' the doctor had said when he had finished.

That was no particular problem when it came to the horny builder, who would certainly have had a raft of friends and acquaintances dancing attendance upon him. But Janey also liked sex, usually on a Sunday morning, and today was Friday. He debated various excuses he could plausibly produce to justify abstinence.

These turned out, however, to be unnecessary. Two mornings later, he emerged from their bedroom to find her sitting by the little breakfast bar. She was sipping from a long glass of something that looked green and healthy and told him that they needed to talk.

'Oh yes?'

She leaned to her left and pulled up a Sainsbury's carrier bag.

'I took a little tour in the garden this morning,' she said neutrally. 'Look what I found.'

She upended the bag on the breakfast bar, and half a dozen video cassettes and a rather greater pile of magazines clattered onto the glass surface.

She had been, of course, angry and humiliated, but she was also realistic. 'Can you really tell me,' she had asked him, 'that this will never happen again?'

He shook his head.

'Then how can we have a future together?'

To that he had no answer.

The next night she had surprised him. 'If we're going for full disclosure now,' she'd said, looking unhappy, 'I guess it's my turn. I've been sleeping with Joe Garton for the past three months.'

He was so surprised that he took a few seconds to say

anything at all. Finally, all he could come up with was, 'I don't recognise the name.'

'He's from the New York office.'

'Oh.'

He was in a weak position to start playing the injured party, but even so, this startling intelligence made it harder to believe that they had much of a marriage to salvage. Over the next few days, their discussions focused more and more upon the division of chattels and the setting up of separate bank accounts. She found a serviced flat in London Bridge and arranged to move mid-December.

'Not one last Christmas together?' Dominic asked.

'No, darling, honestly. I don't think I could cope with that.'

'Perhaps you're right.'

Given that they were busy dismantling their married life, they were startlingly nice to each other, he thought. After Janey's initial (hardly unreasonable) distress, the previous few days had been marked out by a pronounced rekindling of their old friendship and tenderness. On the appointed day, she asked Dominic to stay away from the flat for a couple of hours while she moved her stuff out. Almost as soon as he walked out of the front door en route to the gym, a hired van pulled up, from which two burly young men alighted.

He worked out on the treadmill grimly for forty minutes and swam forty lengths of his very slow breaststroke. By the time he returned, all her stuff had gone.

She stood with him in the little hallway of the flat, with an overnight bag packed. 'I've paid the rent until July,' she said, face creased with distress. 'Give you some time to sort out your plans.'

Dominic held her for the last time while the minicab waited outside. His sense of self-disgust was so strong that day that he could say nothing except that he was sorry.

Chapter Five

Dominic: London and Thailand,
January–November 1990

Self-disgust, however, wasn't always enough to provoke self-betterment. In the weeks that followed Janey's departure, concentration deserted him during his hours in the Round Library, and he felt too apathetic to go to the gym. Instead, he took to visiting Threshers and buying bottles of Bulgarian red for £2.89. A glass or two, he found, helped reconcile him to an evening alone. Maybe three.

The first couple of months of the new year passed unproductively. For the first time, he was some way behind the writing schedule he had devised for himself and seriously doubted he would be able to persuade himself into better habits so long as he was in London. He also couldn't quite forget a recent conversation he'd had with Leon, the gay builder from Stratford, who had told him he'd spent six months in Thailand the previous year, where he claimed it was possible to live comfortably for a few pounds a week.

'And the guys,' said Leon, his eyes bright. 'The fucking guys.'

That sounded all right, he thought. He told himself that he could write as easily abroad as in London. In the middle of March – partly in order to persuade himself his day had not been entirely wasted – he went to Trailfinders, from which he emerged an hour later with a one-way ticket to Bangkok.

A plan of any kind had always galvanised him into action. When he went home, he binned the substantial number of empty wine bottles hanging around the flat, and also threw away a further two as yet unopened. He was going to tidy up his act, here and now. No more solitary drinking. No more assignations with the gay builder or late-night porn on the VCR.

He told his parents he was 'touring Asia' and they appeared to believe that. He would fly to Bangkok; then scoot off to Laos, and maybe Vietnam. See what happens.

'Bit sudden,' his father said.

'I feel like a change.'

'Fair enough,' said his father in his most reasonable and conciliatory tone, before rapidly passing over the phone to his mother. Dominic wondered if he really meant it.

He managed to stay sober and chaste for the five days that he had to fill before his flight. The following Sunday morning he left the Old Kent Road and, rucksack on his back, went to Westminster Cathedral for the early Mass at 7 a.m.

Given the dissolution of recent months, his scrupulous attendance at Mass might have struck others as a bit unexpected, he knew, but it continued to matter to him. The 7 a.m. was also just the kind of Mass he most liked: celebrated, in one of the side chapels, without fuss or ostentation, and with a very small congregation.

Returning from Holy Communion, he prayed more fervently than in many weeks.

I live my life alone. Help me to bear it bravely.

Believing in God, as he very much did – a God of love and redemption – he often found himself baffled by his random appetites and distressed by the insufficiency of his efforts to remain independent of them.

Father, give me the grace to become a better man.

The first sight of Bangkok felt like stepping on to a movie set – nightmare traffic, exotic smells and a strange alphabet that allowed you to get rapidly, dramatically lost.

His *Lonely Planet* directed him towards a modest hotel of the kind favoured by lower-tier executives but a reassuring mile or two away from the red-light district. A couple of days later, jetlag under some sort of control, he perched apprehensively on the back of a moped that deposited him at Bangkok Noi station, from where he took a five-hour train journey through lush wet vegetation to Kanchanaburi.

This was the small town through which ran the River Kwai. On the edge lay the Jeath Museum, a troublingly comprehensive assembly of artefacts, photographs and other memorabilia from the prisoners who had had the colossal ill-fortune to be incarcerated there during the Second World War. Outside lay an original rabbit hutch-like contraption which had housed anyone deemed refractory or otherwise unsatisfactory. Visiting the grass graveyard just a few feet away, in which lay the bones of those who had not made it through the war, Dominic struggled to maintain his composure.

Every inch the earnest tourist, he bought a few pamphlets to study and laid them out in his bungalow. The Ngun guesthouse had been recommended to him by the concierge of his hotel in Bangkok. He'd told him he wanted somewhere quiet where he could work. Cheap too.

'Good, good,' said the concierge. The Ngun was run by his wife's cousin. She'd give him a good price.

She did too, and he liked the look of his little hut, which looked out into the courtyard and into which the sun fell in early evening. There were twin beds, a large teak table between the two windows, and a couple of bamboo chairs. The bathroom had what looked like a Western-style loo without a cistern. A big red plastic bucket was tucked discreetly behind it, just below a cold tap.

He had brought out three blue A4 box files that contained the material he needed to turn his notes into something resembling a book. Six months, he thought, apprehension and excitement vying for supremacy. In six months I can bring this off.

He lasted four days before he had his first drink. He'd been writing all afternoon when a knock on the door revealed a tall and fair-haired young man of about his own age who introduced himself as Adrian.

He was in the hut next door, he said, and a few of them were going for a meal. Would Dominic like to join them?

Of course he said yes. They walked a hundred yards down the road to a bungalow with a veranda overlooking the river. Everybody drank beer and Dominic felt it would be churlish not to join in. Later they moved on to local spirits.

That wasn't quite the tipping point, although when he left his room the next morning it was already 11 a.m. and he had a perceptible hangover. But then, rather to his own amazement, he wrote for a few hours and ran for five miles in the crippling humidity of the late afternoon.

Adrian turned up again later, suggesting a repeat performance. Dominic had prepared his excuses but, at the suggestion that they 'go visit some places', he felt resistance crumble.

'What places?'

'Oh, just places,' said Adrian, smiling but looking in another direction.

It was, of course, in one of those places where he had met Sirichai – a so-called sauna. The stress on its therapeutic qualities (proclaimed in broken English on a billboard outside) was, of course, a gossamer-thin attempt to glide over an uncomfortable truth: this was where men met other men for sex. There was frequently a commercial element to the exchange: if the guy was younger and obviously local, then you bought him drinks, maybe a meal and, if things got serious, Levi 501s. Dominic was not fooled by this hypocrisy for a moment. He did, however, prefer to go through the rituals of courtship simply to handing over quantities of baht.

He had been standing under a shower tap when Sirichai came in, his back to the door. Dominic was aware of someone shorter than himself, and slighter, but in this part of the world that was hardly surprising. He had been soaping his arms and legs industriously, and deliberately didn't move his eyes from the task on which he was engaged. At least, not for about ten seconds when the need to scrub his right leg allowed him to move his head ever so slightly in the direction of the other occupant. A smooth back and buttocks met his eyes and, at the same moment, the other man turned his head so that Dominic saw a strong jaw and chiselled cheeks.

Old enough, anyway, thought Dominic. Twenty-two or twenty-three, probably. He was aware of a pair of dark eyes looking at his own with calm curiosity. Then the man turned to face him, offering impressive evidence that any interest on Dominic's part was fully reciprocated.

The next weeks had been a spectacularly happy time. Sirichai would come over to the Ngun most nights and, in a slightly perplexed way, he agreed to accompany Dominic on some of his sightseeing. They spent a day at the Erewan National Park, and another at the hot springs at Pin Dat. Twice he rented mountain bicycles for them both, and they spent long, sweaty days at Pak Phraek. Dominic recovered a lot of recently lost fitness and again stopped drinking. In the evenings, they ate local food – lots of chicken, in soups or salads; shrimps; papaya salads – first at cheap restaurants and then at the homes of Siri's brothers and sisters, nieces and nephews, parents and grandparents.

This was local living, thought Dominic with satisfaction, although his efforts to contribute to the cost of the entertainment he was receiving were stonewalled. He was apparently expected to do nothing more than eat, smile charmingly and compliment everything and everyone in words simple enough for Siri to understand and translate.

Nobody else spoke a word of English – Siri's was hardly extensive, but he didn't seem to expect conversation. He didn't seem to expect anything much.

Dominic usually finished his meal, with whomever was there, at about eight o'clock and returned to the Ngun to write. Having eschewed alcohol, his head was clear and, confident of Siri's attentions, his morale was good. He would work until about midnight or 1 a.m. or until whenever Siri arrived.

Given the language barrier, conversation was restricted. 'Take picture of me,' was a recurrent request when they went anywhere more than a hundred yards away from the hut. Other recurring phrases included 'today is good day', 'I want Levi jeans' and 'she my cousin'.

It was undemanding, if hardly a prelude to a meaningful discussion of the cosmos. They didn't really talk much. When Siri walked into his hut, his first action (after kissing Dominic) was to brush his teeth in the bathroom. When he emerged, he would stand across the table from where Dominic was sitting, and – without a word – slowly unbutton his jeans. Through whatever cheap pair of underpants he was wearing came the outline of his straining cock and balls. Dominic found that highly erotic and also reassuring.

They only had one row, but that was enough.

After the first blissful couple of months, the third had been marred by a range of lesser requests for cash. Siri's father needed eye medicine (fair enough) and his younger brother an Arsenal football shirt (not exactly an essential, but Dominic coughed up happily). A couple of days after that, they went clothes shopping in the main mall in Kanchanaburi on the entirely spurious pretext that Dominic needed new clothes. It quickly transpired that the rationale of the jaunt was to make good the deficiencies of Siri's wardrobe rather than of his own. At the sight of Dominic's baht, Siri's eyes glistened with an excitement novel to Dominic, and not remotely attractive.

By the end of the day, he had shelled out several hundred pounds and considered himself to have been ripped off. That night, almost for the first time, they did not have sex. There was a difficult chapter he was trying to write about German Communists being abandoned by Stalin, and he said he would prefer to be alone. Siri looked offended, but went off. The next day he arrived unexpectedly at the hut in the mid-afternoon, apparently in high spirits and showing off his new Levi's. He indicated the bed with his eyes and grinned.

'Not yet,' said Dominic. 'I need to work for another couple of hours.' He pointed to his watch. 'Six o'clock.'

'You don't want me?'

'I want you very much indeed. But let's wait. Only two hours more.'

Siri pouted prettily for a moment and then looked serious.

'I want to ask you for money. My mother needs air ticket to see her sister in Manila. Her sister is sick. I tell her you pay.'

Dominic turned round to face him and put down his pen. 'You shouldn't have done that, Siri. You should have asked me first.'

'I ask you now. Will you pay?' His voice was brusque and cold.

Dominic allowed himself to look wronged. 'Siri,' he said. 'I spent a lot of money on you yesterday.'

'So?'

'So I cannot afford to pay more.'

'You are a rich man,' shouted Siri. 'It is easy for you.'

Dominic stood up and Siri registered that his quietness and stillness betokened something serious.

47

'I'm not going to argue, Siri. The answer is no – I won't.'

Siri's eyes brimmed with tears of indignation but he refused to speak any more and left.

Local spirits were cheaper than drinking water and they hurt his guts less. Alone again, he now slept through until midday. The hangover was also less of a problem. It was too clammy to run in the afternoons, anyway, and on the few occasions he forced himself to try, he found his pores stinking of alcohol, which made him sad.

Other tourists came to the guesthouse, some of whom made friendly overtures. He knew how to respond, but he tended to stay in his hut, devouring the Ruth Rendells and John le Carrés that littered the local English book exchanges. His own book languished. Sometimes a few hundred words were written, but usually only when he was half drunk, and they never read well the following day.

He missed the reassurance of being wanted, but never really dwelt on Siri – not least because other, more explicitly commercial replacements could be easily found. There was an initial outlay, of course, but they involved no shopping expeditions. No extended family.

He tried to ration himself at first, appalled by the bloated lechery of the corpulent inverts who constituted the backbone of what they called 'tourism'. But circumspection soon went the way of daily runs and of alcohol-free weekdays. Among other experiences now notched up was a passing acquaintance with crack cocaine.

One morning in early November, the manager of the Ngun approached him looking serious. 'Mr Dom.'

'Hello?'

'Mr Dom, telegram for you.' He handed over a brown

paper envelope.

Dominic, who was drinking coffee, looked at it in a rather bewildered way.

'Telegram important. You open it, Mr Dom.'

'Of course I'll bloody well open it.'

He walked uneasily back to the hut. Its simple order-liness had long given way to a mélange of papers, cheap thrillers, unwashed clothes and stinking bottles. A bundle of unopened letters and cards, mostly from his parents, was part of the general detritus which lay across his desk.

A telegram was, however, something of a departure. Its blunt contents – *Mummy seriously ill stop Ring home at once* – were also sobering. In addition to confronting the alarming implication contained within the text, Dominic now experienced apprehension for his father.

'Jesus,' he said. It must have been three months since he'd sent word of any kind to anyone in the UK.

After two hours' queuing at a post office, he managed to get a phone line and, a couple of minutes later, his father picked up the receiver. His mother was dying and Dominic needed, at once, to return.

Within an hour of hearing the news, he had changed his clothes, showered thoroughly, and packed. Within two hours, he had procured a flight to London for the following day. On that last night, he knew he must not drink and sat alone on the veranda, picking at grilled chicken and trying to prepare himself for whatever lay ahead.

Chapter Six
Dominic: The Midlands,
November 1990–March 1991

Having sat upright and sleepless throughout the flight to London, he discovered his cousin Kate waiting for him in the Arrivals Lounge at Gatwick. She had thrown her arms around him in welcome. Yes, his mother was still alive, she said. But she was in a hospice now and his father was very anxious that they go there straightaway.

'That bad?'

Kate nodded. 'Are you exhausted?'

'I'm not anything really. Too numb. Anyway – here we go.'

She grimaced, and took his arm and walked towards the car park.

When they arrived at the hospice it was the middle of the night. 'You must be Dominic,' said the middle-aged woman sitting behind the desk in the entrance hall. She smiled at him and said very simply, 'Go straight in.' He had turned round to Kate who squeezed his hand, but declined to join him. 'This is your time,' she said.

As he walked into the room, his eyes fell first on his father who was sitting by his mother's side, stroking her hand. Catching sight of his son, he stood up at once and opened his arms wide.

He had not recognised his mother – she had never been a large woman, but the ravages of cancer had led her to shed perhaps three stone in the months he had been away. Her head was propped up on pillows when he arrived, but her glasses had been removed. She lay there with eyes unseeing, her breath wheezy, but not apparently distressed. She was only sixty-five but at that moment might as well have been a hundred.

Contrary perhaps to all reason, it was the sight of his father that most moved him. He looked so much thinner and more aged than when he had last seen him eight months earlier.

Only a few hours later his mother died. In those last moments, they had both held her hands and talked softly to her. When her breath finally shallowed into nothingness it was as though, just as people claimed, she had slipped quietly into the next room.

They did well by each other in the weeks that followed. Never once did his father seek to minimise his son's sense of loss, and never once did he reproach him for months of absence and letters left unanswered. He tried to reciprocate this restraint by unobtrusive, practical support. He shopped and cooked for his father, kept the small house looking like a new pin, and joined him at Mass each morning.

Very often they were asked to lunch and supper by friends and neighbours. He always drove and never drank. Early in February, his old schoolfriend Jack O'Riordan wrote a beautiful, restrained letter of sympathy, and invited both him and his father over to his home for a meal. They ate beef and roast potatoes and there were profiteroles to follow. Jack and his wife Orla, both alarmingly well read, talked books and politics and religion with both Dominic and his father. Then, when Dominic went to help Orla carry plates through to the kitchen, Jack and his father switched on the rugby.

It was a very special evening. He had not been surprised when his father wept in the car on the journey home.

'I think Jack and I can be real friends,' he told his father.

'You always were.'

'Yes. But we're not schoolboys any more. And I feel just the same about Orla.'

'Well. Now you can see more of them. It's only half an hour away.'

On the rare evenings they were left to themselves, they evolved a reasonably relaxed routine in which he and his father took turns to cook while the other served as *sous chef*. In his youth, this would certainly have led to arguments. The elder Mr da Silva, in the full pomp of fatherhood, had had the knack of being both bossy and ineffective at the same time, while Dominic had been thin-skinned and protective of his dignity. Yet, now their teeth had been drawn, they found themselves able to enjoy these occasions, insofar as either was capable of enjoying anything.

There were sorrows too, of course. Sometimes Dominic would turn from whatever he was doing and find his father fixed to the spot – in the middle of chopping beans or watching *Match of the Day* – weeping silently. These moments were not for him, Dominic realised, and he learned to be unembarrassed by them.

They both spoke about the future only with reluctance. Dominic volunteered that he 'supposed' he would go back to teaching, but there was no enthusiasm in his voice when he said it. He also wrote a short letter to Janey, telling her about his mother. The absence of any reply that week, or the next, was wounding.

Eventually, however, one did arrive.

Darling,

Thank you for your letter. I apologise for not having written earlier. As you can imagine, I am flat out at work.

I am sad to hear about your mother. She was very kind to me, and this must be a big loss to your father. Please send him my condolences. I know you will be sad too and I am sorry about that as well, of course.

I hope your trip went well, and that you are getting on with – well, whatever comes next.

Love
J

'Not madly personal,' he said to his father, passing it across.

'No. But don't dwell on it.'

His father's birthday in March was one of those occasions to be negotiated with delicacy. Dominic proposed a meal out, and his father agreed, volunteering the thought that 'the local Thai' was somewhere with no painful associations. For you, perhaps, thought Dominic, for whom the memories of his bibulous and dissipated months were visceral and troubling. But the evening passed happily, all things considered.

A few days later a letter arrived from his solicitor. Mr Hanway explained that he had a cheque for £11,000 to hand over to him – something to do with the sale of a life-insurance policy – and suggested Dominic might like to come down to London to talk in person.

The details were mysterious to him, but eleven thou, he thought, was not to be sniffed at. Now he had another six or nine months before he needed to worry about money again. Or work, come to that.

'Are you all right if I head down to London for the day?' he asked his father.

'Absolutely, old lad.'

On the train to London, he reflected with satisfaction that he had lost a stone in weight and regained, as he phrased it to himself, a ton of self-respect. Pretty soon, he believed, he would be ready to search for work. Teaching, he supposed – but he was going to steer a wide berth away from anywhere posh.

The meeting with Mr Hanway had been easy. He exchanged a few pleasantries, signed a few papers, and collected his cheque. It was only three o'clock when he stepped out into the street. He had an open return ticket, although he had told his father he would be back early evening.

Basking in the euphoria of a windfall and with time on his hands, he felt restless and reckless. There was a bar open across the road and he suddenly felt a huge desire to drink whisky. He drank half a dozen singles in the next hour and a half.

Bugger the expense, he thought, and took a taxi to Euston. He was bursting for a pee by the time he arrived and, standing by the urinal, he noticed, not without interest, he was next to a good-looking young man who was staring very obviously in his direction.

Chapter Seven
Hunter's Chase Preparatory School, 1969–1972

7 March 1969

<u>MY BIRTHDAY.</u> There were letters and cards for me which Mr Reilly gave me in break. One from Mum and Dad which had £1 inside and said 'my real present' was waiting for me at home. It is a game called Frustration. Also there was a card from Kate who also sent a letter which said 'Well done, Cousin! Now you are in double figures'. Grannie sent one for £1 so I am pretty rich. I got a card with a dog on it from Auntie Helen.

I had a big chocolate cake in supper and everyone sang happy birthday. When you give out slices everyone calls out 'me, me' but there wasn't nearly enough for everyone – and I also HATE Syre and Walsh, so they weren't getting any.

4 April

Mum and Dad told me that we are going to move because he is getting a new job. This will mean we will live in Warwickshire. Mummy said I have never been there but we will love it.

17 May

I bought everyone in class a packet of Refreshers. There are 12 boys and they cost 3d each, so it cost 3/- which is a lot. After hot drinks, Hollis said I was trying to buy friends and it would not work.

27 June

We had exam results today. I came fourth out of 20 in English but BOTTOM in Geography.

20 July

Mr Elmley is leaving anyway at the end of term. He told me he does not know where he is going to live. I asked Mummy if we can help, but she said in her letter this week that it would be difficult to put him up because we are moving. He was in charge of supper tonight. One of the fourth form boys who is 13 threw an orange all the way down the refectory. A lot of others then did the same and some people even did it with tomatoes so the walls were splattered red. He tried to say grace after the meal, but most people were laughing at him. I didn't because I actually felt it was all very sad.

21 July

We watched Apollo 11 in Mr Reilly's room. There were about 20 people crammed in with lemon squash and ginger snaps. We all were sent to bed at nine o'clock, which was ages before it really landed.

When we got into bed and tried to go to sleep we heard a noise downstairs. Mr Linstone was giving six to each of the boys who had messed around yesterday at supper. I don't know why he had to do this in the corridor. It was not a nice sound at all.

18 August

Today we moved. I have lived in our house since I was born. In fact, I was 'minus three' when we bought it! I thought Mummy might be sad but she just looked busy.

We have not yet bought a house. The removal vans came from Coventry. There were two of them. I asked her if we would live there. She said: 'Not if we can help it, my darling.' Just for a moment she sounded very sad, so I didn't ask anything else.

We are living in a hotel near our old house until the holidays have finished. There is a table d'hôte menu and an à la carte one. We have the table d'hôte.

Daddy said it was a special day so what would we all like to drink. Mum asked for a Pimm's which made Dad sit up a bit. He said, 'Oh, well, it's not every day we move house,' and told the waiter to fetch it. It looked very fizzy when it came and had straws.

27 September

I am Dormitory Monitor of St Anselm's. There are six of us. I have top bunk. So far, I have not been strict. I did tell Dolan to shut up after lights out, even though he didn't except when he went to sleep.

Everything is pretty well the same as last year. There is a new priest called Fr William. This is because Fr Hadrian got married in the holidays which took everyone by surprise. Mr Linstone told us when he heard this news he went and cried which is (a) rather embarrassing and (b) strange in some ways, since marrying someone is meant to be a happy thing. (My parents like being married, I can tell.) Still, priests aren't meant to do it, I know. Maybe they aren't meant to be happy.

9 November

Morley plays the piano brilliantly and sometimes does performances. He blows hot and cold, as Mummy says. Sometimes he seems to like me, and sometimes he DOES NOT.

Tonight there was supposed to be a film, but there was a problem and we ended up waiting for ages while the reels were sorted out. People called out for Morley to play the piano. He was sitting next to me at the time and he asked me to come up and sing with him while he played. To tell the truth, I suggested I should go up with him, and he said 'Go on, then'.

It was a disaster. Everyone wanted to hear Morley and not me, and they booed. I pretended I did not mind that but of course I do. Morley has been telling everyone he did not ask me to join him, but that I pushed and pushed him to let me. He says that I am sticking to him like glue.

27 November

We are doing a Nativity Play. I am a Wise Man.

6 December

Guthrie's sister arrived from America to take him out. She is quite old (18) but Mr Linstone told Guthrie she had written him a letter asking for permission to take him out which was illiterate.

When she arrived, I was passing the front hall and I saw Guthrie just sort of fall into her arms. It gave me a strange feeling.

31 December REVIEW OF 1969

Yesterday Dad had toothache, but it took a big effort by Mummy before he would take any codeine. She says his new job is going quite well.

This afternoon she saw me reading *The Wooden Horse* YET AGAIN and asked if I was bored. When I said I was she looked a bit unhappy and said as well as doing my diary, I should try and do a 'review' of the past year and write down any ideas that came to me.

The big thing this last year has been moving from our old house in Surrey to Warwickshire. Although we were meant to be coming here because Daddy has had a promotion at work to be a Branch Manager, I don't think we have much money. Mummy has sold her Mini and Daddy is selling his Rover for a Renault.

I hate our new house so much I can hardly write about it. It is small and ugly and modern but not in an exciting way. There is a tiny hall with a little kitchen at the end and a long sitting room on the right. The curtains are bright green but Mum says they will have to do. The village is boring and we don't know anyone.

Mum talks in a very polite way when she meets new people but I can tell she is hating being here. I have NO IDEA what Dad thinks. He goes to the office all day and on Saturday he watches *Grandstand* and *Match of the Day* and on Sunday we go to Mass. He seems the same. When he arrives back from work, he always kisses Mum and they usually have a drink. Dad has whisky and Mum has sherry. During the day, Mum does the crossword and smokes when she isn't shopping and cooking.

I can feel she is angry, and I can feel that Dad doesn't want to think about any of this. All the time I am thinking, and I just can't stop it.

2 February 1970

Mr Reilly asked to see me before lights out tonight. I was a bit worried I was in trouble but he told me I wasn't. I sat down on his sofa and he said, 'Now then, old chap, what's this about you writing miserable letters home.'

I couldn't understand how he knew this, but apparently Mum has been worried and she rang up to ask what was going on. He asked if there was anything bad happening to me, but I couldn't really think of anything. I don't seem to be doing well in anything at the moment. Even though I am in the top class, I am bottom of it. My games are so awful it is a bad joke – that's what the PE teacher says. I am not at all popular. I am worried that Mummy isn't happy in our new house and that Dad's work is going arse about face (that's what Grandpa says when something is going wrong).

I didn't say any of this to Mr Reilly. There was a bit of a long pause and he said finally: 'Well, old chap, it's not very kind to make your mother miserable.' When I went back into my dorm, everyone was asleep. I cried very quietly for a long time.

20 April

I am going back to school tomorrow. I must admit this has been a dull holiday. I have reread a few books and eaten lots of chocolate. Mum is teaching at local primary schools, so she has gone back to work already. The house is in a bit of order now, and the sitting room looks quite like our old one because there are the same chairs and photographs and the picture of Venice above the fireplace. And my parents don't ever seem to change.

15 June

Mum and Dad came up for the weekend. We went to the New Drop Inn which took a LONG time (Mummy was trying to follow the map and Daddy was trying not to get impatient with her). We ate chicken in the basket which was a big improvement from the usual pigswill at school.

Gervase Brooks was also there with his parents but they didn't seem to notice us, which I don't mind because he's not a very nice person and he is one of the older people who sometimes flicks younger boys with a wet towel.

Dad was not pleased that my school suit was so untidy. When we left the hotel he said to me very quietly: 'Dominic, if you present yourself as untidily as that another time, I won't take you out.' I have been at HCP nearly two years now and I don't cry any more when my parents leave. But I did tonight.

29 June

Today was SS Peter and Paul, so we had a High Mass. I was torch bearer and didn't wobble too badly. Then we all went to Chester Zoo, which was quite boring, and Jodrell Bank. When we came back there was a pile of clothes that Mr Linstone had very kindly picked up. These contained my cricket sweater and a gym shoe and rugby shirt.

30 June

I should have realised Mr Linstone wasn't being kind! Today he ordered everyone who had kit on the pile yesterday to see him in his study at break. That was over 70 of us, and every one of us got beaten.

When I went in, he had taken his jacket off and there were great patches of sweat under his arms. He ticked off my name on a list and told me to bend over. Then he gave me three strokes of the ferula. It hurt <u>a lot</u> but I am glad to say I didn't cry. I think he is a bloody sadistic bastard.

6 July

There was a piece of paper on my desk this morning. It had a picture of me in various felt pens and indicating the fact that my shirt was hanging out, my mouth contained specks of drinking chocolate and my bottom was large. Underneath was written 'I <u>hate</u> you. F. Morley'.

I didn't like this much, but I didn't let it show. And anyway, I will get even.

23 August

We have just come back from a brilliant week in Scotland where we stayed at the Peebles Hydro. I went swimming in the indoor pool every day with Dad. Every night in the hotel there was Scottish dancing after supper.

Only one thing is bad which is that Mum took me to get a new pair of trousers today and I am <u>30</u> inches around the waist.

23 September

I am in Form 4B this year. Mr Linstone said he was demoting me from the A class because I came bottom last year. Mr Reilly has left, which so far as I am concerned is bad news. He liked me and looked after me, just as he liked everyone and looked after them. He had a way of getting to know each of us and making us feel we had a sort of special connection with him.

Mr Moro is the new Housemaster, which is bad for me, mainly because he doesn't like me at all. It probably hasn't helped that his new nickname (Mr Moron) seems to have caught on very fast and Philip Brent (whom he LOVES) dropped it into the conversation that I had invented it. This next year looks to be a very bad one.

6 October

Guthrie and I got into trouble for running on Sunday afternoon in the corridor. Mr Colley, who has always hated me (mainly because he was at school with Dad but can't afford to send his children here), sent us both to Mr Linstone. We went at break this morning to his study. Three each on the arse.

Linstone is not very imaginative but he certainly knows how to hurt.

24 November

Although it is against school rules, I have an account at Cat-ling's, the little shop in Hunter's Chase village. Mum has allowed me an account up to £2 a term in order to buy fresh fruit. Mr and Mrs Catling don't care what I spend it on, fortunately, and I can say that there haven't been many apples and bananas this term, but an awful lot of Cadbury's Flakes. I asked Mrs Catling how much I had spent. The answer is £7-12-11.

This is a disaster because if Mum tells Dad, he will go crazy and (he always supports the school) he might tell Mr Linstone who will certainly kill me.

My only chance is to ask for money this year instead of presents. In recent years Aunt Sheena has always coughed up £5. I just hope she doesn't suddenly decide I need a jigsaw or a Meccano set instead. I begged Mrs Catling NOT to send the bill to Mum and promised I would send a postal order by the start of next term. She grumbled and said, 'You need to put your house in order' but in the end she agreed.

2 December

Loder refused to eat his scrambled egg this morning. (I don't blame him – it was truly disgusting – but we're all in the same boat.) Mr Moro sat opposite him until he finished it up while the rest of us filed out past the pair of them. Loder was crying.

Now I have been thinking about that. I know Loder wasn't beaten, but just to make him a spectacle was sadistic. Moro is sadistic though.

December 1970 – REVIEW OF THE YEAR

Well, we are still here in Warwickshire. Dad says his job is going 'as well as can be expected'. I don't quite know exactly what this means but he is just the same as he always has been. When he and Mum come to take us out at school, we behave like it's all a treat and go to the Punch Bowl and eat chicken and chips. They don't tell me off if I don't finish everything in my plate because it's a special occasion.

Mummy is now a teacher at Dingley Hall Prep down the road. I had to spend the morning in the staff room there on Thursday because she was driving us to the dentist's afterwards and it was VERY VERY boring. The school looks a dump (the walls are all crumbling on the outside of the building) but I think she likes it although she says it is very hard work. There aren't many boarders but sometimes she has to go in on a Sunday and look after them all day and she says she feels very sorry for them and for herself because it's such hard work. Anyway with me away in term she needs to keep busy.

Aunt Sheena came to see us for a whole week (a bit long) with Phil, Kate and Andy. We are first cousins, but it is a long time since I had seen any of them. Phil is now at Leeds Polytechnic and has very long hair and a beard. His girl-friend Fenella also came to stay for a couple of days. She sat on the sofa and slept in the little downstairs den. She was very polite and quiet. I honestly don't know what he sees in her. Dad likes Phil being at a polytechnic. He says they are better training than a university. It's the kind of thing he says very confidently but you wonder how he knows.

Kate has grown her hair long and has a maxicoat in green. She stayed in her room most of the day and is revising *La*

Peste for her A levels. Aunt Sheena tested her spoken French sometimes, and I heard her say to Mum 'it's about the only chance she allows me to talk to her'. Andy looked bored which isn't surprising because he doesn't like reading and nothing else is going on here. He went fishing in Mayley Parva one day which meant walking THREE miles.

Fortunately, Aunt Sheena came up trumps, as Dad would say, at Christmas. Five crisp crackling pounds. Grannie gave me £2-10-0, so one way and another I had enough to settle my debts at Catling's. I bought a postal order as soon as the shops opened and sent it off. Mum and Dad have no idea and I sincerely hope they never will.

14 February 1971

The post office is on strike, and so there are no letters. Yesterday I asked Moro for permission to ring my parents. He refused. Later he accused me of disobedience and of having done so anyway. I am innocent and I don't know why I'm being accused of this. We really detest each other. Anyway, he said he is going to send me to Mr Linstone.

You don't have to ask permission to ring home when you get to Big School. Nor do you have bastards like Moro making your days miserable.

15 February

I am in <u>yet more trouble</u>, Mr Williams has found out that I filched Brinkley's Latin exercise book to do my prep. He has sent me to Mr Linstone. D-Day in more ways than just one!

17 February

Linstone began by talking to me quite gently: 'Mr Moro says you are calling your parents at all hours of the day and night. Mr Williams tells me you stole another boy's book. Last term you came fourth in class, but your mid-term position is six-teenth. What on earth is going on with you?' I said I thought Mr Moro wasn't giving me a fair chance, but I admitted that I had stolen Brinkley's book and I was ashamed of myself. I also said that not getting any letters from home really wor-ried me, and made me want to ring my parents.

He just sat behind his desk for ages and said nothing. I could see his fingers tapping and then he stood up and went over to a filing cabinet out of which he took a brown ferula.

'Well. You've used up more than your nine lives, da Silva. Take down your trousers and pants and bend over. You're getting six. I can see you've had a hard time but theft is theft.'

I don't know how far he raised his arm back for each stroke but each one was sheer fucking agony. Ferulas are supposed to be made of rubber and whalebone so that is not very surprising. Fortunately he delivered them fast so there wasn't any time to do more than just take it with your ears screaming. The worst bit was pulling up your trousers in front of him and trying not to make a noise at the same time. I didn't cry at all in fact until I was lying (face down, you may be sure) on my bed.

In some ways, it had been the worst time. The bruises had subsided, though they stuck around for several months, but not the intense loneliness. When Dominic had first arrived at Hunter's Chase two years earlier, he had been an irri-tating chatterbox. Now he had become a tedious fantasist, bragging about the supposed wealth and distinction of his parents: Mr da Silva, the district manager of an insurance company, had been catapulted by his son into the chairmanship of some unspecified multinational, and his grey Renault 16 into a midnight-blue Daimler.

He was one of a hundred little boys, each of whom was coping with their own issues of separation from their families and each required to conform to a regime that was tough but fundamentally coherent. His lies communicated self-distrust, which was disconcerting for others, and a bid for constant attention, which was intolerable.

He knew it too. Notwithstanding his copious lies, Dominic seldom lied to himself. If he had had the courage and clear-headedness, he would have been ready to prostrate himself before his peers and beg them for a second chance. In time, they might have done so – they were overwhelmingly nice kids. But instead he settled for consolation rather than reality. The long lonely hours, after games and before prep or bedtime, were expended on endlessly rereading favourite books (he became a world authority, probably, on *Reach for the Sky*) and he continued to ruin his teeth on copious quantities of milk chocolate.

He still trusted his parents. In the dying weeks of that dreadful term, he had imagined himself fessing up to them – confessing his isolation and misery. He knew perfectly well that they would never send him back if the situation at school were as bad, and as unrecoverable, as he had now come to believe. But the moment passed and again he buried his sorrow. He was reluctant to lose face and had also divined that they too had preoccupations.

He was also more resilient than he knew. Given remarkably little encouragement, his cheerfulness reasserted itself and, with it, the toughness to crack on.

9 June

Common Entrance finished today. The second Latin passage was very hard. It was about Vercingetorix and the last sentence contained the words *Romae, revenit,* and *crudeliter.*

Plattley, who is brilliant at Latin, said the sentence should have read *That night Vercingetorix returned to Rome and was cruelly strangled.* Unfortunately, my translation was *Vercingetorix returned to Rome and led a crude night life.*

14 June

I have passed Common Entrance. Linstone said 'on balance, you have done better than I had feared. Your Latin and science are a disgrace, however.' I put on an 'I'm so ashamed' look, which I don't feel at all, but I know he likes that.

I'm a year younger than most of the people in my year, so (along with a few others in the same boat) I will have to endure another year here. The people in the year below look a pretty nasty lot.

17 August

We are driving back from our holiday in the Dordogne. It has been brilliant. Just Mum, Dad and me. I've read the whole of *Nicholas Nickleby.*

Last night we stayed at friends of Auntie Helen's called the Shapiros who live near Limoges. Mr Shapiro is hugely tall and smokes a pipe and writes books. He was typing on a big table out of doors. You could feel he and Dad were being polite to each other, but it was strange. One of their sons is called Tarquin and when we were all being served supper, he said 'What is this shit, Mum?' Mr and Mrs Shapiro didn't seem to notice but Mum's jaw nearly hit the table, and Dad's eyes bulged.

Afterwards I heard Dad say to Mum: 'Darling, they may be Helen's best friends but I don't want Dominic near them.' We left this morning. Once we were on the motorway, he made us all say a decade of the Rosary out loud, and looked much happier.

22 September

All the other boys who were fourth formers last year are prefects, but not me. I am disappointed and I am also furious. I won't show it because – well, I don't know, you never show what you really feel. I have been made head sacristan. Fr James asked if I was pleased and I said I was. That's another lie, but I won't confess it.

It is because they are all rugger and cricket stars. I wish I was, but the truth is I am not. The only other person not a prefect is Jan van Maryk, who is unfortunately in 4A. I am in 4S, the scholarship group, which is sloshing around with prefects and rugby captains and nobody for me to talk to.

There is at least some good news. Mr Moro has left, for ever I hope. My new Housemaster is Captain Godley. So far I like him and, based on the amount of time he spends in chapel, he seems to live up to his name.

9 October

4S, my new class, has decided that splashing me with ink is the new form hobby. Mr Marden pretended not to notice. He has always disliked me and the class knows it. I think this is because I started the nickname 'Herbie'. His real name is Herbert, but 'Herbie' has caught on.

22 November

We were doing geometry this afternoon and Mr Campbell called Manning up to the blackboard. This is his favourite treatment if you're being slow to get the point and it is bloody terrifying. Campbell kept roaring in his ear and making him write stuff on the board and finally Manning started to cry. Campbell just stepped back and said 'Oh no, not that. It's no use turning the taps on me, my young friend.' A minute later Manning pissed himself on the floor.

Campbell sort of stepped back and the class went very silent. You could see he was shocked. He put his arm on Manning's shoulder and said 'Right, friend, I can see I've gone too far. You come with me now.'

A few minutes later, Fernanda arrived with a mop and bucket and at the same moment Mr Linstone came and told us to go to the library until the period was over. Apparently, Mr Campbell took Manning to Matron. He's back now and I am certain nobody has said anything to him about it, or ever will. There are some things you just don't do, even here.

1 December

High Mass for St Edmund Campion. I was thurifer and had to sprinkle incense on the congregation. Jan van Maryk, who was an acolyte, caught my eye and we both started to shake. I also caught Mr Linstone's eye about half a second later which had the effect of calming me right down. Just as well. In the afternoon, we all went into the woods and I built a den with Jan.

31 January 1972

For the last few weeks I have spent nearly all my free time with Jan. I got him to read *Jane Eyre* and he got me to read *Papillon.*

I can tell he wants to be with me as much as I do with him. Jan isn't popular particularly but he's not unpopular and he's made it clear he likes me.

12 February

Half term. I asked Jan if he would like to come with me because his family lives in Liberia. He doesn't show his hand that much but he said he would like to come. Last night, Mum cooked shepherd's pie and all of us played pontoon by candlelight because there are power cuts. He hasn't said anything at all about our house being ordinary.

16 February

Dad drove us to London and we went to the National Portrait Gallery and we saw the famous picture of Henry VIII – the same one that we have at school. It's by Holbein. Dad says the one at school is a copy. This was bigger. Then we went to a steak house.

On the train back to school, Jan said he had had one of the best few days he had ever had. He told me a bit about his family. His dad works in Liberia because Shell pay the school fees. His mother lives in Beauvais and he does not often see her. She designs people's houses.

22 February

Mum said Jan's thank you letter was the nicest one she could ever remember having. I could have said that Jan being my friend was about the nicest thing I could remember, at least since coming to HCPS.

28 February

Yesterday we built a den in the Infirmary Woods. A few other boys were with us, but somehow the two of us got involved in what we were doing and the others got bored and wandered off. It was much hotter than you'd expect for February and Jan took off his rugby shirt because he was sweating. I saw sweat trickling down his chest and noticed he had hair under his arms.

We didn't talk much – he never does. Time just passed. He asked me if he could call me Dominic and I said that was all right if I could call him Jan. I know now that nothing will ever feel the same again.

30 March

Term ended yesterday. Most people had gone home by car but Jan and I are both train boys and so the two of us were the only ones in the dormitory. When Captain Godley had switched off the lights, we took out cards and started to play.

I cannot stop thinking about him. Since Jan and I became friends, everything feels different.

April 1972 – REVIEW

There's no question I am still pretty unpopular, but perhaps not quite as much as I was. One reason for that is that I don't care so much, so that if (to take a pretty typical example) Francis Morley decides to try to needle me, I just say, 'I'm sorry you're having a bad day, Morley. Can I do anything for you?' If I say it when others are around they laugh at him and he HATES that.

Jan says Morley has tried a couple of times to persuade him to drop me. I'd like to know what words exactly passed, but it's not the kind of detail Jan goes in for, and anyway I just have to trust him.

Another very good change – I seem to have more or less given up chocolate and sweets which is saving me a FORTUNE. I went to Catling's a few days ago to buy batteries for my torch and Mrs Catling called out 'Hello, stranger.'

The good effects of Jan haven't exactly carried over to the classroom. Although he is clever – at least in Maths and Science – he has no interest in studying at all, so in this way he is quite a bad influence. I'm not doing any more work than I have to, and will not do well when it comes to the scholarship exams. To be honest, however hard I tried, I could not possibly get up to the standard of McSweeney and the others (even Morley) so it seems a bit stupid to try. I would rather spend the time with Jan (or, when I'm not with him, thinking about him).

26 May

Term has been pretty unpleasant so far. Captain Godley has changed the dormitories and Jan is a million miles away from me. This is something we both mind very much indeed. He also is in the First XI, and is always having to go on cricket matches and to fielding practice. Needless to say, nobody is putting me in any teams and so I spend a lot of time reading on my own. I am reading *The Last Enemy* and quite enjoying it.

Morley, who is even worse at games than me (if possible), is sadistically happy. 'I could never see what van Maryk had in common with you,' he said to me the other day, 'except you both have silly surnames.'

29 May

Morley had a fight with Gowing, who is a prefect, after morning prayers. Gowing gave him a black eye, which is good news. Better still, they were both reported to Mr Linstone who HATES Morley and gave him a straight six on the arse. Best of all, Gowing got no punishment at all, and so Morley is doubly furious. And now it is me who is sadistically happy.

3 June

Half term. We have just finished the scholarship exams. I am sure I did appallingly. I certainly deserved to. Jan came to stay again and we went swimming at the local outdoor pool. It was absolutely FREEZING OF COURSE (it is unheated) but quite nice for the two of us to be alone. Well, nearly – there were a few other people splashing about. I wished we could have been entirely on our own. I told Jan that and he said, 'I was just thinking the same thing.'

7 June

The scholarship results are out. I didn't do at all well (I'm bottom but one on the whole list) but I did get 86% in History and 82% in English. I'm going to try to forget about Maths and Science – these were APPALLING, or, as Linstone called them, 'the product of a disordered mind'.

Mum and Dad are, as usual, completely understanding. 'So long as you did your best,' Mum says. Well, I didn't. However, we are being given a bursary of £50 a year which will help.

2 July

Yesterday at Benediction I could see Jan had been crying which I have never seen before. I was quite alarmed and afterwards I found him in the locker room looking very sad. He showed me a letter he had from his father which said that he was not going to work at Shell any more and that he could no longer afford Jan's fees. He has a new job in Manchester and Jan will go to a grammar school there starting next term.

Jan told me that when his mother left home to go to her new husband, his father was terribly sad. He knows he has to look after him.

16 July

Prizegiving, not that I had any prizes. Nor did Morley, which was something.

Jan left a week ago. His father is back from Liberia and said that we weren't doing any proper work at school, and he wanted to start seeing more of his son. It all happened very quickly and Jan only told me after breakfast on the day he was going.

I helped Jan carry his trunk downstairs and he said to me very quietly, 'Will you be okay here?' Then he made a sort of choking sound and walked quickly to the car where his father was waiting.

That summer, Dominic and his mother took the coach down to London to visit Harrods, the school outfitters, in order to buy his uniform. It took them a couple of hours, but by the end there were an impressive number of green bags and boxes containing a grey Harris tweed sports jacket, a three-piece black herringbone suit, six collarless Van Heusen shirts, twelve collars, a school tie and two pairs of collar studs.

As Mrs da Silva wrote the cheque, Dominic noticed for the first time the lines that puckered around her mouth.

'Can we go to the Georgian tearoom?' he asked. It had been the site of occasional treats.

'Maybe not today, darling.' They moved through the crowds on Knightsbridge to a cafe near the Tube station. It was raining and remarkably cold for August. As his mother struggled to put on her camel hair overcoat. Dominic noticed that the belt was twisted.

Once settled with the morning's purchases scattered at their feet, he had a Coca-Cola and a toasted egg sandwich. His mother sipped from a cup of white coffee before delving into her rather untidy handbag and taking out a packet of ten Benson and Hedges.

'I wish,' she said, 'that the monks at Hunter's Chase had a year trying to manage a family budget before they start designing a school uniform.'

She smiled at him, trying to take the edge off her words. But the asperity of her voice, and the memory of the anxiety which it revealed, stayed with him.

Chapter Eight
Avila House, March 2014

A few hours after Daniel had left to go home, Dominic started to feel sick. Not in an alarming way, but still enough to ruin his appetite and to make time pass slowly.

On Monday, he took the bus to see his GP who had taken one look at his greenish pallor and promised him 'industrial-strength' medication. It relieved his nausea almost at once, but his head felt it was being bored into by a pile-driver. He retired to bed on Tuesday mid-morning and pulled a duvet over his head. Indeed, he was lying thus when Daniel rang in the middle of the following afternoon.

'I've finished them,' said Daniel. He sounded very pleased with himself – just as he had when he had been a schoolboy, handing in an essay.

Dominic had not spoken to anyone at all in the previous twenty-four hours, and struggled to modulate his response appropriately. 'You've done extremely well,' he said finally.

'You sound so sad,' Daniel told him.

'Really?' said Dominic. 'I can't imagine why. Breda and Maurice have gone caravanning for a week in the Mendips, so I'm blessedly unchaperoned.'

'No, no. You sound sad in the diaries.'

'Ah – the diaries. Yes. Well, I rather think I was. Not all the time, of course.'

'And so young.'

'Undeniably.'

'By the way – what happened to Jan?'

'Who?'

'Jan. Your friend who suddenly went to Manchester.'

There was a silence and then Dominic cleared his throat. 'Oh God – it's rather embarrassing really. I looked him up on Google a couple of years ago and discovered that he owned a bookshop in Lincoln. And, well, this is the embarrassing bit – I sort of contrived a reason to go there one weekend and went into the shop. And there he was.'

'Jesus. Did you just introduce yourself?'

'I did not. My courage failed me and I ended up just buying a paperback.'

'You clot. All the way to Lincoln, and you just bought a bloody book?'

'I'm afraid so.'

'What was he like?'

Dominic thought back for a moment. The bookshop had been disappointingly down-at-heel, and Jan, who clearly had not recognised him from Adam, had been evidently delighted to have a customer. He had complimented Dominic on his choice of book (*Black Swan Green*, he recalled) and had launched, uninvited, into a rather lengthy review of his own. A lonely man, Dominic had thought. Probably anxious for a conversation, although he had noticed a wedding ring on his fourth finger. While Jan had talked, Dominic had surreptitiously taken in details of his appearance – hair still thick, though quite grey, and a noticeable double chin. He was not fat, exactly, but beneath his rather tight and shiny grey suit, it had been all too easy to imagine folds of flesh constrained only by cheap tailoring.

'Like me,' he said. 'Past his best.' As he said this, he remembered momentarily that day in 1972 when Jan and he had swum by the weir.

'Shame.'

'I agree. That's how it felt to me.'

'Is it all right if I start on the next section of the diaries? I want my fix.'

'Wait till you get my email.'

There was a silence. Eventually Daniel said, sounding slightly suspicious: 'What's it about?'

'It's about what you're going to read,' said Dominic, 'you silly bugger.'

'Don't go to all that trouble. Can't I just read it?'

This time it was Dominic who was silent. Eventually he said, 'I know it sounds a bit mad, but I need to do this. That's why I'm only giving you a section of them at a time. Before I hand anything over, I reread it myself.'

'When did you last look at them?'

'I don't think I ever have.'

'Bloody hell.'

He cleared his throat. 'It's proving quite – um – powerful. Takes me back, you know.' His voice trailed off.

'Oh, Dominic.'

'So, you see, these letters are just my way of telling you how I see it all now. It's – it's easier sometimes to write than to say.'

Daniel said that he understood.

Two days later, the email arrived, but Daniel had no time to open it. In that short interval, all hell had broken loose at work. A dissenting judgment from the High Court suddenly cast doubt on the entire legal basis of the case Daniel was leading. He quickly realised that any perusal of Dominic's diaries, not to mention any time spent with his daughters, were going to be casualties of his necessarily altered plans. He was on the edge of ringing him to apologise when he found a voicemail from Fr Maybury at St Asaph's announcing that Dominic had had some kind of haemorrhage and was in surgery.

A few anxious days followed during which Dominic was far too weak and confused to talk. Esther pre-empted much in the way of decision-making by asking her mother to look after the girls and by booking a room in the hotel half a mile from the hospital. It turned out to be spacious and comfortable and an excellent place from which Daniel could work. Twice the following Saturday and three times on the Sunday, he had closed down his laptop and ended his conference calls, and gone instead to sit by Dominic's bed.

By Sunday afternoon Dominic's colour was improving and his blood pressure back to normal, although his speech was laboured. He smiled at Daniel, however, and held his hand.

When Daniel returned to the hotel that night, he finally felt confident enough to print out the email Dominic had sent a few days earlier, and to place it on top of the next instalment of diaries.

Sent: Tuesday 4.15 p.m.
To: Daniel Green

Dearest Dan

Lovely to have spoken earlier. I'm madly flattered you've suggested you're happy to keep going with the diaries, and your voice suggests it isn't a request made only out of a sense of duty. Or maybe I'm surrendering to wish fulfilment as I move into the last phase of life.

It was very shrewd of you to have asked about Jan! I absorbed the news of his departure with stoicism, but I honestly think something died in me as well. During those final weeks of term, we spent almost every spare moment together. His father had given him – with impossible prodigality – a portable cassette player, on which we endlessly played 'American Pie' and Cat Stevens' 'Morning Has Broken'. One afternoon, we went and swam by the weir in a river which ran through the school grounds. 1972 was a miserably wet summer, but the sun shone that day. After we had dried ourselves we lay on the bank, quite silent.

The next tranche of diaries gets a bit redder in tooth and claw, I warn you. When I arrived at Hunter's Chase in September 1972 (we called it 'Big School') I appear to have convinced myself everything was about to change for the better. Talk about the triumph of hope over experience. I was in deep trouble almost before I knew it.

I have occasionally wondered how far my parents guessed at any of the rather lurid narratives which now made up my life. Almost not at all, I suspect. They belonged to a generation that was adept at not even framing the thought, let alone giving words to many of those that may have entered their heads. And, for goodness sake, they had other preoccupations – for one thing, business was bad and they were skint. I bet they felt lonely too.

Shall we talk at the weekend, perhaps? Don't even think of trying to come up to see me. You're too busy and I am rotten company just now: I've just started new medication to suppress nausea. It seems to work, but it gives me savage headaches. Sometimes I think it would be better just to throw up.

Love to Esther and Chloe, and to you especially
D

Chapter Nine
Hunter's Chase, 1972–1974

13 September

Mum and Dad drove me up to Big School. They said they wanted to do this rather than me go by train because I was new and it was a fresh start. Dad has said this so often recently I wonder if he is trying to tell me something.

I made an effort (not too much of an effort, I think) to meet some of the new boys in my year. I sat next to someone who told me his father drives a tank.

The uniform is different (no more shorts, thank God – that was starting to get embarrassing). Using studs to attach a collar to our shirts when you can just buy them ready-made seems pretty bloody stupid. The bogs are truly the most disgusting thing I have ever seen – spit, shit and cigarettes. I'm going to pee in the bushes if I can. It will stop me throwing up.

Supper in the refectory, after a queue which went on for ever. Spam fritters. At least there was nobody to make sure you ate everything up, unlike at prep school. Then we went to a film in the School Hall, because it was the first night of term: *My Side of the Mountain*. Nobody bothered to listen, and some of the older boys were smoking.

Our dormitories are huge – there are about 40 boys in mine – but we each have a small cubicle with a curtain you can draw across. You can put up photographs if you like, but the only decoration allowed on the wooden partition walls is a crucifix.

21 September

There was a class rugby match today – not class as in classy, just each of the six classes in the bottom year had to provide 15 players. Morley was sitting on the touchline, a 'reserve' like me. He told everyone there that Mr van Maryk had decided to remove Jan from the school because he regarded me as a 'weak character and a bad influence'.

22 September

Last night Lennox asked me for a game of chess in his cubicle. He was at HCPS but I never knew him that well.

I didn't know he played chess, but I said all right and we had one good game which I won. We started a second game and I could tell the atmosphere was changing. He wasn't at all unfriendly – just sort of intense. Then it was time for bed and we hadn't finished.

Lennox had a big toothy grin, black curly hair and flashing blue eyes. These attributes, along with enough speed and agility to get him on the First XV, had ensured him a smooth passage at prep school.

He and Dominic were the same age, give or take a few weeks. In the course of the recent summer holidays, he had found himself assailed by longings, the nature of which might have oppressed someone of a more introspective disposition. Lennox was not noticeably cast down; he merely sought relief. With feral acuteness, he had divined that Dominic might be a willing accomplice to the same end.

On this occasion, he waited for about half an hour after the lights had been switched off and then wandered off in the direction of Dominic's cubicle wearing only his royal blue nylon pyjamas. For form's sake, he carried a portable chess set and a pocket torch, but both were extraneous to the entertainment he had in mind.

23 September

The Bible is quite clear. What I have done is a mortal sin and, if I die now, I go straight to hell. I have to go to Confession. We have been told over and over again that the Seal of Confession is sacred and nothing will ever be repeated. But it will be very embarrassing and I think I am very likely to get upset.

24 October

Fr Dolland told us last night to prepare ten lines of Virgil for today's class. I can't say I took it very seriously but in class this morning, guess what, I was called on to construe. The first time I stumbled, there was an awkward pause, and he said, 'But I told you to have this thoroughly prepared.' I blushed and he asked someone else the answer.

The second time it happened, he let me sweat it out in silence for about half a minute. Then he said, 'I think you had better get six after prep.'

So I did. Fr Wharton was on duty and delivered them slow and hard. You put your hands under hot water afterwards and it hurts less. And you mustn't show you're bothered.

6 November

I have become quite friendly with Stephen O'Connor in my form. He went to a prep school in Oxford which he says everyone enjoyed and says he is amazed by how everyone here goes round as if they hated everyone and everything. He also plays the violin and sketches animals.

9 November

This evening Lennox came round to my cubicle with Prebble and said, 'Oliver would like a game with you.'

Dominic had laid out the little blue chess set on the bed and they sat on either side of it, both in their pyjamas and dressing gowns.

'Are you good?' Dominic asked, slightly apprehensively. He was a mediocre player, but disliked being at the wrong end of a rout.

Prebble looked at him speculatively. 'Don't know,' he said.

He was a tall boy, fair-haired and rather passive in manner. But he *must* have known, Dominic thought later. Prebble had been hopeless – didn't know a pawn from a bishop. For the first five or ten minutes, Dominic tried to be understanding, but it soon became clear that the whole thing was fatuous. Wonderingly, he looked across at the other boy who seemed in no way disposed to leave, but peered down at the chess set with an enigmatic smile.

There were heavy footsteps in the room suddenly. Fr Dolland arrived a couple of minutes. 'Lights out in one minute. Everyone in bed?'

Prebble didn't move. The curtains of the cubicle were

closed so, presumably, he couldn't be seen, but Dominic was alarmed, should he be required to do so, at the thought of having to explain this surprising tableau. He sat very still until the priest called out, 'Right. No talking. God bless.'

The narrative that had unfolded thereafter bore a technical similarity to that which he had enjoyed with Lennox some weeks earlier. For reasons understood by neither of them, but shared by both, it had also been much more intense. So was the guilt which followed, of course, but – in Dominic at least – there was a sense of irrevocable change.

14 November

Lennox, Prebble and I now have a code. We call ourselves the Chess Club. Whenever we want to 'resume where we left off', we suggest a game of chess. (Not a very hard code to crack. Prebble thinks it's very funny. I pretend to.)

28 November

Fr Dolland set another passage for preparation a few days ago and then gave it to us to translate in class today on paper. I got 20 out of 20.

16 January 1973

All of us in the bottom year had to go on a run this afternoon – three sodding miles. I arranged to go with Stephen O'Connor. He is pleasant company, and since he is built like one of the pyramids I imagined he would not be in danger of overtaking me. He came 72nd out of 108 runners. I came 106th.

My style is more stop–start than his. Well, more stop than start.

2 February

Prebble and I had a lunchtime meeting of the Chess Club. It went on for so long that I was almost late for class. In consequence, I tripped on the stairs and winded myself really badly, and ended up in the San.

7 February

Robert Barclay has joined the Chess Club – the best player of the lot, and certainly the keenest. He says that there are Chess Clubs all over the school.

16 February

Half term. Aunt Helen and Uncle Roger have come over to London from Hong Kong for a couple of weeks. They are renting a tall house near the Natural History Museum and asked us all down for an evening. The sitting room is on the first floor and is full of modern furniture and on the walls are modern paintings with weird designs.

Before we went out to supper, Roger gave me a Coke and ice in a tall glass that tasted a bit strange. He saw me look at it and he muttered, 'I put in a slug of Smirnoff, but I wouldn't tell your old man if I were you.' Too right I didn't. He looks quite like Dad, but is *completely* different.

Then we went for supper in the revolving restaurant at the top of the Post Office Tower. Roger had foie gras which, as Mum said afterwards, will have cost a fortune. Dad had whitebait. I had prawn cocktail. We all had rump steaks and afterwards baked Alaska.

24 February

Robert Barclay has had his appendix out, so my best chess companion has gone.

26 February

I am in the San, claiming a stomach ache. I don't really have one but I am so bored that I will do almost anything to skip school tomorrow.

What had been intended as a casual deception had suddenly careered right out of control. Dominic had spent the night in the Sanatorium, happy to sidestep the catatonic boredom of his classes. But he must have been a better actor than he knew, because the following morning, the Matron had summoned the school doctor to attend him.

'Looks uncomfortable,' Dr Tracey had said. 'Roll on to your tummy and pull down your pyjamas, please.'

Institutionalised as he was, Dominic had obliged without much thought, but yelped with pain a few moments later, following Dr Tracey's unexpected insertion of a large finger up his rectum.

The medical genius had interpreted this as irrefutable evidence of an inflamed appendix. Matron was sent to ring Mr and Mrs da Silva, and an ambulance arrived a few minutes later to take Dominic to the local hospital, and thence into surgery.

1 March

This is the first day I have felt able to write anything. Every movement hurts like buggery. No sooner had I arrived in hospital than I was shaved and given an injection and the next thing I knew I was lying in a bed having had my guts sliced open and feeling shite. The surgeon wrote to the school doctor to say that the appendix was 'extremely diseased' and was within 'hours, probably' of bursting. I know perfectly well that I was faking, so I have no explanation for how I've been let off the hook.

Dad came up to see me the next day. 'Poor old lad,' he kept saying. And I kept thinking *I don't deserve your sympathy, Dad.* Mum will come on Saturday because she is teaching during the week.

2 March

Robert Barclay is in the room opposite mine. Fr Dennis has been to see us both. No chess, however – the thought of it is enough to kill me. I feel awful in a whole load of different ways.

3 March

Mum came today, as well as Fr Dennis and a few guys from my class. They brought a card and a box of Maltesers. Mum brought a Toblerone and some car magazines.

After the others left, Mum sat by the bed and said, 'Darling, come on. You're exhausted. Just go to sleep. I'll stay here until it's time for my train.' So I settled back, and she said to me, almost whispering: 'You're not yourself, are you, my darling?' and I could feel myself starting to cry. I don't know why. She started stroking my forehead and said to me, 'That's all right, sweetheart. Nothing to be frightened of. Just let it go.'

9 March

I am back at home now, and better at last.

I had an awful night's sleep after Mum left the other day. The next morning my temperature was 103. I thought literally that <u>my hour had come</u> and that God had bloody well had enough of all my fraud sickness and Chess Club and all the rest. At that moment the door opened and the priest came in to give me Holy Communion. For a second I thought it was the Last Sacraments and I nearly freaked.

The fever was caused by a 'stitch abscess'. Any description of the moment when they removed the stitches would be too disgusting to put down on paper.

23 March

I had a music theory class today. Robin Clemo and I both forgot to bring rubbers to class and Mr Bayley ordered us one ferula each. When we went to get them after prep, Clemo suggested we ask for six, since 'a measly single would be too humiliating'. Fr Dolland was on duty. He doesn't like me, I can tell, and I don't like him. The older boys call him 'Sally' and I can see why.

When I asked him for a single he gave me a nasty smile and said, 'Oh well, let's work on quality rather than quantity, shall we?' and brought the bastard implement down on my hand with the force of a fucking freight train.

6 April – REVIEW

It's in the middle of the Easter holidays and I am not that well. I had a terrible nightmare last night in which a burglar was standing over my bed and was about to bring an iron bar down on my head. The next thing I knew was that I had woken up and Mum and Dad were both at my bedside, reassuring me. I know they think something's up with me, and they're right too. But nobody's breaking radio silence.

My report was poor. I got 8% in the end-of-term test for Biology and Fr Hyde described me as 'mentally incoherent' which is about as rude as I guess you are allowed to be. Mum and Dad haven't made any fuss, but they don't need to, because I'm feeling bad enough, and they can tell. The Headmaster's comment didn't cheer me up either – 'Still erratic and still unsettled. I am a bit worried about him, and so should he be.' As Uncle Roger would say, bang on the money.

The biggest problem is the Chess Club, and it's the one I can't seem to do anything about. I've tried going to Confession and, for about an hour, I feel bathed in light and confident I'll never go back. Then I see Lennox or Prebble or one of the others of the Chess Club and looks are exchanged and I feel the old temptations. There are times when I find I can be strong. But often I'm not.

Usually I just say to the priest 'I have been impure' and no questions are asked. Fr Mack gives me a Hail Mary and that's that. Fr Howe said straight out, 'Were you with anyone?' and I said yes. He nearly killed me, and gave me a decade of the Rosary to say every day for a whole month. He also told me that a condition of absolution is for the sinner to have a 'firm purpose of amendment'.

I'm not actually very confident about giving up the Chess Club. But I am saying HERE AND NOW that next term I am going to put in A LOT MORE TIME on my work AND get off the bottom ten in our weekly runs.

3 May

Well, that is one resolution I have at least started to keep. We had one of our sodding awful Year Runs today. I kept going in a shuffle, shuffle way. It felt like about 50 miles, but it was only three. I came 91st out of 106.

21 May

I found a note under my pillow tonight.

The note had read:

Dear Dominic

You want to know who this is from, but I'm not going to tell you.
    Just say I'm an admirer. You've got energy! There's lots of action going on in your cubicle after Lights Out, I know!
    I'm going to come and join you one evening, so stand by.
    If you're sensible (or even if you're just scared), you won't say a word about this. I know too much about you.
    I'll see you later, or at least very soon. We'll have a lovely time.

There had been no signature at the bottom – just an obscene drawing.

A couple of nights later, Dominic had awakened from a deep sleep to find a foreign hand moving into regions most profoundly private, and without permission either sought or received. He was affronted as well as alarmed since, however urgent his cravings had become, he had never thought to embark on a sexual foray uninvited.

The luminous hands on his small travelling clock said it was midnight. Although disorientated by sleep, he found enough strength to attempt a shove. The visitor seemed more irritated than surprised, and returned at once to his explorations. Dominic, now more awake, grabbed a pocket torch which he kept under his pillow and tried to shine it on the visitor's face. Half a second later, the torch had been sent flying and his own face had been expertly punched. The visitor, nonetheless, appeared to have got the message and pushed off at speed. Dominic, nursing a bruise under his left cheekbone, said nothing to anyone, but believed he had seen off the intruder.

A couple of nights later, removing his pyjamas from under his pillow, he found another note which suggested otherwise:

What was all that about, then? Your job is to give the pleasure and mine is to take it. That way we'll be just fine. Remember, if I get found out, so will you.

Unnerved by this escalation, Dominic now reviewed his options. He could have consulted Brother Kelly, a choleric individual who exercised ill-defined powers of supervision over the youngest boys in the school but decided he would do better to rely on the support of someone his own age. Despite the special odium accorded to those dubbed queers, Dominic considered that there was a greater injustice at work here – one which might be recognised even by those who felt little affection for him. Uneasily, he went to consult the boy who slept in the cubicle next to his own. In many ways, he was lucky – Harper was brawny, uncomplicated, and direct. Dominic, after a bit of throat-clearing, gave him a somewhat sanitised version of events, and Harper at once promised assistance.

Nothing had happened for three nights after that – long enough for Dominic to wonder if the mystery visitor was paying court elsewhere. But, on the fourth, he was back: he must have been inflamed by passion or, more probably, by rage that Dominic had proved, thus far, so averse to forming an attachment. But Dominic's preparations had been equal to the occasion and, after a few seconds of struggle, he grabbed the other boy in a most efficient headlock and banged his elbow on to the cubicle next door. Harper duly burst in, showering punches and invective.

1 June

Neil Wade. I can't believe it. I don't even know him. He's certainly never spoken to me.

Wade had wept – great bulbous tears and huge snotty sobs.

'I'll be expelled.'

'You terrified me,' Dominic said, his own anger and emotion rising. Had Harper not been hovering uneasily among them, Dominic might have felt free to enquire – *why didn't you just ask?*

'If you tell anyone, I'll tell them everything I know about you. You'll get expelled too.'

'I don't care,' said Dominic. He registered a freedom in that sudden realisation. 'Now stay away from me.'

It was at that precise moment that Brother Kelly had

suddenly emerged from his room. He was a short squat man of about fifty, easily rattled by complexity, and his natural choler had not been improved by having been woken up by loud and agitated conversation ten feet from his door.

'What the devil is going on here?' he demanded of the three boys.

Wade's head lowered. Harper seemed to feel that this part of the evening was not really his show. The answer was left to Dominic, who was sufficiently indignant not to hold back.

Brother Kelly did not know Dominic particularly, but anyone with a mouth on him always set his teeth on edge. He listened for all of twenty seconds before cutting him off.

'Enough,' he said. He turned to Wade: 'Get to your bed. God help you if you breathe one word about this to anyone.'

There was a glitter of triumph in Wade's eyes that Dominic registered but did not understand. When he had emerged into the silence of the dormitories, Brother Kelly turned again to face him: 'As for you, my fine friend, say nothing about this to anyone – not if you value your place in this school.'

2 June

Nothing has happened to Wade. Nothing at all.

Dominic's understanding of all that had happened suggested to him that he was the injured party – owed, at the very least, an apology. The fact that none was forthcoming, and that Wade remained (so far as Dominic was aware) unrebuked, filled him with a sense of grievance. It was a new experience for him and one he did not really understand or feel free to articulate.

Three days after their big showdown, he had encountered Wade in a corridor outside his classroom. Nobody else was around.

Wade had been walking in the other direction, but turned to face him, eyes glittering with hatred.

'I swear,' he said, 'I'll fucking cripple you before I'm through with you.'

Dominic said nothing, but the threat, crude and unsophisticated as it was, added to his sense of humiliation. By rights, Wade should have been craven and apologetic. Dominic would then have been able to exercise the prerogative of magnanimity and mercy to which, as the victim, he felt entitled. Deprived of this opportunity, however, he decided then and there that he was going to get Wade and, to that end, searched out Brother Kelly, whom he had tracked down, half an hour later, pushing the roller on the Fourth XI cricket square.

'What do you want?' Brother Kelly demanded, not looking at him.

'I've come to ask if you've spoken to the Headmaster about what happened to me the other night?'

Brother Kelly suddenly stopped pushing the roller.

'I have done no such thing,' he said shortly. 'And why would I?'

'Because I was assaulted.'

'Assaulted!' Brother Kelly spat the word back at him. 'You've been like a pig on heat all year long and don't think it's not been noticed.'

Even at this low moment, Dominic inwardly conceded

the point. But he felt wronged too. He lacked the language to say so, but the thought which raced furiously in his head was that his own excursions, however reprehensible, had involved the willing connivance of both parties.

'Wade did this to me, Brother,' he said. 'He never asked.'

This bald statement of fact provoked Brother Kelly into slapping Dominic twice across the face, properly hard.

'You're lucky not to be getting the hiding of a lifetime. Jesus, boy – you go and talk to Fr Headmaster if you're not happy, but I warn you now he's got a rare old right hand and no more taste for queers than I do.'

Dominic stared at him, shock and rage vying for supremacy.

'Oh, I'd like to see the state of you afterwards. You'll be lying on your front for a fortnight, I promise.'

6 July

The bog walls are covered with graffiti about me – *da Silva is a fucking queer* is one of the nicer lines. Being hated gets me down.

Wade is still here, still smoking, still spitting. The alternative would have meant having both his parents and mine called in, and getting 12. I admit it – I'm too much of a coward for that.

13 September

I've really neglected the diary over summer, and there isn't a good reason for that other than me being lazy. Mum and I went to see Aunt Maureen and Uncle Solly in Maine. She's lived there for over 25 years, but doesn't have an American accent.

Their house is big and comfortable, with a swimming pool and a tennis court. Gideon, my cousin, is only 11 but he whopped me at tennis. I also read *The Godfather*, which Aunt Maureen had thoughtfully laid out by my bedside. She's no longer a practising Catholic. Mum would *never* have made it so easy for me to read it, although she's probably never heard of it anyway. Anyway, I finished it in two days and nights and I now definitely want to live in America.

Dad didn't come with us. He didn't say it, but I know it's because he can't afford to stop working for three weeks. Or pay for an extra airfare. He gets bored too. But I could tell Mum missed him a lot.

I took the train back to school yesterday, and smoked half a packet of the Rothmans I had hidden in my luggage on the journey. Nobody was very pleased to see each other so far as I could tell – not me, anyway.

18 September

I've just reread the last entry and must admit that three people, in fact, have been extremely glad to see me. As usual, I feel both guilty (not enough to go, yet again, to Confession) and rather pleased with myself. I like breaking a few rules.

I also like our new form master, Fr Cuthbertson. He's been teaching in Africa and looks pretty old (50 or 60), but speaks in a calm and considered way when he teaches us History. People listen to him, and he never has to ask twice.

7 October

During Mass today, Fr O'Callaghan talked about 'showing the warm hand of Catholic hospitality'. Robert Barclay was in the pew opposite mine and caught my eye. As active members of the Chess Club, we both know something about the warm hand of hospitality.

12 October

Went for a smoke after supper tonight with Nicholas Rowlands. We had quite a nice conversation, smoked two Rothmans each, and then snuck back by the music school, only to be confronted by a quizzical-looking Fr Dolland. However, he said nothing to me, having (as usual) eyes only for Rowlands.

13 October

Fr Dolland sent for me and ordered me six for smoking last night. He also ordered me to 'hand over my supplies'. I had about five Rothmans left so that wasn't such a blow. Let us hope the remaining 160 presently hidden in the Shell boiler room won't be unearthed. I duly picked up my half dozen from Mr Wallace, whose heart wasn't in it, and who delivered them very gently indeed.

I assumed Rowlands had squealed and later confronted him. He claims he said nothing. Nor has he been punished in any way.

17 October

Half-term reports. Fr Cuthbertson asked me to run through my impression of how I'm doing in each of my subjects, going through them one by one. He didn't show me what had been written, but said 'things don't seem to be quite where they should be – don't you agree?'

As I was leaving he said: 'Of course, Dominic, being new here, I can't claim to know you well. But you seem a serious sort of fellow. Is there something going on, perhaps, which is distracting you?'

He said it in a very calm way – just like a conversation – and I replied at once, 'Not really, Father.'

12 November

Chess Club met yesterday. Whew.

Very nearly interrupted by Fr Dolland in the middle of play. Snooping as usual – this time opening curtains of cubicles and peering in with a torch. All in the name of public decency.

14 November

We had a whole holiday for Princess Anne's wedding.

After High Mass (why? I don't know) I tagged along with Stephen O'Connor and spent most of the time at the William and Mary. Drank two pints of bitter and smoked a packet of ten Carlton Premium. Given that we are all four years below the age we're allowed to buy drinks, the landlord must be pretty blind.

Stephen was, as he always is, friendly and easy-going. It was pretty clear, however, from the smirks and sidelong glances around him that nobody else wanted me around. I left early – pretending not to mind, but inwardly very humiliated. I shouldn't have gone. NOT WANTED.

1 January 1974 – REVIEW

As usual I had to go to Mass this morning, even though it's

no longer a Holy Day of Obligation. I wondered for a moment what would happen if I told Dad to stuff it, but of course I didn't.

It's been a pretty dull holiday. We haven't been anywhere, and there were just the three of us on Christmas Day. Perhaps because there's been so little to do, and also because I know I am in a big mess, I have really tried to pray a lot. Maybe, just maybe, I am beginning, perhaps, to take myself in hand.

I told Mum and Dad at the end of term that I wanted to leave Hunter's Chase. They have taken me seriously but the only alternative school is Greystoke, the local comprehensive, about three miles from our house. Mum mentioned she was concerned I wouldn't get very good results from there (I'm doing very badly as it is) but Dad is quite clear he won't send me to another boarding school.

I went with Mum to see Greystoke when term ended and met the Headmaster, Mr Victor. It's awful of me to think this but it just looks cheap and mean and the pupils look pretty rough. I told Dad that later and he said, 'Well, there it is, old lad. You have a choice: Greystoke or back to Big School.'

I think the teaching at Hunter's Chase is bound to be better than at a comprehensive. Also, in my heart of hearts I prefer to think of myself as a public schoolboy rather than some kid at a local school. I know this is AWFUL AND PATHETIC and Mum and Dad would hate to hear I even thought like that. But, at least if I went to Greystoke, I would get a completely fresh start.

I've become very disliked and distrusted at school, and although I've learned always to show a good face in public (it's not like HCPS when I snivelled under pressure), it gets tiring pretending not to mind what people think of you, and it's discouraging. And of course that's the other advantage of a change: no Chess Club.

11 January

Horrible journey back to school. When I came into the classroom, Harrison (who I don't even know) hid under a desk at the sight of me. Not the big welcome.

14 January

Chess Club resumed normal service. I am also up to ten cigarettes a day.

22 January

I felt on the edge of despair today and cut afternoon school. Fr Cuthbertson found me and was kind – didn't say much and didn't punish me.

12 February

I convinced Matron I had a bug and so spent two days in the Infirmary, the boredom of which got me down. Since then I've cut loads of classes. I ought to be amazed I haven't been caught, but I just feel numb. No games, obviously.

I have lost interest in the Chess Club. Lost interest in everything. Even in this diary (and my God do I lock it away carefully), I keep to the code. 'The Chess Club'.

I know what I am. I hate being what I am, and I hate what it has made me. I want with all my heart to be good.

Lots of people I know here have given up on religion, even though we all have to sit through morning prayers, night prayers, Mass several times a week, Confession, Benediction, Stations of the Cross. I can't. God is very real to me and very loving. So I can't see my way clear at all.

15 February

Back at home. It's really the start of a new life. I won't be going back – that is for certain. I'll try and write down what's happened more fully when everything is calmer.

23 February – REVIEW

I feel better, though not exactly normal.

It was a real mistake to have gone back in January. Something had broken in me – I couldn't connect with anyone. I suppose I never did really. The last few weeks I was there just seemed a boring blur.

On the night of 14 February, I was feeling gloomy – but no more so than I had for ages. I was flicking through the school calendar (nothing better to do, I guess) and I saw that it contained a timetable for buses from Slyshaw to Drayborough and it occurred to me – why don't I catch one? I only had 10p on me, but I still had a credit slip from Williams and Glyn's Bank for the £6 I had deposited with them after Christmas. So I thought that if I could get into Drayborough by bus, I could draw out the money from a local branch of Williams and Glyn's and take a train home.

As soon as I thought it, I realised that this would not only be the best, but the only, thing for me to do. Next morning I didn't say anything to anyone, but just plodded on with the usual morning routine: wash, breakfast, Mass. I even went to first period. Then I found Stephen O'Connor and told him I was going home, and not to tell anyone until the late afternoon. I could see by the look on his face he thought it was just a load of guff, but he agreed and we shook hands. Then I slipped out to my dormitory, changed into some home clothes and sidled down the back staircase.

At any point I knew I risked being confronted by a wandering priest, but my luck held. Once I got out of the immediate grounds, I ran like hell to Slyshaw, only to discover that the bus timetable was out of date. But, having come this far, I really wasn't about to turn back, and so I stuck out my thumb and a man in a minivan gave me a lift for about three miles. I still had another two hours of walking, but by 1 p.m., I was in Drayborough and celebrated by spending 6p on a Cadbury's Creme Egg.

After a few false starts, I found a branch of Williams and Glyn's Bank and showed them my pay-in slip. They rang my branch at home who said I could have £5. Just as I was coming out of their front door, I walked more or less straight into Mr Masters – a very scary moment, but thanks, no doubt, to the fact I wasn't wearing any school uniform, he didn't notice me. I moved very quickly to the train station, bought 20 Rothmans and a single ticket to Rugby.

The minute we pulled out of the station, I lit up my first of several cigarettes. It was a very good feeling, and it was almost only when we got into Rugby about three hours later I started to face up to the fact that there were going to be some difficult moments coming up later in the day.

I rang home from a call box at the station, thinking Mum and Dad might be pleased (or at least relieved) to know I was on my way, but there was no answer, and so I decided to take the local train home. It's only an eight-mile journey, but by now it was dark and the ride felt slow.

I was both relieved and nervous when I saw Dad's grey

Renault in the drive and the sitting-room curtains drawn with light peeking from behind them. It sounds pretty odd, but I know I looked at my watch at that moment – it was just before six. I told myself, in a very matter-of-fact way, that my life had changed for ever. I wasn't really worried that either of them would give me a hard time, but I was concerned about giving them a shock.

Mum opened the door and one look at her face told me that the news had broken. I don't think she said anything but she held out her arms and hugged me. At that moment I could see Dad was crouched down by the hall telephone and I heard him say: 'Thank God: he's just walked through the door this moment.' By the tone of his voice, I could tell he meant it.

Chapter Ten
Daniel: Hendon, May 2014

The immediate crisis passed soon enough, but Dominic was considered too weak to leave hospital until the following Sunday, by which point he was a stone lighter.

'That part,' said Daniel, 'I envy you.' He looked down briefly at the unmistakable signs of a midlife midriff.

Dominic did not reply. He seemed to be concentrating on saying his farewells to the various nurses, doctors and healthcare visitors who happened to be around.

'My God, how do you know all these people?'

'They've been great. Anyway, we all need to feel appreciated.' It was a maxim of Dominic's that he had often heard.

Esther had secured permission from Mr Seymour for Dominic to stay with them in Hendon 'for a few days' and they now walked slowly to the hospital car park.

'I've completed my prep, by the way,' said Daniel.

'What?'

'Don't be dense. I've read the next section of your diaries.'

'In that case,' said Dominic, 'the full scale of my disgraceful behaviour is now becoming apparent to you.'

They got into the car and headed towards the motorway. The traffic was dense enough as he negotiated his way out of the centre of town for him to have to concentrate. Once on the M1, however, he turned his head briefly and gave Dominic a complicit smile.

'In answer to that,' he said, 'you weren't disgraceful. Others were.'

'You mean Brother Kelly?'

'Reading about him made me want to throw up.'

'A rather limited individual,' Dominic agreed.

'That's a long-winded way of saying you know I'm right. And as for that boy who sent you those notes and, um, came into your dormitory . . .'

'Wade? Yes – he was a bit out of line.'

'*Out of line?* What are you talking about? He assaulted you!'

Out of the corner of his eye, he could see Dominic thinking and, unusually, taking time to marshal his words.

'He wasn't a criminal,' Dominic said finally. 'It wasn't a gentle place and he'd carved out an image which would have made being gay impossible. So' – he grimaced – 'he went for a soft target. It was a bit opportunistic, but he was only fourteen.'

Daniel shook his head and overtook an absurdly slow Lexus in the middle lane.

'Maybe I'm a bit envious, to be honest,' he said after a pause. 'Not of all the horrible stuff, obviously, but of the fact you were having sex at all.'

Dominic smiled. 'I don't blame you,' he said. 'Those were the years of plenty, little did I know.'

'At that age, the only sexual experience coming my way was a wank in Hampstead Garden Suburb.'

'Oh – bad luck.'

'And that only ever happened when my parents went

down to play bridge at Number 37 with Ruth and Maurice Samuels.'

The banter rather petered out after that and Dominic slept. But, after a few days of family living in Hendon, they could both see that he was looking much better. He even started to walk out into the garden in the late morning, and to listen to music on the iPod Daniel and Esther had bought him.

Chloe came home from nursery school at three o'clock and, so Esther relayed to Daniel, she and Dominic rapidly acquired the habits of undemanding companionship. She was a pretty and sedate child, very much her mother's, who laid out her dolls on the ground beside the bench on which Dominic sat, propped up with cushions. By the end of the week she had evolved a habit of going to sit next to him and of taking his hand in her own.

Daniel was also relieved when Esther told him that she found Dominic an easy guest. That first Monday, when the two of them had been alone in the house, she had made beetroot soup – more as an afterthought than anything else. But he had drunk four bowls and she suspected that he had never learned to feed himself properly. As the days passed, she found herself looking forward more and more to their simple lunches – often almost silent affairs, but the sympathy which flowed between them was palpable. Only now, she said, were the pair of them becoming friends in their own right.

On Thursday, Daniel told Dominic he would like to start on the next section of diaries the following weekend, and later that night, an email arrived for him while he was still in Chambers.

*

Dearest Dan

I am writing this from the beautiful bedroom you and Esther have given over to me – during this time which you have euphemistically described as my convalescence. I've long harboured prejudices about the suburbs (this from a man brought up in West Byfleet!), but Hendon – and more especially your lovely family, your comfortable house and garden – is balm to my soul.

Thank you for persevering with my diaries. The next phase of life took me, for the first time, right out of my middle-class comfort zone. These days, I imagine, anyone running away from a boarding school would be subjected to a battery of therapists if their personal history contained even a smidgen of the colour of mine. These, however, were simpler times. I started at Greystoke County School a fortnight after leaving Hunter's Chase. Third-party intervention consisted of giving me a new school uniform and a leatherette briefcase.

I must say I find myself respecting my parents' outward composure tremendously. God knows what they felt within. No reproach was ever levelled at me, nor at Hunter's Chase. You weren't encouraged to feel sorry for yourself or embrace the status of a victim.

Greystoke was a tough ex-secondary modern: a place in which rural poverty and ignorance were deeply embedded. The vast majority of its pupils left when they were sixteen. In those days, there were plenty of dross jobs open to school leavers who had no O levels or even CSEs. I didn't find the teaching any better or worse than what I'd been used to – a small handful of the staff were good, a few were outright hopeless, and most were sleepy and complacent. You could have said the same of almost anywhere in Britain in 1974.

The social transition ought to have been traumatic, especially since I still tended to talk like Terry-Thomas. In a rare access of caution, I sentenced myself to an almost Trappist silence in those first days which was probably just as well: it wasn't a place for non-conformists. There were about 1,200 pupils when I showed up, of whom precisely one was black (and he took some stick).

As for sex – that went right on to the back burner. I don't think I had ever heard in those days of anyone 'coming out' but, had they done so at Greystoke, they would have been flayed alive within hours. (I must be one of the very few people of my generation whose promiscuity peaked shortly before his fifteenth birthday.)

Sometimes fortune smiles just when you least expect and most need it. On my first day at Greystoke I met Jack – who, like you, became a friend of my heart, and has remained so throughout my life. His appearance made all the difference.

Much love
D

Chapter Eleven
Greystoke, 1974–1977

18 February

Mum and Dad have been very patient. Dad said: 'Big School may not want to take you back, you know.' I said I wasn't going back. Today it's Monday. Dad asked me to ensure I was out of bed by eight o'clock, and to clean Mum's car and sweep the garage, both of which I've done.

19 February

Mum and I went to Greystoke County. Met the Headmaster again who said I had 'a twinkle in my eye' and that I could start at once. They don't teach Latin so Mum has found me a private tutor who will teach me at home. I also have to do metalwork.

22 February

First day at Greystoke. Joined a queue of other kids for the school bus. An older boy asked me my name and if I was good at fighting. He looked such a puny twat that I just smiled distantly.

The school felt noisy and modern but all right. I met

someone called Mr Sherwood who told me he was my tutor, clapped me on the shoulder in a cheerful way and then disappeared. I sort of followed the crowd and ended up bored out of my brains in metalwork. A fat boy with sideburns called Tony talked to me and told me he lives in a children's home. I was home before four o'clock and there is a whole week's half term ahead of me.

2 March

I went with Dad to buy a briefcase and my new school uniform. Yesterday he had to drive all the way to Hunter's Chase to collect all my stuff, and today he is shelling out more money to buy me a blazer and trousers and briefcase. Nothing was said, but you don't need to be Sherlock Holmes: my job is to settle down at Greystoke, however much I may loathe it.

4 March

I was queuing for lunch today and had a conversation with the guy next to me. He looks older than me (he has a real moustache). It turns out we share most classes, and that he's a Catholic. After lunch (burger and chips) we went and played football in the playground. His name is Jack.

7 March

My fifteenth birthday. We had steak for supper. Dad and I went for a walk and I told him about Jack. ('Well, old lad,' he said. 'It's been a very encouraging start.')

18 March

I got a telling off today from the Maths teacher for being late after break. What he didn't know was that I have discovered I can't piss in the boys' loos when anyone else is around. It just doesn't work unless I'm on my own. It's very awkward. Other than that, I'm all right. Jack is coming over to spend the afternoon with us next Sunday. I was nervous about asking and really pleased when he said yes.

24 March

Jack came over this afternoon. Mum and Dad liked him a lot. They are so relieved I seem to have a friend that I think they'd like him however he looked and sounded. He told us that he has six brothers and sisters, and his mother comes from the same part of Ireland as Dad's mother, so that was a nice coincidence. One odd thing. Mum had cooked a kind of high tea (bacon, eggs, toast, and scones and cake), but Jack said he wasn't hungry.

Then Jack and I went out for a walk. What that meant of course was that we went to a pub called the White Horse which is stuck in the middle of nowhere and serves underage drinkers no questions asked. I had a pint and Jack had two. We smoked some menthol cigarettes called St Moritz and then Jack bought us both a shot of whisky each and said we should swallow it in one gulp. I'm not sure I've actually ever tasted whisky before, but it brought tears to my eyes.

2 April

I went into town yesterday to look for a holiday job. Everyone at school seems to have them and it turned out to be pretty easy. I am a Trainee Sales Assistant at Vernon L Crimmings, Bespoke Tailor and Outfitter. Two pounds a day. I start tomorrow.

10 April

Mr Crimmings has told me every day so far about the three paper rounds he did at my age: 'two before school, and one after it'.

13 April

One man bought two suits today and four shirts. The final bill was £159 and he paid the lot from a roll of £10 notes in a crocodile-skin wallet. When he left, Mr Crimmings muttered: 'You may not like the four-by-two boys, but we've all got to make a living somehow.'

2 May

There is a girl called Olive Gee who I fancy, I think. She has olive-coloured skin and large breasts. Her identical twin sister goes out with Gary Pollard, and I certainly fancy him.

5 May

There is a Geography field trip next month for all fourth-form Geography pupils, whether we're doing O level or CSE. Three nights at a youth hostel in Penmaenmawr and three nights at Capel Curig. I asked Dad if I could go. It costs £7.50. There is an arrangement for people to pay by instalments, and he said that is how we should do it.

To be honest, I am pretty sure we could afford to pay in one go, but he doesn't ever want me to think of myself as any different to anyone else, and I think I am gradually getting my head round the fact this is a good idea.

19 May

Fr Donal arrived fifteen minutes late for Mass. Nobody seemed to mind much except Dad who pursed his lips and growled a bit. Afterwards he complained to Fr Donal. Can't say he looked very bothered, but Dad looked pleased with himself. Going to Mass is embarrassing enough. Having a father who bollocks the priest is when I REALLY want the earth to swallow me up.

6 June

The police came to take away a boy called Christopher Chester in the playground today. He doesn't really wear what you would call school uniform and his shoes are tattered. The rumour is that he is queer and certainly he looks as if he gets regularly beaten up.

Apparently, he and all his brothers and sisters and mother have been shoplifting as a gang.

10 June

We read a Graham Greene short story in English today: 'The Destructors'. Mr Martin called on us to read out loud one by one (it was a bit painful, I must admit). When my turn came, I was left to read undisturbed for the remaining 35 minutes of the period. I should have been embarrassed. Me being me, I was also a bit pleased.

23 June

Wales. A long boring coach journey. Alan Belling has brought a bottle of Smirnoff vodka with him. Christ knows where he got it – he can't have bought it because he looks about ten. He has two packets of Sobranies. Now he is cadging money off everyone, because he says he's spent out. I lent him 20p.

25 June

Much pillow-fighting last night, most of it directed at Matthew Phillpots. I don't think he's unpopular – just treated as a joke. I am practically the only person who knows how to make his own bed.

2 August

Had an optician's appointment today. I need stronger glasses. Dad was irritated when I pointed at some hexagonal frames I rather liked, and muttered that I could forget it. He jabbed an impatient finger at the black Bakelite National Health. I said I would pay for them. I have another two weeks' work at Crimmings' and will have the money by then.

Later I heard him tell Mum that he didn't believe for one second I'd stump up 'hard-earned cash on something so bloody daft'.

15 August

I collected my glasses, having paid an extra £3 to have a blue tint added. Dad said, 'I think you're a chump, old lad, but what do I know?'

27 October

I went to Jack's house. We went with his two older brothers and dad to the Working Man's Club and drank Guinness (which was disgusting). I had a pint, and the others had three. Then we went back to the house and his mum and sisters gave us roast beef. Afterwards we went and worked on his dad's allotment. He is growing cabbages and leeks. It was quite interesting.

Maybe I should suggest to Dad that we get one. He watches a lot of sport on the TV at the weekends and could use a change.

17 November

Last night at Sarah Parrington's party in Lorriford. There was lots to drink, including a bottle of Smirnoff Blue Label and another of Noilly Prat. I got chatting up Millie Leckford and it was all going nicely when suddenly my collar was grabbed from behind and I was dragged up from the sofa by some thug who was in the year above me at school last year (but has now left). He's known as Pulp or Gotch – one of those ridiculous single-syllable titles which is meant to show you that he's hard. Well, he is – built like a brick shithouse – and he was suddenly two inches away from my face, bawling abuse and apparently on the edge of killing me. Fortunately, somebody pulled him away.

I sloped off, vaguely embarrassed but too pissed to be half as frightened as I should have been. I don't think I'd done anything. Relative to him (who lives on a council estate), I'm a rich kid. Also a wimp. Also, just at that moment, I was doing well with a girl and I think it was that he hated. His trying to kick ten shades of shit out of me isn't really anything I could have done much to avoid. Thank God I don't live on his estate.

3 December

I asked Rose Redman if she'd like to come out with me one evening. She has lovely hair and a nice smile. Quite a lot of people seem to have girlfriends and so I thought I might. We're going to the Lowther Arms for chicken in a basket this Friday. I thought of wearing the denim suit Mum bought me last summer, but it's about three inches too short for me. Mum says she'll help choose something I can wear. Not sure if that's a good idea.

8 December

Rose and I are now officially going out. It's very nice having someone who is so adoring. I also think that other blokes respect you more if you have a girlfriend.

28 January 1975

The boys at Greystoke seem universally useless at French, and most of them are very hostile to the thought of anyone or anything abroad. Nobody goes there. Blokes who like foreign languages are queers – it's that simple. The girls are a bit better, but mainly they don't like to show it.

4 February

Mr Lipman called Lisa Holden a slut in History today. I was debating whether or not I ought to walk out in protest. I didn't, however. Nor did anyone else, for that matter.

11 February

I was working on my History essay tonight when Nick Walton (who, for some reason, is always known as Boff) arrived. He was trying out his new motorbike – a Yamaha FS1E. It is brilliantly fast (at least 40mph). Fortunately, my parents were out, so Boff took me on the back. I didn't have a crash helmet so it wasn't a particularly sensible thing to do.

16 February

Boff called over again. No chance of another trip out because my parents were at home. I could see my mother taking in the sight of his leather jacket. She tried to chat to him, but Boff doesn't have a lot of conversation so nobody got very far.

21 February

I chucked Rose today. I fancy her a bit but not that much. I told her at break – kept it matter of fact.

26 February

Rose needed a pencil sharpener today in French, and I offered her mine. She said nothing and looked right through me. She's taking it all very personally.

7 March

Sixteenth birthday. I had a cheque for £10 in Mum and Dad's card which is great but it did confirm to me that they had meant what they said about me not having a motorbike. Dad asked me to fetch his briefcase which he'd left in the car.

When I went into the garage, there was a yellow Honda SS50 with a big blue birthday ribbon. Suddenly, they materialised behind me and Mum took my hand and said to me: 'You must promise me, darling, to be sensible with it.' I am not joking when I say that this was one of the best moments I have ever had in my life. Then we went to the Berni Inn for supper (T-bone steak). The bike cost £155, of which I have to repay £100.

'Just one thing, Dominic,' Dad said, as we were leaving. 'If I see you drunk anywhere near this bike, I'll take it away. And you'll pay the full price.'

He didn't say it loudly or crossly. Just matter of fact.

20 March

A bad row in class between Jack and Mr Donaldson. It began with Jack arriving all of one minute late (he'd been at football practice), and moved on quickly to Donaldson shouting and jabbing him in the chest. I could see Jack's face turn grey. He moved his body from side to side, just like a boxer, so that Donaldson kept missing him and wound up jabbing fresh air. He shouted at Jack to stand still but Jack just said to him, 'If you want to hit me, why don't you?'

Donaldson went and sat down at his desk, wiped his glasses and tried to bring his breathing back under control. Jack looked at him without any expression and then, after a few moments, came and sat down at the desk next to mine.

22 March

Rode over to Boff's house. I actually didn't go inside, but we hung around the back where there is a workshop for servicing cars and bikes. There's not much in the way of conversation with Boff. He just hangs around with spanners and monkey wrenches and engine oil. He appears to enjoy having me around, especially if I do imitations (Mr Mackay in *Porridge* is his favourite) which crease him up. The trick is to refuse to do them on demand but slip a few into the conversation. It keeps him keen.

8 June

Leanne Moss's party last night. Boff got off with Tina Watson.

5 July

I started my job at the Ristorante Romana this evening. Tommaso, the boss, is very fat and with dreadful English. He smiled at me and looked vague and busy. His wife, Corinna, is elegant and sharp with black hair, gold shoes and a pair of outsize gazonkas.

12 July

The bit I enjoy most at the Romana is working the pudding trolley. We are told to call it the 'sweet' trolley, but it's like the word 'toilet'– I just can't get my mouth round it. Sherry trifle, crème caramel, Black Forest gateau, and pineapple Romanov (fresh pineapple with kir and whipped cream). There is a dance floor with a three-piece band in the middle of the restaurant. They play Frank Sinatra numbers, and also (endlessly) 'Tie a Yellow Ribbon Round the Old Oak Tree'. I like it because there's a really mellow feel to the place by then. All that music and pudding gets the men sentimental. They hold hands with their wives, start ordering brandies and take out their packets of Slim Panatellas. Ordinary brandy is 40p a shot. Occasionally somebody goes haywire and orders the vintage at a cool 80p.

16 July

As I was serving slices of chicken chasseur yesterday a customer accidentally jogged my arm. Hot oil and lemon juice spilled through my white jacket on to my bare forearm.

When I looked at it later (I only got home after midnight), it was quite a mess. Mum is taking me to the doctor later this afternoon. I rather fancy a night off work, but no sign of that, alas.

10 August

Mum and Dad and I went to Scotland for ten terrible days. Three nights at a retreat centre near Glasgow with Mass every day. Then a week at Tomintoul with Mum's Uncle Duncan. I was too depressed even to write my diary. I read *The Hound of the Baskervilles* and *Ivanhoe*. Hardly went outdoors. It rained all the time anyway.

17 August

Jack and I went to Shirley Yell's party last night. There was lots of Bacardi and the girls were all smoking black Sobranies. There's something about parties I just don't get and never will. How come the same people always get off with each other – as far as I can see, without trying?

The successful ones often don't even bother to talk first. They just end up with their tongues down each other's throats.

Tonight, Mandy Rigby snogged me energetically. I was flattered but a bit confused. Her hands have a terrible texture which is a bit off-putting. I think she was just being sociable.

22 August

Got a bit over-confident tonight and poured gravy on to a green salad, as opposed to oil.

26 August

My O-level results have arrived. Nine grade As. I must admit that I felt pretty good when Mr Victor told me. (Although in a way I didn't because I had a terrible hangover thanks to the fact that Boff and I had each drunk a bottle of his mum's banana wine the night before). I'm guessing, but I bet that's masses better than most people at Big School will have done. I owe my 'success' entirely to my parents and to Jack.

Not everything is perfect. Although I blot it out with hard work and motorbikes and friends, the truth remains that I don't really 'get' girls. I've heard it said that being queer is often 'a phase' but I don't think this is the case with me. I notice (and memorise) immediately the shape and look of blokes' hands and legs. I don't try to – it just happens. Can't see it happening with girls.

Obviously, I am much happier now – for one thing, I feel about one million times safer. I don't have a bad reputation any more and that perhaps is the best thing of all. Nobody here knows anything about what went on. On the other hand, I can't help it – sometimes I miss the Chess Club. At Greystoke anyone who was suspected of being queer – even if it was just the tiniest hint – would be killed. Most of them would be killed at home by their parents, even if they made it through a day at school, which seems unlikely. I could never ever tell Mum and Dad about what goes on in my head: it's harder for them because, let's face it, they are as Catholic as you get and homosexuality is about as bad a mortal sin as there is. Yet another part of me knows with complete confidence that, however bad anything was that I had done, they would always care for me and love me.

So it's all a problem. I block it out as far as I can and I throw out false trails to keep everyone off the scent. Thank God that Greystoke is about a million miles away from Big School – those are two worlds and two sets of people who will never collide. One day, I suppose, my secret will all come out, but by then I plan to be a long way away. The way I see it is that decent brains and a lot of hard work will get me a good job and a decent position. Then I can be myself.

22 September

Boff and I played squash at Bashley Sports Centre yesterday. I lent him Dad's old racquet, but he was a bit confused at first by the scoring. We played for nearly an hour and I just beat him. Then we had a shower. The phrase 'built to last' came to mind.

2 October

Roger Broome has announced he is becoming a Christian – a direct consequence of a talk we had in school last week when a bloke with a beard called Peter told us how the Bible had rescued him from drugs when he'd been in America, followed by the showing of a film called *The Cross and the Switchblade*.

Roger says he feels 'completely certain' that Christianity has all the answers. I wish I did.

19 October

Went out for a drink last night in Boff's Hillman Minx. There were six of us crammed into it, and Boff took the humped-back bridge in Bridley at about 60mph – not a good idea since the car took off and we landed upside down in a field, having rolled over. None of us suffered anything worse than scratches, but the Minx is a wreck. The police arrived, and various parents. Dad came, and was completely calm. Tina's mother arrived and she and Tina did a great deal of sobbing.

We weren't breathalysed. Dad said to me later, 'How much had you had?' I said, truthfully, a pint. I didn't say that Boff had had six or seven. I know what Dad's like. He would have been so outraged he would definitely have driven over and told Boff's parents – or even have gone to the police (whom he loves).

28 October

News today that Boff is joining the RAF and starts his training in Scotland in a fortnight. Apparently, his parents think he's wasting his time at school – which he is – and that he has got himself into bad company. Tina is distraught. They have been going out for ages, and I think she was hoping they'd get engaged

8 November

Boff called over yesterday afternoon – on his motorbike, since the car is written-off. A few minutes later a blue

Datsun pulled up just outside the front drive. Tina was obviously sitting inside, but Boff just scowled and said she was following him everywhere and he was sick of it. She stayed there sulking for about an hour before driving off. Very awkward.

My parents were out for the day and I couldn't help thinking how nice it would be if Boff could be persuaded to share the moment I've been dreaming of for months. But of course he didn't. We had a couple of pints of gassy Watney's at the Queen's Head, smoked a packet of ten No. 6 between us. Then we shook hands, all manly like, and off he went.

8 December

People were talking about the IRA in the playground today, I don't think I've ever heard anyone talk about politics at Greystoke before. Jack was silent for a while and then said, very quietly, 'I support the IRA.' He's bigger than anyone else in earshot, and nobody said anything. I think they might have done otherwise. I didn't react. He's quite scary at these moments.

16 January 1976

After lunch today, Tina was by herself in the Sixth Form Common Room and looked away when she saw me come in. I asked her straight out what her problem was. She shot me a look of real dislike and said, 'You're supposed to be the brainy one. Try thinking it through.' Then she walked out.

22 February

Dad asked me if I didn't think I ought to get a Saturday job again. I haven't had one for ages, since the days of Mr

Crimmings. I reminded him I work on Friday and Saturday nights at the Romana and that I also had homework to do. He grunted and said, 'Jack seems to manage.' It's true – he does. He works all day Saturday at Bainton's Greengrocer's and also serves Sunday lunches at the Romana.

2 March

Mrs Walmsley, who teaches speech and drama part time, asked to see me last week. Her goddaughter, who is my age, can't bear her boarding school and wants to go to a local day school. Mrs Walmsley said to me: 'I know you've done something similar. Would you be happy to talk to her yourself?'

It was arranged that I would meet her today after school. It was a bit formal and embarrassing at first. She's called Julia and is short and very slim with fair hair, and rather nice pert breasts. We went and walked round the grounds (everyone else had gone home) and sat down outside the gym. There was not much talk about boarding school, but I think it is fair to say we are now going out.

27 March

A letter from Julia arrived last week, written on violet notepaper with a lot of hearts and kisses. I like her enthusiasm, as Dad would say, but she seems pretty mad. She told me she has been through three schools in the past five years which makes me look like Mr Steady.

She wrote: 'I am coming home this Saturday and will be very bored because my parents are going out for the day, so it will be just me. Unless you come to visit. PS Come about midday.'

To be honest, that's exactly what I did. Also at 3 p.m. And again just after seven.

Now I am feeling guilty and awkward, and also a bit of fear since we took no precautions.

31 March

Julia tells me her period is due, but hasn't yet happened. She then added, 'I reckon it will be all right.'

4 April

I took out my old missal and went over to St Crispin's on my motorbike, and said two Rosaries and did the Stations of the Cross. Fr Donal saw me, but didn't say anything. If I ever get through this, one thing I will NEVER DENY is the comfort of prayer.

6 April

I biked over to Julia's, and we met on the local rec ground to avoid her parents' suspicions. She is now a week late. 'I'm pretty worried,' she said. We didn't really look at each other. (We don't much like each other, I realise.)

17 April

The phone rang just after I made that last entry. It was Julia, telling me her period had arrived. 'Relieved' doesn't begin to describe what I felt. She told me and then rang off abruptly. I went up to my bedroom, got down on my knees, and thanked God.

'Going out' is well and truly finished between us. It's quite clear she doesn't like me. I don't like her either. I've been trying to think why that is – and I suppose the truth is we have the same faults as each other. I can see she's trying to be someone she isn't. Guess what, she's seen the same in me. SHE'S RIGHT.

I'm queer. That's it. I nearly got her and myself into the biggest bloody trouble imaginable simply because I can't bear being who I am. I can't face that happening again.

13 May

Chip Kendall asked to see me today. I've never spoken to him before and it was hard to call him 'sir' because absolutely everyone, teachers included, refers to him by his nickname. He suggested I should apply for Oxford this year. Apparently nobody from the school has ever gone there. Mum and Dad and I spoke about it this evening. They said that if that was what I wanted, they wished me luck. I said to Jack he should have a bash too (he is MUCH cleverer than me) but he says the philosophy course is better in London.

I think I'll have a crack at Law – I like the idea of being a rich barrister. I'll have to take entrance papers first in one of my A-level subjects (History, for sure) and, if they're good enough, they will give me an interview. Dr Pertwee said he will coach me for the general paper, which is very kind of him.

28 May

For the past two weeks, Dr Pertwee has seen me every few days on my own for an hour and talked through 'general history' essays with me. We have a good discussion and I go away and write one of them in an hour. The trouble is he hates what he reads – he says I lose track of the arguments and fail to answer the question.

4 June

Dr Pertwee came over to my table at lunch today and told me that he didn't think I was anywhere near the required standard and that maybe I shouldn't pin 'too many hopes' on Oxford. He was gentle in his manner and kept on saying 'this isn't for everybody, you know'. I'm not giving up, however. This evening, instead of spending an hour or so writing an essay of about 1,200 words, I spent three hours writing one of about 900. It is full of crossings out and a mess, so I will have to rewrite it again tomorrow. But instead of just writing, I've really been THINKING as well. So maybe I have, for once, answered the question.

9 June

Dr Pertwee said I have, at last, started to show a little spark of what he suspected, all along, lay 'buried under a heap of verbiage'.

21 June

Jack and I went on a day trip organised by the school to Boulogne. It cost £8. Dad got us up at 6 a.m. and drove us to the train station in Coventry, where we met the others. Then we went to London, to Dover and Boulogne where we stayed for two hours. We bought 200 Disque Bleu and drank a lot of Pernod on the ferry and at a bar in the town.

Jack bought a knife. He told me a lot about existentialism. A brilliant day.

12 August

I rang Jack this afternoon and went on my motorbike to the Admiral Nelson. He had a couple of pints but I stuck to orange squash. It only costs 3p there.

25 November

The Oxford exams started on Monday. I took them on my own in the store cupboard behind the library.

European History began badly because Mr McIntyre, who was supposed to be invigilating, decided to type a few letters to while away the time. Later I got horrendously pissed with Jack and can vaguely remember throwing up on Dad's rosebushes.

7 December

At Oxford (Chester College) for interviews. I came here by bus – took three hours, stopping in Aylesbury and Buckingham and Christ knows where else. My room overlooks a quadrangle covered in moss and ivy. It's unbelievably cold but I have put on both bars of the electric fire.

I killed time this afternoon by getting a haircut (Mum has been urging me to do this for ages and this morning gave me £2 for the purpose). I found a poncey place called Fernando's where they put a caftan on my shoulders, served me a coffee and trimmed off my sideburns without asking me first. Bill £4. Thanks a fucking bunch. I look like a monk, and I've run out of money.

8 December

There were two dons for the History interview: one was tiny and sat in a very deep armchair. His little legs didn't even touch the ground. The room itself was large and incredibly grand with a bust of Gladstone on a pedestal (I know this because the name was inscribed on the base). He spoke like a machine gun in bursts of staccato:

'Very well, da Silva. Why do you think Marxist history has no place in university?' You write that class is inevitable: why so? Justify your attempts to rehabilitate Lord North.'

The other chap said that I had written a 'very plausible essay' on why the Carolingian Empire collapsed. His voice was gentle and then he added, almost as an afterthought: 'In fact it's so plausible, I'm left wondering how it ever managed to *stagger to its feet* in the first place.' And so on.

9 December

The Law interview was today. Two men, again. One wore a tweed suit and sat behind a big desk. He was a bit snappy and impatient and kept on using Latin phrases: *mutatis mutandis, sub specie aeternitate, prima facie.*

The other guy looked like Mick Jagger, and spoke with a very posh voice. (This combination of rock star and public schoolboy isn't one I'd expected in an Oxford don and I was a bit thrown.)

Some of the questions were impossible:

What is meant by 'the rule of law'?

What is the difference between guilt and culpability?

Is strict liability an affront to natural justice?

I just bluffed and kept going. Waste of time really. I spoke to Mum this evening and she says that Mrs Kneafsey has a daughter at Cardiff University and that she is loving it.

10 December

There was a drinks party last night for interviewees given by second-years. Everyone drank sherry. Lots of people seemed to have known each other at school. Of course, with my usual luck, the first face I recognised was Francis Morley, the person who more than any other did his best to make my life at HCPS miserable. It turns out he is applying to read Classics. He is short and has bad acne. I don't know if he's a prefect or has rugby colours and it doesn't matter. Here, we are in the same boat.

Once the moment of shock had passed, we chatted reasonably easily. He says that Christ Church is his first choice and that he probably wouldn't accept a place at Chester even if he was offered one. He looked me up and down a bit and said, 'I don't mean that rudely.'

16 December

Dad called through the bathroom door this morning to say that there was a letter from Oxford addressed to me. I could hear he was trying to sound unconcerned. I ran downstairs, grabbed the envelope and took it into my room, taking a couple of very deep breaths. As soon as I saw the first lines – 'Dear Mr da Silva, I am delighted to be able to offer you a place as a Commoner to read Law at Chester next year' – I could feel the blood come rushing to my cheeks.

I took a few moments to try to compose myself, and then went next door into Mum and Dad's room: they were making their bed but looked up at me as I came in. I suppose my face must have told them everything, but I also nodded and smiled and said, 'I've got it.'

I saw Dad's eyes fill with tears, and Mum looked at me

with a kind of long and grave expression, and then they both took me in their arms. It is not a moment I think I will ever allow myself to forget.

The three of us had a meal at the Falconer's Arms tonight (steak, followed by gooseberry crumble). Then Dad said, 'You and I have work to do, old lad.' When we came home, he took out the Basildon Bond and we both wrote, then and there, letters of thanks to Dr Pertwee. Dad wrote another to the Headmaster to thank him and all the staff for their help and encouragement. He hates letter-writing but Mum told me later he would have written both letters even if I had not got in.

29 December

Jack and I met for an early evening drink and ended up chatting for hours. Unlike me, he has no interest in mixing with people from school and going to their parties. He says he can't wait to get out of here and meet people who have 'real' ideas.

Our friendship still matters to me more than any other. When I first met him, I was just incredibly grateful to this kind boy (who was reassuringly big and strong) for making it clear he was ready to be my friend. Now I find him the most interesting and clever person I know. We have never talked about what's going on in my head but I think he's guessed it all – and he isn't bothered. Best of all, I don't fancy him in the slightest. So it's very uncomplicated.

2 February 1977

Boff rang me tonight which has never happened before. In one way of course this is very flattering – Mum says that he must be missing his old friends. Well, I daresay he is, but he sure as hell doesn't have much to say. He kept asking 'what's happening?' to which, of course, the honest answer is nothing at all.

He is a useless conversationalist at the best of times, so trying to sound natural and chatty was a tall order. Nor was it made any easier when, every three minutes, the pip-pip-pip sound went and he kept on putting in another 5p. I was praying for him to run out of cash. After he'd spent about 20p my nerve broke and I told him my supper was ready.

3 February

I have applied to go to a kibbutz for July and August. I like this idea because (a) it is a definite plan for summer and means I can get away from here. I'm getting bored with the place and the people, except Jack; (b) it is cheap. You don't get paid, but your labour pays for your keep; (c) I quite like the idea of a commune where everybody does their share of the shitty jobs but also the good ones; (d) I saw a documentary on one on BBC2 and fancied most of the guys. Clearly I did not tell Mum and Dad about (d), but they have very kindly agreed to stump up my airfare.

4 March

Mr Lovell returned our essays on Philip the Fair today. We wrote them in January. On mine he put a big tick at the bottom and the single word 'excellent'. I can't see why – given his shitty marking, his persistent unpunctuality and lack of any preparation – anyone bothers to pay him.

17 March

Lots of calls from Boff – he rang twice last week, and twice this week. Dad thinks that he's homesick and is very insistent I should not try to rush him off the phone. He hasn't been on any aeroplane let alone a fighter and says he won't since he's a tool fitter.

Last week I overheard Donna Pickard telling some other girls in the library 'she never hears a word from Boff'. I presume 'she' refers to Tina, who certainly looks in a very bad temper at school, and never says a word to me. For some reason she still seems to see me as some kind of enemy.

22 March

Boff rang. He has blown his savings on an old Norton Commando. He says he's 'getting it tuned up to race'. There is a disused airfield, a few miles away from his base, and the farmer who owns it has allowed him to keep it there and make as much noise as he wants. He suggested I come up and see the bike next Saturday and the two of us could camp in one of the farmer's fields. There was a slightly awkward silence after he'd suggested it, and then he said that 'it'll be your half term then'. He has a tent and all I need to bring is a sleeping bag. I said it sounded good.

Later I told my parents about the plan and they thought it was very kind of me – Boff, being so homesick, needs his friends.

12 April

It was a long and boring journey – train, then bus, then a LONG walk. I had expected Boff to be shy when I arrived, and he was. 'You all right then?' was about as far as the welcome went. He had set up the tent just by the tarmac of the old runway, and had a little Calor gas lamp and a cooking ring and a couple of tins of Heinz sausage and beans for supper.

Fortunately the need for conversation ended as soon as he took the cover off the Norton and kick-started it into life. It is a rather beautiful thing, actually, but has a roaring four-stroke that could have been heard ten miles away. Boff didn't say anything: just inclined his head for a second and threw me a crash helmet. I realised that this was a test of some sort, so I put it on and climbed aboard. It did, of course, take fear to new heights – he has obviously been practising cornering at speed, and so I had to lean into every bend with him – my knees about two inches off the tarmac. People wouldn't believe that, but it's true.

The terror had been matched by an exhilaration that sprang from more than terror. When they finally stopped racing round the circuit, Dominic had knelt down by the side of the tent to unzip the opening. As he had done so, Boff had pushed his shoulder so that they had both fallen inside.

For a second they had lain there laughing, high on the adrenalin of fear. It had turned into a wrestle and then, a couple of seconds later, Dominic found Boff's mouth upon his own. The rest had been easy.

Much later they ate supper, their appetites sharpened by the hours spent out of doors, by shared pleasure and also by relief. Boff had made it implicitly clear that he would not welcome any kind of discussion about what had passed between them, and that any sign of tenderness would be unthinkable.

That night, under the light of the Calor gas lamp, he worked late on his motorbike, whistling through his teeth.

14 April

We didn't move much. Raced the bike a bit. Boff keeps tinkering with the engine to improve performance. I read *Selected Poems and Letters of John Keats.*

Haven't felt guilty at all. Even when I said my prayers last night, I had no sense that God was looking for contrition. Opposite of what I felt when I had my thing with Julia last year.

13 May

I was revising hard this morning when the front doorbell rang. I went downstairs to find a very embarrassed gentleman from Radio Rentals there, explaining that Dad has not paid the rent for our ancient black-and-white TV and that he had come to take it away.

'It's not a lot of money,' he said. 'I think maybe Mr da Silva has just forgotten. It's a matter of a couple of pounds.' As it happened, I had £3 on me, so could easily have paid him off but, having been given this heaven-sent opportunity at last to force Dad into getting a colour set, I was not about to pass it up. We are the last family in England still to have black and white. (Dad's excuse is that 'they made better shows when it was still black and white'.)

26 May

Boff has rung a couple of times this week already – it's only Thursday – asking if I want to come and try the bike again. He says he's retuned it. Well in some ways, I would – a great deal. But I am flat out revising and I'm determined to get top grades.

I'm also bothered about Tina with whom (I think) he's still going out. He's never mentioned her to me, and I can't help wondering what she knows.

12 June

I guess she does know.

It was Sheena Doherty's eighteenth on Friday night in the village hall. I didn't really want to go but I've done too much revision recently and I felt like doing something different for a change. Tina asked me to dance, which was a shock – and then said something which I couldn't hear so I bent my face down towards her and asked her to say it again. Then she slapped me – hard enough to hurt a lot, but not so hard that other people were likely to have heard or seen, unless they had been watching.

1 July

A levels finished yesterday morning. A bit of anticlimax really. With an Oxford unconditional offer, I have to get only two Grade Es so all the pressure was self-inflicted. I spent the evening at Jack's. He is going to work in London this summer as a hospital porter. All his sisters were home for his dad's birthday and you could see them petting him – and Jack for that matter. Neither appeared to mind, nor even to notice. But boy, they both get a lot of attention.

We didn't do anything much – watched *Top of the Pops* but gave up when Max Bygraves came on. Then we talked about Ireland and politics. Mr O'Riordan never went to university, just like Dad. But, also just like Dad, he has a knack for putting his finger on the weakness in somebody else's argument. Mrs O'Riordan didn't really join in but made us cheese and pickle sandwiches. They were delicious.

18 July

Israel

The flight was quite long and boring. The nearest to entertainment was when a group of Hasidic Jews in black overcoats went to the front of the plane and started praying. It was about 11 p.m. local time when we arrived. Guess whose rucksack was last off the line? There was a tatty old double-decker outside for all of the volunteers and I found myself sitting next to a rather gruff guy of my own age from Newcastle called Joe.

Israel looks very primitive on the basis of the drive – no modern motorways. Lots of jeeps and soldiers. We arrived at the kibbutz shortly after 2 a.m. In daylight, the kibbutz itself emerged as a compact village set amid a lot of farmland, although in fact we're on the edge of a large town (Nazareth – an Arab town, as it was described to me by one of the volunteers, rather sniffily).

I've been put in a particularly basic room with Joe and two other guys – both (unhelpfully) called Steve. The four 'beds' are really just planks covered by a cheapo thin mattress on which we placed our sleeping bags. There are communal loos and showers – basic, but not a hole in the ground THANK GOD. Breakfast was good if curious: lots of yoghurt and cold meats. After we had finished, we were spoken to by a young guy called Hillel who told us what work we'd be doing. The weird bit was that he had a revolver, and a string of ammunition lying on his desk.

24 July

The days are hot and the work is very hard. We get woken at 3.30 a.m. by some guy in fatigues who shakes your arm and says 'Eh, English, get up'. He has a machine gun round his shoulder so I don't wait to be asked again. Thank God for the very hot strong black coffee on tap in the dining room. A van takes us to the fruit fields where you stand on a portable gantry on top of a lorry which parks between the trees and pick the fruit. Pretty dull, but I quite like the chance to be alone with my thoughts.

At about eight o'clock we get breakfast in a field kitchen. Hot rolls, cream cheeses, cold tongue, hot coffee. Little sachets of Nutella – there's a decadence I never get at home. Then back to work for another three or four hours. Sleep most of the afternoon.

28 July

I'm just back from a day trip with the rest of the group spent touring the Golan Heights. We saw the 'Good Fence' on the Lebanese frontier – a narrow strip of carefully guarded land through which Lebanese workers (mainly women) travel to and from Israel each day to pick fruit. 'For shit wages,' said Hillel, to general laughter.

We travelled in a crappy old bus, and Hillel took charge of the group. He carried a revolver (loaded, I am sure) in a brown leather holster.

2 August

Hillel summoned all the volunteers to a meeting after supper tonight. There have been complaints about shoddy work (in the kitchens), people sloping off early (from the bakery) and also of rudeness of volunteers to Israeli overseers. (Pot and kettle come to mind.)

10 August

Hillel was displeased with the pace of our fruit-picking today and told us we were all useless lazy cunts.

I said, 'Hillel: you were the one who was telling us off for rudeness the other day. You really shouldn't use that word.'

'This is what I mean. You are fucking rude. You listen when I talk, cunt.'

'No,' I said, 'you are rude – as in "coarse" and "ignorant". What I am is "insubordinate". Would you like me to explain?'

Everyone started clapping and cheering.

16 August

My A-level results arrived by telegram. Two As and a bloody B in French. Mum and Dad were full of congratulations and said there was champagne on ice awaiting my return. I'm pretty pleased, but am not saying anything about them to anyone here.

Poker has become our favoured evening activity – nothing else is available anyway. Tonight we played with the help of shots of Mount Carmel vodka (very cheap) and fizzy lemonade. No ice anywhere. God, it was disgusting.

24 August

There was a frightening moment last night when one of the girls started screaming – real full-throated terror, which woke everyone up. It turned out that there were cockroaches on the floor.

29 August

My turn came to do a night in the chicken factory. This involved getting up at 2 a.m., donning a thick pair of gauntlets and a face mask and then taking chickens out of their battery pens and into portable cages on their way to be slaughtered. The chickens shriek and flap and peck at any part of you they can get hold of – I don't blame them.

13 September

Joe and I are just back from Jerusalem. We went to the Dome of the Rock, the Western Wall, the Holy Sepulchre – as Joe said, might as well do three great religions in one fell swoop. Also to Yad Vashem. All the photographs in which Hitler appears have his face gouged out. At the end of the exhibition lies a glass case, in which there are hundreds and hundreds of pairs of children's shoes from the camps. I don't excuse the Israelis' terrible rudeness, but you can begin to see why they tend not to give people the benefit of the doubt.

A Greek Orthodox priest was staying at our very cheap and crappy hotel by Jaffa Gate. He kept on offering us cigarettes which we thought was very nice of him, and then drinks, and then he asked us to follow him to his room at which point we realised he might have another agenda. We declined and said goodnight.

26 September

On the flight home. Joe is asleep next to me. He's a good guy, but Christ! He's gruff. We've made half-hearted promises to keep in touch but I doubt we will.

2 October

The last days at home have been brilliant. I really missed Mum and Dad when I was in Israel. I thought I'd grown out of being homesick, but there were one or two times when I longed for home – partly because I was exhausted by the heat, and fed up of being bitten by mosquitoes. Also (and I know this seems strange), I missed having a few Catholics around.

This week I'm off to Oxford for the start of term. All those people who wrote me off at Hunter's Chase can eat dirt. Mum is very sad because she can't get away from work without causing huge bother (her term began weeks ago) but Dad has more freedom and so he is going to drive me there. I know I get irritated by them about 10,000 times every day, but I also know everything that is of real value I owe to them.

Chapter Twelve
Dominic: Hendon, May 2014

Dominic had been due to go home on Saturday, but Esther asked him to delay his return for a few days, insisting his presence was giving them far more fun than trouble. Had he been in rude health, he would have declined, always super-sensitive to the risk of becoming a burden, but now he was relieved.

There was a conservatory affair at the end of the kitchen and the weather continued to be kind. A comfortable routine had evolved: each morning at about half past nine he would find a place laid for him, and two coddled eggs, fresh coffee and orange juice and toasted bagels. There was also honey and cream cheese, on which he gorged contentedly, dawdling over *Prospect*, *The Times* and (he bought it, not them) the *Spectator*.

Esther tended to leave him alone at this point – he could hear her sometimes go to the study she and Daniel shared. She usually resurfaced at about eleven,] they'd drink more coffee and maybe sit in the garden.

At midday on his last day with them, Wednesday, Esther drove him to Hampstead Heath, where they walked round Kenwood. Dominic was relieved when, after a quarter of an hour or so, she suggested they go to the cafe. Over bread and soup, she asked him if she too could read his diaries. He agreed at once.

He was surprisingly tired after their outing and slept deeply when they got home. Later, while Chloe was having her bath and being put to bed, he took the chance to send a new email to Daniel.

Dearest Dan

I am so pleased Esther wants to try out my diaries. I trust she is appropriately unshockable.

So, now for the Oxford diaries. I went there at a point when, little did we know it, our world began radically to change. In 1977, most Oxford students looked like students everywhere – tie-dyed T-shirts, flared jeans, unwashed hair falling halfway down our backsides. Then came Thatcher, and Chariots of Fire *(the latter the symptom rather than the cause of the huge changes that were starting to shake us all up). By the time I left, many of us looked like extras in* Brideshead Revisited. *I remember investing in a pair of Gucci loafers at about this time – they cost my entire wages for a fortnight's work in a freezer plant where I used to have a holiday job. Honestly, what an arse.*

My college, like most others, was still all-male for the first couple of years. I fell in love at once with the look of the place, although I knew bugger all about architecture. I had all the shock and awe of the provincial for its rituals and assorted nonsenses: gowns, formal dinners and so forth. Hardly surprising: it was the first time I'd lived in a reasonably sophisticated society. I wasn't, however, Alan Bennett and, unlike him, I had no inclination to hide in my room.

Most of the other students came from homes rather like my own and were reassuringly friendly. Of course, there were a few exceptions – young men with floppy blond hair, hacking jackets, and – sober or pissed – capable of being astonishingly unpleasant. My presence seemed to pass them by, but I was shocked and sickened when I saw, on several occasions, how contemptuous and cruel they were to college servants (as they were then called).

Being in their gang was never on my wish list. On the other hand, my social curiosity was intense, and Oxford offered some big opportunities. You'll have to judge the extent to which I was corrupted. I think there was a phase during which my father certainly feared I was selling out to the toffs.

Although I was riven with intellectual self-doubt, I also learned a hell of a lot of academic rigour during my years there – and History, of course. You can't imagine the advantage you had, coming from a school like Groom's – I know that sounds chippy, but it's true. I had to learn how to study from first principles, and Oxford gave me a reason to do so, and thus it effected a liberation on which I've relied every day of my life ever since. How does anyone ever repay that?

The other great gift of my time at Oxford, of course, was the chance to make friends. How could I fail to? All around me were people of brimming confidence and high spirits, and we had, did we but *know it, unsurpassed energy and leisure. The best friends I made at Oxford have stayed with me.*

And it was at Oxford also where I met Ben with whom I fell deeply in love – with an intensity and a lack of equivocation which, hand on heart, I never came near again. (If you are feeling an edge of panic on reading this, please calm yourself. It doesn't get explicit.)

Much love
D

Chapter Thirteen
Oxford, 1977–1981

3 October

Dad drove me to Chester. At the bottom of my staircase there was a big black board with names painted on it in carefully manicured script. Halfway down the list was the reassuring news that they were expecting me: *Da Silva, D.J.F.* I saw Dad looking at it, and taking it in, but nothing was said. He has never had any experience like this. We went for tea at the Randolph and made short work of scones, cream and jam. He was really proud and protective of me, but also anxious not to hang around.

It is strange. He and I are often shy with each other, but (along with all the irritation, of course) there is an incredible tenderness.

4 October

Given that you have to climb five flights of stairs to get to my room, I suspect nobody will ever bother to visit me. I splashed out another £3 on posters at Athena. I also brought a lot of books with me from home, most of which I have never read, but they fill up the shelves. There is even one on economics, though I have no idea what I am supposed to do with it.

Still, this is Oxford: I need to look intellectual and confident, although I certainly don't feel it.

5 October

First day of term. The car park was crammed with Peugeots and Ford Granadas and blokes of my age trying not to get impatient with their parents as they unloaded trunks.

I recognised Marco Godfrey and Arthur Raine from interviews and we went to supper together in the great Tudor Dining Hall. You're expected to wear a gown. Because I'm a 'commoner', mine looks like a crow's turd, especially compared to the luxuriant garb that adorns the backs of scholars.

The setting was grand – dark panelling halfway up the walls and assorted portraits of masters. There was a long Latin grace and beer was served in silver tankards, which was a novelty. The food seemed fine to me (cottage pie and carrots) but a lot of the second- and third-years complained loudly. We then went to the college bar and I had two pints – very cheap and gassy, but you can put it all on credit.

6 October

We were given a week's reading on constitutional law and were told to write an essay on strict liability. At this moment I haven't a clue what it is, but maybe in a week's time I'll be wiser. This term's tutor is Dr Longley, who I remember from interviews because he looked like a rock star. He was wearing John Lennon round spectacles with a yellow tint. The comparison rather collapses when he opens his mouth, however. He sounds like Prince Charles.

10 October

I haven't moved from the Law Library except to go to supper. I am hoping this is not an accurate foretaste of the next three years.

12 October

For the past two days my life has been enlivened by bicycle rides to and from the Law Faculty, by cigarette breaks and by jacket potatoes with Cheddar cheese fillings for lunch. The college Law Library is becoming oppressive to some of us. One of the third-years is an old Etonian who talks about 'plebs' and 'tarts'. His father is a High Court judge.

Two friends-of-sorts are emerging, both freshers and lawyers: Ben Black (he went to Highgate and lives in Golders Green) and Sidney Grant (he went to UCS and lives in Hampstead). I mention these details, because where you went to school seems to be invariably the first question you're asked.

Ben seems alarmingly clever. In our cigarette breaks he holds forth on Middle Eastern politics. I affect more interest in listening to his opinions than I actually feel, because I want him to like me. He is about the same height as me, but much more obviously strong and muscly, and with very long black curly hair.

13 October

Tonight I had my first Constitutional Law tutorial with Dr Longley. Ben and I have been paired off for these. When I'd finished reading my essay, Dr Longley said 'You're a bit windy, Dominic, but there's a very quick mind at work. Keep that up and you'll do well.'

Ben waded in with some criticisms, all of which sounded incredibly powerful to me but Longley kept on accusing him of being 'abstracted' and 'driven by dogma'. When we were walking out afterwards; Ben said he felt 'crushed and useless'.

14 October

A card has arrived in my pigeonhole inviting me to Mass at 5.30 p.m., followed by sherry, at the Catholic Chaplaincy next Friday.

I have just discovered that the 'college representative' at the Catholic Chaplaincy is a third-year called Gerard Forsyth who was at Hunter's Chase. He recognised my name and passed it on.

18 October

Tonight we went to the Union. There was a debate – the motion something to do with the closed shop. The student speakers were dressed up in white tie and tails and looked pleased with themselves. After half an hour Ben whispered that he wanted to cut his throat. So we buggered off to the pub, which was much better.

20 October

There was a freshers' revue in college today. One of them, Guy Robson (easily the best-looking), did a series of imitations. It began with Bill McLaren and Eddie Waring and ended up with one of me! All on the strength of having had ten minutes' conversation queuing for supper the other night. He was good, fuck him.

22 October

I was working in my room last night at about midnight when there was a knock on the door; Ben was standing awkwardly on the threshold, wearing a sweatshirt and sawn-off denims. (If it had been me I'd have looked ridiculous but he has one of those sinewy bodies which seem to mean that whatever you wear looks all right.)

He started apologising for disturbing me but I said I was glad of some distraction and put on a kettle. There was a bit of Maxwell House left and some Marvel. He had just sat down when his head suddenly dropped and his shoulders started shaking. I thought he was laughing, but then I saw tears coursing down his cheeks and realised this was a bit different. I suppose my suspicion was that his father had cancer or something, but none of it. He started to say that I never made anything of it, but that I was brilliant, and he couldn't cope with the intellectual pace I was setting and that he was just getting further and further behind.

'Ben,' I said. 'This is mad. It's completely in your head.'

I don't think he quite believed me, but fortunately I didn't believe him. He is really neurotic. We ended up having rather a long cosy chat and he went off, much happier, about 2 a.m.

23 October

I went to the Mass today. I kept a low profile, but various OHC faces bobbed up. Francis Morley looked ill at the sight of me. I smiled at him rather as one recalling a distant acquaintance.

2 November

I ended up going to Formal Hall tonight. Guy was there and insisted I join him and his rugger-bugger friends. Somebody called Rory was sconced for misuse of cutlery which resulted in him having to drink two and a half pints of beer. A bit ponderous, but it made everyone happy.

Guy brayed and cheered, but he spent a lot of time during the meal concentrating on me – asking all the usual questions you do when you're getting to know someone, but he really listens closely and has a friendliness which feels real.

Talk about not judging a book by its cover. I'd just seen him as a pretty-boy athlete (he is exceptionally good-looking – tall and fair-haired and strong) – but fortunately not in a way which I find attractive. It turns out he is starring in a big OUDS production next term (*Macbeth*, no less) and, as much from what he did not say as from what he did, I began to gather he knows a lot about plays and that he reads poetry for pleasure. He's reading Modern Languages because he says it's easier than English. I suspect he's being modest.

4 November

Ben and I had arranged to play squash this afternoon. The idea of a game between us has been 'under discussion' for a while. I know perfectly well my big aim is to see him in his squash kit. Today he dropped into the conversation that he plays for 'Combined North London Clubs'.

Humiliation beckoned. He had the decency not to make

me feel too much of a loser, however. I took about five points off him in the course of an hour, but only because he was being nice to me. Oddly, he is a much calmer person in a squash court than anywhere else. We had a shower afterwards, and then made toast in my room and drank tea. Neither of us is really bothered about booze (though we agreed it is funny getting drunk now and then).

10 November

Sid has got in with a crowd from Eton. He's bought a pair of crimson corduroy trousers and is wearing a yellow waistcoat he bought at Hall Bros. Ben's line is 'Who does he think he's kidding? Before he came to Oxford, he'd hardly ever stepped out of NW3.'

12 November

Guy Robson was at breakfast today and said, 'Hello you big poof.' He must have seen me pale a bit because he clapped me on the back and gave me a big smile.

He even persuaded me to go and watch him turn out for the College First XV this afternoon. I am such a tart, I know – as soon as someone flatters me, they can do what they like. The rugby was as dull as shit, but the company of sports jocks always leaves me rather envious: everything in their world is clear and defined – in play or offside. No blurred edges.

16 November

Dad had to see a client in Brackley and wrote last week suggesting we met up tonight 'for a bite'. We walked round college, which he described as 'magnificent' (he's right there), and then went to Ben's room for a drink. I really wanted them to like each other. Ben had gone a bit overboard, buying a bottle of college sherry which he thought Dad would like, and affecting an interest in rugby.

Dad was warm and very friendly – all the good things he always is when he's not feeling threatened. He invited Ben to join us for supper but I think everyone was relieved that he didn't. We went to the Star of India, and had a pint of lager each. Dad gave me a tenner and 40 Benson and Hedges at the end.

18 November

I worked late last night on my essay. The Criminal Law tutor, Mr Bates, is much less flattering about my work than Dr Longley. He is even ruder to Ben, however, who reacts by stuttering – something he says he stopped doing when he was ten, except when he's badly upset.

Today Mr Bates was in a better mood than usual and even told us to call him by his first name. (Since he signs himself 'Michael David Bates' we were a bit confused whether it should be 'Michael' or 'David' and, in consequence, just mumbled.) The tutorial itself passed off more or less all right. In our relief, we both lit cigarettes as we left his room and walked down to the vestibule of the Law Library, forgetting smoke detectors have just been installed there. Result: alarms blaring everywhere.

21 November

Sid has given up his Etonian phase and become an intellectual. The waistcoat has gone, and he is wearing glasses and a long greatcoat. On Saturday he persuaded Ben and me to go to a film – *Alice's Restaurant* – which he described (in these words) as 'a really important example of a very particular genre'. It began at 11 p.m., lasted *for ever* and was undiluted shite.

2 December

Ben asked me if I wanted to go skiing during the coming Vac. He's going with his parents and 'a few old friends'. I tried to suppress my jealousy and said I was going to have to work. He said, 'But you can revise when we're there.'

I laughed and said, 'I meant getting a paid job, you twat.'

He said, 'Do your – er, job – after Christmas.'

Bless his heart, as Mum would say. He really doesn't get it.

6 December

Yesterday I went to the Master's Lodgings for 'Master's Collections' – a kind of end-of-term report delivered to the master in your presence. Longley said, 'Mr da Silva is a pleasant young man who makes up for phases of intellectual uncertainty with dogged hard work.'

14 December

I am working nights at Bojo's until Christmas Eve, which mainly involves carrying boxes of frozen food on pallets and packing them into lorries. Everything seems small and unchanged here. The other guys are rough, but I say nothing, so they don't bother me much.

My parents are more of an irritant, Dad especially. I have the impression he feels the same about me.

20 December

Letter from Ben this morning. It's quite long and (to be honest) quite boring. But I forgive him everything because he says he suggests we go back a few days before Collections and says we can spend the time revising just on our own. I daresay my visions of what 'on our own' might mean are a long way off his.

However, his letter certainly has put me in a better mood. I went Christmas shopping this afternoon, and bought a Country Casuals scarf for Mum and an Austin Reed tie for Dad.

24 December

Christmas began at 6 a.m. this morning so far as I was concerned, when I collected my earnings from Bojo's and arrived home. Mum had made me a celebratory cooked breakfast and I was so cold I hugged her in gratitude. We are going to Midnight Mass later.

27 December

Good Christmas – lots of eating, drinking, TV etc. Mum always urges Scrabble and charades on us but we ended up watching the *The Morecambe and Wise Christmas Special*, just like the rest of the country. They gave me a cheque for £25 which will be a very big help indeed.

Things took a bit of a downward turn tonight when Dad and I broke the electric kettle which we were using for catching practice. He gets these moods where he likes to joke around, but his timing was bad today – Mum was furious (not like her). He suddenly changed sides and started saying things like, 'Don't fool around in Mummy's kitchen.'

3 January 1978

Under duress, I went to the Bingleys' appalling New Year's Eve party the other night. Everyone under the age of 25 was required to eat turkey curry in their cellar which, Dr Bingley explained, looking coyly suggestive, had been 'given over to the young'. I have told my parents, politely but seriously, *never again.*

Today Dad very decently drove me to Oxford – he conceded Bingley entertainment leaves a lot to be desired. I have been working in my room all afternoon and evening. As usual, it's freezing even with both bars of the fire on. There is no sign of Ben, nor any word of him, fuck it.

4 January

Ben emerged today. He's tanned on his face and forearms. He said the good bit about a skiing holiday is that it fills the day. He said the minute he came home, his parents were nagging him to do work and have told him that if he doesn't get a Distinction in Mods, he will have brought disgrace upon them. His parents and grandparents and great-grandparents have all been surgeons and university professors.

His mother is also worried that one of his sisters will marry 'out' (i.e., someone not Jewish) or, almost as bad, not marry at all. When his father heard he'd got an Exhibition to Oxford, his first words were 'Why not a scholarship?'

Unsurprisingly, he says he envies me my parents. He was also really curious to hear about my holiday job, and of course the long nights at Bojo's can be easily worked into a story.

5 January

We both put in a decent morning's work, but the good intentions to continue into the afternoon then collapsed. We played squash for a bit, and then I cooked us bacon and beans on toast. It always makes Ben happy when he breaks kosher.

After that, we went to my room and Ben massaged my left shoulder which I had told him, not quite truthfully, was hurting. When he'd done that he said, 'Take your T-shirt off, and I'll do your back.' I saw his eyes checking that the door was locked. He spent about a quarter of an hour massaging my back and shoulders and neck, and it was fantastic.

When he stopped I said simply 'your turn'. For a moment he hesitated but he took off his sweatshirt all the same and lay down. Nothing at all was said. He's probably a stone heavier than me, but he hasn't an ounce of fat. Suddenly everything feels possible.

Dominic had kneaded Ben's shoulders hard with his thumbs and forefingers. When it came to the base of his spine, he had replicated exactly what Ben had done to him. Massage firmly just above the hips and at the top of his white games shorts. He observed the reddened skin where his shorts and underwear had been chafing.

Ben lay with his head face down on the floor.

'You're the best friend I've ever had, Dominic,' he said quite calmly and slowly. 'Nobody else has ever come near.'

12 January

I am so intensely happy. I want every moment to stretch out for ever, and that isn't like me at all. I've given up writing lists, eating chocolate and worrying about work. (Fortunately, going to the library is now so ingrained that I still cycle to the Law Faculty and put in the hours.)

The Chess Club was intense but filled with guilt. Now when B sits next to me what I feel is something like a religious joy.

17 January

Dr Longley returned our essays. I got a beta alpha and Ben a beta plus. He was very cast down and wouldn't be cheered up afterwards.

Guy asked me to join him at the Nag's Head. Quite fun. There were two very bubbly girls from LMH, one of whom was going all out for him. A strange feeling when the other – Eleanor? Emily? – gave me the eye. I wasn't imagining it.

B's light was out when I returned so I went to my own room.

25 January

About midnight last night, I was still working when B knocked on my door and asked if he could just lie down on the floor. He said he didn't want to speak.

I could see he was shaking, but since he'd asked for silence, I wasn't going to break it. After about ten minutes, I whispered to him that I was going to give him a massage.

After about ten minutes of that, he seemed much calmer

and apologised for 'being so weird'. He told me that his mother has been demanding he tell her his marks for each essay and that she had told him to ring home after each tutorial. Apparently when she heard he had only got a beta plus she exploded and said that she and his father are coming up this Sunday to deliver a rocket in person.

(This is one of those moments when I realise that there is no such thing as a free skiing holiday. His parents sound unbelievably awful. He's doing fine. Frankly, the only explanation for my recent run of good marks is that falling in love has sharpened my concentration very nicely, while his has rather slipped.)

He is cacking himself. He hinted, very politely, I should keep well away on Sunday. I think I'll go to Mass instead.

29 January

I did too, though I doubt I'll make a habit of it. Jonathan O'Dwyer was in the same pew as me, wearing Hunter's Chase cricket colours. He gave me a rather cold nod.

From my window on the other side of the quad this afternoon, I could see Ben walking with his parents. They looked much younger than I expected – both have thick dark hair, and his father was wearing a pair of cream trousers under a blue jacket. It looked like his mother was doing all the talking. Ben looked very gloomy and self-conscious and his shoulders were sagging.

2 February

Roman Law is dull, but not too difficult. Anyway, my exams will be over in six weeks (unless I fail them). To blow off a bit of steam, Ben and I and a few others arranged to go to a sweaty disco at Trinity.

Sid was there when I arrived, and a few others from college. We were standing round in that kind of contrived ironic way that comes over blokes when nobody seems to want to get off with them, and periodically joining in when the music seemed good.

No sign of Ben until about 10.30 when he staged quite a conspicuous entrance with a dark-haired girl who was clinging on to him and with whom he proceeded to dance without interruption. He gave me a cheerful wave at one point, but beyond that no sign of recognition. There were lots of people there, obviously, so I had to pretend not to mind – 'pretend' being the operative word.

4 February

Yesterday was a bad bad day. With HUGE self-control, I didn't search Ben out – went to college breakfast as normal (no Ben) and then cycled to the Law Faculty (same). My concentration was CRAP and for lack of anything better to do, I went to see a play in college. *The Dumb Waiter.*

The fact that one of the two main characters was called Ben and the whole play was about waiting for something to happen seemed ironic. It just about took me out of my bad mood but that didn't last when I returned alone to my room afterwards and couldn't sleep but was determined to sit tight.

Dominic's determination had proved ultimately unequal to the task he had set himself. On the one hand, he knew the old saws – neediness was supremely unattractive and, ultimately, the only person you could rely on was yourself. On the other, Ben had penetrated every defence. He could cut a pose as ironic and detached as he liked, but three seconds of Ben's presence was all it took to turn Dominic giddy with desire and weak with love.

At 1 a.m., he had persuaded himself to take a walk through the college gardens on the pretext that it would help him to sleep. Ben's room was on the top floor of the staircase just next to the kitchens. Dominic stood briefly by the obelisk in the garden quad. The sitting-room light was still on.

After a brief and entirely token moment of internal struggle, he had tiptoed in its direction. Inflamed with longing but enough himself to be acutely embarrassed by his ardour, he hesitated on the threshold. The outer door was slightly ajar and he could just detect the strains of *Winterreise* from within.

About five minutes passed. By now Dominic was cold and also becoming aware that his obsessiveness might be considered alarming. On the other hand, he was unsure that he could escape downstairs without at least his foot-steps being audible on the wooden staircase.

While he was debating what to do next, the door suddenly swung open and Ben prepared to step out. He was wearing a dark blue dressing gown and the sponge bag in his right hand appeared to indicate a journey no further than the washroom on the floor below.

It was difficult to say who was more alarmed: Ben was certainly more shocked but Dominic more frightened.

Neither said anything, however. Ben's face registered surprise, followed by alarm and irritation, but he brought himself under control and gestured silently for Dominic to come in. Dominic asked (it seemed as plausible a first line as any) if he could put on the electric fire.

'All right.' He went over and drew the curtains and closed the door.

'Jesus, Ben. It's freezing in here. Don't you ever get cold?'

'I might if I hung around outside your door in the middle of the night.'

'Sorry about that. I couldn't sleep and wanted someone to talk to about Roman Law.'

'Yeah. Sure. That'll send anyone off to sleep.' He stared down at Dominic who was crouching low over the three slowly reddening electric bars, his eyes looking anywhere but in his direction.

'Why are you here?' he repeated.

Dominic looked him straight in the eye. 'Because I think I'm in love with you.'

Ben sat down in the armchair. 'Are you homosexual?'

'Partly. Maybe mostly. I change a bit on that one.' The words came out thickly.

There was a long pause. Dominic stared at this powerful-looking youth sitting hunched forward in his chair, the very essence of effortless masculinity.

'I won't ask if you are,' he said finally, the irony in his voice not quite killing off the undertone of sadness.

'I never even thought about it,' Ben said. 'Until recently. Then I met you, and suddenly I'm not sure.'

Dominic could feel his cheeks burn and his hands trembling. He was still crouching in front of the fire, but turned to face him.

'Look,' he said finally. 'I'm pretty messed up in some ways. But I know my heart all right.'

'I know you do.'

'And I can't help it. I love you.'

'I can't help it either. I feel the same.'

14 February

One Valentine, with a tiny **B** inscribed in very faint pencil.

That night there had been an impromptu Valentine's discotheque in the college beer cellar, and girls had arrived from the local secretarial colleges. Dominic sat with Ben and Sid and a few other freshmen lawyers, while the jukebox blared out ELO and Stevie Wonder. By unspoken consent, they had all decided to take the night off. After two pints, Dominic was in a mood to dance and, after a third, so was nearly everyone else.

The drink made him a little more audacious than usual. At about ten thirty, he had sidled up to Ben: 'Everyone's happy.'

Ben grinned at him. 'Not as happy as we are.'

'No. So I'm going to my room now. Don't say anything. Give yourself another half hour and meet me there. The door will be closed but not locked. Just come in.'

Ben nodded, and Dominic slipped out, to the strains of 'How Deep is Your Love'.

He had thought more carefully about his own appearance than usual when he had returned to his room but, beyond brushing his teeth, he made no big decisions. When Ben arrived, Dominic could smell the beer on his breath.

'Did anyone see you come up?'

'I don't think so.'

'Do you want a coffee?'

Ben looked at him. 'Of course I don't want a fucking coffee.'

'No. Me neither.'

Ben was wearing a Bob Marley sweatshirt which he slowly removed. His torso had been glimpsed by Dominic during their games of squash, and brooded upon during many, many nights of imagining. Now came a new reality.

22 February

I saw Guy walking up the steps of the Radcliffe Camera today, just as I was locking my bike. He said, 'I've never been here before. But I'm in a big fucking mess and I've got to do some work.'

The mess, it turns out, is that he's been told he'll be kicked out of the college (and university, obviously) unless he writes three essays in the next four days. So far he hasn't opened a book (he claims). The trouble is (a) he spends all his time doing sport or rehearsing for plays, (b) he hates German, (c) he detests French and (d) he absolutely LOATHES his tutor.

Later we had a sandwich in Brown's in the covered market. He looked me up and down a bit and said: 'I've just realised what's different about you. You've been fucking.'

I'm sure I blushed and I tried to laugh it off, saying that I wished I had, but he shook his head.

'I *knew* it. You've been fucking. Good on you, mate.' Then he picked up his bag and we went back to the library. Nothing more said.

5 March

Last night I was revising late in the Law Library when I became vaguely aware of somebody coming in and then a voice said, 'Come on – let's go.' There was absolutely nobody around and we had a long and really intense kiss, and it was perfect.

Today, being a Sunday, there was an excuse to sleep late. I slipped out to La Petite Maison and bought some croissants. They cost a fortune but who cares? We didn't move the rest of the morning.

7 March

My nineteenth birthday. It is all happening in a welter of study really – well, study and romance. Tonight, instead of going to Hall for supper, Sid, Ben and I went to the Koh-i-Noor for a curry. Three pints of lager each which put paid to doing any work later.

I had a card (and a cheque for £20) from Mum and Dad, and rang them this evening. Mum said: 'Darling, you sound fantastic,' and I said simply, 'I feel it.' You could hear her take this in – she is very perceptive – and she said simply 'good'.

B gave me a Chopin LP – the pianist is a close family friend. He also gave me a card telling me just what his feelings for me really are. That's not on display (I've put it in the record sleeve for safekeeping).

Three days later, Dominic had been working in his room at teatime. He had been trying to understand an abstruse judgment on the Theft Act 1968 when a knock on the door had surprised him and disrupted his train of thought.

Irritated, he had gone to open the door to find himself

facing a thin woman of about forty. She had dark hair and wore a green suit.

'Are you Dominic?' she enquired. Her eyes showed no warmth.

'Yes.'

'I'm Dee Black.' There was a definite South African accent and she evidently assumed he would register the name. After a couple of seconds, she added impatiently: 'Benjamin's mother.'

'Oh, hello,' he said, smiling his best smile and moving unthinkingly into his be-nice-to-parents mode. 'Is Ben with you?'

'No. Should he be?'

He had retained enough self-possession not to answer that, and watched her mentally registering his unsurprising possessions.

He had been about to ask her to sit down, but she had pre-empted him.

'Benjamin has said enough about you for me to realise you are important to him,' she said, clearly attempting to sound judicious. 'I wanted to meet you myself.'

He could feel a measure of panic rising, but also crossness. There was an acerbic and arrogant pitch here that felt impertinent. He decided not to offer tea, but sat down opposite her and said nothing.

Her voice took on a forced brightness as she asked him about his family. What did his father do? Did his mother work? Where did they live?

Dominic told her, making no secret of his pride and loyalty.

'Were your parents at Oxford?'

'Good Lord, no. My mother went to Edinburgh just

after the war. My father left school without any qualifications.'

'So you are the first member of your family to go to one of the ancient universities,' she said. 'How strange.'

'Why is that strange?' Dominic asked, his voice not quite able to repress the asperity he felt the question merited.

She shrugged. 'I mean that your parents must be very proud of you.'

'If they are,' Dominic said stiffly, 'it has little to do with my being at Oxford. They don't think like that.'

'Indeed. Well, then – how strange.'

She chose that moment to catch sight of the Chopin album lying on top of the bookcase. She hesitated and then stood up to look at it more closely.

'Was this a gift from Benjamin?'

'Yes,' he said. At that moment, the Athena card, which had been secreted in the record sleeve fell out. Without waiting for permission, she picked it up and read.

'It was for my birthday,' added Dominic, even as he watched her face drain of colour. It sounded fatuous even to him.

10 March

Apparently Ben was taken home last night by his mother.

14 March

Ben has not been in college since his mother's visit. He arrived in the examination hall at the very last possible moment yesterday before the paper started and shot off the minute it ended.

After the final paper today, all the first-year lawyers went for a drink in the Bird and Brat – minus him. Sid said to me, 'We won't see him again in a hurry. When Dee Black makes up her mind she wants something, she doesn't let anything stand in her way.'

A car was ordered to drive Ben from Golders Green up to Oxford yesterday and today, and then take him back immediately the exams finished. Sid says he is under orders to see nobody and speak to nobody. (How old is he, for fuck's sake – 18 years or 18 months?)

20 March

You're meant to feel light-hearted when you finish exams, and giddy with relief. Now I can do nothing to escape this misery.

I spend hours lying awake at night. I invent conversations with Ben in which he turns up here and tells me he is sorry and he can't live without me. Sometimes I reproach him, making great speeches. He looks appalled and tears course down his cheeks. In others, I am the one who weeps at the first sight of him, and he takes me in his arms.

Eventually I go to sleep. I am back to having my old nightmare about burglars – the one that always surfaces when I am sad. Of course, I have said nothing. I know Mum and Dad are always there for me. Knowing that is what keeps me miserable, as opposed to becoming desperate.

What could I tell them anyway? That I'm queer. News to gladden their hearts. Perhaps I could just say that I have been unlucky in love. But if I try to say those words out loud, I know I could not stop myself from wailing in anguish and shame. I won't risk doing that. It has always taken me all my energy to keep myself in one piece and I don't trust anyone else to do it for me.

Exams over, Dominic had returned home. A week passed before he found a letter was waiting for him on the hall table by the telephone.

The Maltings
116 Highfield Crescent
Hendon Village
London NW4

Dear Dominic,

I hope the exams went all right. As I'm guessing you've realised, I won't be coming back to Oxford.

I thought this would happen anyway – my mother really never wanted me to go to a university where Jews live just like everyone else. She went to Med School in South Africa and my father studied in New York, and I'm going to Yale in the fall. I will be staying with my aunt and uncle in Netanya until then.

She didn't say much about her visit to you, but I can guess. I think they'd have forced me to leave Oxford anyway, perhaps after next term, but after she met you, she decided I had to go at once. I know you think it's crazy that I'm not allowed to make my own choices. But that's how it is here. The only alternative would mean cutting myself away from everyone I have known up to the time when I met you.

I do feel all those things I felt with you. I also mean all the things I said and wrote. But I'm not sure that I will stay feeling them, and so I can't take that risk.

I might feel a bit less bad if we could speak, but my parents have forbidden this and they won't even let me leave the house on my own. I am being allowed to write one letter to you and they have made me swear that I won't try to communicate with you again or answer any calls or letters from you. If you were sitting where I am sitting, you would realise there are no choices.

I will miss you and always remember you and I will never be sorry for everything that happened between us.

Benjamin

25 March

Mum and Dad have gone to Ireland for a short holiday. I start at Bojo's on Monday but I have had nothing to do this weekend, and nobody to see. This is what I'm like when things are bad. I say nothing to anyone. The only thing I can do is write my diary and even then it is appalling to make myself write the words.

I love him. I want him. I'm not even thinking about his character or humour. Right now I just want to be in bed with him and have loads of sex doing everything and have him hold me for the rest of my life. YES THAT IS WHAT IT FEELS LIKE ALL RIGHT.

Fuck me. I hope nobody ever reads this diary. I keep the

old ones locked up and this one is carefully shut away each night in my desk. My parents are very good about respecting privacy – but if anyone ever saw this I'd be too ashamed to go out of doors ever again.

I have sort of wondered about telling Jack – old mates and all that – and I actually think he would be very strong and sympathetic. But the truth is that if I can't have Ben, the only thing I still want to do is think about him. And that has to be done alone.

27 March

Awful day at Bojo's. Nothing bad in itself – just that the minutes each felt like an hour and I was on a 12-hour shift. It took all my willpower to last out the whole day. I am scared shitless by how unhappy I have become. It's taking various awful forms – nightmares, lethargy, bursts of fear which I try to exorcise by bouts of meaningless activity.

Yesterday, being Sunday, stretched out meaninglessly. I tidied my room (which usually cheers me up) and worked out how much money I have. Doing calculations about everything I've spent and everything I've earned is a brilliant device to get me anxious about something impersonal (like being broke). Then I reorganised my Roman Law file which, since I've finished my exams, seems pretty stupid (unless FUCK I have to re-take). I even did some weeding in the garden and then I went for a run through Holport and Claysford. It's five miles in all and I've done it loads of times but I got so despairing that I stopped outside Claysford, and ended up walking two miles home.

2 April

Mum and Dad appear to have had a good holiday in Sligo. I always enjoy Dad's yardsticks of excellence when he's describing places at which they've stayed: 'very reasonable rates'; 'a most comfortable bed'; 'apple pie served with lashings of cream'; 'piping-hot water'.

He expressed himself in unflattering terms about the state of the house when they returned however.

11 April

My Mods results came through today. Mine were decent, but no better than that, and I am disappointed. My parents, ever generous, are full of congratulation, and I am trying to enter into that mood for their sakes. Dad called in at Peter Dominic on his way home from the office and bought a bottle of champagne to mark the moment.

15 April

I have just finished three weeks of long hours at Bojo's. Still feeling shite but at least I have a bit of cash in the bank. I try to disguise my mood when I am at home (because of late hours I haven't actually seen either Mum or Dad very much). I'm pretty sure they haven't a clue as to what's going on in my head. You can't tell with the da Silvas: difficult questions are generally sidestepped.

3 May

I suppose the fact that I haven't bothered to write any entry for nearly three weeks is a reasonable indicator of how I'm feeling. I'm busy but I'm not feeling a whole lot better. It didn't help that Sid let drop that Ben's parents had given a party for his family and friends before he left to go to Israel.

Thinking about it now, I realise there is no way I could have been asked (his mother would have turned a Smith and Wesson on me at the front door, for sure) but when I found out it felt like an act of cruelty on his part.

Nor at the time could I work out why Sid was telling me – that also seemed sadistic. He came round to my room the following morning and told me he wanted to speak 'within these four walls'. Then he said that he didn't know the truth of what was 'going on' between Ben and me, and that it was none of his business. He said Ben's mother was a well-known dragon and that she took total control over his life and that of his sisters, and that she sensed he was escaping her control at Oxford and 'so she acted'. He also said that, in the end, Ben 'knew which side his bread was buttered' and would never go against his mother.

When he left, I found I was at last clear in my own mind that Ben belongs to the past. For the first time since it happened I found I could cry – which I did, for a long time. Then I went to sleep and woke up feeling better.

I sat next to Guy at supper and he told me that they need someone ('anyone' he said) to make up an eight for a crappy crew he is putting together for Summer Eights. It's called the *Uncoordinate*. On the basis that I ought to do something this term other than Law (and feeling sorry for myself) I've agreed to join. (Me – rowing? Seems pretty unlikely.)

12 May

I am just back from breakfast – after an hour on the river, preceded by a two-mile run. The day began at 6.30 a.m. The blokey pleasures of rowing in a very low-grade college crew have been unexpectedly potent. I enjoy the banter and am feeling fitter than ever before. My friendship with Guy, who captains the boat, is prospering as well. Not intense, but we make each other laugh.

15 May

My tort essay was described by Dr Longley as 'a reassuring return to form' in our tutorial tonight. This bucked me up no end. Sid and I went to the Odeon afterwards to celebrate – *Saturday Night Fever*. Shit, of course, but a whole lot better than pretentious arthouse shit.

1 June

I was browsing in Blackwell's second-hand shop yesterday and found *The Last Days of Hitler* by Hugh Trevor-Roper. I have spent the last 24 hours devouring the whole book. I wish to God I was reading History and not Law.

5 June

Charles St Clair has been sent down. So far as I understand this is because (a) he has done no work of any description all year and (b) he scaled the college roofs last night while off his face, and then smashed the window of a room belonging to a very shy fresher called Thompson and proceeded to trash his room.

Beyond having registered him as someone very blond and swaggering, I have never clocked St Clair but I am very clear in my own mind he doesn't deserve my tears. Guy turns out to have been at prep school with him and says the college has 'completely overreacted'. I said bollocks. Thompson knows nobody and has stayed in his room all year except when he's been at Chemistry lectures. Guy didn't look convinced. ('It was only a joke,' he kept saying.)

7 June

I found myself wondering today – St Clair did History. Might his departure have opened up a space that I might fill?

8 June

I went to see Dr Goddard about possibly switching from Law to History. He was extraordinarily unsympathetic and dismissive and screwed his face up – rather as though I had let fly a particularly noxious fart. He described the idea as 'wasteful and self-defeating' and told me to forget it. What a complete and utter wanker.

9 June

Actually – not. Dr Goddard has been a lot more helpful than he appeared.

This morning he sent me a note to say that he had arranged for me to see the History tutor this afternoon – the famous Harry Peel whom I last met at interview. Peel is about three feet high. He was wearing a tweed suit and smoking a cigar when I arrived, and did not seem to feel the need to go in for any courtesies like 'hello' or 'how are you'. He peered at me fiercely over some half-moon spectacles and said, 'Right, da Silva. Talk.'

The phrase 'coals to Newcastle' came into my head at this point, so I just ploughed on. Peel listened impassively to me

for five minutes or so and then waved me out, telling me
that he would be in touch.

12 June

The following letter appeared in my pigeonhole this
morning:

Dear da Silva,

*Dr Cameron and I have talked long and carefully
concerning your application to switch from Law to
History. We are reluctant to undermine the precedent
that such moves should be anything other than highly
irregular.*

*Mindful, however, that you have acquired a
measure of credibility with your Law tutors this
year, and mindful also of your promise to make up
lost ground, we are prepared to swallow our doubts.
At the start of next term, you will be required to sit,
under examination conditions, two papers: one on
Bede's* Historia Ecclesiastica *(Book III), and the
other on Historical Geography. You will also be
required to send sample essays at intervals during the
summer to Dr Cameron and myself.*

*I trust you have no elaborate plans for the Long
Vac to divert you from your studies. No quarter
whatsoever will be given you when you return.*

Yours
H G Peel

15 June

Last day of full term. The results of the room ballots were announced.

Guy came to find me. I didn't realise it, but he had been due to share with Charles St Clair and had been allotted one of the big sets overlooking the West Lawn. Of course St Clair is no longer around, so he's asked me to join him.

I'm incredibly touched. Guy always makes me feel about five times perkier than anyone else, and I've been spared living in a garret overlooking the Laundry Quad.

23 June

I told my parents about changing to History, and they seemed quite keen. 'I never saw you as a barrister,' Dad said cheerfully.

He was, however, predictably ruthless on the subject of money, and tossed aside all my reading lists with scant interest. 'Just get a job,' he said. 'You can do your reading at night. You will also give your mother £10 a week for house-keeping while you're at home.'

I am starting tomorrow at Marcello's Ice Cream, driving one of their vans.

29 June

I am very bored and pissed off. Very broke too. The weather was shit today. I trawled through endless housing estates, with my windscreen wipers going full pelt, waiting for customers who never showed. This is a problem, since the pay from Marcello's is commission only.

2 July

A very overweight man threatened to kill me today. My offence was to have played the chimes at 11.55 a.m. Legally we're required to wait until midday. He didn't look as if he could have run 30 yards let alone chase a moving van, but he was angry all right and looked rather deadly in his string vest.

23 July

Business has been much better this week: schoolkids are on holiday and the weather is half decent. When I went to Boleyn Street at about 4.30 it took me half an hour to serve the queue.

I noticed an Indian woman in a sari with two little tots. She was completely excluded from all the good-natured chatting that was going on. When she left, everyone started saying things like 'Christ what a pong', 'what they doin' 'ere anyway?'

28 July

An invitation arrived this morning from Julius Dalgetty – or rather from his mother. ('Lady Dalgetty At Home For Julius, Clarissa and Talitha.') Dress is black or white tie. It's not until the start of September anyway, but will definitely be a slice of life I've never seen.

I hardly know Julius except as a rather aloof and smart person in the year above me, but he's a friend of Guy's – hence, I am sure, how I have ended up being asked. On the back of the invitation, Lady Dalgetty has written in great sprawling letters: 'I am so sorry this invitation is coming so late – we had no idea you were a close neighbour!' As Mum said, it depends on what you mean by 'neighbour'. We looked up Lamscote Hall, and it is 22 miles away. I have replied (obviously, yes, not missing out on that, thank you very much).

6 August

The weather is bad again. Almost my only customer this afternoon was a dear old lady in Henty Road. She always buys a wafer whenever I appear because she likes a chat.

14 August

Dr Cameron returned an essay I had sent him some weeks ago.

'Your prose is somewhat addled,' he complains. 'I suggest you read Ernest Gowers' *Plain Words* (at least twice).'

3 September

I went to Julius's party yesterday. As expected, I knew virtually nobody and Guy failed to show up, the bastard. All the guests had supper with local toffs – my hostess was the widow of a High Court judge. A tall blonde girl called Alice was next to me. She had rather popping eyes and a not very good complexion and I guessed we were both low-status guests. She is at a secretarial college in Cambridge.

The dance was loud and boring. Because I was driving I couldn't drink, so the last couple of hours dragged on a bit. My dinner jacket, hired for £7 from Moss Bros, looked new and shiny. (Dad insisted on paying for this, which really touched me.) Everyone else had crappy old hand-me-downs, but somehow your genuine aristo still manages to endow them with a bit of glamour.

5 September

I have given my parents a full debrief of the Dalgetty bash. Although I am pleased to have been asked, it makes me feel guilty: why should I be getting these kinds of smart invitations and not them?

5 October

I hitchhiked back to Oxford yesterday – for reasons of economy. Actually, money has been less of a problem than usual because the weather was mainly very good and Marcello's has proved much more profitable than Bojo's. I have cleared my overdraft and banked about £175.

This morning I sat the two History papers, as instructed. Peel obviously thought I'd do no work unless he put a gun to my forehead, but I think I did all right.

The rooms I'm sharing with Guy are enormous and look very bare. I have a few books to brighten the place up, but that's about it. Guy arrived back a couple of days ago, and so we now have his unwashed sports kit, *Tubular Bells* and *Dark Side of the Moon* to add to Tocqueville's *L'Ancien Régime* and Bede's *Historia Ecclesiastica*. Guy says he's not doing any plays this year, but (although he always claims to hate reading) I noticed he slipped in a few books of modern plays and poetry on to the bookshelves.

I seem to be the only person without a suntan. Guy's face is the colour of ebony. He's been working in a boatyard in

Salcombe for the past three months – he says it was bloody hard work and a complete waste of time so far as bringing his overdraft under control is concerned.

2 November

I am much more sociable this year than last. That's partly down to sharing a set with Guy and partly due to the fact that historians are pretty idle. Our sitting room doubles up as a late night cafe and bar so I am short of sleep as well as of money. Just now Guy's girlfriend, Carrie, is staying with us. Hence, the bar is closed while he slakes other thirsts. She is 'on holiday' from her Art History course in Venice – I'm trying to imagine Dad's face if I told him this.

I try not to think about Ben. Guy, although never passing over the opportunity to call me a shirt-lifter (nice), is remarkably sensitive to my feelings in this matter and side-steps any mention of him.

6 November

Guy has written a series of sketches for a college revue. They're incredibly funny and very clever. As I said to him, he is a world expert at hiding his intelligence. Less surprisingly, the part he has earmarked for me is that of a homosexual clergyman.

23 November

Yesterday I spent the morning working in the library, rowed in the afternoon and did my bit in Guy's play in the evening. Everybody came back here to drink afterwards, but I had a tutorial at 9 a.m. I pulled an all-nighter (literally) in the College Library, finishing just as breakfast began at 8 a.m.

When I arrived at Dr Cameron's room at 9 a.m. there was a piece of paper on the door, apologising that he'd been called away and promising to rearrange. Thanks a fucking bunch.

29 December

Today I spent £3 on a tweed suit from Help the Aged. Then I went to Montague Jeffery and bought some starched collars. I now need to get hold of a pair of brogues (brown or black), preferably without sinking my last capital into their purchase.

I netted about £20 in Christmas money this year, which was extremely welcome. I am back working in the freezer plant for a week on Monday.

12 February 1979

I greatly enjoy Dr Cameron's tutorials. There is always an element of doubt as to whether or not he will remember you're coming for one thing. His sitting room is vast, and books and papers are piled everywhere, not desperately neatly. The question then arises as to whether he will be smoking a cigarette or a pipe when you come in: in case of the former, there is merely a gentle haze; in case of the latter, the fug is rather more intense. He is so shy he never meets your eye or calls you by your name, although he signed a note to me last week 'Hector'. It's his name, after all, and also what everyone calls him – but I felt ridiculously favoured.

Roly Duckworth, my tutorial partner, is making a mission of me. He has so far asked me to two lunchtime concerts (both accepted and enjoyed) and one lecture on numismatics (politely declined). He is much more fun than his very correct style led me at first to suppose, but gets cross when Hector fails to show up.

13 February

I'm moved to write this only because the scene in front of me is so untypical, Guy is writing an essay – almost a unique event – and is sitting at his desk looking martyred. He gets stroppy if anyone knocks on the door which, given that we are known to be open to all-comers, they invariably do. ('For fuck's sake, can't they see I'm working?')

2 March

Just back from a concert at Magdalen that Roly had tickets for. He seems to have a chaste passion for Louisa Garnett who was taking the part of Iphis in *Jephtha* (I am copying this from the programme). I assumed she was a professional, but in fact she's in Brasenose – in the first year. She has a hell of a presence.

5 March

Roly asked me for sherry in his room before supper tonight, an invitation that could be made unselfconsciously by about six people in Britain under the age of 50, and Roly is one of them. Louisa Garnett was there and predictably I told her I'd been at the concert. She just gave me a big smile and said, 'Please *only* be nice to me. I've got a shocking hangover' (she was tippling from a bloody great schooner of amontillado) 'and I *really* don't think I'm up to anything truthful.'

She was great fun, actually, even if her style seems to have been modelled on *The Pursuit of Love*. She's reading Classics, but (like Guy) claims to do no work.

7 March

My birthday. I tried to repress memories of a year ago. Guy and assorted others took me to Brown's for barbecued ribs. We popped into the beer cellar afterwards, where most of the college were queuing to have a go on the Space Invaders machine. I glimpsed Louisa out of the corner of my eye – looking slightly ill-at-ease. She was with Roly. I felt she seemed fond of him rather than enraptured. He just appeared plain uneasy.

Dominic had been unlocking his bike in Radcliffe Square at lunchtime the following day when Louisa had come up to him.

'I haven't exactly been following you,' she had said, eyes laughing, 'but I thought you might be here. Let's get some lunch.'

They had gone to a cafe in the covered market and had a bowl of oxtail soup.

'Not very nice,' said Dominic after the first mouthful.

'Not even a little bit nice.'

'Still. Cold day and all that. Warm us up.'

'I'm about to be cheeky,' she said. 'When I saw you last night, I thought you were looking a bit sad.'

'No, that's not cheeky. Very perceptive.' He looked down at his soup and smiled. 'It's the next question that's likely to be the cheeky one.'

'I'll stop there,' said Louisa. 'The rest isn't my business.'

12 March

We went to a lunchtime concert at LMH today. Louisa was singing extracts from *Dido and Aeneas*. Roly was in ecstasies, and kept on talking about dynamics and the influence of Cavali, for God's sake.

He had to go afterwards, but I hung around. Louisa suggested we go on a bicycle ride. Shorn of hyperbole, this meant nothing more than cycling from LMH to the Queen's Lane Coffee House. I could tell she was nerving herself to ask something.

Louisa's *sang froid* had been dented by his revelation but, sitting over toasted cheese sandwiches, she appeared determined to pursue the conversation.

'If I had been you,' she said, 'I'd have been proud.'

'Proud of what exactly?'

'Don't you see? Proud to have loved someone that much? And proud to have been loved in return?'

'I might have been if he'd stuck around.'

'More fool him.'

13 March

Lou has just been and gone. She stayed for nearly two hours, so I think she liked my company. I certainly enjoyed hers. She exudes confidence when she's singing, or when she's taking in the applause after a recital – but she's quite uncertain of herself and knows it. I asked her if she was good enough to be professional. She reckons that she could probably make a living at it, 'but never a good one'.

Public performance isn't in her genes at all. She only started taking singing lessons when she was about 12, because of a very persistent music teacher who recognised she had some talent. Her father is a farmer in Dorset. I'd assumed from her hair and clothes, even her make-up, she was yet another smart metropolitan. And yet it makes sense: for all her musical training and knowledge, there's something about her that's direct and unaffected. She's also quite strong-framed with a lovely healthy complexion, and looks fit. I asked her if she worked much on the farm. 'Not if I can help it,' she replied, laughing.

15 March

Lou has just left. It's just after 7 a.m. and I am writing this with a cup of coffee.

Once again, she called over last night – that was the third time this week, fortunately coinciding with Guy's play, and hence long and rather intense conversations have not been disturbed. At about ten o'clock, conversation seemed to be running out so I suggested a walk and off we went. She slipped an arm through mine along the aptly named 'lovers' lane' near the Master's Orchard, and – well – one thing led to another. She looks gentle and demure, but she cast all that aside along with her clothes.

I am a bit discombobulated, really, though also pretty pleased with myself, I think. I feel completely comfortable with her and we were both randy as cats. Maybe I'm not so gay after all. If I wasn't it would make like a lot easier.

Very early on, they had both realised that they had the knack of making each other laugh. That helped to iron out a few ruffles. Provoked by a tutor demanding some work from her, or by an inadequate accompanist, Louisa had it in her to become rather grand and haughty. Dominic learned to tease, rather than bawl, her out of these moments. When he became obsessive about completing essays or fretful about money, she made sympathetic noises but did not take his anxieties seriously.

Best of all, she was very keen on sex. Dominic became a much more skilful and confident lover under her tutelage.

21 March

Lou's tutor has given her two spare seats for *Turandot* at the Coliseum on the last day of term – why, I cannot imagine. Certainly not on account of her hard work. Talk about an economy of effort.

17 April

After two weeks at Bojo's (with a lot of overtime), I have rewarded myself with a long weekend away and accepted Lou's invitation to Dorset.

I'd obviously twigged when she spoke about her father being a farmer that he was going to be one of those who drove a Range Rover rather than a tractor. Lord Garnett, in a lofty way, was quite welcoming. He plays the part of the decayed gentleman farmer: elbow patches, ancient corduroy trousers and various protestations of financial ruin. Their son is at Eton – so I am guessing this is wind and piss. Lady G is big-boned and bossy, rides to hounds three days a week, attends gymkhanas, and falls asleep in front of an Aga reading back numbers of *Horse and Hound*. She sniffed me out as an *arriviste* within seconds of my stepping across the threshold. The house is a big Victorian pile.

Lou promised me that they'd 'be doing absolutely nothing', which proved to be absolute bollocks. On Saturday there was a tennis party and we had supper at the home of some local grandee. Lord G was already there by the time we arrived, drinking neat whisky. Lady G eyed him fiercely.

I woke up early on Sunday and headed down in the direction of the kitchen, passing Lord G on the stairs. He was dressed in what an optimist might call a dressing gown but in reality was a long silk frock. He wasn't the least abashed, and asked me if I'd like a glass of whisky.

2 May

Guy and I are going to Spain in the summer. His godmother has lent him her flat in Madrid. It will be a bit of a swansong for us since, like all the other Modern Linguists, he's going to be away all next year. He'd hoped to go to Paris and Berlin, but his tutor (they still hate each other) has placed him in Tours for six months, followed by Dortmund. I told him that he is the kind of person, even in Tours and Dortmund, who can't help making friends and having masses of sex.

Roly has tracked down a small flat in Walton Well Road for next year and asked me to share it with him. There would be big advantages to doing so: I will drink and spend less and work a lot more. Less fun though.

I daresay Lou will be round a lot. Roly is rather proprietorial about both of us, and tells everyone who will listen that he was 'the matchmaker'. Guy doesn't say anything much, but I can he is genuinely mystified by me having had sex with a bloke in my first year and with a girl now.

9 May

I mentioned to Lou, rather too obviously as an aside, that Guy and I were going to Spain 'for July anyway'. She was pretty pissed off and reminded me that, whenever we had discussed going away by ourselves in summer, I had claimed I could not afford it. In the end, it was decided she'd fly out and join me at the beginning of August.

3 July

In Madrid, thank God. Fabulously hot. The flat is small and basic – but it's free and I feel euphoric just being here.

6 July

I cold-called a summer school I tracked down in the phone directory, and they have given us jobs, teaching English to Spanish children. We will start on Monday and should each clear £300 by the end of the month.

9 July

My class consists of a dozen 15-year-olds. I can usually get them to be quiet, but let's face it – they find my attempts to teach them English mind-blowingly dull, poor buggers. The only real challenge are the Garcia Millers, a pair of twins who are imperious to my efforts to keep them under control. Adrian is the lazier of the two, but he makes me laugh. Jesus, his brother, is naughtier. At a disco on Friday afternoon, he allegedly copped off with Immaculada.

Guy is bored witless by the teaching, but – same every-where – everyone falls in love with him. Invitations pour in, from pupils and staff.

24 July

Guy and I were getting a bit tense with each other last week. Heat, boredom – nothing worse than that. He is also pissed off because there is no TV in the flat and so he cannot watch any sport.

I went to Salamanca over the weekend, wanting a bit of space and silence. I phrased the invitation to join me carefully, using words like synagogue, cathedral and art gallery. He said, 'Would you mind if I piked out of that, matey?'

3 August

Last day of our jobs. We were each presented with a fat wad of pesetas and I went straight to the airport to pick up Lou. She is several shades browner than me, having ended up going to Sardinia for a fortnight with her cousins.

Guy tactfully went off for the afternoon, so she and I had the flat to ourselves. Later we went out to join him and various others for an end-of-term meal, sangria and spliffs. Bed about 4 a.m.

7 August

The train journey to Granada on Sunday night from Madrid was knackering. An incredibly crowded train – eight to a compartment and the corridors packed with sleeping bodies. Lou emerged from the WC at one point looking traumatised (I didn't ask for explanations). By the time we got to Granada (7 a.m.) I could see that she was properly unwell and probably had a temperature.

We went to the nearest hotel – very cheap. There's no point in going anywhere further until she's recovered. I am a bit worried about her, but also irritated because her being ill means we have to stay in a hotel and that means spending more money. Another worry. (I know that's mean-minded of me but I can't help it.)

8 August

Lou was a lot worse this morning – sweating and with a ghastly cough. I got the awful woman in reception to call a doctor. She arrived quickly and prescribed antibiotics. I could see her eyes registering doubt when she looked around the shit heap that is our room – which helped me to think more clearly and I said to Lou we had to go to a proper hotel.

The doctor went downstairs and used the hotel phone to ring round. By midday we had moved into the Hotel Angel – bigger, cleaner and more comfortable, just by the Plaza Mayor. There is a pretty little terrace overlooking the rooftops, and a trellis. More to the point, we have our own bath and loo.

9 August

Lou is perhaps a bit better this evening, but still really feeble. I asked room service to bring up something light for her supper – a waiter arrived with a thin soup, tortillas and *tostada*. Lou played with them but didn't really eat much. She has now gone back to bed, but isn't asleep. Too noisy for one thing: there is a brass band playing in the square which we're both pretending to ignore.

10 August

Lou is definitely a bit better today. I rang my father who said, 'Stay comfortable and safe, the pair of you' and told me he was wiring £200 to my bank immediately. It makes me really ashamed for those occasions when I have inwardly railed against him for being tight.

I have been saying to Lou for the past couple of days we really ought to call her parents, but she says her mother will throw a fit and so please hold on.

13 August

We went to the Alhambra today and sat in the shade wherever possible. In retrospect – not such a good idea. Lou is still easily exhausted, with a foul cough.

This evening we rang Lady G who spent ten minutes bollocking Lou for getting ill and ordered her back home 'at once'. I spoke to her myself and she volunteered not a penny of help, nor a word of thanks, nor made any suggestion about how we should effect this mercy dash. Lou ended the conversation in floods of tears and looking dreadful.

15 August

Home – thank God. Lady G met us at Gatwick. She was easily spotted by her Amazonian height, green gumboots and bilious ill-humour. It was not a joyous reunion. My hunch is that Lou needs at least another week in bed.

I came home by coach where Mum and Dad have been full of concerned questions about Lou and oohed and aahed at my tan. My hair has also bleached. I have a month doing nights at Bojo's starting on Monday. The time has come to start repairing the economic earthquake.

29 August

As part of her convalescence, Lord G gave Lou the keys for a small cottage in Devon which belongs to him, and told her she is welcome to use it to live in and to revise. Rather decently he also suggested she ask me along. It was also made clear to her that the matter was not to be discussed with Lady G.

By juggling dates with Bojo's, I have been able to spend four days here. It's called a cottage, but is really a prefab, with a biggish sitting room and one bedroom, and looks out on to the beach. He told Lou he lets it out much of the year and that it gives him a trickle of income of which Lady G is unaware, and on which she cannot lay her hands.

It's been the best time we've ever spent. Lou has divided her days between singing practice (I go for walks during these) and reading Agatha Christies. I read a lot (E. P. Thompson for brain food, Len Deighton for pleasure) and go for easy runs. There's no TV, but good sex takes up a lot of time.

17 September

Just got back from Dorset where I went for the weekend. Lady G had reminded Lou that house rules stipulate separate bedrooms for unmarried couples. It was a bit of a surprise therefore when, in the small hours of Sunday, I was awoken from a deep sleep by the noise of someone opening the door of my room. Vaguely preparing myself for sexual exertion, I switched on my bedside light, only to find Lady G peering down suspiciously. She offered no apologies or explanations, but just marched out.

28 October

Roly and I moved into our new flat in Walton Well Road at the beginning of the month. We have a good view (over Port Meadow) and get few visitors. His self-discipline and sobriety is having an excellent effect on me.

Or it *would* do if I stayed here more often. Lou finds it dull and in consequence I am spending about five nights a week with her in College. It's a slightly schizophrenic way of life for me. Between about 8 a.m. and 8 p.m., I try and be as much like Roly as possible and go to the library and do essays and go for runs. In the evening, I rejoin Lou and do cafe society. She spends her days flitting between rehearsing really hard, chatting with friends and avoiding her tutor.

6 January 1980

Roly asked me to join him this week at this small cottage his family owns in Ambleside. There is bugger all to do except work. It's all very wholesome. He makes us both a cooked breakfast every morning at 8 a.m., and then we work until lunchtime in the little sitting room overlooking the fells. So far we are egging each other on and so work harder than we probably would have done if we were alone. I think I am FINALLY cracking the Anglo-Saxons and the Normans, thank God (but I'll never love them).

We've gone walking every afternoon. Roly knows the names of the places. Today was Red Screes and Dove Crag – a sea of green and mud, and there's been a lot of rain. Nice to be out of doors, though. He is very proud of his knee breeches and walking boots and is trying to persuade me to love fell walking.

We've talked about the future, inevitably. He is determined to join the BBC next year and said he 'presumed' I'd be teaching. I decline however to live on a pittance in provincial obscurity. I've done it already.

17 January

Suddenly everyone is busy applying for jobs. I have sent in applications to various merchant banks and have now been interviewed in five separate hotel suites by an assortment of handsome young men in pinstripe suits and polka-dot ties.

Despite what I assume are good references, I have so far failed to make it to the second round anywhere. I am hedging my bets, and have also applied to do teacher training next year.

6 February

I took a train to Paddington today for the second round of interviews at Grayling Burckhardt Coveney. Felix Sunley lent me his incredibly posh dark blue suit which saved me a load of money and made me feel almost a banker. I'm amazed to have got this far. GBC is meant to be the best of all the banks and they pay their trainees £10,000 in their first year (although quite a few don't last that long . . .).

I arrived at a very grand office in Cheapside on the dot of 9 a.m., along with 11 others. Presumably we are all in competition with each other. It was a gruelling day: there were four separate interviews each lasting an hour. One middle-aged woman wanted to know about school and education, another older guy insisted we talk about Middle Eastern politics (FUCK!!!), then there were two young women. The first gave me lists of data to analyse and the other (very thin, dressed in black and with a strong American accent) wanted to know what experience I had of teamwork. While I was trying to think of what the hell to say, I developed a tickle in the back of my throat, tried to disguise it and then embarrassed myself by needing a glass of water.

It's not going to happen, I can tell.

2 February

Today's interview was at St Ethelreda's Teacher Training College.

About as big a contrast to a merchant bank as could be imagined. It's about an hour's bus journey from Oxford and in terms of the atmosphere (both of the town and of St Ethelreda's itself) feels the other end of the country. The College looks and feels like a 1960s secondary school, albeit one with rather older and less noisy students.

I was interviewed by someone who is due to retire called Mr Leslie. He asked me if I intended to teach in a private school. I said, 'Oh no – certainly not' – which is, of course, a huge lie. He said, 'I'm very relieved to hear you say that, young man. On the basis of that answer, I'm happy to offer you a place here next year.'

I returned to Oxford feeling relieved but, not to put too fine a point on it, uncomfortable that such a big lie should have paved the way to getting a place. However, there wasn't much time to dwell on it because I found a letter from GBC waiting for me – inviting me to the final round ten days from now.

3 March

Final round. The personnel director asked me a few predict-able questions and after about ten minutes put down his pen and said, 'I can't work you out.' He said that he was quite used to interviewing clever young men ('and nowadays even some clever young women') who hadn't a clue what they want, except to be rich.

He said, 'You're a bit different.' Then he added, very softly: 'I'm shooting blind here, of course, but I think you want to be a teacher.' He says I can have a job there if I want, but suggests I brood on my options for a few days more. A wise man. It's a moment of truth.

4 March

This is how I've been reasoning: if I go into the City, my reinvention of myself as an upwardly mobile young man is complete. The old shames of Hunter's Chase will have been expunged. But if I become a teacher, I will be playing just myself.

Truth is – there is no dilemma. I have come home to talk with Mum and Dad. They have urged me to follow my heart.

7 March

Over a birthday curry this evening, I told Lou I had made up my mind to teach and that this would mean another year in Oxford. She said the right things, but I could see she was uneasy.

20 April

A lonely month of revision is coming to an end. Lou has
been up this weekend but just gone home this evening.
Plenty to eat and drink and some lovely cosy times in bed.
Quite apart from anything else it was a blessed relief not
doing any History for a couple of days.

I've stayed living in Jericho all vac – daytimes in the Bod
and evenings at home. Very cheap and, from a work perspec-
tive, very productive. I've kept myself motivated by going
away each weekend – the first, with Roly to the Lake
District, and, last weekend I went home. Mum made me
roast pork and bread and butter pudding, and Dad poured
me a Scotch and talked to me, man to man, about politics.

The middle weekend I went to see Lou in Dorset. Lady G
has thawed – there was something patronisingly kind about
her, which is both unexpected and a bit alarming. I found
myself wondering if she believes Lou is limbering up to give
me the heave-ho. No sign of this happening from where I'm
sitting, however.

26 May

Dilemma. Guy has written from Dortmund to say his
godmother has said we can use her flat in Madrid again
this summer, and is suggesting we do a repeat trip. He
says his German is pretty fluent and that he's loved being
there.

Just at this moment (the pile of papers on my desk is testimony to this) I find it hard to think about anything other
than the Russians' refusal to be drawn into an alliance with
Britain in August 1939 – but I THINK it sounds a brilliant
idea. The trouble is that I know Lou wants us to go away. We

haven't finalised anything, but there's a clear expectation I will be on hand.

4 June

First day of Finals

Two three-hour papers (9.30–12.30; 2.30–5.30), both spent in a blur of furious writing. I worked during the lunch break and this evening. Lou arrived at about 10 p.m. and insisted we go to the pub for a drink.

Same for tomorrow (and Friday, and next Monday and Tuesday)...

11 June

The last History exam finished at 5.30 p.m. yesterday. Police and Proctors were in force in the High, looking self-important and irritated, but they did nothing to stop an artillery explosion of cheap champagne and large numbers of public-school finalists lowering their trousers.

I felt relief, but no euphoria. An acute longing for Ben rather overtook me. All very unexpected and there was, inevitably, nobody with whom to share it.

22 August

Everyone warned me that the first weeks after Finals wouldn't be easy and they were right. I was knackered, and in a bad mood with everyone, especially Lou. As I'd anticipated, she gave me a hard time about my going to Spain again with Guy, since it involved me ratting on a series of outings and invitations she'd arranged for us to celebrate the end of Schools.

Madrid, on the other hand, has been a blast. Guy was already speaking virtually perfect French and German, and is rapidly adding Spanish to his repertoire. As he says, the key is to have regular habits – in his case regular drinking and weed (in both of which I partake modestly) and football and sex (in which I partake not at all).

We're busy at school from about 8 a.m. until 5 p.m. each day, and then he plays five-a-side football. I go out two or three nights a week, but on weekdays at least I prefer to get back by midnight. He's out every night and God knows when he comes home (except sometimes he doesn't). My life is a pathetic remnant by comparison.

I am flying back tomorrow, with all my earnings spent shoring up my bulging overdraft (running at a steady £250 just now). Lou was supposed to be joining me for my cousin's wedding in Hay-on-Wye, but I've not heard a thing, so God knows if she'll actually come.

29 August

Lou rang me on Monday and offered to drive me here for Andy's wedding. We hadn't spoken since I went to Spain, so that was a bit of a surprise – a welcome one, since it spared hassle and expense of a train.

She was a bit cool as we set off and, just a few miles along the M1, said to me that she wasn't 'feeling quite the same way about us'. I presumed this was her building up to giving me the Dear John I have been expecting for some time, but she left the remark hanging in the air. I confined myself to looking politely interested. About 50 miles further up the motorway, she gave me a look under hooded eyes which

(I know of old) basically said she was gagging for it. Very confusing.

No obvious way of doing much about it, however. Mum and Dad have rented a cottage just outside Hay and we arrived about teatime to find that we have been allotted two tiny single rooms at opposite ends of the landing. Dad's work, for sure. Such a plonker.

Later we all drove in to Hay to meet Andy and his fiancée Francesca. Her father is a ruggedly handsome retired naval captain and her mother very much a service wife, with the whole repertoire of conversational lines to fill in any spaces. Lou was a big hit tonight – chatting with everyone. When we got back home, I worked on being easy and cooperative with everyone and everything, laying the table, praising the food, washing and drying up.

30 August

Wedding day. Mum overcame her customary resentment of spending money on expensive clothes for herself. She told me that it took a bit of third degree from Aunt Sheena, but she lashed out on a very smart hat and new outfit (lilac, I think) and looked terrific. Dad always scrubs up well in a morning coat and he looked genial and like the captain of a 747. Lou, always quirky, opted for a rather arresting black velvet creation.

Various relations popped up at the reception which followed. One was my useless godfather Uncle Tommy to whom I introduced myself. His last contact with me was to send me *The Wooden Horse* in 1969. I had hoped that a show of geniality from me might prod him into a burst of remorse and a massive cheque. He put his arm around Louisa's shoulder. 'This pretty gel comes with you, what?' he said, leering at her, and never said another word to me. Old goat.

3 September

Arrived at the new flat Guy has found for us in Cowley Road. Dad has (most reluctantly) raised my allowance to cope with the rent.

10 September

I found Guy in the sitting room this evening with a kitten on his lap. He put on the wheedling voice and sickly smile, so I guessed what was coming: 'Er – hello matey – how would you feel about us getting a kitten?'

12 September

The kitten has been christened Wallop. We have lashed out on cat litter and a tray that she steadfastly ignores.

27 September

Lou and I are in Scotland for Angus Macleod's 21st. Roly drove us up on Thursday in his enormous 1962 Bristol. We left Oxford at 9 a.m., and the further north we came, the more Wagnerian the weather.

Roly was quite undeterred and maintained a steady 90mph while simultaneously conducting *Tannhauser*, sounds of which boomed out from the speakers. We finally arrived at Angus's farm at 3 a.m. He was waiting (getting very anxious) and, mortifyingly, so were his parents. Hot soup, crusty bread and sliced ham awaited us.

I was surprised to wake up yesterday morning and find

myself as lively as I was, given the lack of sleep. We all (except Lou) went tramping up some sodding fell which would, I feared, be humiliating but wasn't. I encountered Lou on my return, peeling potatoes in some kind of out-house. She gave me a sickly grin which translated, roughly, as 'don't get any ideas I'll be making a habit of this'.

We had a lovely late lunch – a great thick vegetable soup (broth, I suppose you would call it) and roast gammon and leeks with a cheese sauce, followed by a jam tart. I ate everything in front of me, which was a lot, and was sorry when it ended.

28 September

Last night was the Ball. We drove about 50 miles to an incredibly beautiful Queen Anne house where we were bil-leted overnight. (This seems to be the way of posh Scots: whenever there's a jolly, all the local nawabs throw open their houses to the hostess's friends.)

Inside was a great stone-flagged entrance hall and an enor-mous fireplace (tragically unlit) with various skewered livestock embalmed on the walls. We were taken upstairs to a drawing room (much warmer, thank God) for more meeting and greeting of the toffs, a glass of champagne taken at a swallow and then politely hurried into a long dining room for supper – a rather stringy casserole and baked pota-toes, none too warm, and that was about it. Matters were slightly enlivened by an old buffer in trews, a couple of places down from me, chuntering audibly about the wine. ('I see Hugh's lashing out on the cat piss tonight.')

After the pudding, everyone suddenly stood up and the ladies retired to powder their noses and complain about the servants, leaving the men to port and cigars. Then it was off to the ballroom (something that looked like a village hall). We were each given a dance card and hours and hours of Gay Gordons, Eightsome Reels and what have you followed. I was completely clueless. Lou found that embarrassing and got pretty impatient. That pissed me off good and proper.

7 October

I met Lou for lunch today and told her I'd decided we've got to split now. I tried to work the line that 'we both know this has been coming' so that it didn't feel like her being dumped by me.

She was very tearful. I was sad about that, but not about the decision. I'm a trainee teacher and she's a fucking land-owner. The implications of that have been becoming clearer to me for a while and, if I had any doubts, our time together in Scotland resolved them nicely. It's time to be myself.

9 October

Today began with a phone call from Lou at about 8.30. She sounded in a state and asked me if I still loved her. A pretty miserable half hour followed and, by the time I put down the phone, I felt like an axe murderer.

I was sufficiently unnerved to ring Dad to whom I gave a thumbnail sketch of recent events. I told him that she had said she would never love anyone again. There followed a brief pause and he cleared his throat a tad impatiently: 'My dear boy,' he said, 'don't flatter yourself. Youth always recovers.'

15 October

I went to a drinks party in Jericho last night and had a long talk with a giggly girl named Leyla who is a research chemist. She has deep blue eyes and great tits, and she laughed at all my jokes. She is clearly up for it, but I have decided to spin things out – just because, smugly, I know that I can.

27 October

Leyla is what my grandmother used to call no better than she ought to be. In the interstices of all the shagging we have done over the past week, I felt it polite to broach the odd bit of conversation with her, and she took the chance to tell me of the existence of a boyfriend who is a pilot in the US Navy. I asked her to give me plenty of notice when it's time for him to get shore leave. She also let fall that some of Lou's snottier chums have been giving her haughty looks. (I said – don't worry about it, but I could have saved my breath. She isn't.)

When I returned to Cowley Road this morning I discovered Guy had pasted a 'To Let' sign on my window. Underneath he had scrawled: 'The previous occupant has expired from an excess of shagging.' He's one to talk.

10 November

My parents visited yesterday. A lovely bright autumn day. We ate roast beef at the Cherwell Boat House, during which my father handed me a letter from my grandmother's solicitors to tell me she had left me £800 in her will. PHENOMENAL!

Tonight Guy and I are going to stuff Chinese food down

our throats at the Opium Den by way of celebration. Prosperity is making me feel confident and calm, and inclines me to love my fellow man.

12 November

I've been doing the PGCE course for a month now. BORING BORING BORING. I turn up for History seminars on four mornings a week between 9 a.m. and 1 p.m., and everything that I have usefully learned to date could have been compressed without difficulty into an hour. So far, I've learned how to write a lesson plan and I have constructed two worksheets (one on Norman Castles and another on Suffragettes). I want to cut my throat.

The people are fine – there are 12 of us in all. The others have no side, no airs and graces, no devouring ambition, and are very easy to rub along with. Not like undergraduate Oxford at all. Most did their degrees elsewhere, and so are socialising with each other madly. They've made me very welcome – but outside classes I keep my distance. Our History tutor (Trevor) is shy and very honest about how much he hated his first two years of teaching and how the kids ran circles round him.

The real killer is the weekly 'professional studies' seminar, led by Neil, who has a really unattractive beard and (it's easy to tell) is infused with a sense of his own brilliance. The seminars are always hijacked by a young woman called Baz who gets in terrible rages if anyone speaks up in favour of fascist practices (like grammar schools or streaming). The rest of us sit in silence anyway, intimidated. She is properly scary.

Neil enraged me last week when he told me to rewrite my

essay on 'equality in education' on the grounds that it was insufficiently researched and 'politically provocative'. He added that he felt the two of us were 'not on the same wavelength'.

23 November

Guy and I gave a Wild West Party last night in Cowley Road. Not a complete success, in that we invited about four times as many people as the house could hold. We had a huge bonfire in the back yard and of course there were complaints from neighbours. There were masses to drink at least, so I don't think anyone actually died of cold.

Leyla, whom I haven't seen in ages, turned up and was especially friendly, so I thought: excellent – she's up for it. However, given the crowds, there was fat chance of doing anything about it.

2 December

I am grossly underworked and my wits reel at the banality of what little is asked of me. Last week it was worksheets on the Black Death for 12-year-olds.

12 December

I signed up for a course to teach English as a foreign language and have spent three hours in class every night for the past fortnight. Coachloads of foreign students visit Oxford during vacations and, if I pass the exam on Monday, it will ensure I have LOADS OF CASH. The classes are intense and – joy and relief after months of mind-numbing banality – have some intellectual backbone.

16 December

I spent all day yesterday revising flat out for the TEFL exam last night – finally learning the phonetic alphabet. On my way to the exam, I got stopped by a policewoman for taking my motorbike up a one-way street and was ordered to report to Oxford Police Station within 48 hours.

I repressed my irritation and arrived for the exam on time. Three hours' intense concentration followed. I think I passed but it's harder than it looks. As soon as I finished, I rode over to the post office depot where I've managed to get night work until just before Christmas. I didn't finish there until 6 a.m. Then I went back to Cowley Road to sleep.

I had a sort of brunch (cornflakes and bacon) and drove over to the police station with my insurance and MOT. A police sergeant cautioned me. I affected as much nonchalance as I could but I was actually a bit rattled.

21 December

We gave an impromptu party in Cowley Road last night – supper followed by charades. Guy invented films and plays with pornographic names and then asked all the girls to simulate them in mime.

26 December

Aunt Sheena arranged Christmas this year and the plan was for Mum and Dad and me to drive down to Kate and Jim's flat in Hoxton in time for Christmas lunch. Dad worked himself into a state about the traffic and unilaterally rescheduled departure for 5 a.m. I think this was done mainly to get a rise out of me, but I had too much sense to protest. In the event, we arrived about five hours earlier than they had anticipated and one look at Kate's face when she saw us supplied me with all the *Schadenfreude* I needed.

2 January 1981

Leyla rang me on 30 December out of the blue to suggest we meet in Cowley Road for a parentless New Year. She concocted a vegetarian lasagne, and I bought two bottles of red from the local Spar. I know nothing about wine but even I could tell it was terrible. It didn't matter, however. She was very giggly and affectionate in her usual mindless way (can't believe she's doing a DPhil). Also very up for it.

5 January

Just back from Gareth Evans' Twelfth Night party at his home near Llangollen. A huge Victorian place – more like a barracks than a house, but perfect for a party and it meant everyone could stay.

'Everyone' included Lou, which threatened to be awkward. She avoided mentioning Leyla, however, and told me that her mother's latest economy drive means that she refuses to burn logs. Christmas has accordingly been colder than usual.

What with her being so jolly and fond, and the booze being so plentiful, I could feel myself starting to get frisky. Indeed, I was on the edge of proposing that we staged a discreet adjournment when some sixth sense alerted me to the fact that she was setting me up for a classic thumbs down. So, exercising more self-control than is my wont, I looked at my watch, yawned and said goodness me, is that the time, what fun, see you soon.

21 January

Teaching practice is JUST like being back at Greystoke, except I'm allowed in the staff room. Even the buildings look identical – utility 1950s and Portakabins in the playground.

A tough school. The deputy head used to play rugby league for Castleford and seems to spend quite a lot of his time pinning bad lads up against walls, whispering menaces. There have been no riots in my classes so far – quite. Classes last for an hour and there are nearly 40 kids in my Year Sevens. The ones I feel sorriest for are the Year Tens. My group is considered too stupid even to do a CSE: difficult, then, to find a compelling reason for them to do a homework on the Cold War.

Life is truly unfair: the most disadvantaged kids are often the least good-looking. They get the worst zits, the hair lip, the squint. They also occupy extremes of physical development. Leanna Bull must wear a 40 Double D whereas Karen Mitchell is quite flat-chested. Martin Batchelor has sideburns and the casual swagger of someone getting sex at least three times a week. Brian Parkin is 16 and his voice hasn't broken.

My head of department spends entire classes with his feet on the desk, apparently doing nothing but eat marmalade sandwiches. He hardly even speaks to the kids except in grunts. Yet all the kids adore him and clamour to be in his classes. Last year everyone in his O-level set passed – a school record apparently. I'm beginning to realise there's more than one way to do this job.

23 January

Lou rang me out of the blue yesterday, telling me she could no longer stay silent about (I quote) my 'gross infidelity' and 'moral turpitude'. I started to answer back but she went shouty, spitting out something about 'you and that whore'. So I replaced the receiver. All very unexpected and I was quite upset.

Guy said not to bother. 'You chucked her. She's just trying to make herself feel better.'

11 February

I'm just back from an interview at Tregowan – crushingly dubbed a 'middle-ranking public school' by the man in the university appointments Committee. The Head of History was kitted out in an aggressive tweed suit, matching yellow bow tie and socks – I could tell at once we wouldn't get on. The Headmaster had a permatan face and brilliantined grey hair and asked me if I had 'any skeletons in the cupboard'.

Off for another interview tomorrow – Saxburgh. I'd never heard of it until I read the advertisement.

14 February

Saxburgh School has offered me a job starting in September, teaching all ages 11–18. It's an ex-grammar school – not exactly the great glittering public school of my snobbish fantasies, but I'm bloody lucky and I know it. (It nearly didn't happen. The Headmaster and I had bristled at our meeting, and he only agreed to call me back because the Head of Department liked me.)

I am not euphoric (I seem destined to live out my days in

the Midlands) but I am relieved. I will now be able to pay my own bills, and to ply my chosen trade. My parents were delighted.

14 March

Degree Day. Graduates met the Dean of Degrees for sherry in the Senior Common Room at midday. Professor Japp was, inevitably, already half pissed, and then got stuck into a decanter of burgundy which was served with some very over-done steak in the Fellows' Dining Room.

I took the booze very slowly and met my parents outside the Sheldonian – they looked truly happy and there was the unspoken thought between the three of us that today marked the end of quite a bumpy journey.

We went back to Cowley Road where Guy had prepared supper for all of us. Beef stew, crème brûlée and gallons of wine. Dad was completely taken with just how nice he was, and made a charming speech. It's considered rather *infra dig* at Oxford to collect one's degree, but I don't give a shit.

24 March

Final day of teaching practice. Craig Greengrass said to me, by way of farewell, 'You'd be all right if you wasn't such a frigging toff.'

9 April

I'm teaching foreign students this week. Leyla has gone to see friends in Ankara and has let me use her room. It is odd to use the room for serious work, as opposed to casual sex.

27 April

I went for a run on Port Meadow today and bumped into Francis Morley. His hair is dyed blond and he was accompanied by a dachshund called Zozo. Slight change of image, but still the same old shit.

2 May

Guy seldom surfaces before 11, and appears to be in denial that in about three weeks' time he is going to be sitting Finals. There is a slim volume of poems by Baudelaire, which he filched from the Bodleian at the time of his most recent essay crisis, lying on his desk. I have not seen him open it, however.

9 May

Blue skies and a blazing sun this morning. Guy dragged out the big blue cushions from the sitting room into the garden in an effort to get a tan. He lay there, vain as Narcissus, looking martyred.

I poured a bowl of cold water on him from an upstairs window and he trashed my room by way of punishment.

1 June

Spending much of last night watching the hustings for the JCR Election in college. Most enjoyable. Left-wing candidates were, of course, in the minority, but infinitely cleverer and serious-minded. As usual, they were the subject of much derision by pissed ex-public schoolboys. Also, as usual, I have friends in both camps.

8 June

Last Friday, I handed in my final essay for the mindless teacher training course. I haven't words to sum up the contempt I feel for the place, but it will give me a qualification and, thus, a meal ticket. Oxford is now officially over. I am celebrating by looking for a very second-hand convertible. Has to be cheap, and so will almost certainly be manky.

11 June

Guy's Finals finished this afternoon. I doubt he will draw a sober breath for a month – nor, to adapt the Liverpool FC chant, will he ever sleep alone. On which sordid note, I had coffee with Leyla this morning, set up by me in the slightly forlorn hope it might rekindle some of her historic enthusiasm for ripping off my clothes. Instead, she announced that she is engaged – not to the US Marine, or whatever he is, but to an actuary called Wilfred who lives in Vancouver. She asked me if I would like to meet him and was a little offended when I said, honestly, not much.

23 June

Proud owner of a nice MGB – British racing green.

Mine for £750. I am trying not to notice rust in sills and underside. (Perhaps it's not that nice, but it's the best I could get with that money.)

5 August

I left my diary at home, accidentally-on-purpose, which

explains the very long absence since my last entry. Once again, Guy and I went to teach in Madrid. We know the routine there so well now that there isn't much to tell. The biggest excitement was that the fridge packed up for a few days which, in weather of about 40 Celsius, was a bit of an issue.

I spent an evening smoking dope with a guy called Armando whom I met at a local bar. At first I declined his offer of a joint because I was nervous about getting arrested. But he wore me down in the end. It was relaxing rather than mind-altering, and I fantasised about sharing a two-man cell with him in the event of a police raid. Back in the real world, the police stayed away and we both went home our separate ways. He had a wonderfully chiselled face and figure, perfect teeth and an angelic smile.

I'm now back in Oxford for three weeks, teaching foreign students. Quite boring, but great money. I have six pupils, each seen for an hour daily. When teaching has finished, I go running. Later I eat crusty bread, cheese, tomatoes and (my new passion) pickled onions. Later still, I make notes for next term's classes until midnight. (The French Wars of Religion are fucking *impossible*.)

11 August

There was a knock on the door at 6 a.m. this morning. When I opened it, two uniformed police officers were standing outside. Was I Mr Dominic Michael Francis da Silva? I had a brief terror that Mum and Dad had been murdered in their beds but it transpired that the MG was stolen last night, and discarded somewhere near Islip. No damage was done, save that somebody has laid a turd on the back seat. Given how cramped the accommodation, its author must be highly balletic. It will cost £22 to clean, but I can't see there's an awful lot of choice.

25 August

All my foreign students went home at the end of last week, so I did the same. Then Guy rang up and asked if he could join us.

I said – of course. He gets on famously with my parents, the old charmer.

29 August

Mum and Dad went to London last night so we were on our own. The TV was all shite and, really for lack of alternative, we began to drink. We sank a bottle of wine, and then liberated a bottle of Dimple in the drinks cabinet and got started on that. Suddenly, when the bottle was about half empty, he asked me very seriously if I had thought about telling my parents that I was gay. I asked him why he should be so sure that I was, but he told me to come off it.

I have replaced the bottle of Dimple – the better to preserve the Old Man's good temper.

Chapter Fourteen
Daniel: Avila House, June 2014

It was another hot day and traffic on the northbound carriageways on the M1 had been slower than usual. Daniel was relieved to see that Dominic looked at least no worse than a fortnight earlier, and had jumped at his suggestion of going to the park half a mile away.

Under the shade of tall conifers, they sat quietly and ate ice cream.

'Nice one,' said Daniel eventually.

Dominic arched an eyebrow. 'What?'

'The Oxford diaries.'

'Oh – those.'

'As if you cared.'

'As if I cared.' He grinned and said, 'Good-oh. I hoped you'd like them.'

'I did too. Blimey, you had fun. Posh friends, masses of sex. You even got a good degree.'

'Not that good,' said Dominic, 'and I don't recall masses of sex.'

'It depends where you're coming from,' said Daniel mournfully. 'And you did cover both genders.'

'Plenty of agony over Ben.'

'Bullshit. Six weeks of hurt feelings. Please don't tell me

you tracked *him* down in a bookshop.'

'No. Learned my lesson there. I did google him, of course. He's an attorney in New Jersey.'

There was a slightly pregnant pause.

'Anything you'd like to add?' Daniel asked teasingly after a little while.

Dominic smiled. 'Not really. Thank you.'

'Was Oxford the best time of your life?'

'No, never that. Great fun, of course. But I was too anxious to be a carefree student, and too stupid to be a really good one.'

Daniel rolled his eyes. 'Bollocks.'

'No. It's the truth.'

'Here, give me that.' Daniel leaned over and took the remains of Dominic's increasingly soggy cornet, placing it in the bin. 'Can we walk for a bit?'

They stood up and moved slowly on to the bridge over the pond in which a few overfed ducks wallowed. Dominic stopped halfway across and looked into the middle distance. 'Of course,' he said judiciously, 'Oxford bowled me over. I hadn't gone to a school like yours. There I was – surrounded by all these clever people. Not to mention the beautiful buildings and wonderful grounds. What's not to like?'

'I know. Wasted on the young.'

They walked on a little more, but Dominic was visibly tiring, and they headed for a bench.

'I'm guessing,' Dominic said eventually, 'that something you've read in the diaries has made you uneasy.'

'Well – since you ask. Your romance with Lou.'

'What of it?'

'It seemed a bit of a charade to me.'

Dominic thought for a moment. 'No – not a charade. We were far too fond of each other for that, and we loved the sex.'

'That's less than a romance.'

'That's true. I think we were both getting off on being a couple. Being young and all that: you're trying on new costumes all the time. We didn't let it run on too long, you know.'

'Did you really enjoy the sex?'

'I absolutely did. We both did.'

'Fair enough.'

Dominic smiled at him. 'Have you only ever felt heterosexual impulses, Dan?'

'I once told you I thought I might be a repressed homosexual.'

'Oh yes – I remember. You were feeling very sorry for yourself, as I recall. I'm afraid I didn't take it very seriously.'

Daniel smiled, and took in the sight of Dominic's yellowing teeth. 'Don't be offended,' he said, 'but I want to take you to my dentist. Your teeth are looking a bit sad.'

'Just be grateful you can't see the rest of me.'

They headed to the car. Once they had settled into their seats, Daniel turned to him. 'There's something else. I'm curious: would you have gone out with Lou for as long as you did if she hadn't come from a posh background?'

'Ah. There you have rumbled me. I'm not sure I would.'

Daniel eyed him sadly. 'I felt that,' he said.

Dominic looked out of the window. 'Going out with someone from a different kind of background was just part of my rather convoluted growing up,' he said. 'I don't think it's that unusual.'

'I didn't do it.'

'You were rather *differently* convoluted,' Dominic said, just a little testily, but he patted Daniel's hand at the same time. 'Still very charming, though.'

Driving home that night, Daniel remembered a moment when he was seventeen and had been told that his cousin had been killed in a car crash near Tel Aviv. The brutal suddenness of it, and the certainty that his aunt and uncle were in every kind of grief, had unleashed within him reservoirs of deep feeling he had scarcely known he possessed. The next day, burying his sorrow under the impassivity he had learned was a shy schoolboy's best disguise, he had gone as usual to morning school.

His first class had been History with the still-youthful Mr da Silva, who had at once seen through his carapace of self-control. Helplessly, Daniel had hung around at the end of class, and Dominic had sat behind the teacher's desk as usual, and smiled at him.

'Old boy. You're not quite yourself today. What's up?'

Daniel remembered that he had looked at him with such patient compassion that his composure had quite broken. That moment had drawn them together. Dominic's articulacy, his effervescence and his empathy, had won him a place very close to his heart.

Of course Lou had succumbed. So, for a time, had Ben. Of course.

Three days later, Esther handed him a letter.

Dearest Dan

Our last conversation has set me thinking. Status anxiety dogged me for years, even after I left Oxford. Very unattractive.

I do hope you enjoy reading about my time at Saxburgh. I tried very hard to be pleased when they offered me a job (the relief of getting a salary rather helped), but, as you already know, I was still slavering for Eton or Winchester. I slavered in vain, however! I didn't have a First, and God knows I was no athlete and so my place in the food chain of independent schools was accordingly modest.

As it turned out, I struck pure gold – it was a terrific school, filled with nice kids and good colleagues, and by the end of my first week I was completely immersed in the place. I was always more ambivalent about the town, the gentility of which rather hit me in the solar plexus. It was certainly pretty enough in a 1950s way (imagine the film set of Genevieve) *but its social DNA belonged to the same period. By way of illustration, may I offer you a true story? During my time there, the* Saxburgh Enquirer, *the town's weekly newspaper, published details of a local wedding under the headline* Bride Wears Floral Dutch Cap. *(My particular sorrow was that there was almost no one with whom to share the joke.)*

Local politics – in this context, school and town were in accord – was brittle unregenerate Thatcherism. You, my dear Daniel, would have been most *uncomfortable, and even a dedicated trimmer like me felt sometimes uneasy. My memories of the sinking of the* Belgrano *were of the delirious enthusiasm it occasioned among my pupils. The riots in Toxteth elicited only their indifference, leavened by irritation for the lily-livered restraint of the police.*

*I might have minded more, but life was so
internalised around the rhythms of school life there
was hardly time to look up. I think one or two of my
colleagues may have assumed I was a man with his
eye on glittering prizes – a headmaster in the making
and all that – but they were wrong. My buzz came
from pleasing people – a beast of a different hue to
raw ambition (although, of course, one every bit as
corrupting if left unchecked). In the effort to swaddle
myself in layers of approval, there was almost no
exertion which I would not undertake, and precious
few indignities to which I would not subject myself.*

*For colleagues, the bumptious newcomer is an
occupational hazard, but it was pupils who had to
bear the brunt of my inexperience. My blunders
(mortifying now to look back upon) mainly arose
when I failed to please and took umbrage instead.
There are two or three people from this time to
whom I wish I could now say sorry.*

*Mainly these were great days. Long ones too, of
course, but I was young and my energy was inhuman.
It also helped to have been surrounded by people of
whom I was fond. Of course, there were more
melancholy patches – I definitely remember framing
to myself the thought that I was lonely. The
happiness of friends and colleagues of my own age
who were settling down with partners was a bitter-
sweet part of the backdrop to being a single gay man
in those days. Especially one in his twenties, living at
a time and in a place where coming out was the very
last option.*

Dearest Dan, I did enjoy our walk in the Park.

Please don't be sad for me. I'm not unhappy, you know – just very tired, and also often not especially comfortable. It's made infinitely more bearable knowing that I love you.

Devotedly
D

Chapter Fifteen
Saxburgh, 1981–1984

3 September

My parents waved me off this morning – in a really nice and low-key way. They promise they will come to see me in October if, they say – 'you can spare the time'. Dad gave me £100 and told me to throw a drinks party at the end of term for 'those colleagues who have helped you to settle in'.

My flat is in Lancaster, a Junior Boarding House, so I'll be teaching older kids and supervising younger ones. Not my choice, but I'm rolling with the punches. The Housemaster and his wife, Vince and Dawn Feather, have gone out of their way to make me welcome. I had a cold supper with them – lettuce, Scotch eggs, beetroot etc. Vince procured a black and white TV for me, which even works. There is also a green Draylon reclining armchair in my sitting room which is comfortable but appears to have an alarming habit of sending you arse over tip if you lean back too expansively.

I am keeping my tape/radio player on all the time I'm in the room at the moment: I'm stuck in a Baroque groove just now ('What beautiful music,' cooed Dawn when I came downstairs later). I thought she said it admiringly but thinking about it now I realise she was hinting I should turn it down.

7 September

Term starts tomorrow. The BBC have thoughtfully screened *The Godfather* and *Godfather II* over the last couple of nights, which has sorted out the problem of what to do with my evenings. I don't imagine that will be much of an issue once the kids return.

26 September

I'm snatching an hour to catch up on what I think used to be my life. It's early Saturday evening and Vince is on duty – for once. As rumour suggested, he's not exactly a workhorse.

Big impressions so far: the kids are friendly but prefer you at a distance. They expect to be worked hard and are re-assured when you comply. I teach seven different year groups, between the ages of 11 and 18. The Upper Sixth make me nervy. It hasn't helped that my predecessor seems, fuck him, to have been charismatic and highly effective.

Colleagues seem unpretentious and quite matey. Chris Carstairs, my Head of Department, is a *diamond*. He looks and dresses – oh, what the hell, just like a provincial school-master: tweed jacket, grey flannels, everything from Burton. Drives a Cortina and takes his family on holiday in their caravan to the Peak District. A few streaks of chestnut hair on a baby face. NB: Will this be me in a few years?

His help and encouragement, to date anyway, have been phenomenal. He runs a department, he's Head of the Middle School, he has a wife and three small children – yet somehow he never looks impatient when I pop round with some inane question. I've been out for a drink with Nick Johnston (always called Johnners) and his girlfriend Sian. At first sight, he seemed your boorish northern chemist, but none of it – high-spirited and a big heart.

I went last Sunday to tea with Alan Lane who teaches French. He's about 30, unnaturally thin – almost an albino. Has a penchant for cream suits and silk shirts in strong colours (Sunday's was apricot), wears a flower in his buttonhole, and a silk foulard handkerchief. Gouache and oil paintings and sculptures of male nudes litter his flat on top of the Art School. Alan has assumed an air of cautious welcome and patronage towards me – in particular, ridiculing my habit of preparing classes and marking work. 'I never do,' he says, rich bass voice etched in contempt. 'It just happens.' Cut from a different cloth, in every sense, from most colleagues.

The other night I overheard two 12-year-olds talking at the end of prep. One of them described me as a 'fucking wanker'. I was a bit taken aback, truth to tell, but it will teach me not to listen in to private conversations.

8 October

I went to the pub with Johnners and a few others tonight (this is rare – Vince, in a rush of generosity, gave me a night off). We were on to our third pints when the Deputy Head walked in and asked if we were all having a good time. Johnners, who had, as they say, drink taken, assured him we were.

'Oh, good,' he replied. 'I'm having a good time too. I'm on *duty*. I'm doing your duty because you have *yet again* forgotten to turn up.'

'Christ, I'm sorry, Tony.' He didn't even finish his drink but shot out of the pub.

Quite an interesting moment. Johnners must be six foot six and is built like the proverbial outhouse. The Deputy Head is bird-like and about a foot shorter. But the advantage, just at that moment, rested with him.

12 October

My first run-in with a colleague – some shortarse in the PE department with bulging pecs who looks like a Poison Dwarf. I was meant to be taking a squash match which clashed with a rugby fitness training session in which two of the team were involved.

Me: I'm sorry about this.
Him: Well, it's ridiculous, that's what it is.
Me: I'm a bit ignorant of what one does in this kind of situation.
Him: I can see you're ignorant.

I decided to take the kids anyway – I hate that kind of rudeness. We lost the match.

14 October

The Poison Dwarf approached me today in the Common Room.

'You fancy yourself at squash then, do you?'

'Not really,' I said. 'I just play a bit.' I looked at him deadpan and he gave a thin smile and said, 'All right. Be in your kit five past one tomorrow. See how good you are.' I agreed, like a total arse. I teach every period tomorrow and lunch is the only moment I get any time at all to myself all day.

15 October

He beat me, unfortunately – but only just. I made him work for every point. We shook hands at the end, but now that a few hours have passed (I'm off to bed in a moment) I can see we'll always loathe each other. Miserable tosser.

24 October

Half term began after school yesterday. I am so used to all my time being used up that the idea of a free day is mighty weird.

I drove to London to see Kate and Caleb (who has all the fun and mischief I would like any son of mine to have when he's three and a half). They live on the eighth floor of a big council block in Dalston and seem completely content. Kate is more like a sister to me than a cousin, and I suppose for part of that I have Aunt Sheena and my mother to thank, since we have always seen a lot of her.

Then, changing the style somewhat, I drove across to see Guy in Camden. He's in a cramped third-floor flat which he shares with two other guys, who I never met but who work with him in the City. As ever with Guy, the flat is a tip and pretty whiffy. He says banking is boring but that it pays more money than any other job he could get. I sense that he's accepted this as the best compromise for the moment, but I'd be surprised if he did it indefinitely – he's not exactly an idealist, but he isn't a hooker either. He's also not sunk in the trough of celibacy, like some of us. A rather slim girl with bobbed hair and a sleeveless puffer jacket called Tish emerged from his room on Sunday morning – I slept on the sofa in the sitting room. Then I drove off to Warwickshire to see my parents – even, in a sudden rush of filial devotion, joining them for Mass.

Since then I have done nothing. Mum and Dad have been very indulgent, encouraging me to take life easy. I haven't emerged from bed before 9.30 a.m. for the last three days, and my greatest expense of energy has been on eating Mum's Danish apple cake and watching videos – *The Deer Hunter*, *Superman* and *Midnight Express*. I'm amazed they've bought a video player. Dad justifies it on the grounds of convenience ('We can catch up on the news whenever we get home'). I think they're just like me and like slobbing out when they get the chance.

In occasional moments of reflection, I have tried to ask myself what, so far, I think of this new life. Johnners is really becoming a mate, which helps. Alan entertains but unnerves me (exactly the same is true of Louis XIV's foreign policy, which I'm meant to have mugged up before Monday).

31 October

End of half term. The boarders returned tonight. Their return was heralded by a compulsory evensong which had the desperate air of an aeroplane crash: many of the younger children green with apprehension, several in tears, and parents looking decidedly shaky. The Chaplain chose to speak on Auschwitz.

2 November

I gave the Upper Sixth what I thought was a terrific class on Louis XIV. The fruits of preparation, I thought smugly, as they all left, A4 magnapads bursting with top insights and info. I heard one of them mutter 'What the fuck was he on about?' as they left the class. Also the reply: 'No idea.'

5 November

I finished reading *The Silver Sword* to the boarders tonight. I felt emotion welling up in my voice as we approached the denouement when the family are reunited with their long-lost mother. I couldn't help looking fleetingly at Nicholas Bampling – aged nine – whose mother decamped from home about a year ago. Expressionless.

16 November

Tonight there was a parents' evening for the Upper Sixth. Tables were set up in the Hall. Staff are required to wear gowns (why is this? To make ourselves recognisable? Or to bolster morale? It seems silly anyway).

To mother of John Coughlin, one of my brightest pupils: 'I must say I'm most impressed by John.'

Her (*doubtfully*): Oh. Good. Of course, he's missing Mr Tyrrell. They had such a good time in History last year.
Me (*rictus smile*): Yes. Yes, of course.
Her: Well . . . (*followed by a couple of deep sighs*) there it is. Nothing to be done. (*Another sigh.*) How is he doing, do you think?
Me: Very well indeed. He works hard; he can argue a point on paper. Very impressive, really.
Her: Oh – well, that's something . . . still, he *does* miss Mr Tyrrell. I mean, they *all* do.

18 November

I observed tonight spots on my back. An unwelcome addition, and also vaguely insulting, since I am also going bald.

7 December

I intended to set the alarm for 6 a.m. today, having gone to bed at 1.30.

Inevitably it was still dark when it rang to get me out of bed. I washed, showered and shaved and sat down and worked for an hour and a half. Then I looked at the clock again. 3.30 a.m. By mistake I had set it for 2 a.m.

10 December

Alan Lane has been much more chummy with me in recent weeks. Tonight he came with me to buy stocks for the drinks party on Sunday. Dad had, I think, rather anticipated something more sedate when he gave me the £100 back in September, but bugger that. Gin is what I want. Can't get fresh limes, so Rose's lime cordial will have to do and we'll cut up fresh lemons on the day.

I can't remember who I've asked: virtually everyone in the Common Room, I think.

13 December

Gimlet Day. Everyone came and everyone, almost, was totally trashed by the time they left. It's the old story: get people properly pissed within 15 minutes of their arrival and any party goes with a whoop.

Johnners set the benchmark high for bad behaviour early

by downing four gimlets within a minute. He's always loud so it made no obvious difference. Alan was staggeringly drunk and kept careering into people and smashing glasses, which he passed off with some aplomb – 'Oh dear, was that me? What a thing.' One older colleague's wife kept on saying, *uber* genteel, 'Well, this is very nice.' However, after she'd slipped down her third gimlet, she became a whole lot livelier. Jeremy Cox went to have a pee to discover a girl already sitting on the loo. He tried to beat a hasty retreat but then struggled to open the door. Hilary York passed into a deep alcoholic sleep in his front porch as soon as he returned home. Only he hadn't. It was somebody else's porch.

14 December

The Headmaster tapped me on the arm after Chapel this morning. 'I gather you had a lively Sunday, Dominic.'

'Er, yes – fairly lively, Headmaster.'

'Yes. So I hear. Anyone left unscathed?'

'Not many, sir.'

'Excellent. Well, I'll leave you to pay the hospital bills and repair the marriages.'

16 December

Last night of term. Our Nativity Play was a big success. Vince, Dawn and all the kids were there. Typically, Johnners showed up. (Equally typically, Alan didn't.) Having done any sort of play has raised expectations, so I am pleased. I am just three and a half months into my teaching career, and properly whacked. But I can't imagine another, or a better, way of life.

24 December

I have been slobbing at the parents' which has been most enjoyable. I slept for the first 48 hours but since then I've gone out each day for a run – a reasonably hard one. A not very satisfactory kind of sexual surrogate, I suppose. While I'm quite proud of my fitness, I can't say I'm particularly reassured by the way my personal life is going. Or more to the point – the absence of any personal life.

Christmas shopping is much more fun since I have enough dosh to buy presents without breaking into a cold sweat. Aunt Sheena arrived this evening with Kate and Caleb and we all seem well and pleased to be together. Mum and Dad are thrilled to have Caleb around. The only drawback is that the house is noisy and that the female members of the family look uniformly exhausted – from an excess of cooking and childcare.

Finding a present for Kate took me longer than for everyone else put together: she is impossible, because she wants nothing. In the end I settled for an ethnic cookbook, a bottle of Beaujolais, and a bat-and-ball set for Caleb, who is now nearly four. I was briefly tempted to throw in an elaborate machine gun and military fatigues which I spotted in the Debenhams Toy Department, but – mindful of Kate's pacifist tendencies – did not wish to challenge the peace of Christmas.

27 December

Tonight, once Caleb was in bed (the subject of bedtime is one on which Mum and Aunt Sheena share strong feelings), we decided to watch a video. I chose *Raiders of the Lost Ark* by which Dad was baffled. After a few minutes, I heard him burble into his chins and he moved off in the direction of a Jeffrey Archer.

6 January 1982

I'm back in Oxford for a conference of 'Young School-teachers' to which the HM suggested I go. Surely the saddest gathering of under-30s in Europe.

I bunked off last night's discussion group in an effort to track down Leyla who, it transpired, was in her room. She'd sent me a card (very surprisingly) at Christmas suggesting we meet up sometime, so it would have been rude not to have followed up. She seemed pleased enough to see me again, at least to the extent of offering me coffee and (come to think of it) shortbread. Thereafter, however, no sign of the old benefits/amenities – though the weird Canadian fiancé has gone west (metaphorically as well as, I presume, literally). She showed me the door at 10 p.m., claiming pressure of work.

I told her I remembered happy times not so long ago when she made it a point of principle to have my trousers off before I'd crossed six feet of carpet. 'Ooh, you liar,' she said, which just goes to show how stupid and self-deceiving she is. I haven't had sex for NEARLY A YEAR.

22 January

I overheard the Poison Dwarf and Mitchell Brown in the Common Room at break talking about a 15-year-old pupil and how they both hated him. Please tell me – why do such people go into teaching? (And why does anyone employ them?)

3 February

Miles Newton hovered around my desk at the end of class today. He made a bit of a show first, asking me some daft question about the Vikings, but he clearly wanted to speak to me. This has happened a few times with him. I think he wants me to have a good opinion of him. He said he is worried his girlfriend is pregnant and wants to know what I thought he should do.

I was at a bit of a loss for anything to say. He says her period is a fortnight late and he's spoken to a vicar – the latter for comfort, I suppose, rather than for contraceptive purposes. A part of me is wondering if he really is worried or just sucking up the attention. I checked on my school list after he left, and discovered he is two months shy of his fifteenth birthday.

6 February

I braced myself for more awkwardness today when Miles Newton asked to talk to me. His girlfriend is not pregnant, but Miles has been warned by her father that if he is spotted anywhere near her, he will give him 'the hiding of his life'.

11 February

There was a hell of a noise coming from the Computer Room after lunch today – so loud I went to investigate and found some little Third Former being jostled by a pair of shits a couple of years older. I dried his eyes (metaphorically) and then told the older boys they could bloody well both go and see their Housemaster and tell him what a pair of thugs they'd been. I left a note in his pigeonhole as well, but I doubt much will happen.

12 February

I made a point of going to see the Housemaster of yesterday's two thugs, but he cut me off as soon as I started. 'No need to say any more. I've just thrashed them both.'

I was a bit aghast. He said: 'They're both villains and well overdue for a whacking. Do 'em a power of good.'

19 February

I've been chatting more with Tom Inskip this term. He's very well-read (as he bloody well ought to be, given he's an English teacher) but I love the fact that he HATES SPORT and doesn't give a fuck who knows it. I don't think I've ever heard anyone say so explicitly in my life. Perhaps when I consider his wonderfully ugly and flabby frog-like frame, I shouldn't be surprised. He's asked me to supper tomorrow.

20 February

I drove over to Tom Inskip's this evening. Alan had been asked as well – he was glad of the lift but slightly sniffy when he heard I'd been invited ('Of course, I'd forgotten, you know very few people here, do you?').

Booze made him mellower, however. When we arrived, Tom took us both to the pub (Lauren stayed at home cooking and looking after their identical twin ten-year-old daughters) and the two of them drank about four pints apiece. We did the usual school gossip and (this is my stroke of luck) other people's drunkenness tends to relax me, so I think I was on pretty good form myself.

The twins were still up when we returned at about 9.30. One looked me up and down a bit and said: 'Tom says you're highly strung.' He and Lauren have adopted that 1960s bohemian convention whereby the kids call their parents by their first names, and say 'fuck off' to everyone else. Lauren is pretty quiet – I wondered if she was pissed off at us for having stayed out at the pub for so long and then having to put up with the three of us talking incessantly. Alan says not, and that's just how she is.

Despite having two children, a house, and having been married for over 15 years, Tom and Lauren have accumulated fewer possessions than anyone I know. It's a very attractive trait, which I wish I could emulate.

1 March

There are two genuinely bright kids in my Upper Sixth class, one of whom decided to cross-examine me today on Jansenism ethics. I hadn't a clue, but I could see others in the class were watching me for a reaction. I tried to look thoughtful and then, as casually as I could, turned to the other clever lad, 'John, do you want to take a shot at answering that?' He did, so far as I could tell, very well.

'Seems fair enough to me,' I said when he'd finished. 'Martin – you happy with that?'

'Yes. Thank you, sir.'

Jesus, if only they knew.

7 March

My 23rd birthday. Not old exactly, I know. There are cards from Mum and Dad, who I rang in the early evening, and also from Kate (Aunt Sheena has told Mum she has split up from Jim and is bringing up Caleb on her own). Vince and Dawn gave me a card, signed by them and all the kids in the House (some of whom will, I am guessing, have signed more willingly than others). They also, very considerately, gave me a big box of Thornton's Continental. Johnners and Sian took me out for a bar meal – pretty quiet (inevitably, being a Sunday).

Part of me is very happy to be here and pleased with all the cards and good wishes. Another part of me feels a bit on the edge of things. Johnners has Sian. Guy has (well, for the moment) Sophie. I can see myself stuck in Saxburgh for years to come – maybe for good. It's fine now – I have a few good mates, I like the kids and earning money, but how will I feel in a few years? I wish there was someone to whom I could talk freely about feeling gay, but there isn't – certainly not here. Johnners is a lovely chap, but we'd both be shy if it came to something very personal. Tom Inskip? He's kind and sensible, but he's much older, and I don't know him very well yet. I also think he'd find my agonising rather silly. No way would I broach anything with Alan Lane. Anything I told him would be repeated, and anyway his answer to everything is self-indulgence.

12 March

I contacted CND a few weeks ago and got them to send someone to speak to the boarders this evening. Most of the pupils in this school would campaign far more readily for nuclear proliferation rather than disarmament, so it was always going to be uphill work.

The speaker, Hamish, told me he was 30 but he looked about 15 – which didn't help. Nor did the Headmaster, who treated him like a bright boy who had fallen in with the wrong crowd.

17 March

Rumpus at supper tonight where I was on duty. A few members of the First XV, having won a match, burst in to the Dining Room and proceeded to push ahead of all the younger pupils.

I threw them out. Just for a moment I could see them deciding whether or not to defy me, but they didn't. Their friends clearly resented it, while the younger ones looked embarrassed and very far from grateful.

20 March

The CCF held an all-night exercise last night. This went, as I understand it, swimmingly – until a 15-year-old corporal pulled out a service revolver that he had purloined from his grandfather, and announced to the platoon of 13-year-olds in his care that it was loaded (it wasn't) and that he'd shoot anyone who didn't follow his orders.

His intentions appear to have been prosaic – an extended opportunity to shout and swear rather than do anything colourful. The young cadets, however, all shat themselves (metaphorically rather than actually), imagining their lives were about to end at the hands of some crazed gunman. When the relief bus arrived to give them breakfast at 6 a.m., the youngsters were found wailing and weeping, instead of being ravenous for bacon and eggs. The result is general uproar and the *putschist* has been sent home, pending a full investigation.

9 April

Very bad spell indeed. I tried to keep myself busy when the holidays began – playing a lot of squash with Johnners, going for runs etc. The truth is that I know nobody round Saxburgh save through the school and didn't want to impose myself, pathetically, on colleagues.

Guy invited me down to London (he's never less than generous) and as always, he lives every moment in a big party atmosphere – banking by day and bonking by night, so far as I can see. Perhaps this air of effortless affluence and mainstream sexuality unsettled me.

My exit route from the sexual Sahara in which I've been submerged amounted to something pretty squalid, starting with a phone call in response to an advertisement in *Gay Times*. I felt pretty apprehensive beforehand – taking a step into a totally unknown world and all that – but also smug. The idea of trampling secretly on all the conventional decencies really suited my mood.

Then came a trip to someone living in a flat off Leicester Square, and a parting with £60. The guy himself was not bad-looking: slight, about my own age, brown hair closely cropped, complexion of someone who spends too much time indoors. A nice smile, but maybe a wary, world-bitten look. Given the nature of the entertainment we had both arranged, I was struck by the fact that he clearly wanted to abide by certain social rituals first. Would I like a drink? There were bottles of Smirnoff and Bacardi, and cans of Coke in the fridge. How had my journey been? He was quite as nervous and as self-conscious as me.

I sat hunched in misery on the Tube on the way home, praying that Guy would be out when I returned. He wasn't.

As I came in, he was sprawled on the sofa. *The Old Grey Whistle Test* was on the TV but he looked bored.

'Hullo, faggot,' he said, glancing up momentarily and smiling. 'Do you want some supper?'

'I'm fine, thanks.' For form's sake, I joined him, pretending to concentrate on the box. I can pretend very well when I need to. It's quite impressive in a way. Outwardly laughing and taking the piss, inwardly screaming. There are times when I despair of myself. I'm writing this now, in real time. This is what I feel – and I have reason to.

14 April

I accept the fact that I'm – at least – bisexual. Feeling totally gay moves in and out of focus a bit, but 'orientation' isn't the point. I behaved BADLY.

I went to Confession today at the Cathedral. The priest was great – no mention of hellfire and damnation, but full of encouragement and comfort. He said I hadn't behaved particularly badly, but was full of sadness and sorrow. That much is completely true.

Then he asked if I felt God was watching over me. 'Completely,' I said, and then – taking me by surprise – hot tears started to pour down my face. It was true: I did.

20 April

Went home. Mum and Dad. Mum came downstairs with what I call her Mass face on – a mixture of austerity and devotion which melds Queen Mary with Audrey Hepburn in *The Nun's Story*. Usually it annoys me, but I'm trying to implement some of the advice given in Confession the other day: to be a bit kinder to myself, and to other people as well.

I joined them at Mass. If they were surprised, no hint was given.

Tonight Dad suggested we all go for a bar meal at the Punch Bowl. We ate scampi and chips and a very jolly time was had by all. I paid, because it's nice to be able to. Is it weird that, given how much I love and admire them both, I still cannot begin to talk to either of them about what's in my mind? They wouldn't be angry or disapproving.

16 May

I am still going to Mass, but today allowed myself an amnesty on impure thoughts. I am much cheered up in consequence which I suspect is to everyone's benefit.

26 May

Prize Day. The Guest of Honour was Melrose Burt, the Headmaster of Lucan Hall. He's the man who thrashed Guy when he was a 14-year-old boy for having sent an indecent letter to his first girlfriend. According to Guy, Burt took a run-up between each of the six strokes. The theme of his speech today was tolerance.

31 May

Kevin Ryland has been gated for a week for smoking. He arrived in my class this morning, following an interview with his Housemaster, in floods of tears – real gulping sobs.

For the first time I found myself thinking a bit more carefully about him – a moon-faced boy who, until now, I've barely registered. I suddenly realised with absolute certainty that he's gay. To be a boarder in Saxburgh, aged 15, with that hovering over you must be purgatorial. No point saying anything to his Housemaster, who would be repelled as well as nonplussed.

2 June

I had to tell one of the little lads in the House today that his older brother is in the local cottage hospital. He's got glandular fever, but, in an effort not to alarm him, I settled for saying that he'd been working too hard and was a bit rundown. He seemed supremely unaffected but was found crying in his dormitory half an hour later by Matron, to whom he relayed the news that his brother had had a car crash.

Memo for the future: don't use the term 'run down' to 11-year-olds unless you mean just that.

7 June

Alan spent half term in Portsmouth with, he tells me, an Able Seaman First Class – which he describes as 'doing his bit'. Despite my recent resolves to be a good Catholic, I felt a squeak of jealousy.

10 June

On the staff-room notice board today I saw a list of boys on 'Punishment Drill', which requires medium-grade malefactors to go and pick up litter after school on Saturday.

Offender: WALLACE
Offence: CALLING PATEL A NIGGER

Some staff have argued that this isn't worth a punishment and that Wallace was only 'joking'.

15 June

The Headmaster asked me to stay behind after assembly yesterday and, slightly to my alarm, to follow him into his study. I haven't been there since my interview. But it was all good news. He says I've done a 'good job' at Lancaster but that he wants me to move next year to be the resident tutor in Romans, one of the senior houses.

I'm delighted – it comes with a good flat for one thing. Vince was his usual phlegmatic self – we've got on very easily but he doesn't really find me *simpatico*. Dawn, however, is irritated. Next year's tutor may not be quite so energised, and in consequence her husband may have to do rather more work.

20 June

Dawdling over the Sunday papers, I came across an article about a virus that appears to target homosexual men in the USA. The paper also quotes someone describing it as 'God's punishment on homosexuals'. A Catholic, I observe with disgust.

21 June

Today I had my last class with my Upper VI. I've put massive amounts of time and energy into their revision and, indeed, into their teaching, but I never felt much of a bond between us. When the bell went, I wished them luck and told them to get in touch if they wanted extra revision classes. Less is more, I told myself. Here was classic English understatement, which could not fail to elicit spontaneous outpourings of gratitude.

I heard a couple of people mumble 'thanks' and then they all buggered off. Un-bloody-believable.

6 July

Last day of term. There was moderate mayhem last night when, following tradition, drunken leavers let off fire extinguishers, vandalised desks, ran underpants up flagpoles etc. It's all boring bollocks, really. My MG was broken into and rolled near (thankfully not in) the swimming pool. There was also some grease put on the door handles – a deliberate refinement to make returning it to the car park more unpleasant. Maybe I'm more unpopular than I realised.

The Headmaster was irritated by the damage. Irritated too, no doubt, by the fact that he obviously no longer has the usual repertoire of sanctions at his disposal. There was a very excitable atmosphere in the School Hall for the final assembly – raucous even. When he arrived, everyone stood up and he said, with an undertone of menace, 'Right. I want a good assembly,' at which everyone shut up. I was impressed. Then he rattled off a few notices, read 'The Desiderata' at about a hundred miles an hour, wished everyone a good holiday and walked out.

Later, it transpired why he'd been in such a rush. The leavers had pooled £50 to get a stripogram to come into assembly and take her kit off – onstage. Somebody had obviously leaked the information, however. Apparently, as he emerged from the School Hall, he saw the girl waiting on the steps in her black leather bikini. He said – curtly, I expect – 'You've wasted your time.'

11 July

Today was the Saxburgh Half Marathon. Dad very gener- ously came up to see it, and me. I took one hour and 43 minutes. I'm glad to have shown him that there is some sport I can do without total ignominy.

15 July

CCF Camp in Yorkshire is proving excruciating. I spent most of today in the Officers' Mess, mainly because there is fuck all else to do and I like being near coffee while I read my book (*Officers and Gentlemen*). I am also trying to avoid the Regimental Sergeant Major. He looks like Windsor Davies in *It Ain't Half Hot Mum*. I could see his eyes freeze in theatrical disgust when he saw me, but he still let fly a terrific salute.

2 August

I've been filling in time by buying furniture for my new flat, mainly at junk stores – a little bureau, a Regency chair in, goodness me, pink velvet, and an old-fashioned standard lamp, which is pure 1940s. All I need now is an old valve wireless to blare out the Home Service, and a tin of Horlicks.

6 August

I have been flirting with the idea of buying an old Porsche 911 which I saw for sale at a garage in Saxburgh. It is a left- hand drive, and the garage only wants £2,250 which they have said is 'a steal'. Finally decided against and was at once very relieved. God, the follies I can commit when I get into tunnel thinking.

11 August

I met up with Roly on Monday and we came up to Oban by train and then by ferry to Mull where we're staying at Harry Peel's house. Harry feels a friend now more than my former tutor. It's an old shooting lodge – mountains behind, sea in the front. Very glamorous setting, but the house is pretty cramped and pokey.

Harry drove us from Tobermory. The single-track roads can be unnerving and he is an unbelievably aggressive driver. His big hatred is caravans. 'If people cannot afford a proper holiday, they should stay at home watching television.'

19 August

A-level results. Overall my set notched up two As, one B, five Cs, two Ds and two Es. One 'O' (Hartman – richly deserved). Chris said he was 'quite pleased' but I'm not.

27 August

For the last four days I've been looking at houses I might buy. I found one today and my offer has been accepted. It's three years old, has three bedrooms, a garage, and a tiny garden.

I feel fortunate, but not remotely excited: it's an ugly, mean, modern house. I am putting down £1,250 in deposit and will borrow £23,750. I am told I can (just) afford it. Let the Debt Begin.

30 August

Last night I was back at home. I had a bad row with Dad. I can only bear to write about it because we resolved it – and in a way which I sense is probably really good for both of us.

He has, for some time, advised me to go for a repayment mortgage and not touch endowment mortgages, which he says are new-fangled, high risk and (very Dad, this) down-right immoral. However, various friends tell me this is bollocks. When I told him that I was going for an endowment mortgage, notwithstanding his advice, he was more hurt than I have ever seen him. He literally froze, which I've never seen him do before, and it showed a terrible pain.

I realised, then and there, I'd made an appalling mistake. I have all these clever friends, starting to earn money he could never dream of, when they're only in their twenties. Choosing a mortgage, however, is a subject in which he has a genuine professional expertise.

At least it led to a hearts-and-minds conversation. Realising I'd hurt him distressed me terribly, and he took that very seriously. I told him that I guessed there were moments when I probably wasn't the son he wanted, but that I loved him more than anything in the world.

Father and son had spoken for nearly three hours. At the end of it all, Mr da Silva had said: 'I'm glad we've talked.'

'We needed to, Dad.'

'Yes, we did, and you were right to press me.' He had looked across at his son with understanding and compassion. 'But listen to me, old lad: in life, you often hope to have the kind of conversation that sets everything straight –

like the one we've had tonight. But it's not always possible.'

'No.'

'The truth is – talking can help, but being constant is what counts.'

'How do you mean?'

'I mean this. If we hadn't talked tonight, I would have gone to bed very sad and I don't suppose I'd have slept very much. But it would never – ever – have made any difference to the love I bear you.'

6 September

Back in Saxburgh. Alan called over last night and roared with laughter when he saw my attempts at interior décor ('Very Derry and Tom's'). He is so pleased by his own virtuosity that he will be repeating his *bon mot* for the next week. He's done nothing all summer that I can fathom, but told me that several of his friends have been ill. One of them, Noel, lives in San Francisco and has been told by doctors he has the HIV virus. Noel has now spent weeks in hospital where doctors and nurses wear gloves and masks when they go into his room. So many people are terrified that they will pick up the infection just by going near him that his only visitors have been his parents.

I asked Alan if he'd be going. He said yes – if somebody paid his ticket. Typical Alan. Not a friend in need. He also corrected my understanding that the disease can only be transmitted through anal sex. Drug users who inject are also succumbing. Well, I thought, that's rotten for them, but I can sleep easy.

And, he added, those who have practised oral sex. I replied, with a casualness I did not feel, surely not.

10 September

The new Upper VI are much more sociable than last year's – there was scope for that. I've also done a lot more reading on the French Wars of Religion, so classes with them are really humming.

14 September

Chris Carstairs popped into my flat this evening, looking slightly self-conscious, to tell me that some of the Upper Sixth have told him that they can't understand my lessons. He was gentle and anxious not to discourage me. A model Head of Department.

Keep things simple, he said. So I will.

16 September

One boy got a black eye tonight, having been duffed up by a local youth – he'd been at the same primary school as the other boy, but had passed the eleven plus.

Romans is a ghastly house aesthetically – a mishmash of Victorian and 1930s utility in which the windows fit badly and condensation is rife. Some of the rooms smell so rank that you gag on entering them.

28 September

I'm having a bit of a stand off with Martin Nelms, in the Fifth Form. He's very deft at what my father used to call 'dumb insolence'. Prep, in his case, is either late or non-existent. I either subside or insist. If I do the first, I look weak, and if I do the second, I look anxious.

3 October

I went to Mass this morning, and vaguely recognised the boy in the pew in front of me – a new boarder, aged 13. He was in floods of tears.

I caught up with him after Mass. His father is in the Navy and the family have just started a posting in Singapore. He is a few days off his birthday, and he knows no one. He has absolutely nothing to do today. I gave him tea and toast in my flat, where he cried solidly for half an hour more.

10 October

Johnners and I ran for ten miles this afternoon – I thought Sunday was supposed to be a day of rest but we've got in the habit of driving each other on, and it's quite satisfying. I threw up at the top of one of the bigger hills, at which he laughed a lot. Still, I must be fitter than I once was.

About a mile outside Saxburgh, we passed Nelms going for a run in the opposite direction. He muttered an acknowledgement – to Johnners, rather than me.

23 November

Woke up this morning with an agonisingly sore throat and feeling shite. No temperature, I could tell, so couldn't reasonably pull a sicky. Taught, marked etc, but deemed myself off-games.

24 November

I rate Pete Spencer-Waugh incredibly highly – I wish I'd had a Housemaster like him when I was at school. He looks quite unmemorable (average height, dull sports jacket, drives a

Vauxhall Cavalier) but the kids here in Romans treat him as a god. I'm not surprised: he's calm, incredibly supportive. Even his blandest aphorisms ('Well now'; 'let me see') are treasured and imitated.

Just now he's exercised about the friendship between two of the boys – one is just 14 but looks about 12 and is very pretty. The other is 18. The two of them seem pretty inseparable. Nuff said, you might think, but I suspect (for once) Pete's instincts aren't correct. Both boys like fishing, and my hunch is that the time they spend by the river is devoted entirely to aquatic endeavour. Saxburgh kids, being what they are, would have pilloried the pair of them long before now if they were entertaining any dark suspicions.

My throat is better, but I have now started a cold. Feel generally crap.

26 November

A dire and dramatic evening. Prep had just begun when I heard running footsteps outside my flat. A Sixth Former from a Day House, looking white-faced and panting: 'You've got to come, sir. Steve Wilkinson's had an asthma attack. He's pretty bad.'

I raced over at once to find a boy I didn't know lying flat on his back. His breathing came only in deep groans, and although his eyes were open they were totally unfocused. To my eyes, it seemed way beyond asthma – something catastrophic seemed to have happened and I rang 999. (Idiotically a debate began in my head: should I have rung the School Matron first? The latter is very touchy if she feels she's been passed over.)

While we waited for the ambulance, we tried very, very gently to raise the boy's head so that he couldn't choke on saliva. A few minutes later, his mother arrived (I didn't call her, and I have no idea who did). Then, about five seconds later, the ambulance. The mother had a patina of calm, but I sensed panic at the edges. The ambulance men put her in the back with her son and told her to talk to him.

After it had left, lights flashing and sirens blaring, the other boys looked around them, absolutely stunned. They came back to my flat and I made them a cup of tea. There wasn't much conversation – they just kept on repeating again and again 'one moment he was fine, then he went down – just like that'. Nobody asked me if I thought he'd be all right. I think they know he won't be.

My cold, which is a stinker, recedes somewhat in significance.

27 November

The HM caught me after Chapel this morning and expressed sympathy and concern over what happened last night. He told me that Steve was quickly diagnosed as having had a massive cerebral haemorrhage, and remains in a coma.

29 November

Steve Wilkinson has died. He had another catastrophic haemorrhage yesterday, and never recovered consciousness. In assembly this morning, the HM told the school and a minute's silence followed. One of his best friends is in my Lower Sixth group whom I taught later this morning – he sat white-faced and silent.

It occurs to me that Saxburgh boys don't have it easy.

They are expected to be stoical in grief without (so far as I can tell) many of them having the consolations of faith upon which to fall back. It's like Hunter's Chase, but without that very singular perk.

3 December

Tim Dooley, in my Fifth Form class, piped up this afternoon: 'It's very sad about Steve Wilkinson, isn't it, sir?'

'Yes. Very.'

'Course,' he said, 'me mum's a nurse. She told me you ever see anyone like that boy, you don't even touch 'em. Worst thing you can do. *Even an inch can kill.*'

There is something about Tim – his little boy face, his wobbly voice and flat Midland vowels – which makes him *believable*. Memories of last Friday rushed back when I tried to move Steve's head ever so slightly, and I began to weigh up the odds of being arraigned on charges of manslaughter.

After class, I went to see the HM (which I never do) and said he probably ought to know what I'd done. He smiled at me paternally and said it didn't make any difference. I suggested he tell the doctor even so. He said he would, but only to give me peace of mind. He also registered my sniffles and wheezing and commented that I wasn't looking a picture of health myself.

7 December

My cold gave way over a week ago to a chest cough and I feel pretty listless and shattered. So I went to the school doctor today, about whom I've heard many stories but upon whom, until now, I had never clapped eyes. With his long grey beard, he looks more like a rabid dissenting minister from the 1870s than a doctor.

Dr Macnamara had eyed Dominic coolly. 'Well, young man. And what is your problem?' Dominic was ordered to remove his shirt and a stethoscope was placed to his chest.

'Bronchitis,' the doctor had said, 'and quite a fruity one by the sound of it.'

He had declined to prescribe antibiotics on the grounds that Dominic was young and fit, and that his own natural resistances would kick in.

8 December

Alan has got a job at Cawley. As he is telling everyone, 'I decided if I was going to teach somewhere grand, it might as well be very grand indeed.' I am taking him out for a meal on Friday by way of congratulation. Maybe by then I'll be feeling better. I can't stop myself thinking of this HIV virus.

11 December

Alan is much enjoying being the centre of everyone's attention, and can talk of little (no, nothing) but the glamour of his new school. He didn't show up for last night's meal – but (a) how typical, (b) it saved me an expensive evening spent enduring Alan's patronage and boasting and (c) it gave me the chance to have an early night, spent firstly in a hot bath, and then snuggling up to a hot-water bottle. My chest is still wheezing. It's true – I'm scared.

16 December

Today was the end of term, and the last day ever at Saxburgh for Clive Styles – one of the older staff (about 50, I guess), who's been here since 1958. He did a degree in physics at Cambridge, but the big deal in his life is sport. He also plays the saxophone, has learned Esperanto and generally exhibits large amounts of unfocused energy. He's shocked everyone here by suddenly handing in his resignation, and is going to teach at a state school in Exeter. His line is that if he ever wants to do anything else before he retires, it's now or never.

Clive has loved Saxburgh, town and school. He read an extract from *The Prophet* by way of farewell to his colleagues. No catch in his voice. Unflinching.

21 December

Forty-eight hours of doing completely nothing. My chest is better, though far from right. I went to London on Friday to stay with Guy and saw *Sophie's Choice*. I came back to Saxburgh on Sunday, in theory to do some reading and noting on 17th-century Holland. In practice, I've done nothing but watch TV and read Flashmans.

22 December

My cough returned with a vengeance last night and I could feel myself getting panicked. With some difficulty, I got an appointment with the doctor who listened impatiently to my chest and said it was 'well on the mend'.

'It wasn't last night,' I said, and for a terrible moment I heard the edge of tears in my voice. I could see him looking at me speculatively.

26 December

A very happy Christmas at home. I offered, seriously, to help Mum with cooking or just as *plongeur*. She plumped for the latter. I quite like spud bashing, as Dad calls it. Aunt Sheena arrived, then Kate and Caleb: the latter's table manners have occasioned some tension between his mother and grand-mother.

My cough has vastly improved, but I don't think it much liked the run I did today. Running is obviously my way of staying sane. My father says I have become addicted to it. In lieu of any sexual alternative, he may be right.

I ache for sex, of course, and often feel that the accepted wisdom – men think about sex once every seven seconds – understates the reality. Celibacy doesn't suit me (I can't believe it suits anyone) but I can't see my way clear here: I think the Church is right and that one shouldn't treat sex too casually. That's a bit of a laugh coming from me, but my experience of casual sex hasn't made for great happiness. Hence all that running.

6 January 1983

Guy and Melinda invited me to a New Year's party last Friday at Lauderdale Hall, her parents' house near Chippenham. I've only met her once before and she's so low-key that I'd sort of assumed she was a nice, quiet suburban girl.

Well – nice she is, but suburban she's not. It's a Palladian house – really knockout. The interior was predictably grand, with two vast portraits in the entrance hall, which had a marble floor and a great sweeping double staircase. In the drawing room were various chairs and sofas which were unsprung, stained Aubusson rugs, all thrown together in an upper-class don't-give-a-toss sort of way. A group of white Christmas cards stood separately on top of a grand piano in the main drawing room, ostentatiously placed to keep their distance from the melee and mess elsewhere. On closer examination, these revealed themselves as photographs of various royals with their monickers appended below.

Anyway, we were made welcome in that kind of effusive, impersonal way that seems to accompany those of great social confidence. It rather reminded me of the glory days with dear old Lou, although this was grander by a good margin. After supper in a freezing dining room, there were charades, amid much stylised jollity. At decent intervals I popped out to pee. The loo was a mahogany thunder box.

Everyone kissed everyone else (along traditional gender lines) when midnight struck. I kept asking myself at intervals what I was doing there. Not because I felt patronised or excluded – merely functionless: a permanent onlooker on the relationships of others.

11 January

I have become the legal owner of 4, Sycamore Place, Saxburgh. The debt (£23,750) is scary and I'm praying that I'll get tenants fast.

24 January

I received a letter from a parent this morning. She asks that her son be excused Saturday's cross-country match because she and her children are going that day to move in with her mother. 'My marriage has broken up,' she writes, 'and our house has been repossessed.'

31 January

Tom and Lauren Inskip asked me over for supper on Saturday with Marina Ransome, the new Physics teacher. She's *exceptionally* nice and oh my goodness clever. Her father teaches engineering at the University of Sussex.

She says – she likes teenage boys, but can't make much headway with them. Not a clothes horse – she was wearing the same black cords she always wears during the week, and a green sweater – but she's quite arresting: slim with beautiful black eyes.

7 February

Marina and I repeated last week's coffee and we enjoyed it so much that we decided to go and have a drink this evening out of town. This meant driving, and I found myself vaguely embarrassed when she saw the MG – I like it, of course, but she seems too fastidious for such frivolous items.

We did the usual chat, the kind used by all those newly acquainted when they're trying to fill in the gaps about themselves – families, schools (I tend to glide over this a bit for obvious reasons), universities. She says she enjoyed Cambridge, but thinks now that she worked too hard. She is far more genuinely cultured than most of my Oxford friends and admits to a 'reasonably serious' interest in astronomy and 20th-century music. I nodded wisely, while trying not to panic. No allusion to a boyfriend, past or present. I like being with someone calm and clever and who exudes decency.

8 February

My Fourth Form this year are the nicest set I think I've ever taught. I wonder if I feel a special tenderness towards this age group because they belong to that time when my life imploded.

10 February

The fire alarm suddenly went off at about midnight last night. It's bloody temperamental and so I rushed out of the flat to switch it off when Tim Tomlinson suddenly appeared at my side and said, 'Sir! Sir! It's a real fire!'

Jesus, Mary and Joseph – it was too – some smouldering curtains caused by Tim having put on a toaster and then forgetting about it and going to have a shower. I had the place evacuated in about seven seconds flat and the curtains doused down within 20.

14 February

Half term. I would have liked to have seen Marina, but she's gone back to Hove to see her family. Tom Inskip said to me on Friday afternoon, just as everyone was going home, 'You do realise that Marina's getting quite fond of you, Dominic, don't you?'

'I'd like to believe that,' I said, laughingly.

'No, Dominic.' He sounded quite serious, which isn't like him at all. '*Very* fond. Had you realised?'

'Not really. She seems to like my company.'

'She does. But I don't think it's just that. Neither does Lauren. You ought to know that.'

Wouldn't it be nice if Marina and I became an item? She truly is as nice and good a person as I've ever met, and I find her genuinely attractive. We'd have great sex, great holidays, my family would take her as their own and perhaps we'd get married. Christ, she might even become a Catholic, and we could have a family. In time, I'd go on to become a House-master and perhaps even a Headmaster.

Come off it: it's me we're talking about. Who am I kid-ding?

15 February

Call from M. She asks if I'd like to go to a concert in Cam-bridge on Friday. I think this is the first time she's rung me and, mindful of what Tom said, I suddenly realised my answer might matter to her. I said I'd love to.

19 February

I never asked Marina what it was she's signed me up for. Given her interest in 20th-century music, I convinced myself it was going to be Arvo Pärt or Philip Glass – some-thing conceptual and impossible. It turned out, in fact, to be an evening of country and western given by a group from Alabama on a tour – and they were *brilliant*. We were both in high spirits when we got in the car, and it made for a mellow journey back to Saxburgh. We didn't talk much but I felt a massive sense of well-being, and I am pretty sure she felt the same.

Since all the kids are away until Sunday night, it would have been pretty easy for us to have gone back to my flat, but as the journey went on I got nervous. I wanted her at least to take the lead but she didn't, and so I ended up dropping her at her flat in Newstead Lane. Now I think I made a mistake. We had time last night, and we won't again – for ages. And will it all have changed by then?

22 February

Jonathan Tyson didn't turn up to cross-country yesterday afternoon. At about 5 p.m. I found a tatty note on A4 file-paper in my pigeonhole saying: 'Dear Mr da Silva, Please excuse Jon from games today. He is not very well. Yours, R. E. Tyson (Mrs).'

Since I teach him, I recognised the appalling handwriting as indubitably his own. This morning after Chapel I duly confronted him with the evidence of his crime. I was laughing because the forgery was so pathetic, and he was laughing because he had been rumbled. I told him to meet me on Thursday after school and join me on a particularly vicious run. Off he went, with the unmistakable air of a villain found bang-to-rights. The Headmaster was hovering in the background and I could tell he had overheard snippets of the conversation. When Tyson had left, he called me over and pressed me for details.

'So what's his punishment?' he asked when I'd finished.

'A seven-mile run with me on Thursday.'

'Oh, no, Dominic. What he did was *forgery*. Send him to me.'

Which, feeling like every kind of worm, I did.

Later, word came back – suspended for a fortnight. Bloody hell.

28 February

Since 4 p.m. on Friday I've been rehearsing *The Crucible* which, in an effort to earn some kudos for myself, I volunteered to direct. Nothing else has been touched – marking, preparation, duties. I actually did teach five periods this morning, which felt, curiously enough, like a blessed relief.

Marina kept on coming into the theatre with cups of coffee, sandwiches etc. We have actually reached the hand-holding stage in the privacy of my flat although certainly nothing more. In the few moments I've been able to think about anything other than the production, I continue to speculate on how to initiate the conversation I know we must have. The kids are so used to seeing her at my flat they have now dubbed her 'Mrs da Silva'. Johnners, leering at me but as ever good-natured, enquired this morning: 'Have you shagged her yet?'

2 March

Marina came over late tonight. I was in and out most of the time, doing beds and saying goodnight to kids, so it was hard to relax. At one point she held my hands and we just sat silently for a minute or so – but I didn't know what to say. Then it was time for me to switch off the Fifth Form lights. When I returned, she was getting ready to leave. The play is on for the next three nights, so I won't really have any time with her until that's over.

8 March

I popped over to Mum and Dad's for my birthday last night. Mum was in shock after giving people supper on Saturday night when the beef Wellington went spectacularly wrong. Dad, protective as ever, insisted: 'But the roast potatoes were done to perfection, darling.'

15 March

I might have been sacked today. My worst moment in teaching, and my most massive blunder – to date.

Background: I suggested to Marina we have a drink last night – we did, but it didn't work. She was even quieter than usual, and that made me gibber. It wasn't the moment for a complicated and candid conversation. I went home quite early and despondent.

And this is what happened: Chris Tatling arrived late for my Upper Sixth class after break, refused to apologise for doing so, and then kept on talking across me. I sent him out and he wouldn't leave. Fortunately, the class ended while we were in the middle of our stand-off, and I told him to wait behind. I told him I expected a written apology and he said (and I quote), 'If you think I'm doing that, you're fucking mad.' I cracked – grabbed him by his collar and tie, pushed him against the wall, and said, 'Don't even DREAM of speaking to me like that, do you understand?'

He's taller and heavier than me, but I could see he was now red-faced and panting and, somewhat belatedly, it began to dawn on me that I was well out of order. I drew myself back, told him to clear off, and went straight down to the office and asked to see the Headmaster. I was ushered in to his study at once to find him looking at me politely perplexed.

'Sir,' I began, 'I've done something stupid.'

I could see his expression shift in an instant to the professionally neutral. Beyond muttering 'that bloody child' when I mentioned Tatling's name, he stayed silent throughout. When I had finished, he looked up a bit more brightly and asked, 'Did you punch him in the face?'

'God, no.'

'Right.' He squared his shoulders. 'Well. Thank you for telling me, Dominic. A difficult morning. Well done. Off you go now.'

I am a bit surprised to have got off so lightly. I am also heartily ashamed of myself, and scared shitless by the explosion of temper Tatling's defiance suddenly released in me.

16 March

Marina said to me she was going to cook me supper at her flat. I said I'd love that but I was on duty. She said she'd spoken to Pete and he was giving me the night off. I could have kissed her I was so grateful. She cooked some lamb chops and baked potatoes and we watched *Dallas* and sort of snuggled.

I asked her if she'd heard about the Tatling business. She said yes, and why hadn't I told her at once but let her find out through the rumour mill. I said I was sorry.

2 April

I'm in Austria, on the Saxburgh Skiing Trip. God knows why. Because it's free, I suppose.

There are 90 kids in all. Staff include Johnners, myself and Alan. The reasons for his appearance are a mystery: he gave up any efforts to ski after 15 minutes. He has let it be known that he 'prefers' cross-country skiing. That means, for him, he sits in cafes and reads.

4 April

A straw poll elicited the information that nearly all of the kids on this trip have paid over half the cost of it themselves. They are evidently loving every minute and show themselves to be enthusiastic if undiscriminating tourists. They haven't, so far as I'm aware, batted an eyelid at this truly shite hotel and the foul food. That's left to people like me, who paid nothing.

10 April

Marina rang me to invite me to meet her family in Hove yesterday. They live in a 1930s semi, and the house abounds in fumed oak tables and lurid oil sunsets on the walls. In fact, it just about ticks every box of all the things that I most dislike – and yet I found I loved it all. Lou's grandeur was part of her allure, but Marina's absence of style is part of what makes her precious to me.

Her mother was shyly welcoming – she's much fairer than her daughter: a slow-speaking woman, disinclined to take the lead in any conversation, and defers to her husband, the university professor, who is quite intense and opinionated. They had prepared quite a formal lunch for me which they set up on a gate-legged table in the sitting room: avocado and prawns, roast chicken with *petit pois* and new potatoes, lemon meringue pie. A bottle of red wine was offered, but when I declined, it stayed unopened. It was a lot of food in the middle of a warm day and afterwards we drove to Brighton to walk it off.

We walked along the pier and Dr Ransome asked polite and sensible questions about my work. I kept wondering when they would bugger off and leave us to walk by ourselves. I honestly felt that the moment had now arrived when I could tell Marina something of what I felt and of what I truly was. But after about an hour, he said, 'Have you time to have tea before you head back?'

Since then, confidence has ebbed and flowed rather. My past rises up in front of my eyes. If I am really to declare myself to Marina, I have a serious duty to share it with her. Can I reasonably ask her to consider me – desperately damaged goods? Around school and in most social contexts, I am so decisive. But not now.

A couple of weeks into term, Dominic had suggested they go to the Red Lion for a drink. It was three miles out of town, so there had been at least some chance of privacy. Radio 2 was being piped into the pub lounge, and the fact that there were only about three other people there made them feel conspicuous. They had drunk their glasses of red wine without pleasure and plodded their way dutifully through conversation. How were her parents? Any plans for the summer? When he had heard himself discussing plans for having his car resprayed, Dominic's nerve began to fail. Five months, he had thought bitterly – five months had elapsed since they had first met. During that time, they had had drinks, meals, enjoyed meetings with each other's friends and families, and had demonstrated, he considered, an interest in one another extended beyond motor transport. He and Marina drove home in a quiet that felt more tense than companionable and he was back in his own flat by 11 p.m.

Later, getting ready for bed, the doorbell rang. He found Marina outside, looking extremely serious.

'Can I come in?'

'Of course.'

She didn't bother to sit down as they went into the sitting room but faced him directly.

'This isn't fair on you,' she said quietly. Her head went down as she said it.

He struggled for an answer for a couple of seconds and then seemed to come to a decision.

'I think I love you,' he said.

'I know you think you do. But you're wrong. You only love men.'

'Jesus Christ,' said Dominic, collapsing into a chair. 'How can you know that?' Then, after a pause, he said, 'Who's been talking?'

'Nobody's been talking. But I can see.' Her voice trailed off as she saw him hunched in his chair, his head in his hands.

She put her arm round his shoulder, but he did not move.

'Dominic,' she said eventually. 'Please.'

'What?'

'Talk to me.'

He lifted his face and stared at the wall. Finally, he said, his voice blatantly on the edge of tears, 'I care for you so much. I wanted us to make a go of it.'

'I hoped the same.'

'We could try,' he said.

'We have been trying, really. We've both been hesitating, but we've never admitted why.'

'Christ,' he breathed. 'I am so sorry.'

'It's not a matter for apology.'

They clung together in silence for a while longer, holding hands. Eventually, she forced herself to stand up.

'Will you be all right?'

He gave her a bleak smile. 'I'm good at getting by.'

'Tell me,' she said, pulling him nearer to her and holding his hand in both of hers. 'Please tell me if you're not coping.'

He shook his head. Soon after that she left. He walked

round the flat in a frozen way for a few minutes and went
to bed.

4 May

There is a part of me which believes that we might have
made a go of it. I am very sad because I was reminded last
night that I am alone, and I think I always will be.

12 May

Alan asked me over to tea this afternoon – out of the blue.
That was an event in its own right because he's a lot readier
to accept hospitality than to offer it. But when I arrived it
was to find everything laid out for a very formal and fat-
tening tea – Minton teapot, Earl Grey, cucumber sandwiches,
coffee eclairs.

Alan was sitting in his battered wing armchair. Stretched
out on the chaise longue, wearing a muffler and with a tartan
rug covering his knees, was Rafe – a friend of his whom I
have met on his occasional visits. Tall, dark and handsome –
but an arrogant and unkind man. Just Alan's type.

'It may seem excessive,' said Alan, 'but Rafe here is prone
to chills, and we are taking no chances.'

Rafe muttered a few cool words of greeting, sipped gin-
gerly at his tea, and ate nothing – in full arctic queen mode.
Alan, for once, seemed to be looking to someone else to
supply the chat. I did my best, but Rafe stayed silent. I
remembered he was a barrister and, after a few minutes prat-
tling, asked him if he had any interesting cases.

He shook his head impatiently.

'Maybe something will come up.'

'The bar and I are over. I'm sick.'

'I'm sorry,' I said.

'Very affecting.' He turned impatiently to Alan. 'Tell him.'

'Rafe has AIDS.'

It transpired that Alan spent ten days looking after Rafe in the holidays – cooking, cleaning, nursing him in every way needed. Much more of a friend in need than I would ever have believed. I think my invitation came because the two of them had exhausted conversation, and I guess I'm a good prattler. Also, they needed a lift to the station so that Rafe could go back to London.

15 May

Richard Jiaow, the only non-English boy in the House, has nowhere to go at half term. I asked Richard Nighy if he had any ideas as to anyone who might offer to take him in for a few days, but he immediately started to look down and shuffle.

'Not as such, sir. I. . . think most people would find it, er, a bit strange.'

'Strange in what way? I mean, it's not exactly strange to want to get out of school over half term.'

'No, not that. I mean having – well, having their kind of, er, person – in your own house . . .'

I knew it. Scratch the surface here, and racism spills out. It's *awful.*

12 June

Yesterday was a killer: teaching till 1 p.m. Drove a minibus 80 miles to a tennis match. We lost, but it took for ever. Kids fractious. Returned at 9 p.m. to piles of unmarked essays on which I made some headway, but won't be finished until late tonight.

(There was a club match being played in the courts adjoining ours. *Fuck* – tennis players can be so beautiful I want to lie down on the ground and weep. So, yes, it *was* worth the long journey.)

18 June

I was umpiring a squash match at home today when Pete Spencer-Waugh suddenly arrived at my elbow and whispered to me that he needed to speak urgently to Liam Wheeler.

'Now? We're about to finish a match.'

'Now. And don't bank on him coming back.'

Well, he's the Housemaster. About two minutes later, I saw them out of the window. They were sitting on the grass and Pete looked as though he was trying to explain something to Liam, who appeared to be uncomprehending. About a minute after that, I heard what sounded like the shriek of a wounded animal. It transpired later that Pete had had to tell Liam that his mother had been killed in a car crash.

21 June

A few months ago, I weakly agreed to do some A-level examining. I now have 600 chunky essays stacked up on the floor of my flat. Somewhere in and among dealing with them, I have to write 180 internal reports, mark 150 internal exams, teach 29 periods a week, and be a resident tutor to 82 pupils. And it has all to be done before the end of term.

The set of scripts has come from Hunter's Chase. One

script belonged to the younger brother of my old persecutor, Francis Morley. I have eschewed any temptation to extract revenge, but only after thinking about it.

23 June

I was on duty this evening – doling out pocket money in between ploughing my way through more scripts. Just before prep, Eric Gibb came to see me with, he said, a complaint.

It took about half an hour's careful listening, since the narrative came out by fits and starts – interspersed by bouts of tears. He's one of a posse of younger kids who are being systematically duffed up by older ones. Today's session was particularly traumatic and another is planned for tomorrow.

I said, very quietly: 'It's all right, Eric. You won't be going. It's over now.'

He was sitting on the footstool in my sitting room and, on hearing that, great heaving sobs came out of him. I waited until he got himself together. After a couple of minutes, he said quietly, 'Can I show you my arm?' It was not so much bruised as battered.

I took him, then and there, to the Headmaster. (I shouldn't have, of course – protocol says to go through the House-master, but I wasn't prepared to wait.)

24 June

Well, the Head has acted – three ringleaders have been suspended until next term. When I arrived in the Dining Room to take supper duty this evening, there was a round of hissing from the senior boys' table when I came in.

Dominic had at once walked over to where they were sitting and said – loudly enough for everyone else to hear – 'Has anyone got something they'd like to say to me directly?'

Heads had gone down.

'You should be ashamed of yourselves,' he said, more quietly. 'You knew this was happening, and you did nothing.'

'We had it done to us when we were young.'

There were nods round the table.

'I know you did. And the proof of the damage it did you is right in front of my eyes now.'

29 August

School trip to Italy for a dozen Sixth Form Historians, led by Chris Carstairs and myself. Chris has organised everything and all I have to do is show up and look jolly. The waiter at our table told us last night that Rome used to be nice, but that now there were too many blacks and Jews. Nice.

31 August

I'm a bit rattled. Clash of two versions of myself – idealised and real.

My air-conditioning packed up last night, which is no joke in this heat. Reception promised to send someone to repair it after breakfast and duly a guy arrived. He wore a tight white T-shirt and a pair of jeans that had been sawn off at the knees and at first I had no idea who he was until he pointed to the air-con unit. I nodded, switched it on and we both made signs of theatrical despair when nothing then happened. He gestured to me to help him lift off the cowling covering the unit. As I glanced over at him, it occurred to me he was a good-looking guy in a Latin way – thick head of dark hair and a friendly grin. Not very tall, but sinewy. My age or thereabouts. I smiled back and gestured to ask him to show me what to do.

And then, suddenly catching sight of his sawn-off denim jeans, I realised that his motives in asking for my help might not be confined to the air-con. I suppose I might say I felt powerless to resist, but the truth is that I felt no inclination to do so. Chris and the kids were still having breakfast three flights of stairs away and, anyway, my door had a very secure lock. I wouldn't describe what followed as romantic or drawn-out, but it was jolly raunchy and extremely good for morale. I didn't feel the usual sense of shame after he'd gone – he gave me a cheerful kiss as he left and a big grin.

No shame at all, actually. A bit smug, to be honest, and enlivened. Despite the colossal heat I expiated any feelings of awkwardness in a long run in the Borghese Gardens.

(Chris said to me at supper: 'My goodness, Dominic. I don't know where you get your energy.' I thought – I bloody well hope you don't.)

27 September

This is my third year here, and I'm determined it's going to be my last. If I want to improve my teaching (and I need to) I have to go to a much more academically selective school. Johnners is a diamond, but really, I'm on my own. Sooner or later, my energy and curiosity will peak and then I'll get less willing and they will look at me a lot more coolly. Better to go now while I've time.

So I've applied for two jobs. One is at King James Grammar. Very academic, not far from London. It's a DAY SCHOOL THANK GOD WITH NO EVENING DUTIES. The other is at Groom's, which is *uber* academic, but also challengingly posh and with the reputation for churning out arrogant kids. (Clearly I should have outgrown the fascination with all that – but I haven't. Also it is not so far out of London that I couldn't go in for an evening if I wanted.)

25 October

King James Grammar have given me the thumbs down, the bastards. If they don't want to know me, Groom's is totally out of court. I can see myself being stuck here for the rest of my life. I'm trying not to panic.

31 October

I have received a letter asking me to Groom's on 16 November. I don't suppose I have a cat in hell's chance, but getting an interview has cheered me up no end.

Johnners and I met up after prep this evening for a drink and the Poison Dwarf joined us, uninvited. Hearing (from Johnners, not me) that I was about to go for an interview, he warned me that the Headmaster's references, good or bad, are well known as the kiss of death, and that I'm stuck here for the next 35 years.

In the midst of his harangue, he held out an empty beer glass, and looked in my direction. I actually said, 'Oh, right. What would you like?'

21 November

Interview at Groom's. Phenomenal buildings and grounds, but very tacky classrooms. I also saw and heard enough to know that the cleverness and arrogance of the kids isn't just a rumour – or the standoffishness of some of the teachers.

The Headmaster, Sir Frederick Hudson, performs like a great Shakespearian actor – he is absurdly good-looking, with a deep plummy voice. The Head of History (mid-thirties, I'd guess) just looked moth-eaten and depressed, and was much more earthbound. I liked him. He interviewed me in a room which looked like something out of a dirty protest in the Maze prison. The kids are *epically* untidy and casual. There was a general air of who-the-fuck-are-you.

Our HM would hate all of it – literally everything. Myself, I loved it, but I'm pretty sure it won't happen. They have more interviewees to meet next Thursday, so I am telling myself to kill any hopes of being appointed.

23 November

I owe various people hospitality (the Carstairs, Spencer-Waughs, Johnners and Sian, Tom and Lauren Inskip). Weeks ago, I arranged for all of them to come to supper this Saturday. Unwisely, at the same moment, I also gave way to a rush of filial piety, and asked my parents along as well.

It seemed an excellent idea, back then. I am not so sure now. If I haven't heard from Groom's by Saturday that will mean I am fucked as far as the job is concerned, and I will be going straight from that thought into giving 11 people supper.

26 November

The postman arrived while I was at breakfast, and a cream Manila envelope lay on the mat, with the Groom's crest embossed. Sure enough, I thought, I'm fucked. But when I opened it, I read instead: *I am writing to offer you the post to teach History at Groom's. My colleagues and I are in no doubt that you are the candidate to whom we wish to offer this position.*

It took me a few minutes, of dry sobs and chest-heaving, before I could think at all clearly. When I did, I decided my first thanks were owed to Chris – the best Head of Department for whom anyone could ever have wished. I walked over to his study and he looked up from his desk in that nice smiley way he has. Instead of saying anything, I just held up the letter and broke down in tears. He was decent enough not to mind.

Anyway, supper this evening was inevitably less of a trial than I had feared – indeed, from my point of view, it was uproarious fun. I bought champagne and bathed in all the congratulations and triumph. Mum and Dad were bursting with pride and pleasure, and that was really the best bit.

28 November

Out of the corner of my eye, I saw Johnners relay my news to the Poison Dwarf today. You never saw such a face of loathing.

29 November

A card from my mother this morning:

Dearest Dominic

Thank you for such a delicious supper, and in such good company. What a terrific fish pie – and your chocolate sponge was a dream! I never seem to get the timing right with mine, so I rely on you to show your old Mum how you do it.

It was so wonderful to be with you as you told us the news about Groom's. Your face told the story of your happiness, and you know that Dad and I share in that. I particularly liked the fact that you said you were determined to give to Saxburgh of your very best until the last moment.

How lovely to have met your friends. They are all going to miss you, you know!

God Bless you, my darling – and may Groom's give you what I know you will give to it.

Always your loving Mum

6 December

Christ, the weather is cold and grim. Freezing rain for the last two days. I was due to take the cross-country squad out yesterday afternoon and they looked at me so pathetically and imploringly, I almost relented – but not quite. After the first mile or so we were so wet that it didn't seem to matter and we did seven miles. This morning, the mother of one of them phoned the school to complain that her son could have caught pneumonia in yesterday's conditions. I am wondering if I did. I feel absolutely shite.

12 December

Same old, same old. Sore throat becomes streaming cold; streaming cold becomes chest cough, which shows no signs of going away. I feel totally wiped out. The euphoria occasioned by the news from Groom's has been eclipsed by exhaustion and nameless apprehension. This morning I went to the ever-lugubrious school doctor, who – perfectly imitating last year's routine – listened to my chest, whistled quietly, described it as 'lively' and ordered me to let 'rest and nature do its work'.

I hope my nature is up to it. Sometimes I wonder.

21 December

I drove home a couple of days after the end of term, having put all social plans on hold because I felt as drained as I can remember and had (I could tell) a temperature. I planned to bluff it out with my parents – and had already prepared a line of being 'a bit under par. Busy term, and all that'. But I was hardly over the threshold before that fantasy was kicked into touch. Mum pretty much ordered me to bed on the spot. By the time I hauled myself upstairs, my case had been unpacked, the covers of the bed were turned down, and there was a hot-water bottle in the bed. Later Dad brought me up a tray with some beef soup and bread and butter. Also (I am a bit embarrassed to admit this) an apple, all sliced up.

Dominic had woken intermittently during the night and came to at about 9 a.m. next day to hear his parents on the phone next door, speaking to their GP.

'Gerard,' his father had said, 'he's absolutely exhausted and looks dreadful. Could you see him this morning?'

He had affected surprise when his father told him an appointment had been fixed for 10 a.m., but didn't bother to go through any charade of reluctance. His father drove him over and, once installed in the doctor's surgery, he had quickly realised Dr O'Callaghan's banter masked a protective concern.

'You look like death warmed up. Did you know that, Dominic?'

'I know I feel like it.'

'Let's take a listen to the old feller then.' He pointed to Dominic's chest and asked him to unbutton his shirt.

'Well,' he said after another minute, 'that's lively enough. I don't know what your old sawbones is thinking of, but you need penicillin, my lad, or you're going to get properly sick.'

'Oh, Christ.' Dominic had closed his eyes and struggled to hold back his tears.

Dr O'Callaghan looked at him in mild surprise and then patted his arm. 'Listen,' he said, 'you've got bronchitis. You're exhausted. It's nothing worse than that, I'm telling you.'

Dr O'Callaghan suggested they bring in Dominic's father.

'Well, Francis,' he said, pointing in Dominic's direction. 'I don't think you should be planning the boot sale of his books quite yet. He's going to be sticking around. It's a pain, but there it is.'

Under the blarney, Dominic heard the tones of unequivocal reassurance.

23 December

I must have slept ten hours last night. And I'm much better – I can tell. Jesus, the relief.

29 December

There are vast swathes of history I've never studied that must be prepared before I start my new job in April. I drove up to Cambridge this morning, bought a load of books at Heffer's and then went on to Saxburgh where I've worked without disturbance for the rest of the day.

I also spent £122 in the process. This had better be the last time I change school. My finances will not survive another move.

3 January 1984

Dad has decided that he cannot go into retirement while driving a two-door BMW. Retirement is still nearly a year away but, like me, he believes in forward planning. So off we went this morning to a car dealer where he demanded something – I am quoting directly – 'comfortable, economical and sedate'.

The dealer proposed a truly terrible Daihatsu. I wanted to die of shame on the spot but had schooled myself to be an impassive observer. He looked it up and down for a couple of minutes and then said, 'I don't think Mummy would find it very comfortable.' Always the deal breaker.

Remembering the days when I was always entreating him to buy Jaguars or Aston Martins instead of Renaults and Rovers (not that it ever got me anywhere), I sensed he found my self-restraint a little unnerving.

4 January

I came back to Saxburgh last night to swot up for term. The phone rang at about 9 p.m. – to my astonishment, it was

Alan. I haven't seen him since he left – what? Six months ago.

For a split second, I wondered if he was calling to congratulate me about Groom's before reminding myself that he recognises nothing about anybody else's life except insofar as it touches his own. But, to be fair, this time he wasn't thinking of himself. He rang to tell me that Rafe died a couple of weeks ago of 'respiratory complications'. AIDS, in other words.

This has provoked some painful heart-searching. I have to accept there is a chance I have AIDS. (What are the odds? Well, it was only the one occasion. Since then, I have had two aggressive bouts of respiratory sickness. Who am I kidding? This is a real possibility.) I'm going to get tested – I don't want to live in fear and ignorance.

The timing, at least, had been propitious: there were still five days left before term started.

Dominic knew that Rafe had been treated at St Mary's Paddington, so it made sense to begin his enquiries there and he was asked to present himself for a blood test the following day.

'You realise that the decision to be tested for the HIV virus is a very serious one?' the doctor asked him when he did so. She was a woman of about thirty, small and softly spoken, but there was no mistaking the gravity of her voice.

'Yes.'

'There is no cure for someone with this virus. If you test positive, we'll be there to offer you every support we can – pharmacological and psychological – but, for the moment, well . . .' The sentence was left unfinished.

Dominic had nodded. 'Should I do this?' he asked.

'I can't tell you that. I can only say that someone who has had unprotected homosexual sex may be at risk – and that he may pose a risk to others.'

She explained he would have to wait a fortnight for the results and gave him a number to call 'in case things are bad'. He thanked her quietly.

9 January

I told Chris Carstairs I needed to be away on 20 January for 'personal business'.

'Of course,' he said. 'Everything all right?'

For a moment, I contemplated saying something. But I didn't, thank goodness.

11 January

The Chaplain has abandoned the use of a chalice for the school's Holy Communion services, for fear of spreading AIDS. The line is that, these days, you can't be too careful.

14 January

Johnners has suggested I join him and Sian for supper at The Feathers on Friday. I said I was away that day. His ears pricked up at once – *Come on, da Silva. Don't be a pussy. Why are you away? You know you want to tell me* – but I batted him off.

15 January

My parents rang tonight. My mother said, 'You must be excited, darling – a propos Groom's.'

'Yes. Very. But . . .'
'But – not counting the days, yet?'
'Just trying to live in the present.'
'Quite right, darling.'
More right than she will ever know. I hope.

Just as he remembered from his previous visit, the waiting area at the GU clinic had been disproportionately full of men. One, of about his own age, was there with his parents. Very few people bothered to read, and nobody talked. When his name had been called, he had been humiliated to find that his legs were wobbly.

The doctor, the same one as he had met a fortnight earlier, went into what was obviously a rehearsed routine: 'Mr da Silva, as you know, you have given us a sample of blood so that it could be tested for the HIV virus.'

'That's right.'

'We have now completed our tests, and the result is, I am happy to tell you, negative.'

Dominic bowed his head.

20 January

I have sent a cheque for £250 to the GU clinic at St Mary's. My usual neurosis about whether or not I can afford something seems irrelevant.

13 February

Half term. I'm fixed up with a fantastic place to live next year, thanks to Guy. His friend Digby Alexander lives in the village of Groom (a rather bizarre coincidence) and is happy to rent me a room.

I drove over to see him yesterday. Digby seems great and the house is a jewel. It's actually the annexe of a beautiful old sandstone manor house owned by his parents, but it's big and wholly self-contained. I get a lovely big bedroom under the eaves and there's a beautiful panelled sitting room. I seem once again to have landed with my bum in the butter.

21 February

Christ, I had a fright last night. About midnight, I was getting ready for bed when my front door was flung open. A Fifth Form boarder, dressed in pyjamas and dressing gown, was standing in the hall. As soon as he saw me he started screaming obscenities. It took me a few shocked seconds to realise these weren't being directed at me but that he was sleepwalking.

18 March

I will miss going to Mass at St Philip Neri's on Sundays. I like the predictability: naff hymns, played excruciatingly slowly; families of all ages, growing up and growing old together in the faith. One of the pleasures is that there are quite a few kids from school at Mass. I enjoy the tacit freemasonry one shares with them. Grossly sentimental, of course.

21 March

My last day of teaching here. I've been overwhelmed by the sweetness (that is absolutely the right word) of the kids, and by the generosity and great-heartedness of colleagues. My Third Formers (who are the soul of amiability, but very dim) presented me with a T-shirt upon which all their signatures had been printed. Saying goodbye to my Fifth Form – we have got on so well – was made that much harder because they were desperately self-conscious and shy. Colin Marsh made a presentation from the House – a tankard, engraved with my initials, and a card signed by all the House. His speech was a bit gruff, as is his way. He arrived in my flat about an hour later with another card, this one signed just by him, and I realised he wasn't without his own feelings.

22 March

My final day at Saxburgh. At morning break, Chris made a generous speech of farewell for me in the Common Room and then came the end-of-term assembly in which the HM made an oblique allusion to the fact that he very nearly hadn't appointed me but said, 'He is now a man with his feet very firmly under the table.' There was a lovely round of applause, but even I became embarrassed and wanted it to stop. Then he did the usual good wishes to everyone for the holiday and the hall emptied. That's that, I thought.

Johnners and I then played squash for an hour, to blow the emotion out of the system. When I returned, I found a note under the door from Chris. It said simply: *Carry on enjoying life, and remain the peacemaker.*

A couple of hours later, I rang my parents. When I told Mum about Chris's letter, I suddenly choked up, which took me by surprise. She gave me time to get myself together. I told her that I didn't want to be overawed by Groom's, because I've seen so much that is good and true here.

'Quite right,' she said. 'And it will stay with you.'

'I know I'm a bit impressionable.'

'You were. Not any longer, I think. Believe in yourself. You deserve that.'

If that's really how she sees it, I'm glad. To me, all my good fortune hangs by a thread. At any moment, I fear I'll be found out. Hunter's Chase is always just around the corner.

Chapter Sixteen
Daniel: London and the Midlands,
July–August 2014

Later – much later – Daniel came to look upon that amble through the park near Avila House as an apotheosis of sorts. Once back in London, life crowded in upon him, as he had known it must.

A bad-tempered antitrust case was shortly to come to court, and the direction of the legal team he would lead consumed most of his days. In whatever hours remained, the demands of Chloe, who had developed frightening bouts of asthma, and of Esther's father, Leslie, who was exhibiting the unmistakable signs of early dementia, had an inalienable priority. Unable to predict when he would next be free to visit, he rang Dominic several times each week. He sounded reasonably content: yes, he was eating properly, and sleeping all right; Fr Maybury and Breda were being very caring and kind; Jack and Orla came to see him almost every day.

To Daniel, these reassuring words sat less than comfortably alongside Dominic's voice, which seemed flatter than usual and more apathetic. But there was no time to reflect upon it: the minute he put the phone down, his mind had moved on to whatever was next. He had been under the cosh before, and knew it wouldn't last for ever, and meantime he tried to suppress the thought that his care for Dominic had lapsed into tokenism.

On the last Sunday in July, almost a month to the day since he had last seen his old friend, he and Esther had planned a supper at home – a minor miracle in itself, in view of the concerns that competed for his undivided attention. But Chloe was almost completely well again, and sleeping through the night. Leslie's new medication had finally kicked in. By dint of having started work at seven o'clock that morning, Daniel had decided he could now set aside a couple of hours undisturbed for his wife.

Esther prepared a rather elaborate salad of endives and asparagus, and Daniel sliced some cold chicken. After a moment's hesitation, he surrendered to temptation and poured them both a generous glass of white burgundy. At that moment the phone rang.

It had been Orla. They had met once or twice only but, in the circumstances, that wasn't important. She and Jack had just returned from getting Dominic admitted to hospital after a traumatic day.

'What's happened?' he asked, alarmed and immediately feeling guilty.

Orla explained. Their visit had been prompted by a phone call the previous evening from Fr Maybury who had suggested, with impressive understatement, that Dominic seemed 'a little confused'. This bland encomium was their first hint that he was, in fact, in a distressed and depleted condition. Indeed, he had failed to recognise Jack at all, and had confused Orla with his mother, who had died a quarter of a century earlier. His little flat, usually so orderly and self-consciously spruce, was in chaos, but when they had suggested to him he might like to come out with them for lunch, he had refused and accused them of trying to kidnap him.

'Jesus,' muttered Daniel, who had been accused by his father-in-law of something very similar only a few days earlier.

Matters, Orla explained, then deteriorated further. Persuaded eventually into the car, Dominic had joined them as they travelled to a country pub of which (they knew from earlier visits) he approved. There he had proceeded to abuse everyone (both of them, the waitress and several blameless fellow diners) and also swept a pile of glasses to the ground with an angry sweep of his hand. Finally persuaded to sit down, he wept and emptied his bladder.

'Where is he now?' Daniel asked, for once pushing away the thoughts of work.

'Hospital, I'm glad to say. We had to call an ambulance in the end. The Lord knows what he's been swallowing, but he can't self-medicate any longer, that's for sure.'

And what then? Daniel wondered, but he said nothing.

'And then we'll just have to see.'

Daniel was only very peripherally involved in what happened next. Fr Maybury, having twigged that Dominic wasn't going to be able to stay at Avila House, had taken it upon himself to contact Digby and Cara, whose number he found in Dominic's flat.

They swung into action at once. Cara called an oncologist friend who assured her 'George Seymour is a thoroughly first-class man.' Within twenty-four hours, Dominic was appropriately medicated and beginning to make sense. Within forty-eight, his temperature and blood pressure were normal and he was reading the *Daily Telegraph*, not exactly willingly but with decent comprehension.

Digby got busy too. His mother was a friend of the Lord Lieutenant of the county and, following a series of phone calls between the two of them, he suddenly managed to procure some residential accommodation for Dominic – the social services were not called upon. This care was discreet, costly and, above all, immediate. They were ready to welcome him as soon as he was discharged from hospital.

Daniel learned of these changes in a series of brisk emails sent daily by Cara. He was relieved but felt vaguely disenfranchised. On Friday night he admitted to Esther: 'I always thought I was pretty well-connected and quick on the draw. Then I met Digby and Cara.'

'You've done plenty.'

'I want to do more,' said Daniel. That evening he sent off an email of his own, committing to contribute to Dominic's care, and, within a few hours, received two replies.

Sent: Fri, 11.44 p.m.
To: Cara Alexander; Digby Alexander

Dear Cara and Digby
Thanks so much for keeping us up-to-date. We've been so relieved you're both around for Dominic.

I'm sure this residential home is expensive. I can help with the money side of things. Please will you and Digby tell me a figure which would cover half the cost and I'll either pay it directly to your account or to the home itself? Jack and Orla are VERY important to Dominic, but I don't think they have any money. So please let me help on their behalf as well as ours.

Best wishes from us both
Daniel

Sent: Sat, 7:01 p.m.
To: Daniel Green

Hi Daniel
Thanks for email. Guy and I really appreciate it. Wingrove Manor – not cheap, but still a lot cheaper than London – averages out £3k per month (he needs nursing so this brings up cost). Could you do half perhaps?? No problem if not.

Truth is we know it's not going to be for ever – Guy spoke to Mr S oncologist who thinks 2–3 months prob.

D seems more cheerful. I hope to get up there Tues or Wed. This weekend is a NIGHTMARE. Any chance you or Esther can go?

Cxxxxx

Sent: Sat, 7:31 p.m.
To: Jack O'Riordan; Orla O'Riordan; Daniel Green; Esther Green

Hi All
Well, D now in Wingrove Manor. MUCH better – chatty and full of fun.

Orla – I know you are going there tomorrow. Can u ring maybe to tell us how he was?

Pls let us know at any time what we can do to help. Hope to get up middle of next week. Will that clash with you Orla/Jack? Presume Daniel/Esther you are in London? How is your case going?

We know we all love him so we must lean on each
other now.
Cxxxxxx

Wingrove Manor was a late-Victorian redbrick rectory,
about half an hour's drive from Avila House. When Daniel
arrived on Sunday morning, he reflected gloomily that this
was precisely the aesthetic Dominic least enjoyed, and the
abundance of grey skies, laburnum trees and rhododen-
dron bushes did nothing to raise his own spirits. Inside,
however, he found himself at once talking to nurses who
seemed confident and informed, and Dominic looking
spruce and unnervingly back to normal.

'I think,' Dominic said, in what was clearly a rehearsed
opening remark, 'my self-medication may have been a little
haphazard.'

Daniel smiled. 'I think it might. You old junkie.'

'I'm awfully ashamed, you know.' His voice suddenly
became querulous. 'I think I got lonely and it made me
careless.' Two tears appeared on his cheeks. Daniel was
relieved to find himself neither embarrassed nor frightened.

For a couple of minutes, the two sat across from one
another, and Daniel gently stroked the older man's hand.

'By the way,' he said eventually, 'I've now read about
your time at Saxburgh.'

'Have you now? Well?'

Daniel sat back, happy to see the kindling of interest.
'Honestly,' he said, 'this was my favourite bit of the
diaries – so far.'

Dominic looked surprised. 'Really?'

'I don't mean that it sounds like anywhere I'd have
liked.'

Dominic smiled. 'You would not. You're *way* too metro-politan. Too much of a pinko, come to that.'

'You don't think they'd have taken me to their hearts?'

'They'd have duffed you up, my boy.'

'It wasn't really your kind of place either, was it?'

Dominic thought for a moment. 'No,' he agreed, 'not where I'd have gone for choice. But there were plenty of pluses: very decent people.'

Daniel nodded. 'I thought your mum and dad were *great*. All that support.'

'Good,' said Dominic very quietly.

Daniel patted his hand. 'Do you remember I chided you last time because I thought your relationship with Lou had been a bit of a charade?'

'I do.'

'I didn't feel that about you and Marina.'

'Nor should you.'

Daniel looked at him. 'I owe it to you to – well, to try to say something I find difficult. When you described breaking up with her, it was the only time I've ever heard you relay the full extent of how sad you've been. The only time.'

Dominic didn't say anything for a while, but Daniel could see he was thinking. Eventually he said, 'I was very sad when I lost Ben.'

Daniel smiled. 'I thought you'd say that.'

'Well?'

'Well – what do I know? I wasn't there. But my sense is that with Ben, you were just experiencing the violent emo-tions of a student romance cut short.'

'A bit of a fantasy?'

'Exactly. He wasn't even gay. Just a bit fixated on you.'

'Very natural.'

Daniel made a come-off-it face. 'It wasn't going any-where – you know that.'

'Bugger,' said Dominic lightly. 'All those years I've car-ried a torch for him.'

'You big softie. But when you faced up to losing Marina, you knew you were staring at a life sentence.'

'Meaning?'

'Meaning, you knew you would always be lonely.'

A carer arrived with tea and biscuits and poured it for them. She was young and spent a certain amount of time chafing Dominic – trying, it seemed to Daniel, to mark out this moment in the day for him. There were freshly cut sandwiches and she handed both of them a slice of lemon drizzle cake. He remembered Dominic's fondness – greed, really – for everything to do with teatime, and affected now not to notice how he left his food untouched.

'I do believe you're getting better.'

'Come off it. I'm just being intelligently medicated.' Dominic pointed to the tea tray. 'And very expensively pampered, of course, thanks to you.'

'Not a big thing.'

'Oh yes it is. And I'm grateful.' He drew out of his bed-side drawer a large envelope. 'Ready for the last lap?'

Chapter Seventeen
Wingrove Manor, August 2014

Dearest Dan

And so to Groom's – the first chapter in the story which you and I have shared.

Even now, I'm conflicted in what I feel about it. Obviously, I was thrilled to have been appointed and was terribly overawed when I arrived. That made me nervous. I had enough wit and self-discipline to camouflage that in front of the pupils, but it came out in the presence of my colleagues. Before them, I rapidly succumbed to my old vice of looking for approval.

Bad tactical error! The Common Room at Saxburgh looked after its own: anyone a bit needy provoked a pat on the shoulder and an invitation to the pub; at Groom's, self-doubt was treated as a source of contagion – and people kept away. Not everyone, of course, but – still – there was a cadre whose behaviour to a newcomer strikes me, even now, as rather unattractive. It exercised an oppressive influence on the better instincts of quite a few more. On the other hand – and it's a big other hand – it was high time I learned to beat a path through my days without somebody cooing reassurances in my ear.

The joys easily outweighed the sorrows. Stan Dixon, your old Latin teacher, became my great friend. He was not exactly the embodiment of wholesome living, but he was brilliant – not just a good scholar, but clear-thinking and a great enemy of cant. I'd arrive in his classroom fulminating at some injustice or snub (I seemed to be finding those everywhere) and he'd make me laugh so hard that I forgot to be indignant.

And, of course, I loved most of the pupils and mainly for the same reasons: you were dizzyingly articulate and (in another big contrast to the Saxburgh boys) unrepentant iconoclasts. Unbelievers to a man or woman, it seemed. The poor chaplain, I always thought, as he tried to quell the simmering resentment of the school as it filed each Sunday into communion. My only regular gripe was that so few of you wanted to do any work. Collecting in essays from most A-level sets was like drawing teeth. You were one of the very few exceptions, I know. Such a good boy.

I am so sorry to have occasioned you much trouble and expense over these last days. I worry that Esther will resent you spending your hard-earned cash on me when you have other and greater obligations. It is lovely to be looked after here, but it is not necessary, you know. Fr Maybury and Breda have been loyal to me for many years, and I don't believe they'll abandon me now.

It was one of the delights of teaching that you never knew which of your pupils might, in time, become important to you. I found you a clever and intense boy, a little anxious to please (takes one to know one) and quite stoical. But I didn't guess remotely that your loyalty and love would colour my whole life – especially in the years when I became no one at all. I have a strong affection for many of my old pupils, even if their names and faces are now occluded by time and weariness. I pray God will let me keep the comfort of your face and voice, and the clasp of your hand, right to the last.

You know, I think, that my days of being dignified and coherent have just about run their course. Don't be afraid for me, please – nor for yourself.

Ever yr loving old
D

Chapter Eighteen
Groom's, 1984–1988

6 April

Digby and Cara gave me supper last night – Digby brought champagne by way of welcome. They're so jolly and warm. I feel very safe here.

10 April

I'm being a bit of a dick – can't stop smirking about living in this house.

Miscellaneous delights: twin battered chesterfields in the sitting room (Digby calls it the drawing room); having a dressing room off my bedroom (not sure what to do here – an over-grand home to my two suits, one Burton, one Austin Reed, both in sale); a stone sink in the scullery; the deep recesses of the window casements; the rich russet and soft texture of the local stone.

Now that I seem to have achieved the mobility about which I've fantasised for years, the main effect is to make me sentimental about my home and staunchly defensive about my family. This is a dialogue which takes place entirely in my head.

Guy arrived to visit us both today. I suspect the fact that

the school has a golf course may have been persuasive. I felt a bit nervous about taking advantage of this amenity even before term started, but was assured by the estate manager this was no problem. He and Digby played nine holes, while I stayed in the little clubhouse and sweated away on the French Revolution.

18 April

First day of term. I felt it was pretty chaotic, but it's a wild old place. Chapel was held in great ceremony and state, but what a shit choir, and nobody sings the hymns. A raucous school assembly followed, after which classes began.

My O-level set met in a sort of deserted book room which, by any other name, you'd call a slum: walls bare, floors steeped in litter. The kids looked at me sceptically. I had expected this and had rehearsed a voice that sought to convey amiability, calm and attention to business. They seemed happy enough with that, but are apparently unused to working. They're good-looking kids with better complexions than the boys at Saxburgh and are no doubt more peach-fed. They're also stratospherically messy, with trailing shirts, ties hanging loose and clothes as dirty and unkempt as possible. I tried not to imagine my ex-HM's face.

No sign of Sir Frederick, who is apparently on a 'fact-finding mission' in Rome. No preparations have been made for me as a new teacher. I asked the Second Master what games I was supposed to be taking this afternoon. He said, 'Christ, man, you're keen. I'd lie low for a few months if I were you.' History Department apart, precisely one other person spoke to me in the Common Room – to ask if I could cover his lesson this afternoon.

4 May

Geoff Wainwright invited me to lunch at Il Napolitano on the High Street to mark my arrival in the History Department. It was very empty – I assume it makes its money at the weekend when Groom's parents show up in search of a good lunch to shove down the throats of their children. I was hungry and enjoyed the menu: avocado vinaigrette; veal escalope with sautéed potatoes; and a strong black coffee to finish.

Food apart, it was quite painful. Geoff was wearing a manky old anorak, and tried desperately to look upbeat and at ease as he arrived. He had booked a table for three, because, he said, 'I wanted you to have a chance to meet Bryce properly' but Bryce stayed obstinately away. Or at least he did until we had nearly finished our starters, thereby causing the waiters maximum inconvenience and Geoff maximum anxiety.

It was, as Geoff had divined, my first meeting with Bryce beyond a hurried handshake over a mid-morning coffee. He wore an elaborate tweed suit and this, coupled with ginger dundreary whiskers, certainly makes him noticeable. Underneath his waistcoat, through which a silver half hunter had been threaded, a great paunch billowed. The motif was high Victorian, but much more that of the bullying mill owner than the aesthete.

He set out not to charm me, but to exclude Geoff. Since Bryce and I both went to Oxford and are both teaching 19th-century history and, since Geoff did his degrees at York and is a medievalist, that could almost have been done under a patina of politeness. But Bryce made it personal and defiant – ensuring he gave Geoff no eye contact and spoke only to me.

After a couple of minutes, I was uneasy. After five, I was squirming. I wrenched the conversation round to ensure all parties were included. Bryce stopped bothering to engage at that point. He wolfed down his cannelloni, said he was busy and left. Scarcely a goodbye to either of us, and not a word of thanks to his host.

Geoff looked at his retreating form and tried to chuckle. 'Quite a character is Bryce,' he said.

'If that's a fair sample of Bryce,' I said, 'I think I might use other words.'

Geoff blinked a few times and muttered something. I looked at him and realised he was trying to control his emotion. Eyes misted. He told me today is the first time since he'd arrived at Groom's two years ago he'd had a proper conversation with anyone in the department. Neil Wallace is a Housemaster, so his preoccupations tend to focus on that, and Jeremy Lyons is rather rich and grand and generally detached from school life. Geoff is completely alone here.

14 May

Passing a Modern Languages classroom this morning, the estuarine tones of a loutish young colleague screaming at a pupil were painfully audible – 'You fucking cunt.'

God only knows what that was about. There's a lot of anger flowing between kids and staff here. Comparisons with Saxburgh run in and out of my head all the time just now.

22 May

I bumped into a boy and girl in the Lower Sixth in a rather intense clinch by the cricket nets this afternoon. I had gone to walk off a headache and affected not to notice. They both left off whatever it was they were doing and the boy gave me a languorous wave: 'Hi, sir. How's it going?'

I don't even know who these two are, but they treat me like an old pal. At Saxburgh, you were honoured if the kids acknowledged you after knowing them two years. The formality between teacher and pupil very seldom gave way.

28 June

Geoff's Fifth Form was completely out of control today. Through the thin partition that separates his classroom and mine, I heard him oscillate between cajolery and threats. My pupils looked at me, trying to gauge my reaction.

I stared blankly back at them and looked out of the window where Bryce was sitting on a bench in the little garden, happily drinking in the mayhem.

I saw Geoff at break in the Common Room, drinking coffee and dunking bourbon biscuits on his own. I sat next to him. He must have known that I had heard everything, but made a painfully brave effort to be cheerful and interested in what I'm doing.

6 July

Founder's Feast tonight for staff and guests.

The invitation had stipulated black or white tie. There is no compulsion to attend, but almost everyone does. Everybody to whom I spoke beforehand whinged and groaned about what a bore it was. This rather cast me down as I had been quite excited. Hugo Mallinson wore a white tie that fell apart within a minute of his arrival. This allowed him to emphasise both his patrician status (white tie) and indifference (filthy tail coat, unpressed trousers et cetera). His Caroline curls fell about his shoulders with a casualness that was wholly contrived.

I wore my Debenhams dinner suit, purchased on 12 months' credit, and looked (no doubt) what I am. To add to the general sense of being out of my depth, I noticed, as I put on my shirt, I have several spots on my chest.

7 July

Not several. Loads, and they have now spread to my face. I have managed to get chicken pox. Digby was rather startled when he saw me this morning, but urged me to attend the drinks party he is throwing at lunchtime. I desisted: too ill, and too deeply humiliated.

8 July

The itching is not too bad, but I have a desperate headache. Digby is terribly solicitous in the manner of a good RAF skipper, encouraging a reluctant member of his crew to believe that the trip to bomb Essen will actually be a lot of fun.

27 July

Mum and Dad really do come up trumps in a crisis. I went home on 10 July looking like the Elephant Man – well, like someone with too many spots to be seen in public. At first, I just felt shite and slept a great deal. Then I enjoyed the spoiling.

On Tuesday I came back to an empty house, since Digby and Cara are on holiday. The only remaining spots are, not to put too fine a point on it, just where I wished they would not be. I brooded about my disfigurement for a couple of days and generally worked myself up into a state, before finally plucking up the courage yesterday to ring Dr Marsh, the school 'medical officer'.

His surgery turned out to be the gables of a large house on the main road leading into Groom village. The waiting room contained one very well-turned-out lady, and many back issues of *Tatler* and *Country Life*. Dead on midday, I was ushered into the presence of Dr Marsh, who sported half-moon glasses and a three-piece suit. There was a decanter of sherry on a walnut sideboard. Having shaken my hand, he gravely bade me sit down in a green wing armchair.

Not like any GP I've known. The thought of asking this fastidious soul to take a peek at my balls was appalling, but it was too late to do a runner. Reassurance (and soothing lotion) was proffered.

2 October

Geoff went to a Barbershop Group that comprised pupils and staff last week and told me he had enjoyed it. He was keen for me to join him there but I said probably not and oh God oh God his shoulders hunched in disappointment. 'Not a problem,' he said, smiling with an artificial brightness that was painful. I pretended to myself that I was too busy, but it's not true. I am frightened the aura of failure surrounding him just now will extend to me if we hang out too much.

9 October

I was so disgusted by my moral cowardice last week I duly turned up at Barbershop. No Geoff. They are musically way too talented for me and the older pupils looked at me with mild contempt, leavened (perhaps) by pity.

11 October

I mentioned to Geoff I'd gone to the Barbershop the other night and had looked for him in vain. ('Oh. Oh, that's a shame. Janice rang to say that Robbie had come home from school with asthma, so I needed to get back.') Further enquiries elicited that said nipper is now better. He admitted that Janice likes him to get home as soon as possible. 'She doesn't really get this being at school in the evenings.' That's going to be (another) big problem for him in a place like this.

13 October

I taught a desperate last period this morning – courtesy of the shite syllabus I've inherited: the Civil Service reforms of Frederick William of Prussia. As usual, there were not enough desks or chairs, and so some of the kids were squatting on the floor. Meanwhile, down the corridor the Head of French served the Shells a glass of Chablis and they stood on their desks, lustily singing along to a tape recording of Charles Trenet.

30 October

I finally got Geoff to bring his family round for tea on Sunday. Digby and Cara had gone off to play golf in Sandwich which, in the circumstances, was a relief. Janice is so shy – catatonic almost – one stranger at a time was enough.

Cara had helped me fashion out a really good kind of High Tea – scones and cakes, a big pot of soup (tomato –

safe enough) and French bread and cheese. The plan had
been we should go for a walk first, but the children (Robbie,
who has Down's, is eleven and Tilda seven) were fractious
and bored, so we lasted only for about 20 minutes. I'd
brought Digby's parents' dog, Bonzo, to entertain them. He
is an epically wet retriever but Janice is terrified of dogs so
that was another nail in the coffin.

I'd hoped the food would liven things up, but it didn't.
With Janice, you give up rapidly any plans of striking up a
lively dialogue. Although he must be used to it by now, her
silence makes Geoff even more nervous. Now I understand
why – notwithstanding having been here for three years – he
seems to have made no friends.

I felt very sad when they'd gone. Washing up is good
thinking time – could, I asked myself, his position at school
be made easier? Answer – probably not. There is a clique of
about four or five men in their thirties and forties in the
Common Room and they set the tenor: abrasive, snobbish,
supposedly cultured. Their instincts are exactly those of the
teenagers over whom we are supposed to set an example.
Anyone who seems to be floundering is shunned.

29 November

A delegation of Shell pupils came to my classroom after
evening school today. They were all jolly and urbane and
said they wanted to talk.

'Of course,' I said, attempting not to look flattered.

'Well, sir, it's about Mr Wainwright.'

My heart sank. There were the usual three-second dis-
claimers ('I'm sure he's a very nice person, sir') before the
poison was poured: he can't keep order; his notes are culled

straight from their A-level textbook; he takes weeks to mark essays.

It's all true, I have no doubt. When you have a depressed wife, a Down's child, and are without powerful friends round here, it's also not surprising.

3 December

I was so upset by the sight of Geoff's white face at break today that I decided to speak to Bryce directly – he is the only other full-time member of the department and he has a big influence over many pupils.

As expected, he was in his classroom, into which I've never before ventured. It's a true gothic nightmare with high-backed armchairs, stuffed fowls under a glass dome, assorted capes and top hats. There were a couple of gaudily framed works of narrative art.

Bryce looked at me with a pair of very unfriendly eyes when I suggested we have a word. I said I thought Geoff was struggling badly, that his home life was hell, and asked if he could suggest anything to help him.

'Yes,' he said shortly. 'Tell him to resign.'

'That seems a bit . . . radical.'

He said bleakly: 'Don't be so fucking pious. He's a walking disaster. We both know it.'

I sat silent for a few moments. 'He's got a family,' I said.

'Boo-fucking-hoo.' He paused for a moment and then said, 'Anything else?'

3 January 1985

I drove back to Groom's on New Year's Day after ten days' gentle living with my parents and am now mugging up the

Enlightenment which I don't get at all. I only agreed to teach it because Helena Crowhurst, a girl in the Lower Sixth, flattered me into it.

Digby and Cara have gone skiing. They asked me to join them, but (a) I can't afford to and (b) being the token singleton in a posse of heterosexual stockbrokers seems an expensive way to bathe in humiliation. I hired a video of *National Lampoon's Animal House* to eke out the evening. That and a packet of chocolate digestives got me through. I'll run tomorrow.

I'm a bit lonely, perhaps.

17 January

I led a group of very apathetic cross-country runners on what was supposed to be a five-mile dash today. Dash, my arse. We got lost in what turned out to be Groom's golf course and the kids were no help at all. Luckily we bumped into Stan Dixon in a school minibus – great I thought – but it quickly turned out he was lost too. So we spent about half an hour in various hamlets on the South Downs. By the time we reached school, we were half an hour late for evening lessons which led to a couple of impolite notes in my pigeon-hole. A particularly acerbic one from that mad physicist Piers Albright. These are, I am told, a rite of passage.

18 January

Stan came up to me at break this morning and apologised for having got lost. I said I'd been just as lost and he'd helped me out, so I owed him thanks. I also said I had had no idea he was a golfer. He said, 'Listen, chumbo, I fucking hate all sport, have you got that? And I particularly hate fucking golf.'

I found myself warming to him. He's pasty-faced and flabby, but you sense a really formidable mind which is always clocking everything that's happening. He's short, too, which helps me not to feel overawed, and quite epically messy (food stains all over his jumper and trousers). We've arranged to meet for a drink one evening after prep.

8 March

Digby and Cara gave a dinner party tonight. I wasn't invited but they punctiliously asked me to join them for a drink beforehand. It was all very courteous and very assured.

9 March

I went for supper with Stan and Caitlin. Given that she is beautifully dressed and aesthetically sensitive, I think we might call these two an attraction of opposites. And, my God, she can cook. Wonderful risotto, with a pickled walnut salad. Mango sorbet afterwards which she'd made. We ate slumped in front of the TV.

The plan had been to watch *Godfather II* but we got diverted. I mentioned Digby and Cara's deft hosting last night and said, in the earnest voice I've noticed gets a rise out of Stan, 'I think that kind of social confidence contains valuable lessons for all of us.' He said that being patronised was the nearest I seemed likely to get to a full-on sexual experience — 'so I suppose you have to like it. For lack of an alternative.'

16 March

The Housemasters here are as snotty and difficult as can be imagined. I sought out Toby Myers at break today to tell him I was concerned about how often John Venning is out of school and he asked me what I expected him to do about it. I said I just thought he should know, given that there are only three months left before his A levels.

'Well. Now I do.' He went back to his custard creams. Grumpy old sod. I typed him a note later, restating our conversation, and left it in his pigeonhole. That will annoy him.

29 March

I'm staying at Kate's for a few days in Hoxton. When she and Jim were together, they had extraordinarily few possessions in their flat. Now she's bringing up Caleb on her own, she has virtually none – just Caleb's toys and clothes. Yet she exudes interest and contentment. Her friends are teachers and social workers. I met several of them during my stay, and they were delightful and unaffected – a million miles from some of the neurotic wankers among whom I've ended up.

Caleb is sociable, affectionate. The only point of contention between them that I have noticed is that he lusts after toy guns and anything that smacks of the paramilitary. I asked him what he wanted to do when he was a grown-up and he said he was going to be a soldier. 'Great,' said Kate. 'And I'm going to be a nun.'

6 April

The truth is that I went to London to meet men. Not hookers – but guys of my own age. I can't just will away all gay feelings in a great slosh of Catholic piety. It doesn't work. On Tuesday I went near Islington Town Hall where there's a meeting for gays under-30. I disguised myself by wearing a baseball cap and dark glasses. This is pretty mad – do I imagine the KGB are following me? I told Kate I was meeting a friend. She's always discreet and completely accepting but I don't want to dump my neuroses on her. The meeting itself was a bit disappointing. Very earnest. A man in his fifties talked about the Stonewall riots and everyone looked sad and depressed.

To be honest, I wasn't there for the chat, but for the action. No sign of that. About 30 people were there in all, and precious few of them were under 30. One or two caught my eye, but I, alas, did not catch theirs. If what I saw was a representative sample, too many gays are overweight.

6 May

Lower Sixth meeting yesterday afternoon for staff and parents. Based on last night's showing, Groom's parents are friendly and charming ('do come and see us in Corsica' etc). There was a fair amount of guff ('Rupert simply adores your classes').

It means, I know, nothing at all. Fierce ambition lies (only just) beneath the bonhomie. I had to field a lot of nasty stuff about Geoff ('Tamara is learning absolutely nothing in Mr Wainwright's classes'; 'I don't believe Hugo's had an essay marked all year') and some vaguely threatening ('Who do I speak to if I want Alexander moved out of his set?').

11 May

I went to see the Upper School production of *The Cherry*

Orchard this evening, which Michael Robey directed. Given he's a Russian teacher, it seemed a pretty natural choice and I enjoyed it. I heard Lewis Walsh on the way out telling his coterie of favourite pupils, 'Do you know, each time I see one of Dr Robey's productions, I say to myself, "That's it: he can't get any worse than this." But no, each time he does.'

2 June

Cara, Digby and I asked all our parents for Sunday lunch today. Given that Cara's father is a judge and Digby's father very much the local grandee, I had a squeak of fear that my parents might be a bit overwhelmed. Not a bit of it. Cara's mother is a crossword addict, so she and Mum settled down to yesterday's *Times* after lunch. Dad and Cara's father talked about police powers, fortunately in accord.

12 June

Digby and Cara are engaged. Their joy shines out of both of them and they spread it everywhere. I'm incredibly happy for them, but (less happily) I now need to find a new place to live.

12 July

I bought a pushbike today. It's the first time I've owned one since I was a kid. I rode it for six miles and retired home, saddle sore and exhausted. When I mentioned the purchase to Mum on the phone tonight, she couldn't quite conceal an underlying scepticism that this might prove to be another of my brief flights of fancy.

15 July

I've bugger all going on for the next month and have decided to cycle solo in France. Today I bought maps and panniers. (What was conceived as a cheap holiday is rapidly becoming an expensive one.) I am taking the train to Portsmouth tonight, with the bike in the luggage van. Then the midnight ferry to Caen.

16 July

Humiliation at Portsmouth Harbour, having forgotten to pack my passport. Back in Groom's.

23 July

In Bordeaux. I have NEVER EVER been so completely DEAD in my life. Any idea of economy has been ditched. I make myself cycle 50 miles every day, after which I collapse into the first hotel I pass. I eat hugely and expensively, and have developed a particular fondness for steak au poivre with haricots verts, pommes frites, and tarte tatin.

4 August

Madrid. Still on a bicycle. I have lost half a stone despite eating like a pig for the last three weeks. I can now repair my own punctures. I have never been even half so fit in my whole life.

24 August

I've returned (very lean, mighty fit, appallingly broke) to an ugly fallout following A-level results. The History Department has more or less held its own, except (and it's a glaring exception) for Geoff's sets, the results for which are really dire. Even Fredo (who regards any analysis of public examination results as common) is perturbed.

I am really sorry for Geoff, but I admit I'm also feeling a bit pleased with myself for getting all the way to Madrid. Once there, of course, I slackened off and holed up in a cheap hotel near Gran Via. Read the whole of the *Raj Quartet* and wrote copious notes on 19th-century British History for ten days. Solitary, productive, a bit bizarre. Then put bike and myself on the plane back.

Yesterday, I moved into my school flat which is spruce, comfortable, and completely anonymous. I've been hanging pictures and filling bookshelves in an effort to give it some character, but it's about as big a contrast to Digby and Cara's place as can be imagined.

28 August

I came up to London yesterday to go to Dillons and buy books on the French Third Republic. Well, only partly that. I came up to London to the Gay Professionals Under-30 Group and in the vague hope of getting laid. Success on both fronts. No hangover of guilt or shame in the aftermath – a further bonus. I have no desire to go to Confession.

3 September

Beginning of year staff meeting. Geoff looks just as tired as in July, and just a bit fatter. He and Janice didn't 'go' anywhere, but he claims that they 'did some nice daytrips'. His eyes implored me not to push for detail, so I didn't. There are four candidates for Oxbridge History this year, which is half the number we had last year.

Toby Myers complained about John Venning's History grade, as I knew he would. I reminded him that I had told him about my own concerns back in March. Toby claimed to have no memory of the conversation, but I drew out of my folder a copy of the letter I had sent him on the subject at the time. Collapse of stout party.

5 November

Stan was complaining today about Sunday lunch at his sister's in Effingham where, so he says, they 'go through the whole fucking palaver'. Pressed for details, it emerged that 'palaver' means they eat in a dining room, that his brother-in-law sits at the head of the table and carves a joint, and that his nieces clear the table afterwards. He described his nieces as 'straight out of The Sound of Fucking Music.'

He says of Caitlin and himself: 'We're not really a couple, you know. Just two people who happened to get married.'

27 November

Storm clouds are gathering over the History Department or, more specifically, over Geoff. Two of our four Oxbridge candidates have not been invited even for an interview. Both have been taught by Geoff who, for reasons unknown, isn't here today. The father of one of them, Titus Bellaby, is a governor of Groom's. (Obviously, with Geoff's luck, he would be.) At teatime today, Fredo was spotted by Stan down by the squash courts in intense conversation with Bellaby *père* – both parties looking grim. Later, I saw them both talking to Bryce.

2 December

Geoff beckoned me into his little office this evening. He is leaving at the end of term. Fredo has allegedly waived the usual requirement of a term's notice 'on compassionate grounds'.

I said I was truly sorry. 'Not a problem,' he said, not meeting my eye. He was knee-deep in A4 suspension files and seems to have chosen this moment to attend, finally, to some departmental paperwork. Only four years late. Actually, he looked happier than I can remember seeing him.

3 December

Cassandra tracked me down at break and told me Fredo wanted to see me. I instinctively searched my memory for anything particularly heinous I might have done. I was duly ushered into what Stan calls the Head-magisterial Presence. Fredo beckoned me to a chair the other side of the fireplace and offered me a whisky. He looked a bit hunted, and said that 'very sadly, Geoff Wainwright has decided that he doesn't feel able to continue here'. There was a rather awkward pause, and he went on: 'I believe he and his wife have for some time now been looking to move to the West Country.'

Then the bombshell: how would I feel about taking over from Geoff as Head of Department? My mouth just moved soundlessly like a guppy fish for a bit, but Fredo seemed to take that as a declaration of interest. He has sworn me to silence *pro tem*.

6 December

I am still shocked. Bryce loathes me, and given that he and

Fredo hang around each other like a bad smell, it is totally out of character that Fredo should have given me the job over him. But, there it is – it's real.

Geoff (who has become virtually invisible) has expressed his pleasure, as have Neil and Jeremy. Good news: since Bryce will most definitely be livid. I need the rest of the History Department on side.

12 December

Fredo announced Geoff's departure to the Common Room this morning, although Geoff himself was not there to hear it. He is still manically filing. There were a few insincere expressions of sorrow from one or two of the Housemasters who have, collectively, done less than nothing to support him. He then said I was being appointed as his replacement. A few people smiled encouragingly in my direction, but most were looking thirstily in the direction of the cafetières, desperate to get a caffeine infusion before the next period.

Then Fredo gave one of his diffident half coughs. 'In another change, Philip Gough has decided to retire as Director of Studies at the end of the term. Very happily, he will be staying on as a stalwart of the Biology Department. Bryce Williams will be replacing him.'

There was some distinctly muted applause in which, reflexively, I joined – my face like parchment, I expect. The Director of Studies is supposed to oversee and support all academic policy in the school, and, above all, Heads of Department answer to him. I therefore work for Bryce. In this one sentence, Fredo has not only managed to annihilate my pleasure in the promotion, but also cut off my balls.

14 December

Term over, thank God. I went to see my parents for a night. They tumbled over themselves with congratulations, but they could see I was very unhappy about Bryce's promotion. Dad always wants to believe well of those in charge and says there has to be a rational explanation why Fredo should esteem him so highly. I said I wished there was. It's inexplicable and, in darker moments, I find myself sniffing out a conspiracy. Mum is ultimately less surprised. I can read her thoughts: *The rich and privileged don't play fair. What did you expect?*

18 December

I wrote to Fredo today:

Dear Headmaster

When you generously offered me the post of Head of History, I obviously had no idea you were planning to make Bryce Williams the new Director of Studies. I know, of course, that all such appointments are at your pleasure alone, but in effect you have made my position impossible even before I begin. Bryce and I distrust and dislike one another. While I'm not proud of the help I gave (or failed to give) Geoff, I believe Bryce has played a shameful part in the circumstances that led to his departure.

If I become a Head of Department, Bryce will, in effect, be my line manager. That is not something I can accept happening. I'm very sad, but I can't now become Head of History. I realise this about-turn will

*be inconvenient for you, and I am sorry for that. But
I am sure of where I stand.*

Yours
Dominic da Silva

7 January 1986

I had a phone call from Cassandra last night, snappishly
summoning me today to meet Fredo. Perhaps it's what being
a secretary means, but she's known to be a barometer of his
moods, so this didn't bode well.

So it proved: there were no enquiries about holidays, no
good wishes for New Year or the like. He was a bit like Lady
Catherine de Burgh: motioned me brusquely to sit down
and said, 'I am trusting you have now thought better of the
extraordinary letter you sent me.'

I disabused him at once, saying I wouldn't accept as my
direct boss someone who should have been sacked, not pro-
moted. The second the words left my mouth, I knew I had
overplayed my hand. Fredo gave me a very cool look, and
reminded me that the terms of my employment committed
me to following all reasonable orders given to me by the
Headmaster. He added that he expected me to turn up to the
Heads of Department Meeting tomorrow 'and play your full
part'.

8 January

Term began today with the usual staff meeting. Fredo was in
one of his tweed suits, with a pale blue shirt and a starched
collar. I found myself watching afresh him tread the fine line
between parody and pastiche. He spoke of the 'academic

garlands that have been bestowed upon our worthy alumni' (*translation*: nine pupils have got into Oxbridge). He hailed the return of 'our intrepid rugby footballers from the rigours of the Antipodes' (*translation*: the First XV are back from a rugby tour of Australia).

He asked all Heads of Department to meet him in the Chaplain's Library afterwards, 'altogether a more suitable ambience for a distinguished company'. I could feel him watching me out of the corner of his eye as he issued the invitation, and told myself – *so long as Fredo takes the meeting, I'll play along. If Bryce is in the chair, I'm off.*

We all trooped across the quad into the library which had been arranged for a meeting with long tables down the middle, each with a blotter and pen, and water jugs.

Fredo said, 'Gentlemen, let me leave you to your deliberations under the guidance of our new Director of Studies.' Bryce, wearing a new black suit (for all the world looking like a Victorian notary reading a will), moved to the head of the long table and plonked his enormous arse on the chair like a bag of soil.

'Very well,' he said curtly. 'Let's get on with it.'

'Not me,' I said, and pulled back my chair there and then, registering a couple of startled faces as I did so. I went over at once to the History block and found Neil and Jeremy (a bit of a miracle since Neil is usually in his House and Jeremy never at school save to teach his classes) and told them I wasn't going to work under Bryce. Neil looked a bit shocked but said, 'I know you're doing the right thing' – he is about the only Housemaster with a conscience in this place. Jeremy said, 'It's a shit job, anyway.' Both were emphatic they have no interest in the job themselves, so I guess someone will be brought in from outside.

My position here looks untenable – I have to start looking for another job quickly. I'll miss Digby and Cara most, and then Stan.

9 January

A notice has been pinned up on the Headmaster's board in the Common Room: 'Until a permanent appointment has been made for Head of History, Bryce Williams will serve as temporary Head of Department.'

28 January

Well, we're in chaos. Outwardly, it all seems normal enough: Neil, Jeremy and I all teach our lessons, mark preps and do whatever else we're supposed to be doing. But Bryce, so far as we can see, does nothing – and that's about to create a shitstorm. The entire crop of O-level coursework has remained unmarked, and the date for submitting it to the Examining Board has now expired.

Bryce likes prestige, not hard graft. Once the full extent of work left undone by the 'temporary Head of Department' becomes clear, all hell is going to break loose among Groom's parents. That means Fredo will get it in the neck – and he'll look for someone to blame.

4 February

Stan and I have brought 24 of Groom's most unathletic boys to Whitby for Lower School Outward Bound week. It's pissing down, of course. The kids have brought Walkmans, cashmere jumpers and new walking boots (hence many blisters). Stan and I drank whisky on the train up here this afternoon to insulate ourselves from the horror.

5 February

Our dispiriting trudge along the North Yorkshire coastal path continues. I draw consolation from conversation with chatty pupils. Stan, whose vocation for teaching surfaces only when in the presence of girls with large bosoms and child-bearing hips, enjoys no such recompense.

We were accosted during the walk today by a man in a very busy-looking cagoule who wanted to know who we were. I assumed one of the kids had been rude and put on my concerned face. Apparently (he claimed) all schools planning a visit should write to the Coastal Path Authority to let them know of their arrival in advance. Needless to say, we hadn't done so. When I explained (politely and quietly) we were an independent school he said, 'You lot always think you're above the law.'

6 February

On Hadrian's Wall. I thought Stan's classicism might extend to a bit of Roman history, but he says, 'I hate them all.' (I honestly don't know whether he meant the Romans or the kids.)

The weather is a fright. In desperation we abandoned walking yesterday afternoon and took them all into Newcastle to watch *Jagged Edge*. An 18 certificate, but most of the kids claimed to have seen it already. Afterwards we went to an old-fashioned chippy. The kids talked loudly about their exotic holiday destinations, gap-year plans, Oxbridge colleges *et cetera*.

22 February

I've been *much* more relaxed this term – no longer expecting anything from Groom's has made my days a doddle. So I've put in for a job as Head of History at San Jose High School in Madrid. No doubt I'm influenced by great memories of all the summers Guy and I spent there (and also of my cycling marathon last year). Teaching abroad isn't what you do if you're career-minded. I think I'm in a mood where I feel like breaking rules.

4 March

I had my interview with Sr Astudillo (Principal of San Jose) yesterday – at the Institute of Directors in Pall Mall. I'd patronisingly expected someone rather disorganised who didn't know the UK educational system, but found myself at the end of a terrifyingly firm handshake from a tall and handsome man of about 40 who spoke perfect idiomatic English. Other than giving me a bone-crushing handshake, his style was very easy and informal. After putting me through my paces on History teaching and running a department for a bit, he grinned and asked what was going on.

Dominic had looked a bit startled, and Sr Astudillo had given a short chuckle.

'I mean, San Jose's a great place, but it's not the noble Groom's.'

'All right,' said Dominic, 'I'll tell you,' and attempted to furnish him with a full and frank account of recent events.

Sr Astudillo whistled softly when he had finished. 'Nasty,' he said.

'Very,' said Dominic. 'And I imagine I've got a crap reference in consequence.'

'You imagine wrongly. Either the famous Sir Frederick

views all this in a less tragic light than you, or' – he gave another short chuckle – 'he's desperate to see the back of you. You shouldn't worry. It's all glowing stuff here.'

6 March

Sr Astudillo rang this evening. He said, 'You and I, Dominic, can do business together. Let's put History on the map in San Jose.' He also asked me to call him Armando.

The money is about the same as here, but there is no accommodation, no health insurance and no pension arrangements, so – in reality – a good deal less. In professional terms, this is not much of a swap. I've asked for 24 hours before I commit.

7 March

My 27th birthday. I wrote Fredo a brief and polite note of resignation this morning – imagining the look on his face was the best present I could have imagined. Decided to tell no one at all, but then weakened at break and informed Stan. He said 'Oh lah-di-fucking-dah' which is (I think) Stan-speak for what anyone else would call 'congratulations'. I was on my way back to class when Cassandra searched me out with an urgent summons to Fredo.

Shorn of circumlocution, Fredo informed me that Bryce has decided that the Directorship of Studies is 'not for him' and Alastair Binney is going to replace him. He asked, in these altered circumstances, if I would now be prepared to take on the Headship of History, starting today.

Slightly to my surprise, I agreed at once, and in consequence have just made a rather cringing call to Madrid. I told Sr Astudillo it had been a difficult decision. He said, 'By the sound of it, not that difficult.'

21 April

Saturday was Digby and Cara's wedding. Guy was Best Man. My role was non-specific and unofficial but of great dignity. On Friday the three of us went to a Greek restaurant in Brighton, sank a bottle of wine each – enough to generate bonhomie rather than insensibility. Back at the house afterwards we drank brandy and (at about 2 a.m.) found ourselves with our arms draped round each other singing 'New York, New York'. After that we collapsed on the marital bed. Hence, Digby will be able to tell his grandchildren that he spent his last night of bachelorhood in bed with two men.

The service was in the village church, where Cara had been christened, and the reception was in a big marquee on the lawn of her parents' house. Blue skies and strong sunshine suggests the Almighty is on their side. I don't usually like weddings very much – too obviously not my constituency – but that day I was mellowed by friendship.

The day was further improved by sitting next to a friend of Cara's called Janey. They went to Cambridge together, but Janey doesn't lard her conversation with that or anything else which might seem to be showing off. The woman on the other side of her was a middle-aged schoolteacher, whom Cara's family have long befriended. I noticed Janey taking quite as much care talking to her as she did to me, or to anyone else.

There was a party later at which Janey and I talked more. We even danced – not my favourite thing, and nor hers, at a guess. She has the kind of tan that I associate with people who spend time hiking on the hills – given that she is a City lawyer, I presume I am mistaken. I rather pompously asked her if she would come to Groom's to talk to our older kids about legal careers.

2 May

Met Janey off the train at Groom station. She looked a bit shoulder padded and City big shot and my heart sank. But the initial reserve fell away in half a minute and we chatted just as we had at the wedding. Rather to my surprise, about 20 kids showed up and she hit the right note at once – calm, informed, perfectly friendly but not trying to impress. Well – she's very much a product of the world to which they belong.

Afterwards we went back to my flat to eat spaghetti and cold chicken, and I put together a tomato and mozzarella salad. Delicious actually, and we drank rosé. In fact, it all began to feel like a bit of a first date – both of us were very concerned to listen to the other. She told me she has only recently emerged from a relationship with an older guy (a partner in a rival law firm). She says what she really minds is that her mother now feels entitled to subject her to endless questioning about her private life. She also says she still gets the odd call or letter from the ex-boyfriend, but is completely cool about ripping up the letters unread or hanging up the phone.

I know she's interested in me. In fact, definite interest registered by both parties.

5 May

History Department Meeting to talk about exams. Bryce reluctantly showed up, ten minutes late. He can't bear being in an environment that he can't dominate – and he also can't stand me. Jeremy and Neil affect not to notice, but the atmosphere is excruciating.

10 May

I went up to London last night to take Janey to *Waiting for Godot*. I'd done all my marking (which meant bed at 2 a.m. the previous day). It's the only way to relax and I wanted Janey to get me at my best. It didn't work out like that – at least at first. The air-conditioning had broken down on the train to Waterloo for one thing and, although we were moving against the direction of travel, it was still reeking of sweat and BO. I arrived at the theatre at 7 p.m. sharp, as instructed, and tried to look svelte and unconcerned at the bar. No Janey. Same at 7.10, 7.15, 7.20 (when we were summoned to take our seats). I thought about going into the stalls and leaving her ticket at the box office, but decided not. Abandonment complex (never far away so far as I am concerned) moved to overdrive.

She eventually arrived at 7.40. There was just me in the bar by this point (plus a few pitying attendants). I could tell she'd been running and her face looked rather sweaty. She was upset, I could see, but really didn't want to show it. Bad day at the office, was as much as she said. We agreed we didn't give a shit about Beckett and went to a very basic Italian place a few doors away from the theatre. The rest of the evening was a breeze and it seemed the most natural thing in the world to take a bus back to her place in Camberwell.

It's a very pretty basement flat. The bars on the windows and double locks on doors that it's not a desperately safe area, but she loves it. There were other things on both our minds, however. Coffee and brandy followed and soon catching the last Tube was no longer an issue. It also meant that I was a bit too pissed to ask myself some of the questions I might normally have done (who was in charge of the contraception? and – not exactly irrelevant – what am I doing sleeping with a woman again?).

But somehow it didn't matter. We suit each other. My God we suit each other. She smells gorgeous, we seem to move in wonderful harmony and we were both spent and pretty rapturous. I got up at 5 a.m., took the early train and was back in Groom's in excellent time to teach my Shell class at 9 a.m. Had a very slight hangover, but my chief feeling was (and is) one of bewildered happiness.

18 May

Janey and I have spoken twice every day this week. She came down yesterday afternoon when, for once, I didn't have to take anyone for games. The weather has broken (not half), so we didn't do anything much but work a bit (this part had been agreed on the phone beforehand) and I cooked a risotto, which wasn't bad at all. It was only the second night we've spent together, and this time we both slept rather more and rather better. This morning came more work, then an hour's walk on the Downs followed by a pub lunch. After that – tragic, I know – it was back to work for both of us.

She left about 5 p.m. and I'm just back from evening Mass, which might sound a bit perplexing to some people, but to me seemed the very best way of acknowledging gratitude.

We've agreed to go away for half term. My initial idea had

been to suggest Paris or Rome, and I even rang Abercrombie & Kent on Friday to see if they could suggest something that wouldn't bankrupt me. But when I broached the idea with Janey, she said, 'Well, only if you really want to.' So I said that I didn't really care where we went – I just really wanted some time with her and nobody else. Good, she said, because that's what she felt too. She thinks we may be able to borrow somebody's cottage in Norfolk.

When we're together, she talks a lot – much more than me. She insists that's not her usual style, however. Just now being with me seems to be releasing something in her.

19 May

One of the big disadvantages of living on the premises is that nobody can visit you without news of it being pored over by others. Stan has demanded details of my weekend and was irked by my discreet précis. More to the point, he is irked by the fact that she is a lawyer. To him, this means that she is 'smug and superior and almost certainly posh'. It's not that he has said this (and in fact has yet to meet her) – but I can tell.

26 May

Internal exams. There is no sign that Bryce has marked the Third Form scripts, although these should have reached me two days ago.

27 May

I tracked down Bryce in his gothic turret. 'You'll get your fucking exams when I'm fucking ready,' he bellowed, in response to my own very polite question.

I raised my eyebrows and said – wholly calm – 'It's a very reasonable request, Bryce. I'm sorry you can't treat it as such' and left, but quite slowly.

It's the first time I've emerged from a row with Bryce feeling I had the upper hand and I felt very pleased with myself. Janey had advised me on tactics when we spoke last night.

29 May

Poor Stan – I've just come from seeing him in hospital. Caitlin was there when I arrived, glowering: she is so bloody enigmatic it's difficult to work out if she is poleaxed by worry for the pain her husband is suffering, or simply seething with irritation he fell down the stairs having had one glass too many of Bulgarian red.

One always thinks a broken leg is a straightforward affair, but his is properly bad and he is in traction and uncomfortable. He had an hour-and-a-half operation on Tuesday and they have inserted a titanium bolt. His theory that life is simply an extended *Carry On* film was given some credence yesterday when a posse of his Fourth Form visited him in hospital *en masse*, and decided to fiddle round with the weights supporting his leg.

7 June

Perfect. Janey left work at lunchtime on Tuesday and we drove up on bad roads but with both of us in very good moods.

We were lent a place on the coast at Burnham Overy: I'd expected something bijou but in fact it was a large 1970s house, with an indoor swimming pool and a sunken bath.

They had left out a glorious supper for us – French onion soup, a cold lobster salad, and masses of bread and cheese. A bottle of champagne on ice and flagons of wine. I don't know why but we were both famished, and we stuffed ourselves.

I suppose it was the booze talking as much as anything but by about 10 p.m. we were both pretty pissed and very, very up for it. I had this idea of doing it in the hammock in the garden. At the time this seemed an excellent idea but it was (a) pretty nippy and (b) not actually that easy to bring off. Still, where there's a will etc – I assume the fact that we were both off our faces helped. There was a brief moment of anxiety when we were sneaking back to the house that we had managed to lock the back door behind us (not in fact the case – that would have taken some unravelling).

Very different tempo next day. Apart from one walk, we spent virtually all of it in bed, talking, just listening to each other with extraordinary gravity and intensity. We talked about families, of course, especially hers. She says she only quite likes being a lawyer, but feels driven to achieve – material success and academic distinction are the only things her mother respects. The relationship between the two of them is very complicated – love and fear and loathing on both sides. When Janey split with one boyfriend, her mother was livid because he was a Fellow of the British Academy.

She's so candid and unafraid that I felt ready to tell her pretty much my own peculiar story – Hunter's Chase; Ben; Marina. About my grinding loneliness at points, and about the Chess Club. She asked me if I'd loved Ben. I said I'd been very fond of him, and enjoyed the subversive quality of our brief liaison.

She then asked who I'd desired more. Ben, I said.

She was pretty quiet for a while after that and finally said she needed to be sure where I stood on the 'sexual spectrum' because we were obviously becoming important to each other and everything between us seemed to be happening quite quickly. I said I would always have deep longings for guys but that, when I was with her, nobody else – nothing – seemed to matter very much. After a bit she said that if I really meant that, she thought we could 'make a go of it.'

Something changed in that moment and we both knew it. I could feel myself on the edge of never being lonely again and, my God, that's a big feeling.

I said I really meant it. She smiled the biggest smile I've ever seen and said, 'Then I'm really glad.'

We hired a kayak on Thursday. Yesterday was much colder: we did an all-day walk on the dunes. I did the supper – two large fillet steaks, chips (homemade – we found a chip pan) and lots of green beans that I remembered to undercook. Comfort is best. Extraordinarily, even though we both knew the next day we had a long drive back (her to London and then me to Groom's), the absolute tranquillity of the week lasted throughout the evening.

I knew that everyday cares were bound to kick off as soon as we left but I also felt that what we'd just had was utterly different from anything I'd ever known. So I said that I knew I was moving probably way too quickly, but that these had been the best days of my life and asked how she felt about us getting married. She said 'actually, I'd love it' and gave me her most perfect smile.

I didn't have a ring or anything and we've agreed our next step is to move in together. I'm going to move out of my school flat, and commute between Groom's and London daily. Long days lie ahead, but in what a good cause.

I honestly never believed this could happen to me. The idea that I'm going to be able to share <u>the rest of my life</u> with someone I find brilliant and wise makes the future feel more – what's the word? More <u>massive</u>, if that makes sense. There are chances for us to live so many different futures. Maybe we'll have kids; maybe we'll live and work abroad; maybe I can even run my own school one day. All maybes, but I can risk allowing myself to look to a future in which it's not only me.

2 August

I am in the depth of the summer holidays – although it certainly hasn't felt restful. I can't claim pressure of business, but it's been high-octane emotion since we announced our engagement.

Predictably, my family is fine – delighted indeed – and, equally predictably, Janey's is not. I wanted Mum and Dad to have a chance to meet us as just a courting couple before anything was said. We drove up for Sunday lunch with them a fortnight ago and they could see at once we were so thrilled with each other that, by the time I nerved myself to say something, it lacked the element of total surprise. Mum looked pretty much as though her heart's desire had been fulfilled and, while the tears rolled down her cheeks, her face had that look of perfect gravity that never fails to move me. Dad unearthed a bottle of champagne and, in a voice cracked with emotion, toasted us both.

Janey is genuinely bowled over by their unqualified and heartfelt welcome and I think they all have it in them to get the best out of each other. It's complicated, however: while she admires its indifference to worldly considerations, every step she takes further into my family feels an act of defiance towards her own. This both thrills and appals her.

The following night, we went to meet her mother and father. Ill-starred in every respect. Janey had had an argument with a colleague at work, and was already keyed up. I had a headache and our Tube was delayed for half an hour at Mornington Crescent. That kind of thing. Anyway, we arrived late. It was my first visit to the house in which she had been brought up – a tall townhouse overlooking Hampstead Pond. Her father looks like a younger version of Lord Carrington, and talks in a series of patrician gurgles. Her mother is a very beautiful woman – flashing smile and sparkling eyes, beautiful skin (looks much younger than her age) and an enviable combination of golden hair and a deep natural tan.

After a slightly laboured 20 minutes or so nursing drinks, her mother went off to the kitchen, and Janey followed her there, while I announced my intentions to her father. He fiddled with his drink, eyes cast down, and then said quietly, 'Are you asking for my permission?' I said quietly that I didn't think I was, but that we both hoped for his blessing. He shrugged and said, 'It's Nicole you need to worry about.' Pretty well on cue Nicole and Janey arrived, both looking flushed and furious. Nicole didn't look at me and said to Robin, 'I've told her it's a mad idea.'

Janey gave no quarter, for which I was grateful. I said little beyond the fact that our minds were made up and that I hoped time would lend understanding. After a couple of drinks, Robin seemed to forget his opposition and said he was hungry. Nicole stayed red-faced and mutinous throughout. Somehow the evening staggered to an end. I haven't seen them since, although Janey had a coffee with her mother on Friday and believes that she is beginning to come round. Just as well, since the engagement will be announced in *The Times* on Monday.

12 August

Janey and I are just back from a long weekend outside Granada. Slightly duplicitously, she had 'forgotten' to mention that a colleague of hers, Lara, and her husband had hired a house a couple of miles away. We ended up seeing rather more of them than I might have liked. Janey played golf with them on two of the three days. I agreed to have a couple of lessons (such are the compromises of impending marriage) but went for long solo walks whenever I could.

22 August

Good news (a): the sale of my house in Saxburgh completed today. I've made about £7,000 profit, having done virtually nothing towards it in the three and a half years I've owned it, save to take rent off tenants. I like this capitalism lark. The money will be a big help now that we're looking for a place of our own near school.

Good news (b): A-level results came in yesterday. We did all right in the end – even Bryce, I was sorry to see. Janey was taken aback by the pressure it puts on me. She is back at work this week, so we're in London. I go to lunchtime concerts at the Wigmore Hall or the Proms, and read about the Glorious Revolution, which is my latest historical fix.

I miss Stan a bit, and our morning poached eggs on toast at the Groom Tea Rooms. He and Caitlin have asked us both to join them in Ireland for the Bank Holiday weekend just before term starts. We've accepted, albeit with reservations on all sides. Stan's perfect woman is a barmaid, skimpily dressed, preferably with an Essex accent. His idea of hell is a Chelsea matron, especially one with a suntan. Janey is neither one nor the other but, let's face it, she's more nearly one than the other.

9 September

Beginning-of-year meeting. Fredo peered at us all, faux benevolent as ever, and said, 'Welcome back – one hardly feels one's had a chance to draw breath.' This from a man who has spent every waking minute of the last two months stalking and shooting.

17 September

We think we have found a house – just on the edge of Groom village, overlooking the South Downs and with a small brook running through the tiny back garden. Just within our price range. It was built in the late 18th century, of the same local stone which I've always loved in Digby's house. The ground floor is pretty well all open plan – which I like – and there are three bedrooms and two bathrooms.

Janey's clear preference for moving out of London has mildly surprised me. So long as we own our own place, however, the school can't quite own me – especially since I'll be moving out of school accommodation.

4 October

Nicole and Robin asked us to supper last night to chat about wedding arrangements. All very stylised – Brook's, Robin's club in St James's.

We kicked off all right – he ordered champagne to toast us – and both of them made a point of asking us about our jobs. Robin's eyes wandered at various points when smart acquaintances of his stepped into the bar. At various moments I was introduced, without apparent reluctance, as his future son-in-law.

Club food: potted shrimps, roast lamb, cheeseboard. During the meal, we got down to business. A brief flurry of concern about bridesmaids' dresses. Over coffee (Robin lit a cigar but didn't offer me one) he told me about Janey's trust fund that, he explained patiently, is hers alone. He seemed anxious lest I imagine I had a claim upon it. I reassured him on this point.

Nicole then asked if my parents had 'settled' any money on me and seemed put out that they hadn't. She muttered, perfectly audibly, something about people 'marrying up'. Janey laid a pacifying hand on mine in anticipation of what I might say in response, but I confined myself to saying that I hoped she would soon think better of that remark. There followed a prolonged and deathly silence which was only broken when, after what felt like half an hour, the waiter arrived to pour more coffee.

We reverted to wedding arrangements. Nicole questioned our decision to get married in a Catholic church. The basis of her complaint was aesthetic (the church was ugly) rather than theological. Janey said quietly that I had a faith which she respected, and that was what counted. Silence.

Eventually, we said our goodbyes. Nicole brushed my cheek grudgingly. I waited for Janey to pass comment on the evening before I said anything. She was pretty quiet on the Tube and then, as we were letting ourselves into the flat, gave a short laugh. 'Mother was on form tonight, didn't you think?'

1 February 1987

We completed on our house last week. I found the business nerve-racking. Janey was much cooler than me, predictably.

We have kept both sets of parents at bay. The idea of them meeting at all, let alone combining to carry a stereo upstairs, is too traumatic for either of us just now. Unbeknown to me, Janey had arranged with my mother to give us the old sofa and chairs from my father's den. They are chintzy and worn and very comfortable. No more eloquent rejection of metropolitan chic can be imagined. I can't wait to see Nicole's face when she sees them.

7 February

Bryce has been appointed Curator of the Groom's Museum from 1 September. It's a full-time job and he will no longer teach in the department. Oh frabjous day.

20 February

We held the final round of interviews for next year's History post today. The glittering candidate has a First from Wadham and a DPhil, but the kids would kill him. An evangelical Christian – bad sign. The one I liked most was Laura Cargill – really clever and sympathetic, but she scuppered herself by telling Fredo she's a militant atheist who refused ever to set foot inside the school chapel. The last guy had the charisma card – Tom Cassidy. Been teaching in Dublin for a year while he finishes a book on the Easter Rising of 1916.

He was quite shy and intense and, judging by the look of his clothes, he needs a job.

23 February

Fredo has come down on the side of Tom Cassidy. He tried to call him, and so did I, but there was no answer, so a letter offering him the job has been sent.

6 August

Written a week after the event, I know – but last Saturday was our wedding – and also the fortieth anniversary of that of my parents. It so happened it was a convenient day for all of us, but we leapt on the coincidence. I also drew great joy from the fact that we married at Holy Redeemer, where they started out their own journey.

In order to comply with the residence clauses, I stayed with Guy in Margarita Terrace last week. On Friday I went to Confession and told Fr Bertone that I couldn't express contrition for sleeping with Janey because we loved each other and it felt right in every way. ('Quite right,' he said, rather to my surprise. 'I don't think the Almighty's any too concerned either.') He has asked me to call him 'Andrea' which feels strange.

I emphatically didn't want a stag party. Guy and Digby joined Dad and me for a couple of drinks in the cocktail bar of Claridge's last night. It was companionable, low key and lasted just over an hour. Guy and I then went back to Margarita Terrace. We watched *The Day of the Jackal* on video after which I slept easily and deeply.

Woke about 6 a.m., at once excited. I put on some jeans and my old trainers and walked across Oakley Street (which was pretty deserted) in order to go to the 7 a.m. Mass in Cheyne Row. This was my private time, and I hadn't told anyone except Janey that I was going to go to early Mass, but she had blabbed. There at the door of the church, quietly waiting for me, stood my parents. I couldn't help myself and felt my eyes fill with tears. My father smiled his shy smile at me and my mother gazed at me very slowly and then held out her arms. Fr Bertone was waiting for me when I came in, with a big beaming smile. Afterwards we went back to the flat where Guy had made us all breakfast – croissants, smoked salmon, poached eggs. I was ravenous and ate everything. We then changed.

It was rather nice being able to walk to the church, and fun to arrive when it was already pretty full. I felt fullhearted rather than nervous, but was impatient to see Janey. Not having seen her dress, and knowing her as a thoroughly independent spirit, I had absolutely no idea what colour (let alone length) she would have chosen. I can't describe dresses, even now. The best I can say is that it was ivory in colour, silk in texture, and long. It was also extraordinarily apt for her – demure at first sight, but packing a hell of a punch. I could read her expression even before I saw her under the veil – ever so slightly apprehensive, but absolutely reconciled to every choice she had made, and to every person to whom she was linked. Robin looked every inch the elder statesman, and Nicole – I will give her this – was completely wrapped up in her daughter and in this moment. Both, you could see, were working hard to keep it together. Though there is a lot I find off-putting about them, I can never doubt that they love their daughter.

Fr Bertone kept the sermon brief (it was about St Ignatius, but I guess only a handful of us picked up on the fact that it was his Feast Day). Janey's voice was calm and clear during the exchange of vows. For me, the overwhelming moment of feeling came when I received Communion, and Janey came and knelt with me. We had not planned that. After the recessional hymn, we walked down the aisle to Handel and out into the sunlight and the slightly brutalising ritual of photographs. It was still warm, although the sky was looking a little less certain than it had been earlier in the day. A magnificent old Jaguar Mk IX arrived and took the pair of us to the Bluebird in great style. I gather there were just under 150 people at the reception, most from Janey's side. Swathes of my past were there – notably Jack O'Riordan from Greystoke, with whom I exchanged a heartfelt promise to get in touch. My old teachers were properly included: Dr Pertwee, Harry Peel. And of course, friends from Oxford, Saxburgh and Groom's were out in force. Stan was in uproarious form, save during the speeches which, good or bad, always fill him with embarrassment. Every part of my life was represented save those sad years at Hunter's Chase.

To my relief, the two sets of parents had obviously worked out a way of being friendly to each other and relaxed enough to enjoy the day. It cannot ever be better than that. I saw Kate (the only cousin we'd asked) being interrogated by Nicole in the reception line, and her eyes (Kate's, I mean) taking on that wary look she gets if she feels uneasy. I raised my eyebrows and smiled in her direction and it was over in a split second. I hope so anyway.

I made Guy run through his speech the day before the wedding and insisted he excise some of the more sensitive allusions – some to Louisa and others to my dithering sexual orientation. He was <u>really</u> pissed off (I know that look). I appealed to the sensibilities of parents, in-laws and so forth.

He just said, 'All right, mate. It's your call.' The way he looks at the world is that the camaraderie of old mates commands the ultimate loyalty.

We had decided months ago we didn't want an evening party. The Bluebird lent us a room in which to change and we were duly applauded as we came downstairs. We spent the night in Claridge's (which had an amazing bathroom). Supper and champagne were brought to the room and nobody thereafter disturbed us.

Next morning, Guy arrived with my car. He looked ghastly – apparently everything had hotted up quite spectacularly after we left. He claims to have no recollection of how he got home from the Bluebird, but says he woke up next to Melinda. Given that they are engaged, that seems prudent.

Everyone seemed to assume that we were off somewhere exotic – I heard the West Indies mentioned by somebody, and the Maldives. In reality, it's Pembrokeshire. As long as the wife's around, I don't care about the rest.

27 August

Tom Cassidy finally rang up today – first sign of life since he wrote accepting the offer of a job. He was all jollity. 'Great, lookin' forward to it all. Hey, feller, any chance the school can give me a bed somewhere?'

Fantastically pompous of me, but I could feel hackles rising: (a) at being called 'feller' by someone of whom I am, after a fashion, boss; (b) at the total dearth of reply to any of the various letters we have sent him over the past three or four months. But I kept my voice reasonable and just said that all bids for staff accommodation had been fielded months ago.

5 September

We spent this evening at Stan and Caitlin's. Lamb curry, a bottle of Rioja, and a video of *The Ruth Rendell Mysteries*. My idea of heaven. Janey enjoyed it a bit less than me, but went along with it.

8 September

Start-of-year meetings. Fredo made an irritating fuss welcoming Bryce as the new Curator of the Groom's Museum. Honestly, he's a librarian, not the British Ambassador in Paris.

Tom Cassidy turned up, rather to my relief. He's obviously bought a new suit. I was mildly unnerved at lunch to see Bryce laying on the charm for him.

24 September

Bill Coote, the Head Porter, has just rung me in my study – it's nearly midnight – to tell me that he has discovered Tom Cassidy is squatting in his classroom. I thought the room smelled.

25 September

I looked for Tom in lunch today and there he was holding forth on Christopher Hill and Eric Hobsbawm to assorted staff and pupils (including bloody Bryce, with whom he's become thick as thieves). When we were on our own, I confronted him about Coote's complaint he's been squatting in his classroom. I took care to try to convey both concern and firmness in my voice. He began with a stout denial which, after a few minutes, trailed off into what I'd call non-specific admission. A long story followed about family problems, lack of money and so forth. I'm inwardly really pissed off, because we told him six months ago that there was no accommodation and he just blocked it out, or convinced himself something could be sorted out when he arrived.

Well, thanks to my weak-mindedness, it has. I've said he can live here while he gets himself sorted out. He is in the guest bedroom upstairs as I write this. I enjoyed his insouciant charm at interview six months ago, but in the three or four weeks he's been here, he's started to unnerve me. Janey is away tonight, and I am brooding as to how to break the news to her that we have a squatter.

12 October

Daniel Green has taken to hanging around at the end of class. He told me today he wants to set up a school History magazine. He's so bright and hard-working that I feel very protective of him. He's not unpopular, but I sense he doesn't naturally draw near to other kids. He's aching to go to Merton, so if he can breathe life into the idea he can always put it down on his application. But I don't think he's being opportunist – just bookish and serious-minded.

I ought to go and get permission from Fredo, but he won't care one way or the other. I said – fine, go ahead. I can always do a mammoth photocopying session in the Common Room at dead of night.

16 October

Janey has gone to Zurich this week, so I have been pleasing myself as to when I've gone to bed, got up, dunked biscuits in my tea etc. I worked late last night and surprised myself by waking just after six, feeling full of life.

I went for a run. All very wholesome, and wonderfully solitary at that time of day. Hence my surprise when, just passing the War Memorial, someone called out to me 'Hi, sir'. It was Daniel Green, who was also going for a run. I said something pretty banal along the lines of 'you're a bit bloody keen, aren't you?' at which I heard a sort of deprecating chuckle, and then he said, 'Do you mind if I run with you?' I had a moment of fear that he was going to want to talk about the History magazine but not a bit of it. I don't think either of us said a word until we came in which was a full half hour later. He asked if we could do it again.

24 October

Janey and I spent the afternoon with my parents, devoted almost entirely to helping them set up the church bazaar. Dad was in charge of the bottle stall and has various supernumerary responsibilities. He looked supremely in charge and chided Janey at one point for carrying a lamp stand carelessly.

In the evening, I joined them for Mass. Dad never talks about his faith, but you can see him slaking it in quiet good works (fundraising for a hostel for the homeless, working as a hospital visitor on two afternoons a week). Mum is more intellectual (she reads a lot of scripture and philosophy these days – books and articles are lying all over the house). She is becoming more outspoken, especially about the Roman Curia, which she detests. Not quite the conformist Catholic of my childhood.

1 November

Tom has gone to see his girlfriend this weekend, and so we had the house to ourselves. Janey amassed a wonderful autumn lunch – French bread, fish pâté, and a massive goulash with spiced cabbage. By the time we'd worked our way through that, we'd had a generous glass of red wine apiece. I then uncorked a rather smart pudding wine her father had given us while she heated up an apple pie. We ended up in bed, whither all kinds of further treats, followed by a wonderfully deep sleep. We emerged about 7 p.m., picked at the remains of the lunch and watched *Inspector Morse*.

The feel-good part lasted until Janey went to switch off the light we'd noticed was still burning in the room Tom has been occupying. She emerged grim-faced about two minutes later and asked me to step inside.

Ruination is too poor a word. He appears to have stubbed out his cigarettes on the curtains; the bedding is filthy and the wardrobes (fitted) have one door hanging off. The remnants of a dozen takeaways left in foil containers lay on the floor. The condition of his bathroom is indescribable. Neither of us has much of a sense of smell, or I think we'd have picked it up earlier.

3 November

Tom never came back on Sunday night, and missed teaching his first two periods on Monday morning. Nor did he ring up or offer any explanation, so I ran around trying to find cover. When he finally appeared at 11 a.m., I asked him to have a word with me in my office and then, door closed, gave him a rocket.

He started to tell me some complicated tale about a sick relative, but I didn't believe a word of it and told him he had no excuse not to have rung the school. 'I didn't know the number,' he said. I rolled my eyes and asked him if he'd ever heard of Directory Enquiries.

He left my office, obviously seething with resentment, to drop his bag – only to be confronted by Janey who was working at home this morning. She didn't hold back by the sound of it: although I have only her version of what followed, she ordered him to find new accommodation by Saturday, and warned him to stand by for a 'fucking great bill'.

7 November

I told Fredo I was 'seriously put out' by Tom Cassidy, and relayed the events of the last weeks to him. He asked how it was that Tom had come to be living in our house in the first place and seemed to have difficulty understanding my explanation (i.e., simple goodwill and desire to tide over a colleague at a tricky time). He refused point blank my request to tell Tom to start sorting himself out.

8 November

Tom moved out yesterday in a trail of Asda carrier bags. Good news. The bad news is that I still have him in the department. Janey has engaged a firm of industrial cleaners to clear up the room and wanted them to send the bill 'to the feral little shit'. I said: please don't – life is complicated enough.

Stan has enjoyed every moment of the whole Tom debacle and tells me 'this will teach you not to play at being Mother

Teresa'. He informed me this morning that Piers Albright has taken pity on Tom, and is letting him use a cottage in the village which used to belong to his mother. That's rich in possibilities: Piers is the most pernickety of all our colleagues and also the one with the most explosive temper. I have already booked a ringside seat.

23 December

Family Christmas at Nicole and Robin's. We arrived last night and have been put in an unheated room at the top of the house – lumpy mattress, thin duvet. Two windows had been left open. Central heating or convector heaters are for the lower orders. I had anticipated something of this kind, so packed an extra duvet in the car and – Nicole would really hate this if she knew – a hot-water bottle.

Janey and I shopped in Camden Market (which I tolerated) and then went for a walk on Hampstead Heath (which I loved). Both were a lot easier than the strained atmosphere at her parents' house. I now have to fashion two entirely different topics of conversation with people who (just now anyway) can't bear to be in the same room as one another. Robin likes talking about wine or cricket, and Nicole about politics. She told me today that she was a socialist. I swallowed hard.

24 December

Nicole and Robin presided over a Christmas Eve party. It's quite impressive. Nicole comes alive as a hostess and makes a virtue out of being startlingly outspoken: 'You don't look like an artist!' that was to Matthew Greenburgh who is a very distinguished one – and 'Aren't you Oxbridge?' – that was to

Stanley Rogers, a professor at Imperial – those were two of tonight's pearls.

She also flirted with the older men – a manifestation of social exuberance rather than of sexual avidity, I guess. They seemed to lap it up. Down at the other end of the table, Robin fiddled with decanters of burgundy and Sauternes, and appeared oblivious. As soon as the last guest had left, they gave up any pretence of civility towards each other.

25 December

Janey and I slipped out of bed at about 7.30 a.m. (Christ – *freezing*) and walked over to Holly Place for an early Mass. A small congregation of mainly elderly and single people. She very seldom joins me at Mass (nor would I expect her to, obviously), but both of us enjoyed it today and I loved her being there.

Nicole was up when we returned. She made no direct mention of Mass, but was clearly irritated that Janey had gone. They don't do presents, but she had decorated a superb Christmas tree in the sitting room, lit only by candles. Rather unnerving, but very beautiful, especially as the light faded and we could see their reflection in the French windows overlooking the pond. Good food too: we ate goose for lunch, and then went for a long walk on Hampstead Heath. Afterwards, we played Canasta and charades. There were no rows, but it felt laboured. Inwardly I longed for *The More-cambe and Wise Christmas Special,* and a box of Cadbury's Milk Tray. I must admit I miss my parents if I'm not with them at Christmas. We spoke to them from a call box on the way back from mass.

In the privacy of our bedroom, I gave Janey a spectacular

black Armani dress she's been coveting. It's very peculiar: she never bothered about clothes at all until a few months ago and now she's reading the fashion pages. Also, much less expensively, *Oscar and Lucinda*. She bought me tickets to hear Ashkenazy at half term, and a very sexy Hackett polo shirt.

13 January 1988

Daniel Green suggested yesterday we should do another early morning run. I said I looked forward to it, but thought I ought to check that his Housemaster didn't mind. So I spoke to Morton Magill who didn't, at all, but was also perplexed.

First he didn't seem to know who Daniel was, and then he asked me if I was quite sure I meant Daniel Green whom he described as 'the little Jew'. I said I had no idea whether or not he was Jewish, which wasn't true, but I didn't feel inclined to share in his brand of prejudice. Eventually he said, 'I never knew he could run.'

2 February

Lower Sixth today. Ned Belshaw said he found calling me 'sir' ridiculous and wanted to call me Dominic. I said I didn't have a principled objection but would find it a bit strange.

10 February

Ilya Grodsky has been set three essays over the past six weeks, and three sets of notes. I have collected in about ten lines of writing from him in total. This, despite invoking the whole canon of sanctions – departmental detentions, house gatings, written warnings etc. Nothing makes any difference. He sits in the back of the room, coal-black eyes burning, saying nothing, learning nothing, doing nothing. He came here from New York where he allegedly inhaled, smoked or snorted every substance on which he could lay his hands, or nostrils. Old habits die hard.

2 March

I have been wondering for a few weeks whether or not Daniel Green's History magazine will ever be more than a short-lived figment of an adolescent imagination. This morning he handed me the proofs for photocopying.

Well worth the wait. Essays on Caxton, Hobbes' *Leviathan*, the Crusades and the Russian Civil War among much else. Book reviews. An interview with Lord Dacre. About 15 pupil contributors in all. This will give some of the other departments something to think about, especially English (who are idle buggers). The boy is a genius.

14 March

Two Upper Sixth Formers came to see me after lunch to complain about Tom Cassidy. The gist was that he hasn't set or marked any work since the end of January; he spends the entire time talking about Christopher Hill and Eric Hobsbawm; he slags off members of staff by name, not least myself. The charges levelled against me, I gather, are that I'm a control freak, small-minded and not very bright.

16 March

Three p.m. meeting with Fredo today. I relayed the conversation I'd had with the two Upper Sixth boys. He said quietly that it was always dangerous to place too much importance on the testimony of pupils. I pointed out that I had hard and fast evidence that he wasn't setting enough work and marking virtually nothing. In which case, he said, speak to Tom directly. I said I had done that and showed him copies of the letters I had sent him on both occasions by way of follow-up.

He looked at me coldly and asked what I proposed. I said that Tom was a probationer, and that we shouldn't renew his contract.

18 March

I was with Stan after lunch today in the Classics office – my God, talk about an Augean stables – when Toby Spencer came in to complain about the C+ Stan had given him in his essay. Stan asked him what mark he wanted. A couple of seconds' silence followed and then, rather diffidently, Toby suggested it was worth an A.

Stan held the pen out. 'Go on. Write a fucking A then. Write whatever the fuck you want.' He often behaves in ways that alarm me and which I could not possibly emulate. But he often has a point.

4 April

The holidays have begun. Janey is busy and I have been at a bit of a loose end. So I decided to come out to West Berlin for a couple of days and trawl the museums and galleries.

That's just what I have done, but it's made me feel a bit self-conscious and lonely being by myself. Restless too – not helped by passing a building near the Zoo station, with a sign in weak neon on the front which proclaimed *Spa und sauna fur herren.*

6 April

Now back home. Janey has made a good fist of asking about how I'd enjoyed myself. She has no historical interest what-soever, so this was partly an exercise in good manners.

7 April

There was a letter from Fredo in my pigeonhole today, marked confidential.

Dear Dominic

I have now had a chance to reflect upon the substance of our discussions concerning manpower for the History Department next year. I have decided that Tom Cassidy will be a worthy addition to the strong department which you lead and I shall be writing to him shortly to invite him to take up a full-time position.

Yours sincerely,
Frederick Hudson

13 April

Janey has gone to Edinburgh. I have been bored and diverted myself today by buying an elderly Jaguar XJ12 from a local dealer.

I have been wondering why. Partly boredom; partly because it was the car for which I ached as a schoolboy but which was way beyond the means of my dad; partly because

Nicole will hate it. She says Jaguars are loud and brash and vulgar.

25 April

One of the Fourth Form told me tonight that he really admired the way Mr Cassidy never styled himself 'Doctor' even though he'd done an Oxford DPhil. I should have loved to have told the said pupil that the nearest to a doctorate Mr Cassidy has done is in being a Blue Riband fantasist – but you can't, can you? I just nodded and said – yes: it's awfully impressive.

7 May

A glorious hot Saturday. Just after tea, I saw a magnificent pale green Mercedes convertible draw up by the library and a handsome boy, whose name I do not know, stepped out of the driver's seat, *en route* for school detention. Daniel Green also observed the scene. He stuck two fingers down his throat and generally did a passable imitation of someone spontaneously throwing up.

12 May

I was picking up a coffee at break this morning when Piers Albright burst into the Common Room and started shouting at Stan. In the grip of temper, he is quite spectacular. His ginger eyebrows actually sweat (which is rather fascinating, but scary). His eyes take on a yellow-ish tinge and his voice rises to a strangulated pitch of fury.

His beef was that Stan had failed to set prep for some of his tutees the other day.

Whereas a normal human being would have raised the matter politely and discreetly (over a coffee, perhaps), Piers shouts.

I know in theory that one should simply tell him to fuck himself but it's hard: he has the bully's instinct for who to attack and when. Within the school he also enjoys a far greater prestige than he deserves, simply because he's been here so long. Fredo never confronts him: his default position is to turn a Nelsonian blind eye to everything awkward.

Later Stan put a photocopy of Piers' note to him in my pigeonhole. There is a curious mismatch between his rather beautiful italic cursive, his intemperate words and his tortured syntax.

*Do you understand that when a prep is due to be set it MUST be set??? This is to happen every time, **NO MATTER WHAT DO YOU UNDERSTAND**. PRA.*

20 May

Stan told me today he is deliberately not setting any prep to any of Piers' tutees. He says that he looks forward keenly to their next discussion.

Lesson for me: Stan DOES NOT CARE what other people think of him. What will it take for me to learn how to do that?

6 June

Meeting yesterday after Chapel for Sixth Form parents and teachers. Niall McLaughlin's mother informed me that it had long been 'decided' that he would go to Cambridge to read History. I told her his marks made this unlikely. I could and perhaps should have added – impossible.

She took the news badly: *How can this have happened? He was a brilliant prep-school historian, his grandfather was an Oxford don.* And so on and on for ten furious minutes while other parents queued behind her, torn between embarrassment and fascination. I tried to adopt the mien of a family doctor breaking bad news – dignified regret and an unspoken exhortation to show fortitude in the face of misfortune.

It didn't work. Rather like a prize boxer (she's built like one) Mrs McLaughlin cut me short, and delivered the equivalent of a left and right, by saying first: 'Mr Cassidy hasn't set Niall an essay all year' and that he never marked last term's exams. Ouch. And before I could start to sound statesman-like, she moved into all-out blaming of me for running a slack department.

All done at some volume. She kept telling me about her close friends in Cambridge to whom she would relay this tale of ineptitude and thus ensure our lasting perdition.

17 June

Nicole rang last night. She put on her *faux*-intimate voice and said that she gathered I was in 'hot water'. I was a bit nonplussed, but it then transpired that the demon Mrs McLaughlin is an old friend of hers and – I dread to imagine *that* conversation – the two of them have been in regular contact.

She was gagging for me to give details but I just said, 'Goodness me, what a coincidence. I'll get Janey.'

7 July

To Glyndebourne last night to see *Jenufa*. Robin and Nicole asked us – I assume we are the late recipients of some corporate hospitality. I took a lot of trouble with the picnic – glorious Parma ham, melon, lamb curry, strawberries. Robin provided the wine, which gave him something to talk about. Nicole studiously avoided any mention of Mrs McLaughlin but expended time and energy in advising us both on our careers. She tells me that independent schools are 'finished' – intel supplied by numerous friends in the shadow cabinet and upper echelons of the civil service. I therefore need to move 'fast' into state schools.

I nodded slowly, affecting the keenest attention. She glowered. Later on we dropped them at the station in my Jaguar which I revved as loudly as possible.

3 August

We've rented a tumbledown house near Uzes for three weeks. The setting is spectacular, the house is cool, and the weather is hot in just the way I like. Every evening, a silent and rather emaciated man of about 80 comes over and waters the plants. He's called Davide – which makes me think he must be from Italy. Beyond vouchsafing his name, he refuses to enter into conversation. He must have been extraordinarily handsome in his youth.

Stan and Caitlin are with us this week. We're not a natural foursome. Caitlin stays downstairs and cooks delicious meals, but prefers you not to engage her in conversation. Janey works in the little room off the terrace and mumbles into a dictating machine. Every couple of hours she comes out to the terrace and suns herself for 20 minutes before going back to work. About twice a day she pops to the phone box in the village and rings the office. I stay on the terrace and read John le Carré. Stan hates the heat, sweats profusely and reads Thucydides.

14 August

My parents have come out for a few days. We've taken them on short trips to Nîmes and Avignon and the Pont du Gard, but the three of us are really at our happiest reading on the terrace. Janey, as ever, works. She went back to London last week to catch up on meetings, but has now returned.

It's so hot that we all swam today – even my mother. I haven't seen her in a bathing suit since about 1970. Although she wouldn't acknowledge it, she deliberately waited until Janey had gone shopping before changing. She feels self-conscious about showing off her old white legs.

27 August

Janey dropped into the conversation that we're giving supper for ten people next Friday – friends of hers – so, I'm sure, lawyers, bankers and their husbands, wives and so forth. I tried to repress the thought of all the hassle, not least because I'll be teaching as usual the next morning, and said 'fine'.

She must have read the anguish in my eyes because she said at once: 'It's only fair. I have had your friends and your parents all summer. It's my turn to have some fun now.' Not actually a very encouraging remark.

31 August

Stan and I went for a poached egg and coffee – our valedictory treat before the holidays end and another school year begins. I told him about Janey's upcoming dinner party and asked (not seriously) if he and Caitlin would like to join us. He said (entirely seriously) he'd rather have his nipples stapled to the tarmac.

1 September

Stan, whey-faced, complained that Janey rang Caitlin last night to invite them next Friday. Now Caitlin is allegedly worked up and has spent hours giving Stan an ear-bashing, demanding to know why they never give large dinner parties. I sympathised and said it must be terrible to be poor.

'Listen, chumbo, I may be poor. But at least I don't have to bring wankers into my home.'

His home (as I was unkind enough to remind him) is a tied cottage and his continued tenancy depends upon the grace and favour of whoever is running Groom's, God help us. I'm the only one of the pair of us who is a property owner.

Still, as usual, he has a point.

3 September

The start-of-year Heads of Department Meeting yesterday saw me at the receiving end of a blast of hostility. I ventured the thought that perhaps those few pupils sitting Oxbridge exams in November might be given a couple of days off school just beforehand in order to revise. It was hardly a very surprising or original suggestion but Piers Albright suddenly exploded at me, shouting that they would just waste their time.

I hadn't particularly cared one way or the other beforehand, but I resent people trying to bully me, especially in public. I said I thought that the issue should be decided on its merits, and not be dismissed simply by someone shouting loudly.

Fredo smoothly intervened: 'I'm sure everyone round this table wants only to do their very best for our pupils.'

After that the meeting lurched on, albeit uneasily, Piers silent but with murder in his eyes. It's all very mysterious.

5 September

I went for a coffee in the Common Room after lunch, and sat next to Roger Rickart and Mary Thomas. I thought I'd exchange a few pleasantries about the holidays but neither of them seemed to want to meet my eye, and within a minute both muttered apologies and left. What the hell was that about? Neither are exactly friends, but both have always been amiable colleagues. So far as I am aware I have done nothing to offend them.

7 September

Roy Venables came to see me after lunch today in the History office. He gave me a tight smile and said he had something to tell me. I could see at once something serious had happened and closed the door.

'This is awkward,' Roy said, sitting down. 'I don't like telling tales, but I also don't like people running down a man's reputation. Not without giving him the chance to defend himself, leastways.'

'Agreed,' said Dominic. 'Let me guess. I'm being slagged off.'

Roy nodded. 'I'm afraid so. By some people who think they're Lord Muck around here.'

'Oh, great. Bryce Williams, by any chance? Piers Albright?'

'Both of them, yes. But it all starts with that young Cassidy. He's at the heart of it.'

Tom, Roy informed him, was busily telling colleagues that he had only agreed to become a lodger in Dominic's house because he had not wanted to offend him.

'Offend me how?' Dominic asked, wide-eyed.

'That's one of the awkward bits. He says you were keen – well, rather *unnaturally* keen – to have him around you as much as possible.'

'My God,' Dominic said. 'Has this man no shame?'

'I don't think he does, actually, and I'm afraid it gets worse. Because he's also claimed that your wife got suspicious of what was supposedly going on between the two of you.'

Dominic shook his head. 'And what then?'

'According to young Cassidy, your wife then invented a tale about him having damaged the property and made you kick him out. *And* he says he was also charged an exorbitant rent all the while he was there *and* that you made him pay all kinds of mysterious bills.'

There was a pause for a few moments while Dominic composed himself.

'It ought to be laughable,' he said eventually. 'I was trying to do that bugger a favour.'

'I guessed that much. But, if you don't mind me saying, you don't want to do people like him favours. They just spit them back in your face.'

'Evidently. I also don't like the fact it's become a story doing the rounds among our colleagues.'

'I don't blame you. That's why I'm telling you. I noticed Piers Albright has worked up a big head of steam about it, and he's telling everyone now as well.'

Dominic then asked Roy if he'd be prepared to tell Fredo what he'd just told him.

'I'd be glad to,' he said. 'A few people here need taking down a peg or two, don't they?'

9 September

Shortly before midday I saw Fredo climbing into the head-magisterial Mercedes. He didn't return my greeting, and deliberately looked away. Tom has obviously been spreading poison everywhere, and Piers Albright is proving a very willing conduit. It's intolerable.

12 September

Janey was asked for a drink at the Connaught on Thursday by a senior colleague. She agreed – reluctantly, because she thought he might be trying to hit on her.

It turned out it was a bit of an ambush, in as much as, when she arrived there, she found herself facing four of the firm's head honchos. She has been offered a partnership, subject to a probationary period lasting about two years during which she'll be worked to a jelly.

I have been sworn to secrecy. There is a whole raft of other associates in the firm, older and more experienced than her, who are slavering for partnerships and they'll be gutted, poor bastards. In addition to being desperately overworked, she'll also be the focus for a lot of resentment.

I don't think she can help being a bit pleased, but she won't admit it. She says she's worried what it might do to us. She warned me, as she's done before, that she won't have a lot of headspace to spare for me.

She looked so severe when she said it that I almost shelved the idea of telling her that I was really worked up about Tom

Cassidy and Piers. But in the end I did, and she was much more patient than I had expected.

I said I was finding it unbearable to work with Tom and asked her if I was getting matters out of proportion. She said simply, 'Yes, darling, I expect you are' – but added she was happy to get someone in her firm to send a letter to Tom and Piers, threatening them with an action for defamation unless they back off.

Strong meat. I said the fallout would probably poison the atmosphere here so badly that it could cost me my job. She agreed, but pointed out we can survive financially and it will be far better to go down in a blaze of glory. A bit Wagnerian?

14 September

I was collecting in GCSE preps today when Sebastian Rogers looked anxiously at me and told me his was not done. I sensed distress behind his rapidly blinking eyes and asked him very gently to wait behind after class. The minute we were alone, he burst into tears, which was very out of character. It transpired he went home for the weekend and that his parents spent the whole time having a big fight.

15 September

I sent a letter to Fredo this morning which I won't be able to retract.

Dear Headmaster

My wife and I appear to have become the targets of what really deserves to be called a smear campaign. Rumour and innuendo always fly about in institutions, I know, but there are good reasons to believe this one is vituperative and defamatory.

May I come and see you, please, as a matter of some urgency?

Yours sincerely,
Dominic da Silva

He rang me at home this evening. He wants to see me at 10 a.m. tomorrow. He must be rattled.

16 September

I arrived on the dot of 10, and Fredo, looking irritated, asked what the problem was. I had schooled myself to stick to the facts and stay dispassionate, but it didn't quite work out that way. There were a couple of moments when I could feel myself on the edge of tears and had to be very firm with myself about not giving way. Fredo hates that kind of thing.

He asked me what I proposed he should do. I said – nothing. I was informing him out of courtesy, but that Tom Cassidy and Piers Albright would soon both be receiving lawyers' letters along the lines Janey had outlined.

'I don't advise the step you are contemplating,' he said quickly.

So I asked him what he would suggest. 'Grin and bear it,' were his words. He added that I worried a great deal too much what other people thought of me. 'This week, you're the story. Next week, it will be someone else.'

I'd intended to have a showdown and to walk out feeling that I'd got him rattled. It hasn't worked out like that at all. Bugger, bugger, bugger.

'I don't know what to do,' Dominic told Janey that night.

'Darling. Do what you want, please. We have enough money. If you want to make a fresh start, we can.'

He sat uncomfortably in the armchair by the fireplace. 'I don't know what I want.'

A few days later, he sent Fredo another letter:

Dear Headmaster

Thank you for seeing me last week.

Please accept this letter as notice of my intention to leave Groom's at the end of next (spring) term 1989.

I'm going to take a spell off teaching – maybe to write a bit – and just freewheel for a while. We're going to sell our house here and move back to London.

You were quite right in saying that I mind too much what other people think of me. It's time I grew out of it, and I'm certain I can't do it here.

With best wishes,
Dominic da Silva

Chapter Nineteen
Wingrove Manor, October 2014

When autumn came, Daniel felt that Dominic wasn't going to last a lot longer. As he acknowledged to Esther, it was a matter of divination rather than of hard and fast evidence. A barrister's gut feeling? she asked, her eyes smiling and sad.

Knowledge of impending separation impacted upon his professional concentration. He wasn't hopeless, obviously: he could read a judgment, talk to a client, pile through his emails – all that. But there were never more than a few minutes at a time when he didn't reach out in his mind to his old teacher.

'I am lucky in my friends,' Dominic had told him. 'Just you and a few others, of course. You don't need many when you already have the best.'

Daniel had pooh-poohed a bit, but in truth he too had been impressed and moved by the unobtrusive devotion by which Dominic had been sustained. Jack and Orla had borne the brunt of looking after him during the weekdays, along with Fr Maybury and the Devlins – endless round trips of 30-odd miles, four or five times a week; Cara and Digby had poured into him care and loving imagination, as well as stumping up half the costs of the home: they had come up every other weekend and (in a stroke of genius, Daniel thought enviously) the three of them had watched together the RSC's production of *Nicholas Nickleby* on YouTube. He and Esther came up virtually every weekend.

Each of this tiny group of intimates knew Dominic a little differently, but Daniel intuited best that the business of being ill – of being almost always on the edge of nausea, and prone to strange and undignified afflictions all over Dominic's body – was taking a fearsome toll on his spirits.

For the first six weeks or so that he had been at Wingrove Manor, Dominic had seemed remarkably content. Perhaps he wasn't exactly institutionalised, but he was apparently unable to prevent himself succumbing to the stimulus of society. Partly that was physical: insofar as he was capable of enjoying food by this point, he seemed to like what he now ate, and to appreciate the relief from having to think about catering for himself. It was also social – eating all his meals in the company of other residents brought to the surface those same instincts that had made him such an effervescent young teacher, albeit muted by time.

As he had explained to Daniel, the other guests were not natural soulmates, being drawn off that prosperous rump of Midlands society to which he had never had access. They were fund managers and directors of IT businesses, partners in big Birmingham law or accountancy practices.

Strangers they may have been, but Dominic loved to talk about them. In their now nightly phone calls, it became clear to Daniel how this latest tranche of people in Dominic's life had kindled his curiosity and excited his compassion.

'What do you talk about?' Daniel asked him. 'Politics?'

'Christ, no. We've all given up bothering about them.'

'Sport? You can't have much to say there.'

'No. It's families. Nearly always families. Lots of pride, lots of angst, a fair bit of heartache. It always comes back to families.'

'I suppose so. Do you feel left out?' Daniel asked uneasily.

'Silly sod. Of course not. Family is just another word for love, you know. Why would I feel left out?'

That had been a good conversation. In others, he had been slower and more halting and it wasn't hard for Daniel to work out that the effort required to retain a semblance of reasonable spirits, even of composure, was drawing heavily upon depleted resources. The next day – it was wet and grey – a message came from the Matron at Wingrove for Daniel to call.

Sent: Wed 2.29 p.m.
To: Daniel Green
Cc: Esther Green; Jack O'Riordan; Orla O'Riordan; Digby Alexander; Cara Alexander

Dear Mr Green
Thank you for your phone call this afternoon.

As I explained, there has been no crisis or collapse, but Mr da Silva is not in very good spirits.

Until this week he's been a great attender at meals and always show an interest and concern in other residents. Over the past few days, he's missed several of these (we've given him meals in his room) and has become very withdrawn. He's also given up his after-noon walks and told the physiotherapist on Tuesday and this morning he wasn't well enough to see her.

Today he didn't want to be weighed! We can see he's

getting thin and he has also told us he's not sleeping well. I'm afraid these are all symptoms consistent with someone whose condition is advancing quite quickly. But so far as any of us can see he's not in any real pain, although there are several areas of local discomfort.

Dr Barrons will be in tomorrow, and we'll make sure he sees Mr da Silva on his rounds. After that I will let you know what he says.
Best
Sian Aitken SRN
Matron, Wingrove House

Sent: Thurs 11.01 p.m.
To: Daniel Green; Esther Green; Digby Alexander; Cara Alexander

Dear All
Sorry this is being sent so late.

Jack and I went over to Wingrove this afternoon and found D pretty much as Matron indicated to Daniel – awfully low, poor soul, and trying so hard not to show it. He says his feet are hurting – which seemed strange. I went and bought some oil and rubbed them. No idea if it helped, but he said (as usual) nice things!

Dr Barrons eventually arrived (about an hour later than D thought he would, but that may have been confusion). He spoke to Matron rather than to me, but I think the gist is that D is on the edge of depression and too exhausted to do much about it.

The *physical* signs of his deterioration are pretty clear to me in that he's painfully thin, not eating, skin waxy etc. Jack said, rightly in my view, he probably hasn't a lot of time left when we can expect him to be very coherent or indeed in a mood to say much. But you may find him different.

I think he's also *very scared* and that's one of the reasons why he's quieter than usual. If we all come round too much that may add to it. Maybe I'm wrong? I honestly don't know.

At the same time he needs one of us to look in every day. I'll go on my own tomorrow. Is anyone able to do this weekend at all? We *can* go, but I think he's getting very bored of us as it is – so maybe a fresh face might help? But I do understand you're all incredibly busy.
Love
Orla

Sent: Friday 9.04 a.m.
To: Orla O'Riordan; Jack O'Riordan

Dear All
Thanks Orla – we'll go up tomorrow. We should arrive mid-afternoon and will 'report back' afterwards.

Digby rang me a bit earlier and they're both going on Sunday arriving teatime.
Best to you both
Daniel

Dominic was sitting rather vacantly in his armchair, looking awfully thin but there were tell-tale signs he had prepared for the visit. He was wearing a very smart maroon cashmere V-neck and some rather expensive-looking midnight-blue corduroy trousers.

'Oh, I see,' Daniel said, happy to have an excuse to banter. 'Cara's been shopping.'

Dominic grinned.

'Where are the loafers, then?'

'Wardrobe.' He gestured with his eyes. 'My feet aren't up to new shoes. Silly, sweet girl – wasting her money. I did tell her.'

Daniel sat down opposite him. 'Esther's gone to the loo,' he said. 'She'll be along. Have you had any lunch?'

'Lamb shank and cherry tomato roulade,' Dominic answered precisely.

'Enjoy it?'

Dominic paused momentarily. 'Quite,' he said.

Daniel reached out and took Dominic's hand. He had spent fifteen minutes before he appeared at Dominic's door getting a more detailed update from Matron. She had explained that ulcers had been running across his gums for some weeks now and had spread under his tongue and into his throat.

'What can we do?' Daniel asked.

'Nothing, dear boy. You're doing it already.'

Daniel said nothing. Matron had already told him that she had arranged the day before for Dominic to have a simple lunch of tomato soup and stewed apple in his room. He had finished it up, but she said it would have been an effort. Later, she had passed by his room and spotted him sitting in his armchair, looking out on the briskly trimmed gardens, weeping silently.

Daniel looked at him. 'I think I'm going to be done for speeding.'

'Really? A bit of a non sequitur if you don't mind my saying so.'

'Not at all. I thought you might be interested.'

'Oh, I am. Awfully.'

'I overtook a caravan on the inside lane and the speed camera flashed.'

'My parents had a caravan,' said Dominic.

'Bet they didn't.'

'All right, they didn't. But we did have a trailer tent.'

'Christ. Your childhood.' He kissed the top of Dominic's head, and tasted briefly a sick man's sweat.

Dominic tried to stand up when Esther arrived a few minutes later but she leaned gently over him in the chair to kiss him, and whispered to him not to. It had been a fortnight since their last meeting and in that time, she guessed, he had lost over a stone.

'Where's Chloe?' he asked.

'At my mother's.'

'Oh, sweetheart, you shouldn't have to do this. She'll be fretting without you.'

'She'll be stuffing her face with chocolate more like,' Daniel volunteered.

Esther rolled her eyes. 'It's good for both of them to have time without us. Just a shame about the dental mayhem.'

She brought a chair over and placed it so that Dominic was in the middle of them. Daniel leaned back and said casually, 'I want to talk diaries, if you don't mind.'

Dominic laughed softly. 'I'm relieved to hear you say it. The timing's getting a bit tight.'

'Well, I'm a bit confused, to be honest. You seemed to be powering away very nicely at Groom's. You gave no indication of being unhappy or restless. Quite the reverse: totally committed and positive.'

'You are a nice fellow.'

A pot of coffee lay between them on the low table,

although Dominic sucked water from a straw. His voice had developed a new tremolo and his exhaustion was evident. A couple of times Daniel asked him if he was up to talking and, in his slightly unaccustomed soft and quavering voice, he insisted that he was.

Esther asked him how Fredo had reacted to his letter of resignation.

'Terribly emotionally. Floods of tears.'

'*Really*?'

'No, Esther, not really.'

Decent History teachers lay thick upon the ground, and so he was easily replaced. When news of his departure had been announced, the Common Room steward had explained to him the protocols governing the departure of colleagues: he would be entitled to a drinks party, but not to the formal black-tie dinner in the Great Hall that was the preserve of those who had served the school for a decade or more.

In the event, a couple of dozen people had shown up as Stan, moving with unaccustomed discretion, had spoken a few vapid words of farewell. Janey had been working at the time and could not be there.

'So what happened with Janey?' Daniel asked.

'We went back to London.'

'Go on.'

'Oh, I see. Well, we got distracted.'

'By work?'

'In her case, mainly, yes.'

'And in yours?'

'Well, I was finding myself, wasn't I? Heterosexuality was an early casualty. It wasn't much fun for her. She had a fling herself.'

'So you don't blame her?'

'Janey? Never.'

Esther shook her head. 'In all the years we've known each other, I've never heard you blame anyone.'

'Then you'll need to read the diaries more closely. Read what I say about Bryce Williams. Or my mother-in-law.'

Conversation had perked him up. After twenty minutes or so, Dominic asked if they could take him into the gardens. There was a smattering of blue in the sky and no sign of imminent rain.

The business of putting on his fleece and then manoeuvring him into the wheelchair and outside took some time. They both thought he would be exhausted by the time they reached the Victorian sundial which looked out on the lawns, but his face acquired a little colour and his voice some animation. They sat on the wrought-iron bench with him beside them.

Daniel leaned forward. 'The anxiety, Dominic – that restless anxiety. It's on every page of your diaries.'

'Yes. Well – that's me.'

'Why is that, do you think?'

'Honestly, I'm not sure.' Dominic looked across at him. 'My best guess is that when I was still very young I somehow took on the knowledge that both my parents were lonely. I suspect that made me feel very sad and powerless. Also very ashamed. I buried the thought very deeply for many years.'

'I understand that,' said Esther.

'That would be a context to make anyone anxious, don't you think?'

'I'd always had the idea that your parents had loved each other very much,' said Daniel.

'You were right: they did. And they loved me too.' He paused for a moment. 'You know,' he said, 'we shy away from admitting it. But if happiness is what you're about, you need more than love. You need a hefty dose of natural confidence.'

Daniel nodded.

'Well, my lovely mother and father weren't particularly confident people. I think they found a lot of interest in life and a lot of purpose, but they weren't exactly carefree. I'm just not sure how often they were happy.'

'Finally,' said Daniel, 'I understand. You took their sorrow on to your shoulders.'

'They never asked me to.'

'Christ – listen to yourself: you're still doing it now. Of course they didn't – I'm just saying it's what *you* did.' He looked at Dominic. 'That's why you suffered in silence for so long at Hunter's Chase. You never allowed yourself to admit the validity of your own unhappiness because you were too busy worrying about theirs.'

'Perhaps.'

'You poor bugger.'

'Come off it,' said Dominic, but his voice was gentle. 'As you may recall, I found ways of consoling myself.'

'And of beating yourself up.'

'Ah. I think the guilt was there anyway. The sex just gave it a supporting narrative.'

Esther shook her head. 'I still don't understand what you had to feel guilty about in the first place.'

Dominic looked down. 'I couldn't take away their loneliness.'

There was a longish silence. Finally Esther said, almost conversationally, 'Do you wish you hadn't been gay?'

Dominic smiled his old smile. 'I don't wish anything at all. It took me a while, but I learned to get along with myself very nicely. It's a great way to enjoy life.'

It was nearly time for them to go, but for another minute or two the two men sat calmly and quietly while Esther unobtrusively rearranged the blanket around Dominic's shoulders.

'If you think,' said Daniel, 'of the various women in your younger life, is Janey the one you cared for most?'

Dominic slowly nodded his head. 'I loved my cousin Kate,' he said, 'and Janey.'

'Do you know where Janey lives now?' Daniel asked.

'North London, I've no doubt. I haven't seen her in twenty-five years. You can google her, I daresay.'

'I think I'll do that.'

'Why are you interested?'

'We have to be fair,' Daniel said neutrally. 'She was your wife. She deserves to know about you.' He repeated: 'We have to be fair.'

Dominic slowly lifted his head, and looked at him. 'Right,' he said dully. 'Things are bad, aren't they?'

Daniel tried to answer but suddenly the words would not come. He held out his arms, in a perfect echo of that moment, so many years earlier, when he had been assailed by grief and had turned for comfort and understanding to his teacher and friend. Now, as then, Dominic gazed at him in profound pity and was suffused by pride that he had been so favoured.

It had always been his reflex to embrace the whole company. He took Esther's hand in his own as well as that of Daniel and thanked them both.

Chapter Twenty
Avila House, January 2015

The funeral, rather as Dominic had anticipated, had been overlong, and the liturgy punctuated by too many readings and vapid hymns. For most of those present, the emotion of the occasion had been dissipated by boredom. Only a lusty rendition of 'I the Lord of Sea and Sky', as the coffin was led out of the church, offered much in the way of catharsis.

The congregation had also to contend with one or two moments of anxiety. Luke, a long-established resident of Avila House, was entrusted with carrying the collection plate, from which he seemed reluctant to part. Then, during the exchange of the Sign of Peace, Mrs Doyle wandered the length of the nave with a view to getting to know some of the congregation rather better than they might have wished.

But Fr Maybury held everything together with dignity and apparent unconcern. He also presided at the graveside, where the motif was one of decorum. Kate had managed to get home just a few days before Dominic died, and she, Daniel and Esther were joined there by Jack and Orla, and by Digby and Cara. Air-traffic control were on strike in Melbourne where Guy was presently travelling on business, and so his frantic efforts to get to see Dominic in time had been thwarted.

At the funeral tea, past and present residents of Avila House pulled out all the stops. Mourners were greeted with a veritable orgy of egg and cress sandwiches and of chocolate cake with buttercream icing, each consumed with relish and despatch, often by the same persons whose hands had fashioned them. There were also two urns of strong tea and a large jar of Maxwell House. Jack and Orla, frequent visitors over many years, moved comfortably among the throng. Digby and Cara, although less familiar, worked the room with every indication of ease. Digby's booming laughter broke out every few minutes. Esther and Daniel were more diffident, but did their best.

It took about an hour and a half for the party finally to disperse. Kate was staying with Jack and Orla for a couple of nights and, after the last guest had gone, she and the three couples walked out together to their cars. They exchanged kisses and hugs and proclaimed their intention to keep in touch. Fr Maybury arrived at this moment, and calmly joined in the adieux. As he shook Daniel's hand, he handed him an A4 envelope.

'What's this?' Daniel enquired, eyebrows arched.

'No idea,' he said. 'I'm just the messenger boy.'

Esther had already offered to drive back to London and so Daniel sank gratefully into the passenger seat. He said nothing as they drove out of town and, sensitive to all he might be feeling, she stayed quiet herself. It was only when they approached the motorway that he asked her if she'd mind him putting on the passenger light.

She heard the sound of an envelope being opened

and noticed, out of the corner of her eye, a few sheets of handwritten A4, each in a transparent pocket wallet.

'More diaries?'

'Looks like it.'

My beloved Daniel,

Maybe not that interesting, but anyway.

As you know, I gave up writing my diary when I left Groom's. After that it was only very rarely that I found myself drawn to record the odd incident or to make the occasional reflection.

What you see here is all I could find. There's been no cull – no edit. I thought you might want to add them to the rest.

All love
Dominic

2 November 1989

I was locking my bike against the railings in Bedford Square this morning when I heard some loud and disconcertingly familiar voices, most of them rather clipped. I didn't even need to look up to identify them: Groom's A-level classicists were on their way to visit the British Museum, led by Stan (looking shabbier than ever).

I was wearing a cagoule and a woolly hat and nobody noticed me, which was a relief. If I'd been recognised, I'd have had to get into a conversation, I'd have been required to keep up an appearance of bluff cheerfulness. I could have done that all right, but it's an effort and one I don't feel like making just now. So I decided to work at the London

Library today instead and cycled round to St James's Square. Faded into the landscape.

Inwardly I felt a great wave of sadness. Kids don't realise how much teachers can love them. It's nothing unwholesome: you simply care deeply and miss them when they're not around. A diluted version of what it's like to be a parent, I guess.

I didn't tell Janey – I'm not sure she'd have understood, nor that she'd have sympathised. Her line is that we should crack on and not look back. I'm not convinced myself.

31 March 1992

It was a year yesterday since my appearance in front of the magistrates. Life at Avila House is physically and emotionally too demanding to allow me time to navel-gaze very much. But I have a fair bit to show for this past year – I feel useful, which matters to me.

I am also sufficiently sure of my peace of mind that I have finally replied to Daniel Green's letter, suggesting that we meet when I'm next in London. This was rather disingenuous of me. I no longer have any reason to go there! So if it ever comes to pass, he will have been my only reason for going. But I won't tell him that – it would embarrass him, poor boy.

13 October 1992

Oh goodness – I _did_ enjoy that.

Daniel is a young man now. There are obvious continuities: he's still earnest and disposed to be intense, but big differences too. There's nothing of the schoolboy any longer – far too trenchant and, in most respects, self-assured.

He got a First – something he dismisses as 'a fluke' – and he's studying for the Bar. He has a very good tenancy lined up, and will no doubt earn a lot of money one day! We went to lunch at Pierre-Victoire (very cheap) and he tried to pay. I said no – we'll split it.

But he wasn't really very keen on talking about himself which (thinking back ten years) was all I was ever capable of doing. He wanted to know all about the hostel and the kind of work I do. He asked if he could visit. He's such a lovely and steady sort, I said – yes, I'd be delighted, so long as he wasn't going to feel sorry for me! I said it as a throwaway, but saw at once the remark worried him.

Until then he had avoided any mention of my court appearance, so it seemed like the right moment for me to do so – to thank him for his extraordinary delicacy in writing to me. At that, all of a sudden he *did* look like a schoolboy, because he blushed to his roots. I told him that I still feel mortified by the fact that what was essentially my private stuff became very public. He said it hadn't made any difference to him, although his voice became very husky as he told me this, which rather suggests that it had.

14 April 1994

Dad drove over and we went to Mass. The timing of his visit was bad insofar as I had forgotten that there was a workshop at midday to help our residents apply for independent housing. I obviously had to be there and, rather on the spur of the moment, asked him to help out.

It's been an eye-opener for me. He's shown himself to be really good at this – not just filling out the forms, but getting whoever he's talking with onside. There's a really fine line to tread here. If anyone gets a sense of being patronised or bossed, trust can unravel very fast. Dad didn't miss a trick and he obviously enjoyed himself too. Definite repeat invitation to follow.

He left with a real spring in his step, and that perked me up too. It certainly featured in my prayers last night. Talking of which, I've acquired a better habit of prayer in the last few months. I say mine mainly last thing – a sort of review of the day: what I've enjoyed, what I haven't; where I'm at ease, and where I'm struggling.

I think my biggest fault is greed – greed for praise and attention, and greed for sex. I am adept at getting the first, and resentful at missing out on the second. Still taking refuge in chocolate and cakes by way of compensation.

10 September 1995

Daniel rang on Wednesday and asked if he could come up this weekend. I said please do. I can tell his mood in a moment and knew something was up. Anyway, he drove up on Saturday and very kindly took me out for a meal. It took a while before he unwound.

As I'd suspected, he and Hilary have split up – the holiday in Sharm-el-Sheikh didn't go well and they both realised they 'hadn't enough in common'.

He asked me if I'd ever liked her! I said, certainly I did. I desisted from adding that I'd long thought they were no more than fond of each other. On the other hand, since I only ever saw them together in rather contrived situations – meals out, visits here and so forth – I don't trust my judgement.

He is a conundrum, bless him. So self-assured intellectually and (evidently) professionally. Startlingly diffident in most social contexts, however. He told me that he'd had 'not much sex' before he met Hilary. God, that made me feel old – I held back from saying that that much was pretty bloody obvious anyway.

He looked so miserable that I tried to straddle irony and sage advice. Told him I would do this once, and only once, and then proceeded to enumerate his advantages: he's only 24; his career is taking off; he's a very nice-looking guy. (Which he is, although I've never really allowed myself to dwell on that. Once my protective and quasi-parental instincts are engaged, I go into another place. Very fortunate.)

He looked at me unconvinced and said: 'I've been wondering if I might be a repressed homosexual.'

'Fucking hell, Daniel,' I said. 'If that's true, would you mind looking me up, because I could get interested!' We both laughed at that, and it certainly moved the conversation along. I've never met anyone less gay in my life.

11 March 2001

Went to a concert at the Inner Temple on Friday – Bartók (Romanian Folk Dances), Brahms and Franck (Sonatas) and some Ravel. I enjoyed it a lot, though perhaps too highbrow for me. Esther, who gently underplays her own achievements, volunteered she felt the same. The real fascination of the evening came in Daniel's utter absorption, especially in the Bartók. A real window into his soul.

As soon as the interval arrived, and when we moved into the reception afterwards, he was intensely self-conscious. I wondered (rather stupidly) if that was because he might have been embarrassed by me – I looked and was dressed like someone who was definitely unused to these hallowed halls –

but it wasn't that. Esther says his shyness is intense and that it takes weeks of persuasion to get him to go out in the evenings. 'The only person he'll really make any social effort for is you,' she added.

16 August 2002

Dad's funeral. For a man so resolutely private, the neighbours turned out in force. I have had over a hundred letters from people who describe themselves confidently as his friends.

I've reflected much during these past months, watching his life slowly ebb away, on the privilege I've known in being his son. I was uneasy with him as a boy, of course – typical for sons of my generation when fathers were unembarrassed by being authoritarian. But he made a huge effort to nurture my independence and to respect my individuality.

The Murphia were out in force. Eight priests on the altar. Dire sermon by Father Trimble (in the grip of early dementia, for sure. Quite embarrassing actually: he went on and on. In the end Canon McDonagh had to whisper gently in his ear to move on. Christ!). Dad wouldn't have batted a hair. He had no interest in panegyrics.

Black humour was further intensified at the graveside when, for one rather scary moment, the coffin couldn't be lowered into the freshly dug grave. I saw the head undertaker looking a bit panicked. They tried again and it worked.

I love the idea of him reunited with Mum. Goodness, they'll be delighted to catch up.

Once the house is sold, there will be easily enough money left over for me to buy a small flat. A strange feeling: I am used to having very little in terms of income (or capital, come to that) but I'm not poor. My needs are always met and I gave up wanting anything much in terms of clothes, cars, or holidays once I came here. I've also always had a stream of treats thrown my way by Dad and my old friends.

Not sure I feel easy about having a substantial sum of money for myself, nor any property.

17 June 2005

Kate asked to come up because she said she had 'news'. I found a vegetarian restaurant which she liked (a lot of pulses) and which I endured.

Caleb is now 25 and as determined to become a Dominican as he was at 18. He's been accepted and will be starting his training this autumn in Glasgow. That's not the news, she said, as I began to congratulate her! Since he is now launched in his own life, she too has more choices. She's decided to train as a lay sister in the Order of St Teresa of Ávila, and will be going to live in South America.

Single mum becomes a nun at the same time as her son becomes a monk. How very 21st century!

3 February 2009

Daniel and Esther's little girl was born on Saturday. Today I took the coach to London, and then a Tube and a bus, and finally arrived at the Royal Hospital in Hendon. What a bloody awkward journey – I wish they lived near Victoria coach station! However, it was well worth the trouble: Chloe is a beautiful little girl and her mother and father are bewildered by their happiness.

Or at least they *were*, until the talk turned to feeding routines, at which point Sharon became startlingly bossy and

Esther looked very crestfallen. After a few minutes Clive interrupted her (thank God, I thought, and not before time) and proceeded to instruct them both about how and where their daughter should be educated.

I could have killed them both – and I was also fed up with Daniel for not shutting them up. He's hopeless about standing up to his parents. He walked me to the bus stop when it was time for me to leave, and so I took the chance to give him a bit of a wigging on the subject.

He claims a row with his parents will be followed by weeks of hurt silence. I know, I said, but you've got to put Esther first.

21 November 2013

Guy and I had supper last night – he's incredibly hospitable about searching me out whenever he comes back to the UK. We went to a sushi place in Kensington. I caught a glimpse of the prices and felt faint. Oh well, bless his big heart and his fat wallet.

He says he hardly recognises London – did I not remember how shabby it was when we were growing up? Yes, I said, but London isn't typical. I told him that he should try seeing where I live and work. He nodded solemnly, but he has *no* idea – he and Melinda have been surrounded by cooks and drivers and nannies for years.

Our friendship seems to have prospered, however polarised our lifestyles. I have an historic attachment based, I think, on the fact that he was the first person who both identified me as being gay and was completely unfazed by it. Doesn't sound much today, but back in the day it seemed astonishing.

He's also the only one of my friends who talks about sex frankly, and routinely asks me about *my* sex life, insolent devil. I said I'd have liked more than I'd had.

He replied, with some feeling, 'You, me, and every man over the age of 50.' He said to me that the enduring mystery was why I'd never paired off with anyone.

'Well, I did,' Dominic had said. 'You were my Best Man. Or had you forgotten?'

'That was Restoration comedy.'

Dominic raised an eyebrow. 'Didn't seem that way to me.'

'Really not? You're a faggot.'

'Ah – but I was trying hard not to be. Oh my goodness – I wanted to be straight. Play your games. Wear your outfits.'

'Why don't you have a steady guy now?'

Dominic looked at him a little shiftily. 'Not so easy, old boy. I'm the warden of a hostel run by the Catholic Church. Slightly cramps my style.'

Guy shook his head before shovelling *miso dengaku* into his mouth. 'Stop diving for cover. Why are you still alone?'

Dominic went quiet for a few moments. 'Because,' he said eventually, 'I never learned to trust. Not like a real person.'

'And why was that?'

'I can't be sure,' he said, looking down. 'I can only tell you what I think.'

Guy nodded. 'So – tell me.'

'Well, then. When I was still very young – a couple of months shy of my third birthday – I suddenly came down with pneumonia. And I mean, really badly.'

'Nasty.'

'It was, I believe. My parents were in despair. The GP raced me to hospital in his car.'

'And then you recovered?'

'I did, but it took a couple of weeks. And I think it's what happened then which did the damage. You remember what it was like when we were kids: hospitals kept parents at arm's length. There was no question of them staying overnight. Anyway, I obviously believed I'd been abandoned.'

'But surely they came to see you?'

'Yes – as often as they could. No doubt about that. But I can only infer that it wasn't enough to reassure me. I was very ill, of course, and so presumably pretty distressed. The funny thing is' – his voice tailed off at this point – 'I don't actually remember them being there.'

'Do you remember any of it?'

'Bits and pieces. Injections being shoved into my butt; howling for my mother.'

Guy had stopped eating and was looking across at him. 'And you say you never got over it?'

Dominic smiled. 'Well, you know, it was a horrid thing to happen – but hardly unusual. Kids get ill and go to hospital. I can't really say why I took it so tragically, but I think it had something to do with the fact that, once I was home, we never talked about it.'

'Stiff upper-lip and all that?'

'That was the *zeitgeist*, wasn't it? It was 1962. Now, of course, I can see that they were in trauma as much as I was and, anyway, they weren't the kind of people who would have owned up to that in a conversation. So there was a bit of a conspiracy of silence.'

'Did that make it worse?'

'It wasn't intended to, but I think it did. Trust was the casualty.'

Guy nodded. 'What about when you were older? Was it never mentioned?'

'Once. I was about twenty.' Dominic averted his eyes. 'My mother and I were alone at home at the time and, lo and behold, all of a sudden she started to relive it – describing me getting more and more ill, and her calling the doctor. She suddenly said, "I knew I was losing you," and her voice cracked and – oh God, Guy – how she cried.'

His own voice had thickened in the telling. Guy shook his head and said very quietly, 'Your poor mum.'

'Yes, indeed. Then she pulled herself together and went off to dry her eyes. It was never mentioned again.'

Sent: Saturday 23 November 2013 6.09 p.m.
To: Guy Robson

Hello dog breath
Sorry this is being sent so late. Loved our evening. Thank you so much.

And what a fab meal. I always eat so much better when you come to the UK. If it's ever awkward for you to fly to London, please have no inhibitions about just sending me cash instead.

Thank you also for getting me to spill my emotional guts. Very cathartic. I should have added that solitude (much like marriage, I imagine) becomes the natural state of being after a period. There are occasional low days, but not many.

Sex, or absence thereof, is more of an issue than loneliness. I find that my libido is slowly ebbing – but longing remains. The distinction would make no sense to an adolescent, would it?

Longing can feel like a knife in my guts – yet it's also longing which has given my life much of its urgency and savour. And, ultimately, I can't regret something so integral to the person I am.

Got a pain in my left tit. How weird is that? I'm seeing the consultant in January.

All love to you and Melinda
D

20 December 2013

Went to Confession for the first time in ages. Fr Maybury was very gentle with me, bless him.

I wish my religious stance were a bit more mainstream. I take great comfort in the Mass and the sacraments, and certainly in prayer, but I have no very clear sense of heaven as a destination. Even less of hell – that just seems vengeful.

I cling to the words of St John of the Cross: 'as for what happens when we die, I don't know. I believe. I believe only that a great love awaits me.'

Anyone who has known love has already had a taste of paradise. All that's left is to pass it on.

Supporters

Unbound is a new kind of publishing house. Our books are funded directly by readers. This was a very popular idea during the late eighteenth and early nineteenth centuries. Now we have revived it for the internet age. It allows authors to write the books they really want to write and readers to support the books they would most like to see published.

The names listed below are of readers who have pledged their support and made this book happen. If you'd like to join them, visit www.unbound.com.

Ebby Adhami
June Aitken
Christopher Alcock
Rachel Anderson
Jonathan Andrews
Yin-Fung Au
Anne Ballard
Nick Barrett
Elspeth and Chris Barrie
Thomas Barrie
Anthony and Deviani
    Barrons
Annie Bayley
Clare Bentley
Veronica Berman
Bertone family
Nabeel Bhanji

Alexander Bishop
Cecile Bott
Claire Bruce
Ed Burgess
Dennis Burton
Carlos and Amanda
    Conceicao
rcope99@icloud.com Cope
John Crewe
Sandy Crole
Marianne and Mike
    de Giorgio
Amanda de Lisle
Alexis de Longevialle
Angela Dean
Helma Diffey
Alexander Donger

Elizabeth Donger
Thomas Edlin
Erica Engel
Mark Feltham
Shoshannah Fenner
Adam Fenton
Arthur Fincham
Rory Forsyth
Luisa Fulci
In loving memory of Fabian
    Garcia Miller
Adrian Garcia-Miller
Tim Gee
Kate Gibbons
Mary Gibson
Jonny Glassberg
Daniel Godfrey
Benjie Goodhart
Matthew Greenburgh
Rachel Grigg
Chris Guinness
Daniel Hahn
Christine Hanway
William Hanway
Oscar Hard
John and Evelyn Hargreaves
Paul and Barbara
    Hargreaves
Mary Hargreaves and Peter
    Wright
Evadne Sara Harrity
Gavin Henderson

Jeffrey Herd
Philip Hewitt
Claire & Robin Hilton
Jennifer, Nicholas &
    Frederick Johnson
Dylan, Carey, Harry and
    Alex Jones
Jack Kember
Dan Kieran
Jennifer and Ewan Labrom
Alan Leibowitz
Alex Letts
Chris Liddell
Ning Lim
Robert Lister
Antonia and Ashley Long
Cecilia Loo
Andrew Lownie
Ewen MacArthur
Gareth Mann
Helen Mann
Penelope Jane Martelli
Russell and Annabel
    Merrett
Mandy Merttens
Andrew Miller QC
John Mitchinson
Claire Morrell
Isabelle & Andrea Morresi
Joe Mulville
Toby Mundy
Carlo Navato

Serena Nuttall
Malachy O'Keeffe
Margaret-Louise O'Keeffe
Ahana and Amara Ogle
Oldhams
David Owen
John Owen
P & B
Alex Panayides
Steven & Mary-Clare
   Parker
Justin Pollard
Stuart Proffitt
Richard Pyatt
Stephanie Rackind
Henry Raine
Edward Randall
Issy Rawlinson, Jane Heath,
Simon Rawlinson
Matthew Reid-Schwartz
Dermot Reilly
Marina, Ulrich and Carl
   Rietschel
Robson Family
Jenny & Neil Rodgers
Harry Rose
Suzy and Colin Rose
Will, Gen, Josh and Amelia
   Rosen
Christopher Rowe
Varsha Saraogi
K J Scanlon

James Scott
Ben Shillito
Yugene Shin
Elizabeth Sinclair
Stuart Southall
Aidan Sproat-Clements
Simon Stanley
Dennis Stevenson
Katie Sunley
Jean E Suvan
Keith Tompkins
Kevin Walsh
James Wan
Barbara Weiss
Tom Weisselberg
Nicholas Welsh
John Witney
Nancy Wood
Tim Woods
Simon Wurr
Richard Wynne-Griffith
Alina Young
Ned Younger
Sam & Annie Younger